Dear Readers,

Welcome back to the world of the Sazi, and to a whole new chapter in the world. Those who have come to love and fear Tony Giodone will get to meet a brand new alpha male this time. The readers have spoken—and you'll get to learn more about the enigmatic Monier clan (or perhaps you'll only discover new questions to ask!).

Antoine Monier is the representative for the werecats on the Sazi council. He is a powerful cougar, a seer of future events, and he is *very* used to getting his way. But when he discovers a gorgeous Turkish-American woman named Tahira Kuric in a German jail, he learns that not all the shapeshifting cats in the world answer to him. Tahira and her brother Rabi are part of the Hayalet Kabile, a mysterious "ghost tribe" of Caspian Tiger shifters from the Iranian/Turkish borderlands. Featured too will be the oh-so-bad representative for the snakes, Ahmad al-Narmer, as well as a host of other people who live in the Sazi universe.

One of our goals for this alternate reality is to show that despite cultural differences, country borders, and prejudice, people are people, whether human, shifter or somewhere in between. For every bad shifter, there is a good one, and gray is a far more frequent occurrence in the real world than simple black and white. Evil can lurk in the hearts of the best of men, and there can be some nobility in the darkest of souls. But there's one difference in our world—always, but always—love conquers all!

We hope you enjoy this next installment in the Sazi world. And never fear! Tony will be back sooner than you can say *Mafioso*!

Captive Moon

CATHY CLAMP
and **C. T. ADAMS**

TOR®
paranormal romance

A TOM DOHERTY ASSOCIATES BOOK
NEW YORK

This is a work of fiction. All the characters and events portrayed in this book are either products of the authors' imagination or are used fictitiously.

CAPTIVE MOON

Edited by Anna Genoese

A Tor Book
Published by Tom Doherty Associates, LLC
175 Fifth Avenue
New York, NY 10010

www.tor-forge.com

Tor® is a registered trademark of Tom Doherty Associates, LLC.

ISBN-13: 978-0-7653-6268-1
ISBN-10: 0-7653-6268-6

First Edition: August 2006
Second Edition: October 2008

Printed in the United States of America

0 9 8 7 6 5 4 3 2 1

DEDICATION

As with everything we do, we dedicate this book first to Don Clamp and James Adams, along with our family and friends, who have offered patience and unswerving moral support through the years.

Special thinks go to our agent, Merrilee Heifetz, the wonderful Ginger Clark, new friend Claire Reilly-Shapiro, and always to our terrific editor, Anna Genoese, at Tor.

Without all of you, this wouldn't have been possible. We know that words aren't enough, but they're what we do best.

ACKNOWLEDGMENTS

We would also like to thank those people who helped make this world the best it could be: To our terrific international author friends, Wendy-Marie Förster of Stuttgart, Germany, for city details, and to Cheryl Sallick and Carmen Evans of Australia for turning our new Aussie character, Matty Thompson, into a true blue, dinky-di Sydney mate! Thanks also to Antje Rettig and Laurie Thayer for their help with details about Germany and France. We hope we got it right, but if there are errors, blame us, not them.

Captive Moon

Chapter One

THE SWEET STENCH of rotting flesh on the breeze assaulted Antoine's nose, even before the buzzing of flies reached his ears.

"We are nearly at the site, Herr Monier. We are fortunate that it was cold last night. The carcasses have apparently been here for several days. The smell isn't nearly as bad as it could be."

Antoine stepped over a log hidden under the melting slush and stopped just short of a clearing. He could see uniformed officers and even a few members of . . . the *harbor patrol*?—taking photographs and measurements under the towering beech trees outside of Stuttgart, Germany. The sun was about to crest the top of the nearest peak, but the shadow of the full moon still lingered on the opposite horizon. The gentle, sultry pull reached for the animal under his skin. His senses were still intensified by the invisible magic that played over his body. At any other time, the forest scents would be too intense for him to remain near prey long. But the death smell of fellow predators that permeated the valley stilled his natural urges.

The uniformed officer behind, with the weighty tang of his blood sausage and porridge breakfast still hovering on his breath, couldn't smell the log under the snow as Antoine had. He tripped and dropped hands first against a tree.

Antoine stopped, his nose sorting out the history of what had happened here. He caught Simon's scent and knew he was dead. The two-year-old tiger had been one of Antoine's favorites. A stab of pain and sadness rushed through him. *And I failed him. What sort of Rex can't protect one of his own cats?*

Kommissar Reiner turned and raised one bushy brow, which disappeared under the brim of his cap. "Herr Monier? Are you well? We do not have to continue if you do not wish." The man's English was heavily accented but far better than his French.

Antoine squared his shoulders and tucked a few loose strands of long blond hair behind one ear. *If Simon could endure his fate, then I can stand witness.* "I'm fine, Kommissar. Please show me the animals."

He entered the clearing and could only stare in shock and rage at the carnage. Big cats of every description lay in bloody, decaying heaps around the edges of a makeshift slaughterhouse. Bits of flesh, black with slow-moving flies, were splattered haphazardly over the ground.

Officers wearing masks and gloves photographed the area. Crows peered down from the branches overhead. Their raucous caws, combined with the constant buzzing, set Antoine's nerves on a knife edge. Thankfully, the scent of fear and pain from the animals' final moments had dissipated. He wasn't sure how he would have responded to that.

"We believe the poachers were trafficking in tiger organs for the Far East black market. But we are not sure about the other great cats. Perhaps they could not find enough tigers to meet the demand."

Perhaps. But there's more here than meets the eye. A Sazi was here. I can definitely smell an injured female were-tiger. While Antoine's nose wasn't nearly as sensitive as his twin's, the female shapeshifter who had been in this clearing had left her mark. *Sandalwood and tiger musk, with a hint of patchouli.* A quick sniff. *No, she's not among the dead. She was taken from here, very much alive.*

He'd identified as much as he could with his nose. Now his eyes began to take in details. Fiona and the rest of the council would want to know everything he saw, heard, and smelled. If necessary, one of the Sazi seers could touch his mind and describe it at the meeting.

"Were you able to apprehend any of the poachers, Kommissar? How did you come to find this place?"

One of the police officers, looking a bit green around the gills, approached Reiner as they carefully skirted the bloody, makeshift tables. He removed red-stained latex gloves before saluting.

Antoine could tell that the Kommissar was going to ignore Hermann in favor of him, their annoying, high-profile visitor, but one look at the officer's face dissuaded him. He made a small motion of his hand. "One moment, Herr Monier." Antoine nodded politely and wandered a short distance away.

Was ist los, Hermann? Reiner lowered his voice and turned his back on the visitor; he couldn't know that it didn't matter. Antoine's supernatural senses would have been able to hear a conversation back inside the squad car.

Ich habe gerade Nachricht erhalten von Dietrich und Shapland, Kommissar. Sie sind ein wenig nervös wegen des Tigers auf dem Revier. Sie haben Zweifel, ob der Käfig hält. Sollen sie das Tier betaeuben?

Antoine stiffened while struggling to appear not to understand: "I have just received a report from Dietrich and Shapland, Inspector. They are nervous about the tiger at the station. They are worried that the cage will not hold it. Should they tranquilize the animal?"

It was so much easier to eavesdrop when the police believed he didn't speak German. Playing the part of the haughty Frenchman had been a useful idea. But the inspector's words dropped with the weight of lead. *They had a tiger at the station? Could it be the female Sazi? If they tranquilize her and the moon sets . . . Merde!*

Das waere ratsam! Wir müssen den Antrag stellen, um das Tier zu entsorgen. Bitte bring meine Nachricht zu Dietrich. Er hat die Lizenz für die Tranquelizer!

Antoine deliberately wandered around the far edge of the scene, careful to take in every word with his supernatural hearing. "Yes, that would be wise. We'll have to file the proper paperwork to dispose of the animal. Please relay my instruction to Dietrich. He is qualified with the tranquilizers."

Putain! What to do now? This could easily become a diplomatic incident. He began tapping his fingers on the front of his designer slacks. Who should he call? He wasn't qualified to handle this. But he knew of no weretigers to contact in Germany, or any other species of were-cats, for that matter. *No, I need proof that the cat is Sazi—*

The Kommissar's voice, louder now, startled him. "Herr Monier, I am sorry for the interruption. What was your question?"

It was hardly a plan—reckless and bold. The council would never approve. Antoine took a deep breath and spoke quickly so he wouldn't lose his nerve. "I was asking about the cats. These all appear to be male. There are no female cats here. Where have you put *those* bodies?"

The Kommissar frowned and his eyebrows knitted into a single, formidable line across his forehead. "Female? But no—you distinctly said you lost a *male* cat. It is in my report."

Antoine rose to his full six-feet-plus height and

crossed his arms over his chest. He pushed the tiniest bit of his magic toward the other man. The Kommissar visibly shuddered. It was a risk, and it could go badly. Humans seldom reacted well to powerful Sazi, and those in positions of authority sometimes treated them as a threat. He would hate to wind up behind bars himself.

"*Non!* I most certainly did *not* say it was a male. My lost tiger is *female*—mother to a pair of cubs who will die without her. Why on earth else would I get up at such an ungodly hour to follow you through a forest to see . . . this?" He swept his arm out wide, and set his face in tight, angry lines.

Without a word, the inspector stepped over to one of the men and grabbed a clipboard. He stalked back to his former position and turned the clipboard so that Antoine could see it. The powerful scent of his anger filled the air. *It does smell a bit like burning coffee. How very strange I've never noticed before.* He fought not to sneeze.

"You see, Herr Monier? It distinctly says *male* in my report—"

Antoine waved his hand airily in the general direction of the clipboard without bothering to look. He knew full well what it said, but that didn't matter. "Your report doesn't interest me, Kommissar Reiner. Whoever took the details was mistaken. I am missing a *female*. Do you have a female tiger for me to view or not?"

Reiner looked at his report again and frowned deeply. Antoine sent out tendrils of magic to eavesdrop on Reiner's thoughts: *The report says male. But I am to "cooperate." Diplomatic courtesy, they told me. He says a female was lost. There is a female, and she has been especially difficult to handle.* An oddly amusing thought crept into Kommissar Reiner's mind. *There would be less paperwork to fill out if the Frenchman took the cat. Wilhelma Zoo has not yet opened. Perhaps the tiger and our guest deserve each other.*

"Very well, Herr Monier, if you would like to see a female tiger, we were able to rescue one. It is at our station house, awaiting transport to Wilhelma Zoo. If you can identify this cat as yours, you are free to take it."

Antoine frowned. "*Identify* it? What would you consider identification? I certainly don't brand or tattoo my cats."

Reiner shrugged. "You said it was nursing. That should be obvious, at the very least. But any particular feature you remember—a missing claw or damaged ear. A distinguishing feature that *we* can verify before *you* see the cat."

The words were very clear and seemingly innocent. But Antoine understood the inspector perfectly. Now he would just have to decide how to make good on his puffery. How in the world would he be able to positively identify a cat he'd never seen?

Well, Fiona always said I was the creative one in the family . . .

Antoine turned on his heel and started back to his van, shaking the snow from his designer slacks after each step. Over his shoulder he shouted, "As you wish, Kommissar. I will meet you there and we will collect *my* cat."

TAHIRA WOKE TO heat burning her skin. She tried to lift her front leg, but the drug still coursing through her made it difficult. Again she pushed against the door of the wire cage. It was weakening, bending outward, but she struggled against unconsciousness with each attempt. At least she'd been able to remove the dart quickly and had only pretended to be unconscious until the men left. But she'd never tried to hold her form beyond dawn, and it was already long past. Sunlight was slowly crawling up the wall, throwing shadows of herself, and her prison, across the floor.

I can't pass out. I must hold my animal form or they'll kill me. Well, they or her family. It hardly mattered which. She drew in a painful breath, snarled lightly, and searched ever more desperately for the waning moon magic. Every muscle was in agony, and she could feel her bones straining to break and re-form to a human.

The heat was unbearable and she looked longingly at the bowl of water just a few feet away. *But I don't dare move. If I concentrate on anything but holding this form, I'll lose control. I've endangered us all with my recklessness. Rabi wouldn't have wanted this, no matter what his fate.*

She scanned the room again for the hundredth time since she'd been brought here. There must be *something* she could use to free herself. If only the cage wasn't wire mesh. With bars, she could turn human and slide between them to free herself. If she was at full strength, she could easily break open the door; but the drugs from the policemen, combined with whatever her *original* captors had given her made that impossible. She could barely open her mouth enough to pant to cool herself.

Why had she planned this so stealthily that *nobody* knew where she was? If she had just told Grandmother or Uncle Umar, they would have supported her. It was only stubbornness that had caused Grandfather to refuse to send a rescue party for Rabi in the first place. Apparently she had inherited that stubbornness.

She readjusted her paw and winced. The light tingling under her fur was turning into prickling—stinging pinpoints as though thousands of tiny ants were crawling and biting every inch of her body. The heat was increasing, too. The constant whir of the exhaust fan buzzed in her ears. An abrupt crunching, grating noise sounded directly overhead. She jumped when two sharp metallic slams echoed through the room. She recognized the noises. She must be in a basement, and the parking lot was directly above her. Voices now, in that harsh language that she didn't recognize. She wouldn't be able to hold out much longer. What was she going to do?

Hallo, Tiger. Was ist Ihr Name?

Tahira looked up and around. Nobody was in the room. She glanced at the barred window, but the sunshine was blinding to her sensitive eyes. The language was the same as she was hearing outside the door, but she didn't understand where it was coming from. Was there a microphone in the room?

Parlez-vous le français, le Tigre de Madame?

Was that French? Tahira shook her massive head. If she was starting to talk to herself in delirium, shouldn't she at least be able to understand the language? She growled again, and a startled yip followed when her jaw snapped. It was starting. She couldn't hold it off anymore. She was going to change right here in front of witnesses, and her family would be hunted like rabbits and slaughtered.

Do you speak *English*, tiger? We're running out of time!

For heaven's sake! The voice *was* in her head! There was a distinct American accent to his words, and relief flowed through her. She tried to think of what to say. Well, not quite *say*. She thought the words in her mind: Uhm, yes—I speak English. Where are you? *Who* are you?

Merde! At last! My name is Antoine and I'm in the outer room. Listen to me carefully. You are Sazi, correct?

Her head raised in unconscious reaction and she roared loud and long. I am *not* Sazi! I am Tahira Kuric of Hayalet Kabile!

* * *

THE GUARDS IN the outer room with Antoine jumped with the tiger's roar . . . *Hayalet Kabile.* Where had he heard that phrase before? *Hayal . . . Oh for the love of—* How could he forget? It was just mentioned at the last council meeting. The Hayalet Kabile were known as the "Ghost Tribe." The were-tigers that lived along the Turkish/Iranian borderlands had declined to attend the great meeting of shapeshifters all those centuries ago.

They were mentioned at the Sazi council meeting because Ahmad had brought along a clipping from the Discovery Channel Web site that said there had been a sighting of a supposedly "extinct" species of tiger, the Caspian, just last fall. The annoying were-cobra, representative for the snakes, had asked what *Antoine* intended to do about it, since the Caspians were well known to be shifters, and he was the representative for the cats.

But the Hayalet Sahip, the head of the tribe, had refused an invitation to talk. Now there was one in the next room. Based on the roar of pain, she wouldn't be able to hold her form much longer. She was about to break the primary rule of both the Sazi and the Hayalet cultures. What a diplomatic nightmare!

"*Merde!*" he whispered harshly.

"Did you say something, Herr Monier?" Kommissar Reiner said, his mouth curled slightly in disdain. "Are you ready to make your identification of *your* cat?"

Antoine drummed his fingers on the table sharply. If he could only talk to the tiger, make her understand what was at stake . . . *Yes, perhaps.* He turned fast and reached for the doorknob, startling the inspector. "One moment, Kommissar. I've forgotten . . . my . . . uh, I'll be right back!"

He raced outside and pressed outward quickly with his waning magic. The tiger was directly under him.

Tahira, please listen to me. We don't have much time.

No response. But he could smell her fear just behind the bars of the window.

Tahira of the Hayalet Kabile. I am Antoine Monier of the Sazi. Will you please speak to me? You are in great danger.

Another roar, powerful and haughty. *You need not worry about me, Sazi. I will end my own life before the humans see me in my day form.*

This doesn't have to happen, Tahira. I can help you. I've convinced the police that you're one of my *tigers. But I need your cooperation.*

A snort of derision, but hope was replacing the fear. *And who are you that you believe you can* own *a tiger?*

Antoine walked out toward the van. A pair of pigeons pecking at gravel exploded into the air just as he reached the door. He managed to stop himself from unconsciously leaping into the air after them. *It's a complicated story, Tahira. But I and my cats entertain in shows all over the world. One of my tigers, Simon, was killed in the woods where you were held. But I have another Bengal named Babette. She just had kittens. I've convinced them that you are Babette.*

Her voice sounded suspicious but intrigued. *But even a human can tell the difference between a nursing and non-nursing tiger. Uhm . . . can't they?*

Antoine opened the van door and reached inside to grab a clipboard. He flipped his long braid back before swinging the door closed. He smiled and paced quickly along the edge of the carefully cleared walkway, expanding on his daring plan. *I don't know many humans who are willing to get close enough to check. But I'm an alpha and have excellent illusion abilities. It would help if you have any other identifying marks—perhaps ones that the officers have already seen? I* promise that once the police have released you and are no longer watching, I will get you back to your *Kabile*—your tribe.

Her soft alto was sad. I will be dead to them. I'm already an outsider. I disappeared without permission, trying to save my brother. But I didn't find him, and now I have bargained with a Sazi. I will be exiled . . . or killed.

I *have* bargained with a Sazi! She planned to cooperate. Thank heavens. A crunch of gravel behind him said another vehicle was arriving. He turned to see the occupants. Several of the members of the team from the forest were returning and he was out of time. So you will allow me to assist you? The moon magic is nearly gone, but my power can hold you in form—if you'll allow me to. But I need something to identify you.

I . . . you can hold someone past the dawn? But only sahips hold that much power! Still . . . if you believe you can—I am missing part of my left ear.

Curious. What could have damaged a Sazi—a shapeshifter enough . . .

A touch on Antoine's shoulder made him jump. Annoying that he hadn't heard or smelled the inspector walk up behind him. Distractions could be costly at this stage. "Herr Monier? Are you quite ready? The zoo is now open and if the cat is not yours, we must make a call to them."

"Yes, of course, Inspector. Sorry for the delay." As he followed the inspector through the door, he threw a burst of magic ahead of him. He felt it penetrate the steel door in front of him and cover the tiger in the cage. The illusion was subtle, but he had to cast it broadly. Even Tahira would be able to see it when the time came. But he felt her shifting stop.

"Are you ready to identify *your* tiger, Herr Monier?"

"Of course." He thrust the clipboard toward the inspector with feigned annoyance. "These are the customs forms for my animals. I thought you would want to see that I do indeed have a female Bengal with kittens."

Kommissar Reiner shuffled through the papers that Antoine recognized as the bill of lading, and confirmed for himself that Antoine had several different species of cats of both genders. And, yes, there was a female Bengal.

"There are no identifying features mentioned on this form."

Antoine forced his voice into a slightly condescending tone. "No, there are not, Kommissar Reiner. As you can see, there is nowhere on the form to insert them. It might be something to consider mentioning to the appropriate department. But, Babette—my female—is missing a piece of her left ear. And, as I said, she recently gave birth and is nursing."

He stared blankly at a print of a famous painting on the wall as the Kommissar questioned his men. No, they didn't notice whether the cat was nursing. That would require contact far too intimate. Even the dart didn't put the cat completely under. Yes, there was part of the left ear missing. It was in the report. Antoine suppressed a smile as the inspector reviewed the form.

The Kommissar smelled disappointed to find the written note about the defective ear on the paper, but he dutifully cleared his throat and removed a large ring of keys from his pocket. "It appears we *are* in possession of your tiger, Herr Monier. But I would like to see for myself that the cat is nursing. Tigers often fight in the wild and in captivity, so a damaged ear is not terribly—"

"Uncommon?" asked Antoine, with a sly smile. *He really doesn't want to let me win. But I already have. Thank God.* He concentrated on Babette and the cubs, let the memory of watching her nurse fill him until it was fixed in his mind. He felt for Tahira in the next room and let his magic bleed outward, blur the image of her belly until it matched the one in his mind. He shivered as the magic tied them together. He could almost see her in his mind now.

Reiner raised his brows. "Indeed." He swung open the steel door on oiled hinges and held it open so that Antoine could enter first. The negative pressure fan that kept the parking lot exhaust from filling the room assaulted Antoine's ears and he wondered how Tahira had managed to stay sane.

He stepped inside and got his first look at the woman, the tiger, he was helping. Her wide golden eyes looked startled as she inspected her chest and stomach. A burst of surprised scent quickly disappeared into the fan's flow. Antoine followed the stare and he swore under his breath. He'd said it himself! She was a *Caspian* tiger, and that particular subspecies has a mane similar to a lion's, with *long belly fur*.

Before the Kommissar could get past him to see, Antoine concentrated carefully and blended the memory with the reality, like melting photographs into a single image.

He could see her surprise as her body betrayed her eyes. It was only when she ran her own nose over her fur that the illusion was dispelled. She froze when he spoke into her mind again.

You will need to greet me as though we are friends, and— He felt embarrassed to say the next words, but it had to be done. Well . . . I will also—and I do apologize . . . but I will have to touch your stomach to prove to the inspector that you are nursing.

TAHIRA STARTED AT the statement and immediately looked up. She felt her heartbeat race when she finally saw her benefactor. He was incredibly handsome, slender, and fit. His blond hair was slicked back from his face, and the confident green-gold eyes grabbed her attention. He was so very young looking! Could he really be a sahip at such an age?

Then she looked more carefully. No, perhaps not so young. His heart-shaped jaw did bear a small golden beard, just covering his chin, and small wrinkles at the corners of his eyes made him at least in his late twenties. The eyes sparkled when he continued. I normally wouldn't ask, came his voice, but I don't think the Kommissar will believe you are mine otherwise.

What he suggested did make sense. But he would have to put his hands on her naked chest. The form didn't matter, and he very well knew it! She would have frowned in her human form because he didn't seem too upset by the idea, either. But as a tiger all she could do was glare and pull back her lips in displeasure.

But one glance at the officer with him, the Kommissar, put the matter to rest. The narrow face was cold and his dark eyes serious and suspicious. There would be no discussion about the issue. He would have to see the evidence for himself, just as her father would. Nobody else's word would do. But then a thought occurred to her. She hated that the words came out sounding a bit desperate.

If I am supposed to be a performing cat in your show, shouldn't I be able to obey commands? Couldn't you instruct me to roll over, or something like that?

She was a little annoyed at his chuckle. No doubt she smelled distinctly of embarrassment and fear. But his reply was polite and professional.

Is there room in there? I am quite certain that the Kommissar will not let you out of the cage, but I don't want to make you uncomfortable.

Tahira looked around and realized the Sazi was correct. There was barely room to stand and no room to make a full turn. If she tried to roll onto her back, she would be stuck there. *No, I suppose there isn't. But do only what you must—I warn you!*

He dipped his head slightly into a bow and remained serious, but his scent said something else entirely. He was amused at her discomfort. *As you wish, my lady.*

He walked toward the cage with Reiner at his heels. She could hear his heart pound as he got closer, and she struggled against an increasing pressure that made her bones ache. She felt an uncomfortable pop and realized that her bones were trying to re-form. Why did it seem more difficult for him to keep her in form the closer he got?

"So, Herr Monier. Is this your cat? Can you prove your claim?"

Tahira watched the man—Antoine—offer a patronizing smile to the officer. "Of course she is." He turned to her and with complete confidence on his face, said, "Babette, are you all right, girl?" He stepped forward and reached past the cage grate to stroke her face. His hand was soft and gentle and smelled strongly of fur, along with a wonderful cologne that reminded her of freshly mown grass. She tried to offer a look that might appear adoring to the uniformed inspector. He was watching the interaction carefully, but not stepping too close to the cage. She rubbed her face against Antoine's hand as a house cat would and made soft kitten sounds. Hopefully, the officer would have no concept of proper greeting methods.

"Come now, Babette. I'll take you home to your cubs. Can you show the nice officer your belly? That's my girl." He turned to the Kommissar. "It's perfectly all right, Kommissar Reiner. You can step closer. Babette wouldn't hurt a fly. You wanted to see evidence of nursing, and you can't do it from back there."

Tahira struggled to remain completely passive while Antoine removed his hand from the cage and eased it through a lower square. He very carefully placed his flat palm on her side and let it remain there motionless as the inspector nervously stepped forward. The inspector reeked of fear, though he tried to hide the fact. She tried to fix her mind on the tangy scent of terror, remembering the tall grass that slid past her body as she stalked the old, limping deer. But her last hunt dissolved abruptly as Antoine ran a slow hand along her side and flank.

"You see, Kommissar? Here and . . . here."

His touch made her skin tingle. She'd never felt the touch of so powerful a sahip, and presumed that the tingling was an after-effect of his magic. But when his fingers slid through the fur of her belly, she suddenly knew better. It was magic, all right, but of a whole different kind.

Don't think about how good it feels. There's too much at stake. Rabi is counting on me. Rabi is countin—

But her body wouldn't cooperate with her brain. Her stomach, and parts lower, clenched as his fingers skimmed along her fur. She closed her eyes and a small growl of pleasure slipped out. But just when she had decided to let herself revel in his touch, it stopped. Her eyes flew open in time to see the two men stepping toward the door. She hadn't realized that his hair was long. A wheat-colored braid hung almost to his belt. *What kind of cat is he?*

Antoine turned to her and winked. If she was in human form, she would have blushed.

We'll be right back. I appreciate your cooperation. We should be out of here in a few minutes.

"There is some paperwork for you to sign, Herr Monier," said Reiner as they closed the door. His voice sounded much friendlier. No less professional, but the tone and tenor were relaxed.

A few minutes later, she heard their voices again—this time in the parking lot above. "And you are certain that this van will hold the tiger, Herr Monier?" The man called Reiner must be inspecting the Sazi's vehicle, because she heard the squeaking of car springs, and then rattling metal.

"Without question, Kommissar," Antoine replied confidently. "We use this van frequently to transport our cats, and it has been inspected and approved by your government on numerous occasions. I do have the paperwork, if you wish to see it."

Reiner responded without a hint of worry. "No, I see no need. It is obvious that the cat knows and trusts you. It was quite calm when you entered the room and handled it. It reacted *completely* differently with my men."

Antoine laughed. "I don't doubt you! She is quite stressed right now. She needs to return to her cubs and have a meal and some quiet."

But shock filled her as Antoine stepped back into the room holding a *collar and leash*.

I am not a pet to follow along after you, Sazi!

For the first time, he narrowed his eyes and dropped his head into a defensive position. Here, was the true sahip showing through. He expected to be obeyed without question. His gold and green eyes burned bright with intensity and a burst of magic hit her hard enough to sting each and every hair on her body.

The words that seared into her head were terse and angry. No, you are not a pet. What you are is a dangerous wild animal, and these men are afraid of you! They have guns and there are more of them than I can reasonably defend you against. I would suggest that you keep your annoyance to yourself and allow me to get you to safety. I can't hold your form indefinitely, you know.

Both his tone and the truth of his statement made heat rise to her face. But her parents, her grandparents—they all said that the Sazi would use any excuse to subdue the Kabile, to subjugate them and turn them into shadows of humans with no free will. Yet Antoine seemed to be trying to help. Or was he merely afraid to be found out himself?

There was no way to tell, but in freedom there is power. So she lowered her eyes when the cage door was opened and allowed the collar to be placed around her neck. When Antoine pulled on the leash she stepped out of the cage and followed him through the police station. But then she saw the man who had kicked her head through the cage so the other could inject the drug. A snarl rose from her chest without warning. It was met with a sharp tug on the collar and another burst of biting magic.

Tahira fought down her anger. There was no time. *I should be thankful that I'm getting out of this alive so I can find Rabi.*

The guards followed them out to the van with hands on weapons, remaining until the rear doors were safely shut and locked. Tahira took a deep breath. The van was filled with the scent of other cats, large and small, some shapeshifters and some wild cats. But it smelled of comfort and peace, rather than anger or fear. The cats who had passed through this van were content. It was a shock. She'd heard horror stories about the treatment of cats in circuses and shows, and even worse stories about the sadistic Sazi.

A wave of relief made Tahira sigh as the police station grew smaller in the rear window. She jumped and turned as something lightly struck the back of her head. A cream-colored silken shirt lay at her feet.

"I'm about to change you back. I thought you might want to cover yourself."

She looked up at the sound of his voice and caught sight of his eyes in the rearview mirror. The annoyance in his eyes matched his scent.

"I'm sorry for snarling back there, but—"

ANTOINE TURNED ANGRY eyes back to the road. The very American accent in her voice was a worry. "It doesn't matter *why*. You nearly ruined your own escape. If you were Sazi, I would be forced to . . . but no, that doesn't matter right now." With a thought, he released the flow of magic, and forcibly ignored the scream of pain as she shifted back to human form. She must be *quite* young to still scream.

There was a shuffling of fabric against skin and when he glanced back again, a fully grown, stunning woman was finishing buttoning the silk shirt. It stretched tight over the generous swell of her chest. She tucked slim, permanently tanned legs under her so she could rise to her knees. Thankfully, the shirttail was long enough to cover everything, but Antoine found that he had to force a very appreciative gaze back to his driving. He wished he could ignore her enticing scent as easily.

He cleared his throat, and fought the customary attraction to a beautiful woman. "I . . . ahem, I expected you to be . . . *younger*, Tahira."

She half-crawled to the grating so she could see him as they talked. She dropped to a sitting position next to the grate, feet tight against her thighs. When he glanced in the mirror again, he couldn't stop his eyes from opening wide at what he saw. Without planning to, he laughed out loud. She was looking down, and her hair spilled over her face and shoulders. Wide portions of her hair were colored the bright russet of her animal.

"You have . . . *stripes*."

Tahira looked up with shock on her face and immediately pulled her hair back and tucked it in the neck of her shirt while blushing furiously. Her scent was hot embarrassment and anger, and she wouldn't meet his eyes in the mirror. "I'll dye it immediately when we reach a town. I swear. Please don't look badly on the kabile for my defect."

Defect? Why on earth—

He softened his voice, let the amusement drop from it completely. "I don't consider them a *defect*, Tahira. I've simply never seen them appear before in human form. They're really quite lovely—as are you, by the way. Who told you they were a flaw?"

After a few moments of silence, where her scent was a mingling of emotions that included being worried and flattered, she responded. "Oh. Um . . . I . . . *thank you*. But in our tribe, they're looked down on as being low-caste—nearly as bad as a *sifena*, a halfling that must change on each of the three nights of the moon. Anything that would be noticed by townsfolk on casual inspection is a danger. If I lived with my grandparents, I would probably be put down for these stupid orange hairs. But since I turned late in life—I only had my first change at twenty—they're hoping it will pass. But it's been two years. . . . Normally, I dye my hair during the moon. That's really easy at home in California. It's harder here in Turkey. I wear a head scarf a lot of the time to cover my hair, even though I'm not Muslim."

"What do you mean, Turke—" Antoine saw her face in the mirror and noticed a large bruise that covered one eye and stained her cheekbone an angry red. He turned

·his head to confirm what he saw and exclaimed, "*Merde!* What happened to your face?"

She rose up to look in the mirror, which brought a grimace and a gentle probing with one finger. "It *does* look bad, doesn't it? That's why I snarled at that guard. He kicked me in the face through the cage."

Antoine's hands clutched the steering wheel until his knuckles were white and the plastic creaked in protest. Fury boiled inside him. The thought of someone— "He *kicked* you? *Pauvre con!* Why didn't you tell me at the station? I could easily have '*discovered*' it when I examined you and had him disciplined."

Tahira shrugged and sat down, carefully smoothing the fabric to cover her thighs. "What good would that do? Even if you'd made an accusation, they'd just claim that the men who'd captured me had done it." She pushed against her ribs and felt an answering twinge of pain. "And they did plenty—you just can't see the bruises anymore. Besides, I'll heal."

A shadow of a smile passed over his face. Their cultures might be very different, but they were also much alike.

She sighed and looked out the window through the grating. "I'm just hoping to get back to the village by nightfall. I'm not very good at directing people there when it's dark. Grammy must be beside herself. I've been gone since before dawn."

Antoine nodded. Ah, yes. Back to the subject at hand. "Where do you think you are, Tahira? Do you know what day this is?" He asked the words calmly, without any emotion attached, but wasn't surprised when she regarded him suspiciously.

"It's Friday, which—" She wrinkled her brow, and her face in the mirror grew more worried by the second.

". . . is a holiday in Turkey, and the police station shouldn't be open. The police weren't speaking Turkish, either."

"No, it wouldn't, and they weren't," Antoine agreed. He decided she needed to figure this out for herself before he intervened.

She looked out the window as another building flashed by. "Van is the closest city of this size, but the architecture is wrong."

A car ahead braked to avoid a small animal and the rear end skidded on the icy road before moving forward again. Antoine took his foot off the gas pedal in response. They slowed several kilometers an hour to a more appropriate speed. Yes, they would both *survive* an accident, but why risk one?

He listened to Tahira mumbling under her breath. Her scent was a blend of panic and worry that made him clench his jaw. "Damn! I should have paid more attention in class. Franco? Grecian?"

"Baroque, mostly," Antoine offered. "A bit of Bauhaus in a few buildings." He decided to take the bull by the proverbial horns. "We're in Stuttgart, Germany, Tahira. And it's Thursday."

Tahira slumped against the expanded metal grating with a dropped jaw. It took two tries before she could get words out of her mouth, and even then they were a coarse whisper. "But . . . I was captured on Friday, and it was the first night of the moon. It can't . . . the moon can't last for a whole week, can it? I mean, strange things happen around Halloween, but not *that* strange."

Antoine sighed heavily and felt his shoulders slump. If she really had lost her brother, there would be no hope of finding a trail after this long. He hated to tell her, but better now than later. "It's the second week of December, Tahira. I closed my show early so my troupe and I could return to America for a long holiday. Can you remember *anything* about your captivity? Anything at all?"

"A *month*? But I couldn't have been a prisoner for a full month! What about Rabi?" She wiped sudden tears away with an angry hand. He could tell she was trying hard, but her chin quivered and her fists clenched as she fought to control her emotions. And there was no hiding her scent.

Antoine's voice was soft and gentle. "I'm so very sorry, Tahira. I hope your brother is still alive. When we get back to the show, you're welcome to full use of my satellite phone or the Internet to make some calls."

The next curve brought the old tunnel into sight in the far distance. They were only a dozen miles from their camp. While Antoine had planned to stay near the auditorium where the show had been performed, the hotels were all sold out from a second convention, and they would have had to split the troupe. That was bad for morale of the cats, so they had obtained a special permit to set up the living trailers and an animal exercise tent in a field on the outskirts of the city.

He tried to ignore Tahira's wracking sobs in the back of the van. The reality of her situation had sunk home and there was little that could be done for the moment. By the time they arrived—

A light caught his attention and he flicked his eyes to the driver's side mirror. There was a police car on their tail and the blue lights were flashing. Well, perhaps it wasn't for him. He slowed and moved toward the edge of the road to give it room to pass. But there wasn't much room to move. The plows had been busy and the towering pile of ice-covered dirty snow could easily take off his side mirror. But the police car also slowed and moved to the side. *Merde!* What now?

"Take off the shirt, Tahira!"

He said it harshly enough to stem her tears and look up in shock. "What?"

Antoine applied his foot to the brake—just enough to show compliance but still stall for time. "The police are behind us again. They will be expecting a tiger, and I happen to like the shirt you're wearing."

She turned and looked out the tinted rear window. "Oh!" She hurried to obey, not even noticing that he would see her naked.

But his eyes were only on the police. He pulled the car over and sent a powerful burst of magic into the back of the van. "I'm sorry, but this is going to hurt."

He had to watch to make sure that the timing was right. She grunted but didn't scream as raw energy ripped across her body, literally *pulling* the tiger inside to the surface. Bones broke and fur flowed like a waterfall over sharp rocks. It was over in seconds, leaving her panting and shaking on the carpet before the van had even come to a complete halt. He kept feeding power into her until she roared in protest. He was surprised when a shock of fear scent flowed from the back. But there was no time to ease her fears.

Antoine rolled down the window and forced a smile onto his face. It was difficult. The strain of keeping her in animal form seemed to be increasing. He could feel sweat paint his brow and start to roll down his temple.

"*Guten tag.* Is there a problem, officer?"

Tahira fought back a growl, and he noticed. It was the same man she'd growled at in the station—the one who had kicked her. The officer noticed the tiger's complete attention. He unconsciously backed away from the window a half step. "You forgot to sign a document, Herr Monier. All of the documents *must* be signed."

Antoine bit back his first response. He couldn't afford

to give the officer any reason to detain him further. He couldn't understand why it was so difficult to hold Tahira's form. It hadn't been like this earlier, but the more power he gave, the more she required. It was quickly draining him. His eyes were growing unfocused as he stared at the paper and the spot where the gloved finger pointed. He nearly dropped the pen from limp fingers while signing, and the German noticed.

"Are you well, Herr Monier? You look very pale suddenly. Should I follow you to your camp?"

Antoine's mouth felt dry and hot, and he had to lick his tongue over chapped lips. He managed a small smile and nodded. "I'm merely tired. I was up late performing and had little sleep before I received the call from your Kommissar." He pointed at the tunnel mouth. "But our camp is just on the other side of the mountain. So there's no problem. I appreciate the offer, but I don't believe I need an escort."

The officer wasn't buying it. Tahira must have seen his indecision, because she suddenly threw herself against the side window and let out a vicious roar, making the entire van rock. The officer blanched and stepped back in alarm. It was enough of a distraction. His eyes moved quickly between the large tiger and Antoine's pale face. "Very well, then, Herr Monier. I will leave you and your cat to make your way back."

Another roar and a powerful leap against the rear grate as the officer returned to his car made him drop the clipboard and scramble to pick it up. Antoine rolled up the window. "His reaction alone tells his guilt. That one is all muscle, with an intellect rivaled only by garden tools. His Kommissar wouldn't have been so easily distracted."

A dark chuckle that ended with an animal snarl came from deep within his chest. Tahira regarded him with a sideways glance. "Don't worry. I have few ideas to *thank him* for his treatment of you." Antoine stepped on the gas and quickly increased the distance between the two cars. "And now I think it's time for you to turn human again."

He threw a wave of power and waited for the change to occur.

But it didn't. Instead, the heat began to increase so quickly that his head began to pound. He started breathing painfully and noticed that Tahira was as well.

"Why aren't I changing?" Her speaking voice in animal form was nearly an octave deeper than when human. There was a delicious dark snarl at the end of each word.

"I don't know. Something is wrong. But just a few more miles—"

By the time the tunnel loomed in front of them, Antoine was having a hard time keeping the car on the road. *Just a few more minutes. But why can't I stop my magic?* Sweat was pouring freely down his face, stinging his eyes with salt. He heard Tahira collapse to the carpet and begin to pant heavily from exhaustion.

He leaned forward on the steering wheel to keep himself upright. His magic, his very life force, was being sucked away, and he didn't know why. Already spots of gray and white were edging his vision.

The darkness ahead seemed to stretch out, the light at the end narrowing to a pinpoint that disappeared into an inky blackness the headlights couldn't pierce. What in the name of—?

Twin red slits appeared above him and a gasp choked his throat as the eyes blinked and became the red irises of a giant snake. They were driving right into its maw! Antoine turned the wheel frantically and slammed on the brake. He heard a distant scream and tearing metal, as though he was underwater.

Bone-jarring pain now in his shoulder, his leg, the side of his head.

More images passed in front of his eyes. He fought, as he always did, but the shimmering reflections entered him, filled him, and he couldn't turn away: A veiled woman dressed in black and gold moved in a slow, sultry dance to music he couldn't hear; men and women, chained to rocks screamed and shriveled into husks of paper-thin flesh that stretched thin over twisted animal bones; lips pressed against his that tasted of cherry jam and sandalwood. A hole appeared in a stone cliff covered with brush; water, and a need to breathe so strong it seared his lungs. Blinding pain in his chest seemed to flay the skin from his bones from the inside out; and through it all, the eyes—those fiery eyes that his heart knew would burn his world to ash if he didn't intervene.

The images rushed forward, enveloping him in sparkling power before everything disappeared into blackness.

Chapter Two

"ARE YOU CERTAIN that you wish to meet with these men, my lord? I can complete the transaction without your involvement."

The steady drip of water from the mineral stalactite against the cave floor punctuated the seconds while Nasil waited for a reply. The quiet murmur of chanting from the next chamber seemed to take on the beat of the droplets.

A deep chuckle made Nasil shiver in the cool dampness. The measured voice when his master replied held a note of amusement that didn't bode well for the interaction. "No, Nasil. I believe that I would like to meet these men. I always prefer to personally deal with those who *fail me*."

The words became a whip and Nasil flinched as though struck. He dropped to his knees on the smooth stone and bowed low at the feet of his seated master. "Their failure is mine, my lord. I did not think it necessary to be specific as to the tiger we sought. I didn't realize that there was another tig—"

Nasil heard movement but held his place. He was born to serve this man—trained to take whatever punishment was determined. He would honor his calling regardless of his fate. His heart quickened when the rustle of cloth stopped next to his head, but he didn't move.

The voice was pleased, and he breathed a silent sigh of relief. "The scent of your fear, and your quiet acceptance of my judgment move me, Nasil. You have served me well for many centuries. This small defeat will not reverse your lifetime of service in my eyes. You did *exactly* as I instructed, so the fault is mine—"

A clatter of rocks in the distant tunnel stopped them both. The baritone lowered to a whisper. "Stand at my side once more, Nasil. We will greet these . . . *poachers* as one, as we always have."

"As you command, my lord Sargon." He rose to his feet after the other man had seated himself. Nasil stepped behind the rock where Sargon reclined on a cushion.

The ammonia scent of panic was almost visible as the chanting grew louder beyond the curve of the cave but wasn't enough to cover the rattling of the chains as the subject struggled to free herself. The press of magic seemed to fill the room in a wave and then flow back out in a rush with the power of a tsunami. Nasil struggled to keep his feet as the tide rushed past him, pulling his own magic through his very pores. His skin began to ache then burn as more power was drained. Even Sargon was affected by the magic drain, but Nasil noted that a slow smile was curling his master's lip.

Perhaps they had finally succeeded. Perhaps—

A piercing scream filled Nasil's ears and made him flinch involuntarily. Sargon stood and turned his attention to the flickering torch light that illuminated the other chamber. The scent of his anticipation, his joy, brought pleasure to Nasil's heart. But then the scream abruptly cut off and his master frowned in the silence.

"What was that?" came a male voice from the darkness ahead to their left. "Was that a scream?"

"So what if it was?" another man replied in a bass

rumble. "None of our concern. Hey, there's a light ahead. Maybe we've finally reached the end of this stinkin' cave."

The first voice, a thready alto, quavered a bit. "Let's just get our money and get out of here, Alan. Getting tigers is one thing, but I don't like this. It feels like a setup."

Nasil saw the men first, and stepped toward them. Sargon didn't turn to the arrival of the poachers. He continued to watch the torch, waiting for any sign. A woman appeared from the lit chamber, followed by a huge black man with long dreadlocks and a bare chest. Nasil stepped back so Sargon could approach them.

When the poachers rounded the final bend, Nasil held up a hand to stop them where they stood. The tall, stocky poacher who had been identified as Alan started to open his mouth to say something but stopped when Nasil moved forward like lightning and flexed a hand around the man's throat tight enough to silence him.

"Be quiet or *die*!" He let some of his remaining power flow toward the men and hissed the words into the poachers' faces so his master would not be interrupted. The men glanced at each other nervously but obeyed. Nasil took a few moments to check the men for weapons with his free hand. The fools had honored their bargain. Each was unarmed save for a small knife.

Sargon stepped forward until he was within inches from the woman. The metallic scent of blood hung heavy in the air. "Dr. Portes? What went wrong *this* time?"

The tiny Guatemalan woman shook her head and wiped the smear of red covering her hands off on the front of her smock. Nasil noted that the thin poacher paled a bit at the look of *annoyance* on the woman's face.

"The same as happened *last* time, my lord. She was

not the one. We had hoped to expand her abilities through the ritual, but the power consumed her."

Sargon's voice was calm and soft, which Nasil knew was when he was at his most dangerous. "Is she still alive?"

The harsh laugh from the black man was quickly eaten by the cave, just as the scream had been. It was as though the cave itself fed on their presence. No echoes would reach the outside world.

"She is *not*," he replied harshly. "She was torn apart before the ritual completed. I told yo—"

Sargon had the African pinned high against the wall, his neck held at a painful angle before he could complete the word. The flow of magic was stifling and it was all Nasil could do to keep the poachers from bolting from sheer terror. The scent of their fear was powerful enough to bring a disturbing gleam to Rachel Portes's eyes.

"You do not tell *me* anything, Zuberi. You are here only at my sufferance, and you will hold your tongue or I will turn you over to the doctor for an *appetizer*. Do you understand?"

Nasil was pleased to see the nearly living fear in Zuberi's eyes. He *should* be very afraid. He nodded with what little movement Sargon allowed him.

Sargon released his hand and his magic, and Zuberi dropped unceremoniously to the floor. Were it not for the human poachers present, Nasil knew that Sargon would have used only his magic to punish the man, so as not to soil his royal hands with the likes of a *cat*.

Dr. Portes stepped forward quietly. "The room should be cleaned before the next attempt, my lord."

Sargon held up his hand and she fell silent. "In a moment, Doctor. Let me first greet my *guests*. Nasil, release them and bring them before me."

Nasil led Alan and his friend to where Sargon once again rested on his pillows.

Alan rubbed the red marks on his throat and pointed a long, black metal flashlight menacingly at Nasil. "You and me, buddy. When this is done, we're going to go rounds for that little stunt."

Nasil doubted that *he* would be given that honor, but smiled the tiniest bit and nodded to the fool.

"So," the man strutted forward toward the master. "You're Sargon, huh? Well, you got your tiger. Now we get our money."

Sargon's face lit up with a broad smile. "I'm afraid that you're very confused. I do *not* have my tiger, so you get no money."

The thin man with the ferret-like face finally got over his fear enough to smell angry. "Whoa! You wanted a tiger, and we got you *three* tigers. Don't jack us around, asshole."

He started to step forward aggressively, but stopped when Nasil was suddenly in front of them, blocking the path to his master.

Alan stared him down, despite the scent of fear and twitching of his eye muscles. "Me and Mickey worked our butts off to get those tigers and we're taking our money, even if we have to take it off your dead bodies."

When Sargon stood and put a hand on Nasil's shoulder, he stepped back with a bow. The master's voice began light. "There's no need to argue, gentlemen. While I can *assure* you that you did not deliver my tiger, I'm certain we can work something out. The error was mine. I did not tell you the *specific* tiger we wished you to deliver. You did actually capture her, but then *left her* to be discovered by the authorities. *I was not pleased.*"

His voice had dropped nearly an octave during the speech and ended with enough scorn to cut through the anger of the men. They watched the tall, olive-skinned man with nervous eyes as he stepped closer and closer.

Sargon let his angry magic leak out until it was a suffocating cloud that the men wanted to run screaming from.

But just when they were ready to bolt back into the blackness of the cave in terror, Nasil was surprised to see Sargon stop and smile.

"But, as I said, gentlemen—we can work this out." He reached into the pocket of his tailored slacks and removed a leather bag tied with a strip of rawhide. He held it up for the men to see and shook it. The richly toned clinking inside made the men's eyes light up greedily. "In this bag are gold coins equal to *half* the money you negotiated with Nasil."

The pair looked at each other. "Hey!" Alan nearly shouted.

Sargon raised his hand in a seemingly placating manner. "Never fear, gentlemen. The gold coins inside this bag are very old and *very* rare. While the actual value as a metal is indeed half, the value as *antiquities* might be double what you anticipated—with a little work on your part to find the right buyer."

Alan gave a knowing smile. "So, for leaving the fourth tiger for the Germans to find, we have to pad shoe leather to get all of our money, huh?"

Sargon raised one brow. "Precisely."

The ferret-faced man named Mickey looked suspicious. "I want to *see* the coins first. I know a little bit about gold."

"As you wish." Sargon tossed the bag to the ferret-faced man. "But I would be very cautious not to get your finger oil on the coins."

The poacher waved away the comment. "Yeah, yeah. I know." He loosened the leather thong carefully and eased one of the coins into view, using the leather top of the bag to hold it. He stepped closer to the torch and squinted as he turned the captured coin to see the reverse.

"So, whatcha think, Mickey?" Alan asked as Sargon returned to his cushions with a small smile.

Mickey let out a slow whistle and looked excitedly at Alan. "Man! Either this is the best damn forgery I've ever seen, or this coin is an honest to fucking God Spanish doubloon. This freaking bag might be worth a *fortune*."

Sargon raised his hands and leaned back. "As I said."

Sargon took the moment to stand and walk over to Mickey. He licked his palm slightly while the other man wasn't looking. "Do we, as you say, have a deal?" He held out his palm to Mickey, who was almost too busy staring at the coins in the bag to notice. But when Sargon cleared his throat, he looked up and the dry heat scent of embarrassment found Nasil's nose.

"Oh, yeah. Sure." He shook Sargon's hand and then returned his attention to the coins.

"And you, Mister, er—Alan?" The tall man was shaking his head, little movements that betrayed the fact that his instinct was telling him something completely different from what he was hearing. But he finally shook Sargon's hand.

"Then our business is at an end. You may go." The look on Sargon's face made Alan turn back more than once as they stepped into the cave.

Nasil smiled quietly as Sargon released Rachel and Zuberi before the poachers had reached the end of the torchlight.

Sargon raised his voice and called out to the poachers. "Oh! And gentlemen? One more minor detail."

They stopped and turned around. The beams of the powerful flashlights hurt Nasil's eyes, but he wanted to see the looks on their faces, so he squinted and kept watching.

Nasil could see the growing concern on Alan's face at

Sargon's smile. How little these foolish humans understood their kind.

"Yeah? What else?"

Nasil felt a burst of power tingle his skin as Rachel readied herself to transform into her animal form.

The low chuckle from his master tightened Nasil's throat again as Rachel stepped forward. Sargon ran a slow hand down her leg. His voice was soft, but Nasil knew it would carry to the men's ears because he had their full attention. "The poison that is now seeping into your palms will begin to affect you soon. In about thirty minutes, you'll be completely blind."

The two men stared at their palms in abject horror and began to rub them frantically against the fabric of their pants. Mickey dropped his flashlight and scrambled to recover it, all while keeping his total attention on Sargon.

"If you make it to the entrance of the cave, the gold is yours to keep. Of course, you'll be sightless, but what is that small detail to a millionaire?" Sargon stood and stepped toward the torch. He pulled it from the holder in the wall and ran his hand through the fire until the flame glowed green from both his magic and the venom still on his palm. He carried the torch back to the cushion.

The poachers were slowly backing away, trying to keep from stumbling but wanting to make sure they heard every word. "You're insane, Sargon! We'll go to the cops! You'll wind up in prison for the rest of your life."

Nasil chuckled and Sargon let out a laugh of fierce joy. "Prisons have crumbled to dust around my feet while I still remain, gentlemen. You should probably leave now. I believe that Nasil timed the journey from here to there at twenty-two minutes—if you *run*."

Sargon looked at them with the cold, unfeeling eyes

of a snake. But the pair *truly* understood the nature of their deal when Rachel completed her transformation. The sudden horror on their faces was worth the pain in Nasil's head from the flashlight and green fire.

"But I don't believe it will be a problem for you to beat Nasil's time, since the lovely Dr. Portes will be chasing you. I wouldn't suggest you let her catch you. I've heard she's quite a . . . handful. I'll be magnanimous and give you to the count of ten. One—"

With a rush of air that sounded quite a bit like a scream, Alan and Mickey turned and ran at full speed into the darkness of the cave. "Two . . . three . . . oh, to the devil with it—*ten*." Sargon stroked his hand again down one of her legs, one of the many that surrounded his cushions. "Bring back the gold if you would, my love." He put his lips close to her mandibles and licked a drop of poison from her fang, while the spider leaned into him. He shuddered briefly as the venom burned his lips and tongue. He ran his teeth over the small hole it cut into them.

"Ssshall I allow them to reach the light, my lord?"

Sargon smiled, but there was no emotion in his eyes. "Consider them a reward for your efforts with the ritual. You must be quite drained. Do with them what you will."

The nearly silent scuttling of her feet against the stone as she started the chase unnerved Nasil.

"My lord Sargon?" Zuberi's voice was small and quiet from the wall where he still remained.

"Yes, Zuberi?"

"I do not wish to seem too bold, my lord, but the poachers failed."

Sargon sighed and turned to the big Swahili. "They did indeed, Zuberi. And I suppose you are hoping that I will allow your plan to proceed?"

Zuberi dropped to his knees in front of Sargon's pillow and remained prostrate. His words were slightly muffled by the stone touching his lips. "I believe it's a good plan, my lord. I will not fail you as they did."

Nasil watched sweat form on the broad, dark back as Sargon pondered the situation. "I will give you a chance—but only *one* chance. Bring her to me before the next full moon rises and you will have repaid your debt to me. Now, if you're quick you may join Rachel in the feast."

Zuberi raised his head with a smile. He kissed Sargon's slippered foot before melting into the darkness of the cave in a blur.

Nasil waited until Zuberi was out of earshot before he stepped to Sargon's side. "I believe it unwise to trust them."

"I know you do, Nasil. But Rachel Portes excites me as no woman ever has, and Zuberi has undeniable skill for this particular venture. He has reason to bear a grudge against the Monier clan, so all eyes will point to him and the fools will not even *look* further. Besides, they're both expendable."

Nasil acknowledged the fact with a dip of his head. "But their kind are untrustworthy—"

A man's scream from the darkness was swallowed by the sacred cave, and another followed in seconds.

Sargon chuckled. "Yes, Nasil. Aren't we all?"

Chapter Three

"Do you plan to sleep away the day, little cub?"

Antoine turned his head to the familiar voice and struggled to open his eyes. It wasn't as easy as it should be, and that worried him. His senses returned first, and he felt a slight breeze overhead, heard the stuttering whir of a mechanical fan and the clinking of tableware. He took a deep breath and held it for a moment. Coffee with chicory, fried bacon, eggs, and bread. But underlying the food scents were other ones. Clean linen with a hint of dried blood, his older sister's musk perfume, and the soft fur scent of *Grand-mère*.

He realized he was lying in a bed because of the cool thickness of the sheets under his hand, the fluffy pillow that threatened to smother his head, and the weight of blankets over him. But he shouldn't *be* in a bed. Should he?

A tapestry that covered one entire wall was the first thing Antoine saw when he could finally focus without pain. The rich blues with gold, greens, and vibrant reds that portrayed scenes from Chaucer's *Canterbury Tales* demanded recognition. So, he knew *where* he was, but couldn't figure out for the life of him how he'd come to be here. He snaked one arm from under the quilt and put it to his eyes to discover a cloth bandage encircling his head.

Merde! What in blazes happened to me? But then the

memories slowly started to filter into his brain—the police station, the dead tigers, the girl and—

He sat bolt upright in a panic. "Where is the girl, *Grand-mère*? Where is Tahira? Is she safe? What happened?"

A tiny, white-haired woman, a lynx in her animal form, stepped to where he could see her. She uttered an exasperated breath. Although Giselle Bertrand was not a blood relative, she had raised Antoine after his mother died, and he would always think of her as his grandmother.

"Pfft! Would I not have told you immediately if the young woman was *not* safe, *petit fils*? She was in the van with you, *somehow* still in tiger form after moonset. You lost control on the icy road and crashed into a tree near where we were breaking camp."

"How did we get to Charles's mansion? Where are my cats and the troupe?"

She clucked her tongue and jumped up lightly to sit next to him on the thick down mattress. She patted his leg and he moved it to give her room. "We *are* competent to run the show without your continual presence, Antoine. The cats, save for Babette and the cubs who are housed in the basement lair, and most of the performers have returned to America. Charles and your sister stopped by for a visit on the way to their winter home in Siberia. He foresaw your accident and sent us to you. Amber made certain that the girl was changed back to human form and you were both put into a sleep until you could recover."

Antoine touched the bandage again and Giselle noticed his concern and the quickened beating of his heart. She laughed brightly. "Ah! No need to worry, little cub. Margo instructed Matty to bandage your head so the linens wouldn't be ruined while you slept. The cut on your head was quite deep, but I've no doubt it's healed by now."

"I need to see the girl, and then Charles." He started to slide out the opposite side of the bed when Giselle grabbed his arm.

"*Non*, Antoine. The girl is still asleep and Charles has gone. You must rest, regain your strength. Amber said you were badly drained."

Antoine's brow furrowed. "He *left*? Why would he—?" He shook his head with annoyance. "Then I'll have to call him. It's imperative that I speak with him."

It would do no good to explain to *Grand-mère* about the vision. She couldn't grasp the concept when he was a boy, and little had changed other than a grudging acknowledgment that he actually *was* a seer. No, he needed to get an interpretation of some of the images from his mentor because he was certain it involved the girl.

He was surprised when Giselle didn't remove her hand from his arm. Instead, she tightened it and pulled him back. "Once again—*non*, little one. You forget your place. Charles is fully aware of everything, as he always is. He left specific instructions for you regarding the Hayalet girl with Margo. If you will not rest, then you will *eat*. The telephones are not working because a road crew cut the underground lines. We're fortunate that Charles maintains a generator for electricity or we wouldn't have that either."

She removed her hand from his arm and patted his cheek. "Eat the meal that Matty prepared. It's simple but filling. Then you may dress and join us by the fireplace in the great room downstairs. We will be here for a day—perhaps longer. The radio reports the storm is large."

Antoine nodded his head but didn't respond. *Grand-mère* could scent a lie, so it would do no good to agree to follow her instructions if he didn't intend to. But he would contact Charles, and quickly. The chief justice might be a seer like himself, but he couldn't know what

Antoine had seen, nor realize how critical it was that they move quickly. Antoine couldn't say why, but he knew it was so.

Giselle's chin dropped, her arms crossed over her thin chest, and she stared at him with suspicious eyes. Antoine only just managed not to flinch under the intensity of her gaze. "I know that look, Antoine. While I may no longer be able to physically *prevent* you from making a fool of yourself, I hope that you will at least display the common sense the heavens gave a prey animal. Speak with Margo before you do what I know you plan to do."

She was right, but he hated it. He shook his head in annoyance and clenched his fists. "*Grand-mère*, I'll talk with Margo. But I must first see for myself that the girl is healing."

Giselle threw up her hands in frustration and lightly leapt down to the floor. "Always the stubborn cub! Well, it will do no harm, I suppose. The magical sleep that Amber placed her in will only end when she is healed. If she is awake, she is healed. As you choose, my esteemed Rex." She bowed her head in subservience and backed away from the bed.

Antoine shook his head again. She was not lying, nor being condescending. *Grand-mère* was just stating the truth. But he wished he could believe it. He *was* the leader—at least in name—but could seldom do as he chose. He slipped from under the covers and started to stand, but then jerked his bare feet back from the cold stone floor and put on the slippers conveniently by his bedside. No doubt Margo's doing.

Rex. Councilman. I'm supposed to be the leader of my people, but I am still a cub in their eyes. Worse, in my own.

By the time he'd taken a long, hot shower, had a shave, and completed his other bathroom chores, Antoine had banished some of the demons that seemed to lurk in his mind whenever someone referred to him by title. The cuts on his head were healed. Only a long, faint scar remained near his temple from what he supposed would have required a number of stitches on a human.

He dressed for the dreary day and his dark mood. Black slacks, charcoal turtleneck, and a simple rubber band for his hair. His clothing had been transferred from his trailer to an exquisite Louis XV armoire. The rest of the furniture matched the wardrobe. While gaudily ornate, Antoine loved everything about the furniture: the carved cabrioles, embellished shell and acanthus leaves on the cartouche, and thick beveled glass on the armoire. Someday he would convince Charles to sell him the set for the estate in Strasbourg.

But for now, it was time to face the day. He slipped quietly from his room and immediately heard a loud thump and voices from downstairs.

"I swear, Matty, if I catch you with your feet on that one more time, I'm going to—" Antoine could hear the frustration in Margo's voice. "Do you have any idea how much that table's worth?"

Antoine could smell the faint scent of sandalwood and musk through the door next to him. He opened it a crack and slipped inside the room. The pale light that edged the heavy curtains was enough for his sensitive eyes to see in after a blink or two.

He heard his Australian friend laugh downstairs as he moved silently to the bed. "Probably big bikkies. I'm not a drongo, Margo. I already promised Charles that I wouldn't muck around while we're here, so relax."

Tahira's thick hair was splayed over the pillow, her breathing slow and eyes closed. She seemed fragile and very . . . *human*, despite the sleek, powerful cat who had shaken the van to the frame with a single blow. He studied her face for a moment. Her slightly rounded face, broad nose, and luxurious brows were common in weretigers. But her lips were thinner than other cats he knew, including the Sazi Bengal agent in Wolven. There was some cross-breeding there that made her face unique and . . . lovely.

He wished he could see her eyes. A person's eyes told him so much—sometimes even more than their scent.

Are they green or hazel in her human form, or perhaps nearly amber like mine?

Tahira's nostrils flared for a moment as though she could scent him. He started to step away, but she turned on her side and dropped back into her magical sleep. Her hair fell back from her neck and he could see that more than half of her left earlobe was missing. The edge of the damaged area didn't appear ripped. It had been cut. Perhaps it was a Hayalet tradition? He wanted to ask, wanted to know what brought her to this place.

But *Grand-mère* was right. There was no reason to wake her for the moment.

He reached for her before he realized he was moving, gently brushing a few strands of hair off her cheek, letting the silky strands glide over his sensitive palms. A new scent rose from the fire-colored hair. He bent down slightly and sniffed, then lifted some of the dark to his nose. How strange. The highlights had a different scent from the rest—a smoky, spicy cinnamon that was different from anything he'd ever smelled.

He was startled that touching her hair had been so unconscious, but a part of him was pleased when she sighed peacefully and dropped back into her dreamless sleep. He left the room before he accidentally woke her, being careful to turn the doorknob before pulling the door closed with barely a whisper of sound.

He turned and stood at the balcony overlooking the massive entry room. Although typical of the building practices a century ago, it still startled him that the cathedral ceiling in the entry was actually *necessary* when the owner of the house turned on the moon. Antoine had only seen Charles Wingate in his animal form a few times, but it had been more than a little startling— not to mention *intimidating* as hell. Charles was a polar bear that could stand flat footed on all four legs and look in the windows of a two-story building. Each of his razor sharp teeth was nearly as broad and long as Antoine's forearm. But it was why Charles was the chief justice of the council, and had held that position for longer than anyone could remember.

As he started down the gray stone staircase that was flanked by banners of the many countries and cultures that the Sazi represented, Margo spoke again. "A person would think that we both spoke the same language until you open your mouth, Matty. That Australian slang is going to be the death of me. What in the world did you just say?"

Antoine stepped into the doorway of the large, lavishly furnished main room. A fire roared in the walk-in fireplace, and muted daylight streamed in from a dozen windows on the south wall. Margo was seated at a desk, her laptop computer open on several programs. Her comforting odor of . . . hmm, *peaches with nutmeg* made for an odd combination with Matty's underlying . . . yes, dill weed and tomato scent. That young wolf in Chicago had gotten him hooked on this *"personal scent equals food"* concept, and he was finding it surprisingly true. Tony had promised to send a list of his discoveries to date for Antoine's amusement.

Matty was—well, he seemed to be *whittling*. Bits and chunks of fragrant pine were flying through the air each time he stroked the wicked-looking knife blade along the length of wood.

"He said that the furniture is probably very expensive, that he's not stupid and that Charles made him promise not to have any accidents. How are you today, Matty, and what in the world are you doing?"

Margo looked his way and heaved a visible sigh of relief. "Glad to see you alive and well, boss. You gave us a scare yesterday."

Matty turned a grin to Antoine as well. "G'day, Antoine. I'm doing good, thanks mate! I see you managed some shonky bizzo so we could all stay over."

Antoine walked to the couch next to the fireplace and plopped down into the soft cushions. He let out a small chuckle. "Yes, I'm quite good at wrecking the van and faking head wounds just to be a guest at the chief justice's home. I presume that the van *is* wrecked?"

Matty smirked and then nodded. "Yeah. It was quite a bingle, mate! We just managed to get you back here before the coppers showed up."

Antoine's light mood evaporated. "The police were involved?"

Margo looked up, away from the screen, while her fingers continued to fly over the keyboard. "Only until Charles arrived. I doubt they'll even remember showing up."

"Speaking of Charles—" Antoine inclined his head a bit toward Margo. "Do we need to speak alone? Where is *Grand-mère*?"

"Not for me," replied Matty. "I was in the room when they yabbered, so no worries. Giselle is out hunting rabbits in the storm. You know how lynxes are—can't keep 'em out of the white stuff."

Margo nodded in agreement. "We didn't discuss any council business. It was just regarding the girl."

Matty laughed. "Ace sheila you cracked onto, mate! She's not a dog."

Antoine gave him a sharp look that ended the laugh abruptly. His voice was harsh with anger. "I did not '*crack onto*' her, Matty. She was a prisoner—first of the same men who killed Simon, and then of the police."

The other faces showed shock, and then the scent of sorrow made him remember that they hadn't known. Margo spoke first. Her voice quavered with surfacing tears. "So Simon is really *dead*? I'm so sorry, Antoine."

Matty winced. "Your Dale is going to be mad as a cut snake that someone done him in, Margo. Probably best that he went back with the other cats."

Antoine tried not to remember the scene in the forest, but they deserved to know the basic details. "As far as the police here are concerned, the girl upstairs *is* Simon. Well, actually, she's supposed to be *Babette*."

Margo looked at him quizzically. "So Babette is *Simon*?" She shook her head. "I'm afraid I don't understand, Antoine."

Matty showed a pained smile. "Yeah. Bit of a shock for her cubs, mate. Simon wasn't known for his nursing skills."

"Matty!" Margo's voice showed her outrage at the comment.

But Antoine knew that Matty was trying to use humor to cover the pain. The big cat had been a favorite of his, too. Being the veterinarian for the troupe, he was accustomed to injuries and death, but slaughter was something else entirely.

"It's a very long story, my friends, and I only have bits of it. The police here discovered a tiger organ smuggling operation. The police took me to the site. Simon was among the dead."

While Matty retained his outward composure, his

scent gave away his horror and anger. A small muscle at the corner of his jaw started to twitch from his clenched jaw. Margo was likewise affected, but the wet cloud of sorrow blanketed the anger.

"But I smelled a Sazi female—or what I *thought* was a Sazi female." He brushed a few chips of wood from his pants. Matty's whittling was getting more aggressive as he got angrier.

"Who is actually a Hayalet. Charles told us," concluded Margo. "I don't know much about their people, and I called *everyone* after he and Amber left, but nobody else knew anything either."

Antoine shrugged gracefully. "I know little myself that isn't classified. Their people live in the mountains on the Iranian/Turkish border. They were nearly wiped out by the Russians back in the 1950s, when the Caspian tigers were hunted to near extinction."

"I thought they were hunted *to* extinction," Matty replied. "There haven't been any specimens to study since the early 1960s, well before my time."

Margo turned her chair to face the men. The old wooden desk chair squeaked noisily with the movement. "There have been sightings from time to time over the years, but nothing confirmed. There were a few reports last fall on one of the animal channels, but nothing since."

She crossed her arms and tipped her head down to stare at Antoine over the top of her wireless glasses. "Charles said that we are to keep the girl here until her family comes for her. You are absolutely *not* to allow her to leave alone. You are *not* to let her family take her. We're supposed to sit tight and 'wait for events to unfold,' as the chief justice phrased it."

Antoine frowned and held up his hand. "Wait. We are supposed to hold her here until the family arrives, but *not* let them take her? That makes no sense!"

"Yeah," Matty replied. "I said the same thing. But he just gave me that *look* with those beady little black eyes, and I did the bolt."

Antoine ignored Margo's confused look that always seemed to follow Matty speaking. "That *look*?" But then it occurred to him, and he answered his own question. "Ah! The look that says, 'You're barely an appetizer but keep being disagreeable and I will be more than happy to have a snack.' *That* look?"

Matty shuddered and the knife flashed even more quickly. "Yeah, that'd be right. Like I'm a mozzie that needs squashing. I've never seen the bloke in his animal form, and don't *ever* want him to bail me up. I'd mind my own bizzo on his reasons if I were you, mate."

Several of the wood chips popped up, arched over the couch, and hit Margo in the face. She reared back when it struck her and the back of the chair slammed into the laptop screen. She stood in a rush and stalked toward Matty. "Would you *please* stop that ridiculous project! This whole room is going to be ruined! Just *buy* a boomerang and be done with it."

"A *boomerang*?" Antoine asked. "What in the devil do you need with a boomerang?"

Matty apparently didn't hear the question, or didn't care to answer. He continued shaving chunks of wood from the rapidly slimming log and glared up at the woman. "It's *not* a boomerang, Margo. I've told you that five times now. This is a *kylie*. Totally different weapon. I only have a few weeks to get everything made before I leave."

Antoine stood up, walked over to the couch, and yanked both the stick and the knife from Matty's hands before he could react. He threw them against the wall hard enough that the knife buried itself to the hilt into the window sill with a squealing sound.

His words took on the thick French accent that always occurred when he was angry. "*Je m'en fous!* I do not *care* what it is called! Things are happening, friends are dying, and I am being ignored! It will *stop*! I have very little humor left in me today, so I want to know what is going on—*now*!"

He didn't often let his Sazi magic leak out accidentally, even this close to the moon. But he could tell by the flinching from both of his human employees, and the sharp scent of their panic that he had done just that. Their eyes were too wide with white showing. He put fingers to his temples and closed his eyes. Then he bowed his head, took a long deep breath, and let it out slowly. By the time he had finished counting to ten, his magic was safely tucked back inside his own skin and the scent of terror in the room was a bit less.

He sat down on the couch next to Matty, who didn't move a muscle. Antoine placed a hand on his shoulder and was pleased that the vet didn't try to pull away. "I apologize, *mon ami*. I did not mean to press my anger on you." He turned his head to include Margo. "On *either* of you. But the last two days have given me many questions and few answers. Before we try to learn the meaning of the Hayalet or of the workings of our chief justice's mind, let us start in our own house. Matty, why are you carving a kylie and why are you leaving in a few weeks? Where are you going?"

Margo and Matty looked at each other in surprise. From their expressions, he should *know* what was happening, which meant that he'd been ignoring, or forgetting, things he'd been told. But with the unscheduled trip to Chicago for the council meeting, the *thing* they killed there, and the loss of Simon, he hadn't been paying proper attention. He was about to correct that oversight.

After a few moments, Matty laughed. "Strewth! No

wonder you've been staring at us like we had kangaroos loose in our top paddock! Yeah, well, this will take a minute. Charles put some VB in the fridge for us to watch the footy match this arvo—if we can get a signal. Care to share a slab?"

Antoine nodded and Matty rose to go to the kitchen. Margo called after him. "And while you're in there, could you maybe figure out how to tell your story in *English* for those of us who don't speak Australian?"

Margo turned back to Antoine and had just opened her mouth when he put up a sharp hand to stop her, and then a finger to his lips. He heard movement, and it was coming from the stairs. With all the stealth and grace of the cat inside him, he stepped to the doorway. He could tell who it was by scent, and by the shadow she cast on the floor. How long had she been listening?

Margo remained frozen in her chair as he stilled even his breathing. For a few long seconds, the only sounds were the crackling of the fireplace, the raging wind outside, and the sound of clinking glass in the kitchen. Then there was a quiet footfall as the person listening outside stepped a bit closer.

He stepped around the corner with supernatural speed. "Would you like to join us?"

"I'm sorry!" Tahira exclaimed. He could hear her heart pound frantically. "I didn't mean to eavesdrop. I woke up and just wanted—"

She wasn't faking her fear, that much was obvious. The clothing she was wearing seemed too large for Amber, but might well be left over from Fiona's last visit. She had a healing cut on her arm, but the angry bruise on her face had faded so he could finally notice her eyes. They were hazel, flecked with gold and green. Warm, intelligent, and quite lovely.

He swept down into a deep bow and gently took her

hand. "My humblest apologies, dear lady, for frightening you." He very lightly kissed the back of her hand and then stood. Her face showed confusion, but the tangy scent of her fear was dissipating. "Please, join us near the fire, and allow me to pour you a glass of wine to settle your nerves. One of my employees was about to tell us about a trip he's taking."

TAHIRA STOOD SILENTLY for a moment, her mind reeling from the roller coaster of emotions that were battling for dominance. Fear, anger, embarrassment—combined with a warm spot in her stomach from his smile and the feeling of his lips on her hand. But which was the lie and which was truth?

Antoine held her hand and smoothly led her farther into the brightly lit room. When he stepped away to remove a glass from a heavily carved wet bar, she glanced out the frost-edged windows. The raging blizzard she'd seen from her bedroom window looked even worse at ground level.

She thought of Rabi lost somewhere in this storm and tears again threatened. She had to find him. But while she *should* be able to track in snow, she didn't know how. Their kind came from a line where fierce winters were common, but she grew up in California. She had no skill, only instinct. Grammy hadn't gotten that far in training before she had gotten herself . . . *captured.*

She still couldn't believe that she had no memory of an entire month, but bits of things kept popping into her head and she couldn't ignore the implications. There were too many memories of rancid meat being shoved through cage bars, memories of chains on her wrists and ankles and around her neck as a tiger. There were too many fragments to have occurred in one day, or even a week. She had no choice but to believe what the Sazi had said.

"Tahira? Are you all right?" She turned away from the window, startled. Antoine was holding a crystal glass half filled with pink liquid. He held it out to her. "The blush was open, but if you prefer red or white, I can uncork a new bottle."

She took the glass from his hand, again noticing the tingling of her skin when it touched him. The air around him seemed almost electric, as though her hair should be standing on end. "No, blush is fine. Thanks."

He nodded slightly and smiled. "Would you like to meet the others, or would you prefer to be alone for a bit? We could move to another room."

She turned and saw two other people in the room. The woman had short honey-colored hair and bright blue eyes behind small rectangle glasses. The man who was just entering through the far doorway was carrying half a dozen beer bottles of a brand she didn't recognize. He moved with an easy swagger and his tanned, leathery skin spoke of countless hours in the sun. He seemed to exude that same devil-may-care attitude of some surfers she knew from back home.

"No, no, you shouldn't have to leave. But I'm really tired still, so I might just sit by the fire and listen if that's okay."

He inclined his head just a bit and stepped back. "But of course. Whatever you wish." He walked over to the bar once more and removed a brandy snifter that was warming over a small alcohol heater. He swirled the small quantity of amber liquid around the wide bottom for a moment to cool it. He waved the glass under his nose and sighed.

The dark-haired man walked past her and set a beer bottle on the bar next to Antoine just as he drank down the contents. "There you go, mate. Something to wash the taste of that slop out of your mouth."

Antoine laughed and put the glass back on the bar. He snuffed out the flame and picked up the open beer. "That '*slop*' is hundred-year-old cognac, Matty. You know full well cognac is the main reason we even stopped in Stuttgart."

The man named Matty flopped down on the chair and put his feet up on a low table with legs carved in the shape of dragons breathing fire. The honey-haired woman let out a strangled sound that caused him to roll his eyes and lower his feet back to the floor.

"Yeah. Some bloke found a bottle of old wine that you're going to pay out your arse for, just to put it in a dusty vault under your house. Waste of money and good grog, mate." He raised his bottle in salute. "You need to stick with throw-downs. Just as right for a Sunday barbie in the backyard as an arvo in front of the telly watching the footy."

Antoine's eyes twinkled merrily as he stepped toward the couch and swept his hand to indicate that she should precede him. "First, let's dispense with the formal introductions. Matty, Margo, this lovely young lady is Tahira Kuric. She's a member of the Hayalet Kabile from California. She and her brother were staying with their grandparents in Turkey when the abduction took place." He glanced at her for confirmation. "Correct?"

She was taking a sip of the wine and lowered the glass suddenly, since he seemed to be waiting for an answer. She was startled that he remembered everything she'd told him.

"Yes . . . um, that's right." She raised her hand and gave an embarrassed wave and then bit her lip for a second when Margo smiled and smelled of amusement. She set her jaw. *No, I can do this. I managed debate club and school plays, and I'm an adult member of the kabile. Time to grow up and play with the big cats.*

Antoine dropped his chin a bit in acknowledgment. "The gentleman on the couch is Matthew Thompson. He's a large animal veterinarian from Sydney, Australia, who cares for our cats."

Matty tipped an imaginary hat, smiled quietly, and then popped the cap on his second beer. "G'day, Tahira. Sorry our introduction isn't under more pleasant circumstances."

She smiled at him. His underlying scent reminded her of a summer picnic in the park and it reminded her of home. She already knew that the phones weren't working, but she needed to contact her folks as soon as possible to let them know that she was okay and find out if they'd heard from Rabi. *Maybe he's already escaped and I'm the only one still missing.*

Antoine's voice showed a small amount of humor that made her look up. "The lovely lady at the desk with the dropped jaw is Margo Ritzman."

Margo was staring at Matty with something approaching awe. He turned his head and regarded her with a bit of challenge in his expression.

"You spoke *English*! Real, understandable English!"

He laughed. "Thanks heaps! I *am* a uni graduate, luv, with a couple years of grad school in the States. I talk to Antoine that way because it's comfortable and he understands it. Well . . . and of course, because it bothers *you*." He turned to Tahira again and winked. "I'm a true blue, dinky-di cockroach, darls, but for *your* benefit, I'll pretend I'm a Yank."

Tahira laughed. She liked Matty! "We had an exchange student from Queensland when I was in school, so I'll try to follow along."

"A banana bender, eh? Yeah, well they're sort of Aussie, I suppose."

She took a sip from her wine and said with a small amount of teasing, "Strange, he said the same about people from New South Wales." She nodded to Margo. "Nice to meet you. Are you by any chance on the internet? My parents must be frantic about me. Maybe I could send them an e-mail?" She bit her lip hopefully. Margo looked to Antoine significantly and he took a slow breath. Either he was really good at hiding his emotions, or he wasn't concerned, because he didn't smell of deceit.

"I think we might arrange that if we have a connection," Antoine said, which caused a brief look of surprise on Margo's face. She quickly turned back to the computer.

"I'll check to see. It wasn't up a few minutes ago. I've been working on some other things off-line."

While she opened the programs to try to connect, Antoine waved Tahira to the couch. "Why don't we sit down and be comfortable. Matty, I believe you were going to tell me about your trip."

Tahira sat down on the couch closest to the fire with her wine and curled her legs under her. She was surprised, and slightly pleased, when Antoine sat down next to her, nearly touching her slippered feet. The clothing that had been waiting in her room when she awoke was obviously expensive, in current style, and fit fairly well. The slippers were hand-knitted and wonderfully warm. It was almost as though she had been expected, which was a bit eerie. Sort of like being around Grammy, a *ruhsal* who *knew* things.

* * *

"HOW LONG WILL you be gone?" Antoine continued. He noticed that Matty had started to put his feet back up on the table but stopped himself with a look of frustration. He tried to readjust his position on the couch, but they were for built for Charles's massive form, not an ordinary human.

The cushions were deep but firm, and sloped a bit toward the front. Antoine noticed it was difficult to stay seated *without* putting his feet on something. With a wink and a deliberate smile at Matty, he lifted his feet and placed them on the table with a dull thump that caused Margo to turn around viciously in her chair. Her mouth had just opened to reprimand Matty when she paled at the sight of her employer's heavy leather boots on the table instead.

He raised his brows innocently. "Is there a problem, Margo?"

She shook her head, probably not trusting herself to speak, and turned back to her computer.

Matty mouthed the words, "Thanks, mate!" and gave a thumbs up. He lifted his feet and let them set gently on the table, then leaned back a sigh.

Antoine continued as though he hadn't been interrupted. "We'll have to arrange for someone to care for the cats while you're away."

"Yeah, Margo's working on that part. I know a bloke at the Taronga Zoo who wants to get out of Oz. He might like to visit the States for a turn. The plan is to only be gone for two weeks. But you know what they say about plans."

"Of course, it's not my business where you take your vacation, but you seem a bit . . . worried about it." Actually, he smelled worried but excited at the same time.

"For good reason, mate. Do you remember the letter I got from the barrister in Sydney before you left for the States?"

Antoine nodded. "The one that was dated months before and had traveled to a dozen different locations, following our show around?"

"Yeah. Well, I finally got hold of the bloke and it seems that I had a grandfather I didn't know was still alive . . . well, actually, he's *not* alive anymore. That was the point of the letter."

A light fog of sorrow drifted to his nose from Tahira. "Your grandfather died? I'm sorry. My dad's father died just last year."

He nodded in thanks. "Yeah. It would have been nice to have known he was about. Mum never told me about any of my dad's family. But the barrister told me plenty. It seems he was a jackaroo out in the bush—" He turned to Tahira and amended, "That's a station hand at a farming operation down in the Australian outback." He noticed Tahira's understanding, and continued, "But he inherited a bit of land in the outback, about five hundred hectares, a click or so from Lake Mungo. He left it to me in his will."

TAHIRA WAS SIPPING her wine and nearly choked. "Five hundred acres is a *bit* of land?"

Matty shook his head with a chuckle. "Not acres, luv. A hectare is about two of your acres. It's closer to a thousand acres. And yeah, that's a *dinky* bit of land in the outback."

Margo turned on her chair. "Actually, the bequest was for 506 hectares. There are 2.47 acres in a hectare, so you inherited 1,249.82 acres." She shrugged when he beat his fist into his forehead. "Hey, precision is what I do." She glanced at Tahira. "Our satellite link is still down, but I'm trying to reroute through the cable television link-up to the house. There's supposedly an internet subscription that came with it, according to Amber. I should be able to get in touch with your family in a bit."

Antoine smiled brightly as Tahira heaved a sigh of relief. "But Matty, this is wonderful news! You've always said you would like to start a wild animal clinic."

Matty took a final draw of beer from the bottle in his hand, set it on the table, and grabbed a third. "Yeah, but that's not the whole story. The part that gobsmacked me was that a good bit of the land is part of Dreamtime and the Aborigines want it back."

"Oh! I've heard of that!" Tahira sat up straighter and became more animated. "I had to do a report on Aboriginal legends in my mythology class in high school. So the land you inherited belonged to the Koori from before the time of living memory?"

Matty nodded with a pleased expression. She turned to Antoine when she caught the scent of his curiosity. "See, Aborigines have been on the Australian continent for at least fifty thousand years, and there are skeletons that have been found as old as forty thousand years. In fact, I think it was found near Lake Mungo. The tribes did pictograms but had no written language as a group. Each of the five or six hundred tribes have a different language and dialect. But the sacred lands of Dreamtime are the one thing that they all agree on."

Realization came to her slowly and she winced as she turned to Matty. "Uh-oh! They're going to fight tooth and nail for that. Will the courts find they have any claim? I know they've had a rough time reclaiming sacred property in the past."

"Bloody hell!" Matty exclaimed. "I wish you would have been here a week ago when *I* was trying to find out all of this. Yeah, I guess it's been a battle in the court for nearly a year. The QC—the Queen's Counsel—has been arguing the High Court for free claim to the property for the heir, which is me. But they couldn't find me, and finally the justices said that if they couldn't find an heir, the land would revert to the tribe."

"But now you've been found," Antoine said quietly. "So what does that mean?"

"Well, one of the blokes in the firm actually got on with the grandson of a tribal elder, who had been doing translations. After we talked, the barrister told him about me and what I hoped to do with the land. Daku talked to his granddad and they offered me a deal—if I would do a walkabout on the land as my grandfather had done, then they would withdraw their claim and I could build the clinic on the part of the land that isn't sacred. So, that's what I'm going to do. I've got until the next corroboree ceremony to do a walkabout and perform a bora initiation."

Tahira cocked her head and the glowing red coals made her hair shine the color of her animal. Antoine caught himself looking at the hair and her slimly muscled legs tucked up against her chest.

"But a walkabout isn't anything, is it? Doesn't that just mean to wander around—sort of like a vacation?"

"Yeah, that'd be right. Except it turns out that a walkabout used to have more of a meaning. I talked to Daku, and we nutted out what I had to do. I'll be spending two weeks hunting and gathering on the land, dropped off without food or water. I can bring with me a boomerang, a kylie, and a woomera spear thrower for getting food and for protection. There's a billabong on the property—that's a small pond or watering hole—so I won't have to dig, but I'll have to make something to carry the water in. I got the impression that I had to make and decorate the tools myself. I have to walk the boundaries of the land and do meditations so the land will accept me. Daku said the elders will *know* if the land accepts me. Some sort of seer stuff, I suppose. I'm learning plenty about *that* rubbish from being around Antoine, so cheating won't help any."

Tahira glanced at Antoine in surprise. He acknowledged the fact briefly with a nod of his head and then turned his attention back to Matty.

Matty shrugged and readjusted his feet so his heels were against the table edge. Margo held her breath as the table moved slightly toward Antoine and Tahira's side of the room. Antoine lifted his feet a fraction without anyone noticing, so his heels didn't scratch the finish as the table moved. It was one thing to put Matty at ease by letting him put his feet on the furniture. It was another entirely to have to pay for the table if they ruined it.

He noticed that Tahira was having a hard time taking her eyes off him since learning he was a seer. But she apparently was still listening, because she nodded and added, "Aborigines believe that land doesn't belong to man—man belongs to the land. If the land rejects a person, he or she has to leave. Have you chosen a totem?"

Matty shrugged. "Daku said that it will find me. Apparently, my grandfather's totem was the carpet snake. No surprise, I guess. Both sides of my family are Sazi. We're all snakes. But I didn't get the right genes, so I'm just human. I'm not much into the 'Earth Mother' bit, but my uncle had survival training in Nasho, and taught me a thing or two, so no worries. It's just the carving and decorating thingos that has me feeling a galah."

"A '*galah*'?" Margo asked.

Matty turned his head back. "A bit of a fool. I'm studying hard *how* to make them, but I'll be bloody amazed if any of the things I carve will actually *work*.

I've built snares and have a knife, though. As you Sazi blokes say—*I'll live*, even if I get my share of dingo breakfasts."

Tahira laughed. "I've actually heard of that one before! A yawn, a leak, and a long look around, but no food."

"Just right, luv. It'll give me time to learn to play a couple of instruments, the didgeridoo and the boomerang, which apparently is a percussion instrument that keeps time with a ritual dance. I'll have to perform at my bora initiation well enough to please my totem." He shrugged once more. "And I'll have to bring a gift of something I've hunted or gathered to the tribal elders. Daku said a few rabbits would do. So, as soon as I have all the thingos prepared, I'll train whomever we find to care for the cats in Reno, and then catch a plane to Sydney."

He pulled his feet off the table and spun around to rest them on the couch. He set the bottle on the table and looked at Tahira. "But, that's enough about me, other than to know that you'll all be putting up with sawdust around the house until I finish all this bloody carving. How about you, Tahira? What's a knockout sheila from the States doing in a jail cell in Germany?"

Antoine cleared his throat in annoyance, and Matty flushed a bit and fidgeted. "That's not our business, Matty. Tahira is our *guest*, and is not required to explain herself."

"No, it's okay." Tahira smiled, a bit embarrassed at the compliment. She straightened out her legs and leaned forward to put her empty wine glass on the table. *So, I'm still in Germany—not that it helps much to know.*

A burst of frigid air on her neck made her shiver. A

glance to the left told her why. The fire had burned down to coals and icy wind was coming down the chimney. She stood up and walked over to a hammered copper wood box and selected a few triangular pieces of pine while she spoke. "I don't mind, because I really need to try to remember what happened and why I *am* here. Talking about it might help."

She moved the logs to one arm and grabbed an iron poker to stir the coals. But the walk-in fireplace was deeper than she expected. She had to step nearly into the coals to reach the grate. The heat from the coals made her face hot as she leaned far inside the stone cavity.

Tahira felt movement behind her. She smelled Antoine's scent and felt the light tingling of his power as he touched her arm and pulled the logs from her grasp.

"Allow me to help, *mon chat du feu.*" The words were quiet and warm, meant only for her ears. She didn't know what the last part meant, but it sounded *amazing*!

She turned her head and saw intense amber eyes that glowed golden from the coals. Her heart started to pound in her chest, and the swirling smoke caught the thick scent of piñon, pine resin, sand, and Antoine's strangely sweet musk. They stared at each other for a long moment and it didn't even occur to her to move until the smell of her palm scorching from the hot metal made her jump. She nearly dropped the poker. One corner of his mouth turned up and his scent was amused. She quickly stirred the coals and backed up, bumping into him as he bent down to add the logs to the fire.

She was strangely flustered when she returned to her seat on the couch. Matty was studiously ignoring her, staring at the ceiling. Margo had a small smile on her face that disappeared when she saw Antoine's warning expression as he returned to the couch.

Tahira cleared her throat and glanced at the dark red

mark on her palm that was already starting to fade. "So . . . um. Well, I guess my story starts right before Halloween. Rabi—that's my older brother—and I had been staying with our grandparents for about a month, trying to learn how to be proper tigers. We had gotten into a habit of going running at dawn, before our grandparents started breakfast. That way we could talk about things. They trained each of us differently and we wanted to make sure that we were both learning the same things."

"Why would they teach you differently?" Antoine seemed innocently curious, but Grammy's words echoed into her head: *Tell a Sazi nothing they can use against you.*

She shrugged and lied. "I don't really know." She waited to see his reaction, but there was none. He just continued to watch her passively and she couldn't smell a single emotion over the thick scent of his musk and cologne.

"We were supposed to be leaving to go home for the holiday in the afternoon, but Rabi didn't show up for our run. I'd seen him the night before with two friends he'd made in the village. They were drinking and playing cards. I waited until after breakfast was over for him to show up, and then went and told Grandfather that I was worried. But he wasn't. I guess other men in the village wander off for days at a time and nobody thinks anything of it. But Rabi wouldn't do that—or at least I didn't think he would."

Matty sat up and took a drink from his beer. "Did you ask his friends? Could be it turned into a rip snorter and he was still rotten."

Tahira nodded and scratched at a spot where her palm had started to itch as it healed. "Yeah. One of the men was really nice. Basir took me to where they last were drinking and swore Rabi had been fine when he had gone home. But I didn't trust the other man, Kemil. I always worried when Rabi spent time with him. Kemil said that Rabi had decided to stay after he went home. I didn't believe him. He was lying about *something*, but Grandfather wouldn't do anything. He wouldn't send a search party and told me I was a . . . well, he said I was overreacting."

There was no need to repeat that her grandfather had called her a bitter, overprotective spinster. Her grandparents had been shocked she wasn't married with several children at her age. Oh, it was fine for *Rabi* to still be single—

Antoine was nodding as she came out of her thoughts. "So, you thought you would look for him yourself?"

"Not until the next day when he still hadn't returned. He has the potential to be a *sahip*, one of our leaders, so I wasn't really concerned he would get hurt in the wild. But we missed the plane, and he had been so excited to go home. It seemed . . . *strange*."

Margo had abandoned her attempts at the computer and was listening raptly. "It should. If he was raised in America, he knows better than to leave for days without contacting someone."

Tahira hoped that nobody had heard her stomach growl. But there was clattering in the kitchen, so perhaps not. While there had been a tray on a table in her room when she woke, the food had been cold. "It was Gram who finally convinced me to go. Normally, she bows to Grandfather's will, both as her husband and as the leader of our people. But she had a . . . well, she's a *ruhsal*, one who sees the future. She said that he was being held by bad people and that I could find him if I hurried. She told me of a green truck she saw and the clothing of the men who had taken Rabi. So I set off in the direction she told me, and by the end of the day, I'd found the truck."

A female voice called out from behind the kitchen door. "Dinner is ready!"

Antoine clapped his hands against his thighs, startling her. "On that note, I believe we should find some lunch and hear the rest while we eat. It sounds as though *Grand-mère* has returned from her run. Shall we see what she has caught?"

Although Tahira was hungry, she didn't want to presume that she was invited and didn't stand when the others did. In reversed circumstances, she wasn't positive that a stray Sazi would be offered food in the village.

Margo and Matty walked toward the kitchen doors, chatting amiably. Antoine started to follow but stopped when he noticed that Tahira remained seated.

"Will you not be joining us?"

She felt heat rise to her face. "Well, I didn't know if—"

HE CROSSED HIS arms over his chest and raised one eyebrow. "You are a guest in this home, Tahira. Why in the world would you think you would not be shown every courtesy? Yes, I heard your body protest the lack of food and I am famished as well." He took a step closer and with a sweeping motion, held out one hand, palm up. "Come, let us eat a good meal, if not as *friends*, than as companions by circumstance—at least until you complete your story."

He winked and smiled, and that same fluttering started in her stomach. Why did she feel like she recognized him when he did that? There was something about him that was familiar, but it was just out of reach.

She nodded and held out her hand. "Okay, if you think you have enough."

She waited for the familiar tingle, but it wasn't there. He must have pulled all of his magic inside him. Her grandfather could do that so it didn't bother humans they interacted with in trade. His hand was just a hand—but it was warm and firm with only a few calluses where his pads would be in animal form.

"So," he said, as he tucked her hand next to his body. "Besides being a cat, what do you do for a living?"

At last, a question she didn't mind answering! "Both my father and grandfather run export companies. Dad ships different kinds of berries—strawberries and blueberries and such—to Canada and Mexico. Granddad ships apricots and grapes all over the Middle East. I work in the office, handling shipping contractors, supplies, and stuff. It was nice to have the background from Dad's orchards because Granddad's operation really needed updating. He didn't even have a *computer*!" Antoine opened the door with one hand while keeping his full attention on her. She felt both flattered and strange that he seemed to be hanging on every word. Her stomach growled again as she caught the scent of fresh meat. *How long has it been since I've eaten?*

"How were they managing? Is it a small operation?"

She took a deep breath and tried to focus away from all of the scents bombarding her nose. "No, actually, it's quite large. But everything was being done manually, so suppliers were robbing him blind because they'd insist on an instant answer when he didn't have time to dig back through his records to see what they charged the previous delivery. It was a mess."

He nodded and released her hand as they neared the table where the others sat. "It sounds like you're quite organized. You and Margo have a great deal in common. She's very much my right hand. Since my own operation has grown so large, it's difficult to keep track of meat suppliers, costumers, venues, and such. It's gotten to the point where my secretary needs her *own* secretary."

Margo laughed as she overheard the comment. "And don't forget I need a raise. *Never* forget about the raise!" Tahira laughed and sat down as Margo held up a roll of paper. "By the way, the new posters arrived just as you left for Chicago, Antoine. I'm not certain I like it. I think it's too flashy for the Midwest, where our next show is. I think we should consider using it just for the East and West coasts."

"Nah," Matty said as he bit into a thick sandwich that smelled of the same meat she'd noticed when she entered. "It's ace, mate! The cute little sheilas that storm the doors will steal 'em right off the wall. That's the sort of exposure you need where you don't have the big press to push the show."

Posters? Storming the doors? Yes, he'd said he had an animal act, but this was sounding larger than she'd imagined. Antoine took the rolled paper from Margo's hand and opened it on the countertop. She was just curious enough to ask. "Can I see?"

Antoine turned his head. "Hmm? But of course. You're nearly the right demographic the publicist was hoping to reach. Tell me honestly—would this entice you to attend a performance if you'd never heard my name?"

He turned the poster around and Tahira's eyes grew wide. No *wonder* she seemed to recognize him! But his clothing yesterday and today were so elegant and tasteful, his hair held back to give the illusion of short hair, that she'd never connected the name to . . . She felt her mouth open with surprise, and Antoine started to chuckle.

"You're Antoine the Magnificent? The guy with the sold-out, mega-bucks shows in Reno? *No way!* You were on TV every other *hour* last fall. I can't *believe* I didn't recognize you!"

But there was the poster, right in front of her—filled with flowing, golden hair and a white-sequined jumpsuit that hugged every tanned muscle and matched the sparkling teeth. He stood confident and commanding in front of snarling cats of every description. Those intense amber eyes with flecks of green seemed to grab her gaze and hold it.

"It's—I mean, uhm—"

Margo spoke first. "Yeah, a lot of people who meet him in *real life* don't match the two up. Terri, his publicist, just *hates* that he is so damned low-key off stage."

Antoine snorted lightly. "It wouldn't be *possible* to be as visible as Terri would prefer. Already it's a danger to have so many public performances while being Sazi." He turned to Tahira. "At least Margo is able to schedule performances in locations so that the venues we choose truly aren't *available* on the moons. It saves so many embarrassing questions."

"It's hard enough to explain away your disappearances for meetings," Margo commented while Tahira continued to stare at the poster, lost for words.

Antoine released one end of it, allowing it to roll up. "So, what is your opinion, Tahira? Since you're from America, I'll heed your counsel. Is this poster as equally appropriate for downtown Los Angeles or New York, as for Des Moines, Iowa?"

The question brought her back to reality. It was a good question. Her family had lived in a small Kansas city for a year before completing their migration to California. How would this poster be received at the Safeway in a tiny, conservative town?

She thought seriously about it for a moment, as a small white-haired woman quietly placed in front of her a bowl filled with steaming meat and vegetables in a rich broth. The woman must be Antoine's grandmother, but they didn't smell alike. They seemed to be different cats. Still, the scent of the stew in the bowl was enough to make her salivate.

No! I need to ignore the food. She was being asked a question that was important to him. "Can I see it again?"

He nodded and stepped forward, offering the curled end of the paper to her while holding the top edges. She pulled the paper flat and looked at it carefully while he watched her with serious eyes.

Her eyes darted across the poster from side to side and top to bottom several times until she was satisfied. "The background color is good. It draws attention to your eyes and the eyes of the cats. The hair—" She shrugged and continued to talk to no one in particular. "Eh. It's a little over the top with the wind machine blowing it, but it's not offensive or anything. The smoke around the corners gives it that David Copperfield 'magical' look, which isn't a bad thing. Play on those who came before."

She released one corner and tapped the center of the poster. "Now, see . . . here's your real problem. The jumpsuit has too much skin showing. It's flashy and will play well in L.A., like Matty said. But you might have your printer run a second batch for distribution to smaller towns after airbrushing the white a little higher. Go to about mid-chest, rather than to the belly button."

She caught him smiling out of the corner of her eye and looked up. "You don't *like* my belly button?"

She managed not to blush, despite the intensity of his gaze and the thick French accent that slid along her skin like silk. He seemed to be able to turn it on and off like a switch. "It's lovely, but Grandma Mabel in eastern Kansas might hold her hand over her eight-year-old granddaughter's eyes and *forget* to tell Mom about the show, which won't help your box office. First impressions are everything with advertising. I've lived in both places, and the attitudes are different. It's not good or bad. They're just different."

He pursed his lips and nodded thoughtfully. "You raise valuable points, and I'm grateful for the input. Thank you. We live with this every day, and sometimes we forget about the first impression. Since the promotion company suggested a road show, I haven't had much time to stop and think about the image of it. It's useful to have outside impressions from time to time. You seem to know a great deal about marketing. Have you had schooling?"

Tahira shook her head. "No, but how people think when they shop has just always made sense to me. Dad asked me to help him think up new ways to get repeat business a couple of years ago, and the things I suggested seemed to have worked. His receipts tripled last year."

She couldn't stand the scent any longer and released the poster to pick up her spoon. The stew had cooled to just the perfect temperature and the first mouthful was sheer heaven. When she finally swallowed she exclaimed, "Oh, my God! This is *amazing*! What kind of meat is this? I've got to get my mom to make this!"

The white-haired woman walked up to the table, wiping her hands on the bottom of a cotton half-apron that was far too big for her. She was beaming from ear to ear at the compliment. "This is old-fashioned rabbit stew. The recipe was my great-grandmother's. Jackrabbits are a little lean this time of year, but they cook quickly. I always pan fry the meat before putting it into the broth with vegetables. That way it doesn't soak up too much salt."

With a movement almost too fast to follow, Giselle reached across the table and yanked a basket out of

Matty's hands, ignoring his startled expression. "I am so glad you are feeling better, young tiger. You had us quite worried. Please, try some of the bread with the stew before our bottomless pit eats it all. It's black bread with sunflower seeds."

She reached over and gave Antoine a light slap on the arm with the back of her hand. "Since my insensitive grandson didn't bother to properly introduce us, I'm Giselle Bertrand. I'm the healer for the troupe."

Antoine smelled a bit embarrassed, and gave a lopsided, apologetic smile before walking to the stove to fill a bowl with stew.

Tahira raised her eyebrows and spoke after swallowing a bite of bread. "I'm Tahira Kuric of the Hayalet Kabile. My brother, Rabi, hopes to be a healer some day. His skills aren't strong, but he's learning. We have very few healers, so any skill is welcome."

She felt another flush rise at the surprised scent from Giselle. *I'm being too free with information. Grandfather will be furious for what I've already said if he learns of it.*

The older woman had opened her mouth to speak when a small sound caught Tahira's attention. She turned her head toward the room where they'd been earlier with her head dropped defensively. "Do you hear that?"

Antoine turned and listened. "I hear nothing but the wind, but my nose is better than my ears. *Grand-mère*?"

Giselle nodded slowly, and suspicion began to fill her face. "Yes, I hear it, too. It sounds like someone is trying to open the front door. I locked it when I returned from my run. Are *you* expecting guests, *petit fils*?"

Antoine's face darkened ominously. He lowered the bowl and placed it carefully on the counter. Power began to roil from him in a wave that made Tahira shiver. "None have been *invited*. Let us go see who is calling on us in such a storm."

Chapter Four

WHOEVER WAS ATTEMPTING to get in wasn't trying very hard to hide their presence. The knob was rattling furiously and someone was throwing their weight against the wood.

Antoine held up a hand to stop the rest of the group from advancing farther and sniffed carefully next to the door. Recognition of the people on the other side was immediate despite the draft guards that prevented cold wind from seeping into the house.

But what in the blazes are they doing here?

He quickly unlocked the deadbolt and opened the door to find two shivering men bundled to the point that they could barely see through the wrappings. A burst of icy wind sent swirling snow through into the entryway.

"Come in, come in! You'll catch your death out there." The pair was happy to comply and nearly dove through the door into the warmth of the house.

Antoine started to close the door when one of his animal keepers, Bruce Carmichael, managed to stutter out through blue lips. "S-see if y-y-you can get the key out. I-it's frozen in the lock."

His quick inspection proved Bruce right, but only a bit of Sazi strength was necessary to extract it in one piece. "It must have gotten warm in your pocket and then froze when you inserted it in the lock. Why didn't you just knock?"

Another round of stuttering followed without making any sense. Finally, Bruce's companion, Larry Medina, explained, "W-we did. But we were both too c-c-cold from walking from where our car stalled to knock loud enough."

Antoine noticed that *Grand-mère* and Tahira both furrowed their brows, but they let the comment go. There was no scent of either of the two lying. But it did seem odd that they would hear the rattling knob before knocking. Still, it didn't matter. They were here—for whatever reason.

"You must get out of those wet things immediately." *Grand-mère* took control of the situation. She stepped behind the men and pushed them toward the great room and the fireplace. She barked orders over her shoulder. "Matty, please go fetch clothing for them. Antoine, gather some blankets. Margo, be a dear and boil some water for tea, please."

"And I'll get some of the stew," Tahira added. "They must be hungry."

It was only a few minutes before the men were in dry clothes in front of the roaring fireplace. The group gratefully ate spoonfuls of the stew and sipped hot tea with honey.

"I can almost feel my fingers again," said Bruce. "Man, that storm is *brutal*."

Antoine squatted down next to the fire so the others could have the second couch. "Why on earth are you still in Germany, and how did you find us *here*?"

Bruce released the blanket long enough to motion with his thumb to the other man. "Larry thought of checking Charles's house. We decided to stay over an extra day in Stuttgart because Larry had an aunt on his mother's side who had invited us if we ever visited. But when we got there, she'd gone out of town. She left a note with a neighbor with a key, telling us we could stay over and perhaps she'd be home today. But that was before this storm. Everything is closed down—airports, buses, restaurants. When we drove out to where we'd staged the camp, everybody was gone, but a tow-truck driver was just returning from bringing the van here and asked if we were in trouble."

Larry interrupted. "And we knew that if someone was hurt, you would come to Charles—well, actually to *Amber* before getting on a plane. It wasn't too hard to find out where he lived, even with my rotten German."

"But your car broke down? You've walked all this way in the snow? What about the tow truck?"

Bruce laughed. "It didn't *break* down. We didn't need the tow-truck driver when he first showed up, but we sure could have used him later." He waved his hand toward the window. "It's out there somewhere, buried in the snow. We came around a curve on the private entrance and *wham*! Right into a snowbank that had blown over the road. The engine stalled and we couldn't get it started again. It took half an hour just to walk the quarter mile here to the house, but at least the car isn't out on the main road."

Tahira had been sitting quietly on the couch and was watching Larry with carefully observant eyes. "You're a snake." Her voice had deepened an octave, nearly to her cat voice.

Antoine could tell that she was struggling to keep the distaste from her voice. All of the Sazi cats had a difficult time with the snake shifters, but it spoke well that she didn't attack him on sight. It was still close to the moon, and he knew just how difficult it was to fight the instinct of the animal inside.

He watched her closely, looking for any danger signs. Larry had been around the cat show long enough that most of the animals knew and trusted him. But he was understandably cautious around strangers. Fortunately, he was also very fast when he needed to dodge attacks. Larry's voice was carefully neutral when he responded, but his knuckles were white from clutching the spoon in his hand, and his scent held the light tang of fear. His smile didn't match the look in his eyes. "Yes. I'm a rat snake. My family emigrated from the UAE to America when I was an infant. Does it help any that I'm harmless? Or are you going to eat me in my sleep?"

His voice had a lighthearted tone, but the question was serious. Antoine noticed that he and Bruce were waiting tensely for a reply. It had been hard on Bruce all these years, having his partner constantly under suspicion. But Larry was a good soul and people eventually saw past their initial instincts. As with several of the Wolven members who were snakes, it was just a matter of education.

"I can vouch for him, if that will help, Tahira," Antoine offered. She didn't take her eyes off Larry, and was breathing with flared nostrils, but she wasn't being openly aggressive. He turned to the two men. "Tahira isn't Sazi, gentlemen. She's part of a splinter group of shifters called the Hayalet Kabile. Her tribe doesn't often encounter our people other than their own kind."

She shook her head a few times as though clearing her mind. A deep breath seemed to calm her. "But I'm from America, land of the weird, and home of the strange. Heck, I've spent most of my life outside of San

Francisco. There's not *much* that can surprise me. No, I don't plan to eat you in your sleep. Although—" she admitted ruefully, "You might keep your door locked tonight. It's the third night of the moon. I don't *have* to change, but my senses go wacko."

Around the room, everyone relaxed. Larry nodded. "I usually do anyway. Even Antoine gets a bit—snappish."

"*Moi?*" He held up a hand to his chest in innocent surprise. "Is it my fault that *you* smell like dinner a few days a month? I think it speaks well that you've been with us for nearly a dozen years."

Larry snorted lightly. "Yeah, it says that I'm fast on my feet and can slither into small places."

"Speaking of dinner," Matty said with a sour expression from the kitchen doorway. "I don't suppose there's any chance anyone has sweets? I just fossicked about and there's nothing even resembling bikkies in the place. I'd even settle for some fairy floss right now."

Bruce lifted a hand and cut short a sip of tea. "Actually, *you* have some sweets, Matty. The postman stopped by the vacant field while we were talking to the city driver, not realizing the show had left. You got a package from your friend Paul in Sydney, and I'll bet I know what's in it."

Antoine nearly laughed at Matty's expression. Everyone has their drug of choice, and Matty's was chocolate. But not just any chocolate. No, it had to be Tim Tams biscuits—for which he would spend every last dime he earned, and often did.

With a move that would do any Sazi proud, Matty blazed a path to the soaking wet backpacks and dug through both in a frenzy. Finally he pulled a slightly rumpled box covered with stamps and stickers into view with a triumphant cry.

"You're a *prince*, Bruce! A bloody angel!" Matty pulled at the sturdy tape that completely covered the brown-paper covering while everybody watched in amusement. When he finally resorted to tearing at the tape with his teeth, Antoine removed a small folding knife from his pocket and tossed it to him.

Giselle stared at him significantly. "You plan to *share*? Yes?"

Matty's face grew panicked and he clutched the package to his chest as he looked from Giselle's stern expression to the five other people around the fireplace. It was obvious to Antoine that he hadn't even considered the possibility before *Grand-mère* spoke.

He didn't answer until the package was fully open. The Australian's sigh of relief moved his entire chest, because there were two packages of the biscuits under the wrapper, rather than just one. Kicking the wrapping to the side, he walked across the room and handed one package to Giselle with a flourish. "For you, my dear lady, and the rest of the crew."

Tahira picked one of the biscuits from the tray when it was passed by her. "I've never heard of Tim Tams. Are they cookies?"

"Fuck me dead! Bite your tongue, woman!" Matty exclaimed after finishing his third biscuit. "Tim Tams aren't *cookies*. They're manna from heaven. You Yanks have no concept of what a true joy you're missing, thank the good lord."

Margo leaned closer to Tahira. "They're not sold in America, so Matty has to beg friends to ship them. They usually make him pay out the nose for the trouble. But he is right. They're terrific!"

Tahira bit down into the biscuit and Antoine watched her reaction. "Wow! These *are* good. Chocolate cookie with chocolate cream and covered in chocolate. Rabi would probably eat the whole package in one sitting. He was insane for chocolate."

She stopped mid-bite when she realized what she'd said. Everybody else, save for Bruce and Larry, noticed as well, and the scents of sorrow and sympathy nearly overwhelmed Antoine's nose. The two men on the couch looked at each other and shrugged.

Margo placed one hand on Tahira's shoulder, but she smiled and shook her head. "No, it's okay. That was just a slip because I'm stressed. I really believe my brother's still alive. He's out there somewhere and I'm going to find him and take him home."

Antoine stood and walked over to the fireplace to add more logs. "Bruce, Larry—you should know what's been happening. Tahira's brother was captured by persons unknown and she was also abducted while trying to save him. I was able to spirit her away from the police when they raided a tiger poaching operation. But Simon is dead, and Rabi's body was not with the other large cats. You haven't finished your story, Tahira. Did you ever find your brother?"

Shock set into the face of both Larry and Bruce, but they didn't ask any questions. Tahira nodded. "Well, like I said earlier, I followed the tracks and his scent until I found the truck. I saw him for a moment, caged with another tiger, a leopard, and two lions. All of the cats were fighting, and the men were using stun sticks on them to break them up. I was able to sneak closer because they were busy and he saw me, too. He warned me off when one of the men started to turn around, but they were getting ready to leave, so I decided to *isim* and move closer."

Antoine held up his hand. "*Isim?* What is that?"

Tahira immediately blushed and stammered, "It's . . .

um . . . that is, it's a way to move closer. It's something Grammy taught me."

Matty opened his mouth, but Antoine shook his head. He was going to let it drop for the moment. "Go on, please."

She took another bite of the Tim Tam and collected herself while she chewed and swallowed. "Anyway, I *isi* . . . I mean, I moved closer and let the air out of one of the front tires while they weren't looking. I planned to go back to the village to get Granddad while they fixed it."

"Obviously, something happened before you could?" Margo's voice was hushed and nervous, like listening to the calm before the storm.

"When I moved back into the brush to wait for them to notice the tire, I was still in tiger form. I didn't realize they had a third man in the truck with them, who had wandered off into the brush behind me. Before I could even turn around, he hit me with two darts in my hip and I was out for the count. But I *know* that Rabi was still alive, and if he wasn't with your Simon, then he's still alive. He's strong. He could have escaped on his own."

Antoine nodded. "Definitely possible. But you don't remember anything of your time with your captives? No clue that might help us find them? I presume that they knew you were a shapeshifter. You couldn't have remained in tiger form for a full month."

Tahira clenched her hands into fists and stood with a frustrated sound. She slammed a fist on the mantel above the fireplace hard enough to make the antique clock on it wobble. She quickly reached for it and stopped it from falling with an embarrassed scent that didn't quite overshadow her frustration.

"Not enough. I've been trying, but all I get are

flashes—being fed rancid meat through a cage, shackles on my hands and feet; so yes, I had to have been human for some periods. But I can't remember faces or even scents. It's driving me nuts! I know that if I could just remember *something*, I could find Rabi. I won't give up. I have to at least get out there and *try*."

Antoine shrugged. "There is little any of us can do until the storm ends, I'm afraid. Hopefully tomorrow we will know more and can reach the outside world. For now, I have some contract details to work out for our next show, and you should probably get some more rest. Bruce, could you perhaps show Matty how to feed Babette? He needs to learn the proper method, and you and Larry should rest after your ordeal."

Margo sighed, slapped her thighs with her hands lightly, and stood up. "And I need to pay some bills, if I can get online, or we won't have any electricity or water by the time we get back to Reno."

"Yes, and if you would, Margo, if we have a connection, please help Tahira reach her family in America. They must be terrified having her missing this long."

Tahira's eyes lit up and she smiled at him warmly. Perhaps he couldn't allow her to leave, but neither could he just stand by and let her people worry.

If Charles saw that the family would come for her, then somehow they must learn she's here, after all.

In a few minutes, the room was emptied of people and Antoine sat down at the computer. Margo and Tahira would use the spare already hooked up in Margo's room.

A few clicks of the mouse later and he was already shaking his head. *Merde! Sixty-seven e-mails in a day. However did we survive before the internet?* Contacts from his attorney, publicist, council business, plus a variety of spam. He was only interested in two at the moment. One was from his online chess partner, who was his source for the rare cognac, and the other showed no sender name.

He clicked to open the message from Leland Behr, "chssmstr" in his online persona.

"O-O-O +" read the first line of the message, and Antoine swore under his breath. He had hoped Le wouldn't see that move. Castling to the queen's side placed the white rook in position for an attack on Antoine's king. He was in check. *I'll have to set up the board again and think about how to get out of that move.*

He continued reading.

```
The bottle reached me, and I believe it
truly is one from the first run! :D But he
still will not provide information about
where he found it, Antoine, and that
concerns me. If he discovered an entire
case, he could flood the market and the
value would drop into the dustbin. Are
you still in Germany and can you come to
my home in Berlin? I want you to see it
with your own eyes before I release the
funds to him. Pressing my thumbs for
you. —Le.
```

Antoine leaned back in the chair and tapped one finger on the mouse without clicking the button. Leland was correct, as usual. But he could own one of the original bottles of cognac produced by Hugo Asbach in a small basement distillery before partnering with Albert Sturm and creating a dynasty. Yes, even if a full case existed, it might still be worth the price of three thousand Euros.

He clicked on Reply.

As usual, you have the better of me on
the board, old friend. My plans are in a
bit of an uproar right now, so my response move to your check on my king
must wait a day or two. As for the
bottle—I will trust your judgment. I
don't want to risk the transaction for
days of indecision. You're the expert,
or so say the auction houses. <g> Release the funds after withholding your
commission and keep the bottle until I
know my plans. I will try to make it up
to see you before we leave here, but, as
I said, things are happening quickly. I
will gratefully accept your pressed
thumbs for luck! —A

Antoine sent the message and moved on to the next
e-mail. As usual, Tony Giodone, using his new alias of
Joe Giambrocco, leapt to the point without prelimi-
naries.

I thought of another one. Fear smells
like hot and sour soup to me.
   I tried your suggestion on the case
file that got destroyed. It didn't work.
Apparently hindsight doesn't work on
someone who just *read* the information
in the past. Oh, and I can't seem to
turn it on and off well enough to inter-
view the suspect. Based on what I've
seen, I'm pretty sure that if he thinks
we're sniffing at the door again, he'll
bolt and I'll have to take him out. Although, that *would* solve the case.

Nikoli asked me to remind you that you
still owe him for the chair. Apparently,
it rode the boat with him from the
motherland and he's been a PITA to deal
with since it got clawed to toothpicks.
Never mind that we saved humanity. Pfft!
Let me know if you have any suggestions
about the hindsight.

Joe

Antoine furrowed his brow. Chinese soup has the same scent as *fear*? He tried to think back to the last time he'd made hot and sour soup. It had been a number of years, but it hadn't reminded him of any particular emotion.

He took another sip of the fine Cordon Bleu from Charles's bar, took a bite of chocolate biscuit, and considered the concept.

It would be an interesting experiment to find scents to match emotions. He'd never tried before. He was actually enjoying corresponding with Tony Giodone. He understood the wolf's frustration with a gift that was just as often a curse. Antoine just didn't think he could help him. Hindsight wasn't anything like foresight. One could be controlled, the other couldn't.

The only other seer with hindsight was his own sister. Antoine couldn't understand why Charles didn't simply have Tony train with Josette. Then again, Tony was a trained assassin, and his sister was prone to making people mad enough to kill. *Pity that Charles is so blasted honorable. Somebody ought to put Josette down.*

"Antoine?" Margo's quiet voice from behind him interrupted his thoughts. "Tahira's family sent a reply e-mail. How would you like me to respond? I don't know if I'm allowed to give out Charles's phone number or address."

His voice was harsher than he'd planned, but thinking about his older sister did that. He didn't turn around and opened his clenched fists to let blood flow back to his fingers.

"Absolutely not! This address and phone are private and unlisted. Tell them that if they wish to send someone, they can contact us when they arrive in town and we will meet them."

Margo's scent held surprise at his tone, but it passed quickly. She was accustomed to the quick temper of cats, both wild ones and the Sazis that surrounded her. Her tone was quiet and respectful, intended to soothe. "Of course. I'll send a reply. But," she said, putting a light hand on his shoulder and lowering her voice even further, "you might want to explain your reasoning to Tahira. She would like to speak to them by phone when the lines are back up. She's excited and also worried, because nobody has heard from her brother yet. He's still missing."

Antoine leaned back in angry frustration, muttering things so foul that even in French, he could smell Margo's embarrassment. She quickly removed her hand from his shoulder. He ran his fingers through his hair, gripping the strands in clutched fists and pulling them from the band. The rubber band was removed and replaced so quickly that he doubted Margo even noticed. But the hair was becoming annoying. Bet or no bet, he would be cutting it soon.

He took a deep breath and closed his eyes. "Very well. Is she still in your room or in hers?"

"Actually—" Margo paused for a moment, causing Antoine to drop his head farther back so he could see her face. She winced and bit her lip. "She was quite upset, so Giselle suggested she wait in your room."

His eyes widened and he leaned forward and turned the old chair on the pedestal. "*Pardonne? Grand-mère* allowed her to go into *my* room? The room where my briefcase containing sensitive council documents is sitting in full view?"

"She did take out the briefcase, and apparently . . . all of the chairs. I think she was hoping that Tahira would be forced to sit on the bed. Specifically, the *quilt*."

Antoine pursed his lips. It was actually quite a good idea, and one that hadn't occurred to him. He smiled. "She is brilliant, as always. How long has Tahira been in the room?"

"Probably about ten minutes. Is that long enough?"

"Let's give her another ten. I'll respond to this e-mail, and you go up and tell her I'll speak to her in a moment. If she's not on the bed, suggest that she lie down, or even sit on the bed with her for a moment. In fact, take up a glass of wine for both of you. Between the quilt and wine, she should be quite calm when we speak."

Margo let out a small laugh. "That will probably do it. But you might have to wake us both up."

He turned back to the keyboard and clicked on Reply. "Even better. Oh, before you go in the room, stop in the television room and put on a classical music CD on the player—your choice. My room is auxiliary speaker D."

"Wow! You want her *completely* comatose. If I fall asleep and forget to pay the bills, don't whine that you have to pay reconnect fees."

He turned his head and winked. "I have complete faith in your attention to your job, Margo. I doubt we're anywhere close to late on the bills. But if we are, I promise not to utter a single comment."

When she'd gathered the glasses and bottle and left the room, Antoine turned his attention back to his student's message.

Thank you for adding to my repertoire of scent references. I'll definitely try them out to see if I agree.

Tell Nikoli that while I'm sorry that I destroyed the chair, I question the value he's placed on it, heirloom or not. Please tell him to contact me directly with any *evidence* he might have, such as a dated appraisal, and I will be pleased to pay the actual value.

Antoine smiled wickedly as he wrote the words. Tony would probably laugh. While the esteemed pack leader of Chicago might say his dusty old chair was worth eighteen thousand dollars, Antoine suspected he was just annoyed and wanted his strip of hide in cash form.

I'm sorry that your gift is not being cooperative. They're often like that. I remember my sister once mentioning that she found it useful to find two other people who shared a significant event with her and "read" them. Naturally, they must know about us and be willing to participate, and the event has to be something that will evoke strong emotions. But if you talk about the event enough to recall it in each of your minds, and then touch them, it's possible that you might be able to see the same event from multiple points of view. Then, since you were there, you can decide what information from the others is valid and what to discard. Consider it your assignment for the week. Let me

know what happens. My regards to your
lovely wife. —A

Antoine glanced at his watch as he hit the Send button. It had been almost exactly ten minutes. He closed
down the internet connection and walked upstairs. He
expected to hear voices and music, but there was only
the light crinkling sound of paper coming from inside
his room.

That was not a good sign.

Chapter Five

ANTOINE OPENED THE door, expecting the worst. Instead, he found Tahira alone on the bed, completely oblivious to his presence. She was sipping a glass of wine and smiling as she poked at a portion of the quilt, causing the wad of gift wrap inside to rustle enticingly.

The quilt *Grand-mère* had made all those years ago was a masterpiece of style, form, and function. It was nice to see that it still had the same effect on cats as when it had covered his and Fiona's beds when they were children.

"I'm glad you're enjoying yourself," he said lightly.

Tahira started and looked up as her glass nearly leapt from her hand, causing a few drops of wine to fall on the pillow.

She put one hand to her chest and sat up. "God! You nearly gave me a heart attack." She noticed the spilled wine and reached for a tissue while placing her wine glass carefully on the bedside table. "Well, at least it was Chablis. It probably won't stain. I shouldn't even be sitting on the bed, but there aren't any chairs and I was tired of standing and looking out the window."

Antoine walked to the bed and sat down next to her. "Don't be concerned in the least. This quilt is intended to be toyed with. It's the purpose of it."

She stopped pressing the tissue into the pillow. He

noticed that she didn't move away from the spot where their legs nearly touched.

"The quilt has a purpose?"

Antoine nodded and scooted farther up onto the bed so he could lie on his side with a bent arm under his head. "Indeed. *Grand-mère* made this when my twin sister and I were just children. We both had our first change very early in life and were very tense and nervous near the moon. It was difficult to sleep. This quilt was made to help us relax."

Tahira smoothed her hand over the top of the quilt. "It's certainly gorgeous. It must have taken a long time to make. It's a crazy quilt, isn't it? There are so many different fabrics: lace and velvet, brocade and satin, and all the embroidery that connects the pieces. I saw one like this at the state fair. It won the grand champion ribbon, and it wasn't *nearly* as intricate as this one."

Antoine nodded. "Ah, but this has more than just a beautiful exterior. The *interior* is what makes the quilt so special. There are many secrets in this quilt, some that even I haven't uncovered."

"Secrets in the quilt? What sort of secrets? Is there more than just batting under the top layer?" Tahira tried to turn her head to see him, but his position made it impossible. She hiked one leg onto the mattress and turned her whole body to face him.

Antoine smiled. "Well, you already found one secret—the wrapping paper that rustles when you move it. There are few things more enticing to a cat of any sort than crinkle paper hidden from view. *Grand-mère* found that wadded gift wrap works the best. It doesn't flatten up as much as grocery sack paper." He poked at an overstuffed pocket next to his head. "Another secret is this bit right here. Smell it."

* * *

TAHIRA WAS SUSPICIOUS of his amused expression and scent, but leaned forward and put her nose to the cloth. An amazing rush of scent cut straight to her brain and conjured images of every description. There were so *many* scents, each one of them distinct and pure. It was like walking inside a flock of birds in an English garden near a forest at the sea. There were flowers and herbs, trees, moss, and salt water. The smell was enchanting, intoxicating, and she found herself wanting to pick it up like a bouquet of flowers and carry it around with her.

"How in the world?" She turned to look at him. His green and gold eyes were startlingly close and were twinkling with the same amusement that turned up one corner of his mouth.

"*Grand-mère* is both a healer and probably the world's first aromatherapist. Fiona and I were forever catching birds as kittens and *Grand-mère* would insist that we bring them to her to remove the feathers before we ate them." He grinned sheepishly. "Sometimes we even did. I *still* have a fondness for squab."

Tahira laughed brightly. "Leave it to the French to come up with a fancy name for *pigeon*. But it's not like I can talk. Sparrows are my weakness. Mom keeps complaining that she's filling a *bird* feeder, not a cat feeder. But there's just something about those quick little movements." She could almost feel herself drooling at the thought of stalking one. "I know it's sort of sick—"

Antoine's eyes were bright as he watched her, and his scent was thick with amusement when he shook his head. "Not really. It's difficult enough to fight down our instincts not to chase *humans* for sport, and I doubt that sparrows or pigeons will become extinct because of us. I must admit, it's quite nice to meet someone who shares my somewhat *unique* indulgence, and understands it's not horrible. Oh, and 'squab' isn't a French word. It's Scandinavian, and it's served in restaurants in Europe."

"I doubt the restaurants serve them with the *feathers* though. I have the feeling you don't wait for the butter to melt." She was teasing and he didn't seem to mind. In fact, he appeared to be enjoying the banter. "I don't know if it's horrible or not, but I doubt my high school friends would understand my snatching one out of the air in front of them." She looked again at the quilt. "So there are more than just one sort of feathers in these pockets?"

He nodded. "Indeed. In that one little pocket, there are feathers of probably a dozen different birds, from cardinals and sparrows to ducks, geese, and quail. Wherever we would stop for a show, more feathers would be added to the quilt. And there are herbs, too. Chamomile and rosemary, cinnamon, dill, and a dozen others scattered throughout the quilt. You would think they would conflict, but they don't. The quilt is meant to quiet a frantic mind. It helps a person relax and think clearly. Amber keeps it in this room for when I visit. I'm often very stressed."

"But if Giselle made this quilt when you were a child, then it's twenty or thirty years old. How can it still smell so strong?"

Antoine laughed and a bright burst of sweet citrus blended with the herbs from the quilt. He raised up onto his elbow. "Thank you for that, but I'm a touch older than you might think. As for her methods, I don't think anyone will ever know the answer. *Grand-mère* has her own secrets, which she will take to her grave." He reached over and brushed a stray hair away from her face, making her skin tingle. "You seem much more calm. Do you feel that way?"

The question startled her, but as soon as he said it, she knew it was true. "You're right. I just feel relaxed. Sort of like after a day of reading a book under a shade tree. It's a nice feeling. Thank you."

His smile was warm, pleased, and suddenly very enticing. Before she even realized what she was doing, she leaned forward and placed a soft kiss on his lips. He didn't react like she expected. The part of her that thought of him as a famous, unreachable persona expected that he would pull back and either chastise her or pat her head like a little girl.

She hadn't suspected that he might *want* her to do just what she had. She suddenly found herself tight against him with strong fingers kneading her hair and the back of her neck. His other arm slowly slid up the back of her shirt and squeezed tight enough to make her stomach clench. His mouth began to move against hers, his tongue exploring, teasing, encouraging her to do the same. He tasted of sweet, heady brandy and chocolate, and his natural musk was growing stronger, filling her nose and turning her brain to putty. The scent tightened her body, arousing her faster than anything she'd ever experienced.

His fingers began to contract on her neck, and she could feel his fingernails bite into her skin. He took a deep breath and then let out a small growl. The kiss deepened just a bit, and she could feel the golden hair on his chin rubbing against her skin. Each time his fingers padded, nails dug deeper into her skin. It was unlike anything she'd ever experienced, and the sensation made her writhe in pleasure. When he lifted his hips to press against her, he was fully erect.

The knowledge of what might happen if they continued panicked her for the briefest moment. There was something raw and powerful about Antoine. Somehow she *knew* that he would slowly carve the pleasure from her with nails and teeth. For the first time in her life, the tiger rose to the surface and wanted . . . *needed* the frantic claws and hisses of another cat during the moon.

She gave herself to the sensation, willed him to continue, and then suddenly felt every inch of her body bathed in a burning roil of magical energy that both surrounded her and pounded against her like jets in a spa. The combination of the hungry kiss along with the skin-prickling power made her pulse race and her body weak.

She slid her fingers through his hair, marveling at how it could be coarse, thick, and silky all at once. She was suddenly light-headed and desperate to feel his hands touching her bare skin—somewhere, anywhere, *everywhere*.

The power intensified until her skin became as hot and swollen as after a midday run in the summer. Antoine seemed to notice, because he placed his palm flat against the back of her neck for a moment and then against her cheek. He moved his mouth from hers and ran his lips along the line of her jaw while she remained frozen, letting the sensations wash over her body as she struggled to breathe.

His whisper near her ear made her shiver. "Suddenly, I'm not nearly as relaxed as I was, and neither are you, *mon chat du feu*. We should stop now, before we wind up doing something we both might regret—as enjoyable as it would undoubtedly be."

He eased his hands off her and moved her away just enough to allow him to sit up. She opened her mouth to say . . . *something*, but he put a finger to her lips with a small smile.

"Shhh. There's no need to speak, Tahira. It was

lovely, and I thank you. Just accept it for what it was.
But I still have contracts to read, and you still need rest."
Antoine paused, and took a deep breath, as though men-
tally switching gears, Tahira thought. "I've asked Margo
to contact your family and they will probably arrive as
soon as the airport is accepting flights. When they get
into town, we'll give them directions here. The address
and telephone for this house are very secret, as I'm sure
you can understand. I would appreciate it if you would
not call them for now. Too many people have caller ID
or could trace this location and I can't allow that. You're
welcome to sleep on the quilt if you like. One of us will
wake you for dinner."

She nodded dumbly, and watched him stand up and
walk to the door. She couldn't figure out what to say or
whether to say anything at all. She didn't feel quite real
yet. Her skin was still vibrating lightly and aching, feeling like it should be able to crawl right off her bones.
She could swear that bees were buzzing in her ears. As
he reached to close the door behind him, he caught her
eye and winked. Her heart skipped a beat and her body
clenched.

She dropped backward almost bonelessly onto the
quilt, hoping for the same lazy feeling as earlier. But
everything smelled like him now. Her hair, her skin,
even her clothes. She could still taste musk and brandy
on her lips, and it made her shiver with anticipation,
along with a fair helping of fear. She was *so* not relaxed
anymore.

Even after ten minutes, Tahira's muscles refused to
unclench, and she was sweating bullets from the magical energy still heating the air around her—and she was
beginning to worry.

This isn't normal. Attraction is one thing, but this is

just freaky. There's something seriously weird going on and I need to find out what it is.

A wave of dizziness hit her as she sat up. She took slow, deep breaths. When the light-headedness passed, she stood. It was time to get some answers.

Chapter Six

"WE NEED TO talk."

Antoine jumped as the angry female voice brought him back from his thoughts. The contract on the computer screen was already on page eight and he couldn't remember a single word of what he'd read. Blast it!

He turned to look at Giselle. When he did, he noticed that there were deep gouges in the arm of the big wooden chair. He hadn't even realized he was clawing the arm to splinters, but he wasn't surprised. The situation with Tahira was becoming a great concern. He'd had another vision. Two in less than a day! But what a vision it had been! For the first time, he'd had sensory input other than visual. He could hear his own growls; smell and feel the sensation of her naked body under his, the scent of her hair as he clenched her neck in his teeth. No, that was a vision better to avoid than encourage. While he had exited the room gracefully, the power drain during their kiss had cost him a great deal. He hadn't fully recovered from the first time. Combined with the vision, the kiss had been enough to leave him weak and . . . more than a bit nervous.

He lifted up his hand and crossed his arms over his chest. "Better?" His voice was just short of annoyed at her tone. Her return gaze was disapproving. "I suppose this was a gift from you to Charles. Do you plan to turn me over on your knee?"

"I think we're well beyond that stage, Councilman Monier." Giselle's voice was serious. Each word ended with a slight snarl. "I'm not concerned about the chair, although it *is* a symptom of the underlying problem. I just spoke with Tahira."

"*Merde!*" Antoine stood and pushed back the chair hard enough that it hit the wall with a loud thud. He threw his hands in the air, turned, and walked toward the fireplace. "Please do not lecture me about women, *Grand-mère*! I *agree* that it was a mistake to kiss her, and one that I do not plan to repeat. Does that satisfy you?"

Giselle dropped her chin a fraction, and the burning caramel scent of her anger filled the large room. Antoine could swear that he saw her hair fluff defensively. "I don't believe you have any clue what might satisfy me at this point. But that is what I am here to discuss. Did you know that Tahira is *glowing*, Antoine? And I do mean that *literally*. She has absorbed so much energy from you that her skin is red and she is in a great deal of pain." She paused to see how he would react.

She was in *pain*? How could he have not noticed that? He started toward the door, but *Grand-mère* blocked his path with supernatural speed.

"Leave her be. I healed her skin where the blisters had formed and sent her downstairs. She has been instructed to swim in the pool to cool down and expend the excess energy. Matty and the others are there. They promised to notify me if there are any problems. I thought that best, since you and I need to have a serious discussion."

Antoine felt magic begin to roil up from her small frame, making her seem more powerful than usual.

"It was both thoughtless and *dangerous* for you to have left her in that condition! What were you thinking!?"

Antoine felt himself flinch from her tone. How easy it was to drop back into childhood roles. But it honestly hadn't occurred to him what might become of the energy that had been taken from him. He opened his mouth to respond, but *Grand-mère* held up a hand before he could speak. She moved closer, forcing their auras to touch. Fury vibrated her body, clawing along his own magic.

"*Do not answer*! It's obvious that you *weren't* thinking. Just as you weren't thinking about the chair, or the visions that have been haunting you. And just as you haven't been thinking of the decisions you've made on the council of late! All that is about to change, Antoine. You will be thinking a great deal about these and other things in the next few days."

She was right. So many things had been occupying his mind lately that he'd ignored others. Like not personally ensuring the safety of his cats, or knowing about Matty's trip. He sighed deeply. "*Grand-mère*—"

She shook her head, and frustration and determination edged out the scent of her anger. "No, Antoine. Today I am not your grandmother. Today, I am Giselle Bertrand, leader of the lynxes. I am one of your subjects—and I am planning a palace revolt."

He felt his brows raise. "*Pardonne*?"

She clenched her fists and took a deep breath. Antoine could hear her heartbeat slow a bit from the angry pounding that matched her scent. "I had hoped that thrusting you into your present position would build you, make you accept and embrace your Sazi abilities. But there is too much of your father in you. Your sisters apparently received all of your mother's best traits, so . . . a change is needed."

Antoine sat down on the arm rest of the couch near the fire, keeping the distance between them that she had established. "I do not understand Gran—I mean, *Giselle*. What is it you're trying to say?"

Giselle stared at him, searching his face for . . . something. She apparently didn't find what she was looking for, because she sighed and dropped her gaze to the dark leather upholstery with a sad shake of her head. "Even yet, you don't grasp the situation. Very well. You were a dauphin, Antoine. You were the first surviving alpha male of either the lions or the cougars in a very long time. It was believed that you would rule over the cats and bring peace to us."

He shook his head just a bit with confusion racing through his mind. "And I *do* rule the cats—"

She laughed, and her bitterness smelled like unripe lemons. "You do not know the *meaning* of the word! You sit on your throne as Marie Antoinette sat on hers—unknowing and uncaring for anything save your own comfort. Perhaps we protected you too much. Your childhood was traumatic and your seer gifts made it more so. But others have endured trauma and survived. They have *grown*, as your sisters grew in skill and responsibility. But you have *not*. You play with your wild cats and entertain the humans, ignoring the trials and needs of your people. Twice now you've left Tahira to face her fate, unknowing, *uncaring*. You have no curiosity about what brought her to us, nor why she is able to absorb magic—"

Antoine felt his own anger rising. "That is *not* true! Perhaps *you* don't understand all that is at play here! Tahira is of another culture, one the council is trying to establish friendly relations with. I am quite concerned about her welfare, which is why I allowed her to contact her family, and hope to return her to them. It is why I have fought *against* my curiosity, out of respect for her privacy. It is—"

Giselle let out a harsh breath, close to a laugh. "A game to you. Nothing more. You have not *tried* to contact her family. You have waved your hand airily and instructed your *employees* to do so. I read the papers in your briefcase." She saw his shocked expression and shrugged. "Do not leave them in view if you don't want me to look. You invited Tahira's *sahip* to visit your estate in Strasbourg. *Putain!* How did you expect them to do that? Do you believe they have *wings*?"

He frowned as his fingers began tapping his leg almost of their own accord. "I would have been happy to meet with them at a location of their choosing."

Giselle tapped her temple. "Again, you did not think! The kabile is poverty-stricken but proud. So they declined the meeting rather than admit they could not *afford* to travel to France. But you took their refusal at face value. You never even considered the possibility of dirtying your linen trousers or scuffing your fine shoes to seek them out. But even that I could forgive. *This* I cannot."

She reached into her pocket and extracted a small brown envelope and threw it hard enough that it hit him in the chest. "Go ahead. Look inside. See what you have done to your people—to those you supposedly lead. I found this waiting on my pillow when we arrived here."

Antoine opened the clasp and pulled out a thin stack of photographs. He flipped through them and his first thought was of revulsion. A small pride of lions was lying under a sole shade tree on a vast savanna. They were barely alive, with ribs showing and patches of hair missing. The sores on their legs were black with flies. "What are these?"

Giselle's voice shook with emotion when she responded, but there were too many scents coming from her to sort. "*Those are your people*. They are your mother's tribe. Once they were strong and proud, masters of their domain. But you saw fit to end that with the stroke of a pen, from a thousand miles away."

He put the photos back in the envelope and tossed it back to her. She didn't reach out to catch it, so it dropped to the couch and bounced onto the floor. "How is this *my* fault? I have done nothing to these people."

Her jaw set and her eyes flashed with the same anger of her scent. "Precisely. You have done *nothing*. When the Sazi hyenas moved onto their land, you did *nothing*. When Angelique, the representative for the raptors, made motion for the rights to a small pond—which happened to be the only watering hole for miles on the savanna—*you did nothing*. You did not visit the area, although you *do* have the means. You did not ask what effect losing a watering hole might have. You simply voted in favor, so that you could return to your comfortable home in time for your next show. You did *nothing*, and now your people suffer and die. You actively chose their fate by your inaction."

Tears were rolling freely down her face, and Antoine could only stare at her with rising outrage. "I have never willingly harmed any of my people! I absolutely deny any malice toward these people, whether or not they were my mother's tribe. I work very hard at knowing the facts on issues before I vote. How *dare you* insinuate that I do not take my responsibilities seriously!"

But she waved off his statements. "I was *willing* to talk to you, make you aware since you were born with so little curiosity. But then Tahira came to us, and *still* you do nothing. The poor child is a power well, and you leave her to suffer. But her suffering will soon become the suffering of all of us. You know it. You have seen it—for weeks now you have had visions, but you silence them, ignore them because they are *inconvenient*. That is, until your seer gift would tolerate no more interference and forced you to see, at the risk of both of your lives and anyone who might have been unfortunate enough to be on the road."

Antoine held up his hand. "What is a 'power well'?"

"Something that should not exist. A gift, or curse, that is the stuff of legends and fables. There are small references in a dozen books, but no guides—no instructions on what to do or how to deal with the abilities. *That* you will have to learn for yourself, before the eyes in your dream swallow the world."

His hand clenched the couch arm. "But how could you . . . my vision . . . you can't know what I see! Besides, my visions have nothing to do with my duties. You are deliberately changing the subject."

She looked at him with contempt, but her scent was filled with pity. "Acting on your visions is *part* of your duties, Antoine. The subject remains the same. Do you *really* believe that the council would allow me to raise you and your sister—two powerful alphas even as cubs—without some small abilities of my own? I am a sensitive, and a good one. I was a member of Wolven when your sister called us. You probably do not remember, but it was I who removed you from your hiding place in the wall after your mother had drowned your younger siblings. It was I who helped the other agents, whom you now know as Lucas and Jack, put your mother to rest at last. It was I who helped your sister Aspen deal with her various seer gifts before they could destroy her mind as they did your mother's. It was *I* who helped develop Fiona's powers, and though I have desperately tried to help you realize yours, you will have no part of it."

His head was swimming. All these years of believing her to be his confidante, the one person he could trust in the world, and now . . . "You *killed* my mother?"

The confusing blend of scents rising from her included anger, surprise, comfort, and concern. "She was *insane*, Antoine, and too powerful for her own good. You were very young to have remembered it, but it took all three of us to put her down. Yes, you watched the death of your infant siblings, but you didn't see the six deaths of those who preceded Amber and Aspen, the ones she claimed to be *accidental*, and the ones in between that we learned about from your sisters. Did you never wonder why there is such a large age gap between you and your older sisters? There were others, many others, Antoine."

Her eyes were filled with pain and sadness, but her voice was calm. "Times were different. We believed her when she told us of tragic illnesses and crib deaths. Death is not uncommon in Sazi children as they struggle to reconcile the beast inside. We didn't know what psychiatrists now understand about postpartum depression. But that is neither here nor there. The issue today is *you*. I am sorry for your difficult childhood. I wish it would have been otherwise. But it was no worse than my own, and I have recovered. It is time for you to do the same, or face the consequences."

Antoine stood up and felt power rise in him, matching his anger and outrage. He stood and advanced a step toward her. "Consequences? You speak to me of *consequences*? You stand there and inform me that you killed my mother, tell me you have lied to me for a hundred years about my past, and I am the one to face consequences? *Je t' encule pauvre con!*"

Without even thinking, he extended his hand and threw a vicious blast of power at her. To his surprise, she quite calmly blocked the energy and sent it veering into the wall. Rock exploded outward, raining down on them both, knocking the laptop to the floor. She didn't even flinch at one of his best attacks and had no scent of fear. How was it that he had never noticed this side of her? How long had she been reading his documents, watching his visions, and following his council career? Who *was* this woman in front of him?

Giselle crossed her arms over her chest, and her voice was both sour and angry when she responded. "This is just like you, Antoine. You react without thinking, and blame all but yourself. *À méchant ouvrier, point de bon outil!* Your sisters all know the story. They asked long ago. I have *never* lied to any of you. You are the only one who has never wondered—never *cared* about the *why*. You cling to your memories as though reality of the past will somehow bend to your will. You remember Sabine as sweet and good, rather than the wild-eyed killer she was at the end. And in taking offense at actions from a century ago, you gloss over your own failings, which are every bit as bad, if not worse. I brought a murderer to justice to save innocents. You have *slaughtered* innocents through your indifference. Which do you believe is worse?"

Antoine could only stare in shock at the force, and the truth, of her words. He ran his fingers through his hair and then rubbed the bridge of his nose between his eyes. There was too much to think about, to consider. "I do not blame my tools for my failings, Giselle, if indeed I have failings. I . . . I need time to think about all of this."

He was startled when steely determination filled her scent. "And yet, there is no time. As you said earlier, things are happening. People are dying. So, be it known that I hereby challenge you for your council seat. If you will not act, then someone must in your place."

He was already stunned from the revelations and had to catch himself on the fireplace mantel to keep from falling. It took several tries to get words out. "Wha— what did you say?"

She stood up straighter and raised her chin, eyes filled with fire. "I believe I was clear. At the next full moon, unless you have proven yourself capable of leading our people, we will battle in animal form for the right to represent the cats. One of us will not survive, as a leadership challenge is to the death. I am willing to risk that to protect our people. *Fais ce que je dois, advienne que pourra.*"

He held up his hands in shock and resignation. This was becoming ridiculous. "I am also more than willing to, as you say, 'do my duty, come what may.' But if all you want is my council seat, Giselle, and feel you can do a better job, then take it. I offer it freely. I never *asked* for the job. It was thrust upon me against my wishes, as you well know."

Giselle shook her head. "*Non*, Antoine. That is not the way this can end, as *you* well know. I am sorry if the truth hurts—*Il n'y a que la vérité qui blesse, petit fils.* But by *accepting* the post, you became Rex to our people, and the cats would never willingly follow one who *negotiated* for the throne. But you still have an option. I have made it clear in my challenge that if you are somehow able to live up to the responsibility of your post—to learn how to control and use the power well to save our people from the death and destruction that is about to occur—then you may remain in your seat."

He opened his mouth to respond when the sound of someone hammering on the door made him turn his head. A low growl rose from his chest and he fought not to let out a piercing cougar roar. All of this stress on the third night of the moon was forcing his magic too close to the surface. He would probably have to change into cat form later to compensate.

He stepped toward the door. "Who in the world can be calling in this storm? *Grand-mère*, we can discuss this potential challenge later. You have *not* made the terms clear to me, as you seem to believe."

She stepped from around the couch and a small smile turned up one corner of her mouth as she passed him in a blur, reaching the door first. "I never said I made the terms clear to *you*. I have already filed the formal challenge with the council and chief justice". She sighed suddenly, her voice and scent determined but sad. "This has been a long time coming, Antoine." She avoided his hand when he reached out to grab her arm. "Our visitor should be the person who will officiate the challenge. I was expecting him when Larry and Bruce arrived, but he wouldn't rattle the knob as they did. He would simply walk in. He apparently was delayed by the storm, since he intended to be here before I challenged you."

"Who in the world would agree—?" But he didn't need to finish, because he *knew* the one person on the council who would brave the fires of hell, the depths of the ocean, or a winter blizzard in Germany, to watch one of the Monier family fall in combat. Antoine felt both a snarl rise in his chest and a sinking feeling rumble the pit of his stomach. "*Merde!*"

"Ah, you have guessed," Giselle said, as she unlocked the first deadbolt on the door. "The battle will be offici-ated by the worst enemy the Moniers have ever known, save *themselves*: Councilman Ahmad al-Narmer, repre-sentative for the snakes."

Chapter Seven

"NO, NO. HIGHER, Matty! She needs to have to work to reach it."

Tahira toweled her hair as she watched Bruce and Matty preparing to feed the large female Bengal, Babette.

A sudden sharp pain made her let out a startled yelp and pull her foot away from the male cub, who had decided that her toes were chew toys. He immediately pounced on the retreating prey, so she picked him up by the scruff of the neck and nipped his ear with a small growl. The cat hissed and spit and struggled to free himself while Tahira held him at arm's length with a smile. The cubs were just darling—so feisty and playful.

She and the cub both turned their heads at the sound of Babette's light series of grunts and chuffing. Tahira set the cub on the ground, and he bounded over to his mother and began to feed. His sister climbed from the shallow, running stream that led to the pool, shook herself, and quickly nestled in beside her brother for some milk.

"That high enough, mate?" Matty asked.

Tahira shook her head in wonder. She knew they were in a basement, but the underground lair was simply amazing. A small man-made stream ran through the cattails that hid an aerator. They fed a small pond that looked, for all the world, as though it should be in the middle of a summer meadow. The stream wound its way to the opposite corner and fed into a large, deep pool, with molded plastic sides and walls. The blues, grays, and white created an arctic landscape. Everything was lit with recessed, full-spectrum lighting with dimmer switches that could bring full noonday sun or twilight to the room. Tahira had chosen the glacier pool for her swim. The impression of ice had appealed to her when she'd changed into an apricot one-piece suit that matched the highlights in her hair. She was overheated and sweating after leaving the bedroom and talking to Giselle. But she hadn't noticed that the water was chilled to near freezing by a refrigeration unit until *after* she'd jumped in.

The long string of screams and swearing when she surfaced made the three men laugh and one cub try to climb the walls. Only one thought had flowed through her mind as she shivered and tried to catch her breath. *What in the hell sort of animal does the owner of this place shift into?*

Giselle had been right about needing to cool down. So much steam rose when she hit the water that the humidity in the room rose by half. Her hair was going to be a frizzy mess. But it did cool her down enough that her skin was nearly back to its normal color.

Just remembering the water made her shiver, so Tahira turned her attention back to the men. When Bruce nodded, Matty tied off the rope to a nearby hook. There seemed to be hooks and pulleys all over the place, along with a variety of floor textures, from Astroturf to sea-grass mats to rubber. Both she and the wild tigers were finding the room quite entertaining.

"Charles must have known that we were coming. I can't imagine that he normally stocks sika deer and antelope in the walk-in, but Babette will be thrilled." Bruce was looking at the antelope with a pleased expression.

The skin and hooves were still attached, and it was swinging slightly in the breeze from the vent.

The whole notion of "presentation" of food to Babette interested Tahira. Since she'd become a tiger, she had been hunting live game on the moon. She'd never really stopped to think about animals in captivity. The drive to chase, hunt, and kill was still there. She knew that she would become quite depressed if, for every meal, day after day, a steak or part of a deer was simply tossed in a bowl.

"Right. She should have a fair go at that. Will she fossick it by herself, or do we call her attention to it?" asked Matty.

Larry laughed as he walked up to the pair holding the kylie that Matty had just finished carving. "Don't worry. She's been watching you two the whole time. She knows *exactly* where it is. But the cubs come first. She'll find it in a bit, when it's a little warmer and smells stronger. Here's your kylie. Sorry it took so long for me to get it pulled out of the wall, but that's a long climb to the ceiling!" He smirked when Matty reddened and smelled of dry embarrassment. "You do realize that a kylie is called a 'rabbit stick' because it's meant to be thrown at *ground* level, right?"

"Yeah, I know, mate. The trouble is that I *did* throw it at ground level. Guess I need to work a mite on the angles."

Tahira rubbed the towel against her face as she struggled not to laugh. She had been thankful that she could duck under the water to avoid being hit by Matty's various failed attempts at hitting an archery target next to the door. The odd sound of wood wobbling through the air, combined with a panicked "Down, mates!" had been enough for her to stay in the pool until the kylie was safely embedded in the foam wall two stories up.

Larry was kind enough not to rub it in. "It's a shame that we didn't think to bring Babette's diet sheet in our packs, Bruce. We should have remembered she couldn't travel yet. Does she need some vegetables today?"

"I think I saw a couple of small pumpkins in the walk-in. She'd probably love to chase them in the pool."

"Wild tigers eat pumpkins?" Tahira couldn't help but ask. Of course, she loved pumpkins, raw or in pie, but it hadn't occurred to her that wild ones would as well.

Bruce nodded and walked toward her, pausing to give Babette an affectionate scratch behind one ear on the way.

"Well, it's more about touch and smell and the game of it. Pumpkins float and Babette likes to jump into the water to chase them around. Then she'll nose it and chew on it like a bone. It's just about head sized and squishes under her teeth and claws. But they're high in vitamins, too. I don't want to spoil her too much with all of this fun food in one day, though. I've already hidden two of the rabbits that Giselle caught behind some rocks in the cattails for her to find. There's also grass growing in one corner of the enclosure in the next room, and we'll add in some crickets and white worms at dusk. The cubs will like chasing them, and Babette will eat the ones they squish."

"This is an amazing basement! It must have cost a fortune to build," said Tahira. "I guess the owner is pretty rich, huh?"

"Charles has had this place for a very long time. He's built it up over the years to entertain the animal side of the various dignitaries in the Sazi world." Bruce bowed slightly. "And now to the Hayalet as well."

Tahira moved her head a bit ruefully. "Technically speaking, you probably *shouldn't* be entertaining a Hayalet. Unless my parents step in, it's pretty likely that the people in my grandparents' village will want me to be either killed or banished if they find out. I didn't tell my folks that you were Sazi when I told them I'd been rescued, because there's been a blood feud between the two cultures for centuries."

"I'll be stuffed!" Matty exclaimed, while Larry shook his head angrily. "Do you really think they would? Hurt you, I mean? Just for staying in a house with us?"

"It's not like the Sazi can talk, Matty, and you know it." Larry's voice dropped several notes.

Matty shrugged and sighed. "Yeah, I suppose that is tall poppy syndrome. We can't really talk about being vicious when we're up ourselves about whether we turn on the moon. Lots of family members back home in Sydney who won't ever be Sazi get spewin' mad at the way they're treated. Still, we're not all arses, Tahira. You're welcome back if they give you the boot. I'm sure Antoine would say the same. He's a high mucky-muck councilman, so he could get you settled somewhere."

"That may not be true for much longer." Antoine's voice took all of them by surprise. It was as though he had magically appeared behind them. Nobody had heard him enter the room. Matty jumped several inches because the taller man was directly behind him when he spoke. "I'm afraid that all of our lives have just taken on a distinct . . . twist. Tahira, could I speak to you in private for a moment?"

Tahira felt a shiver that had nothing to do with air temperature or a cold pool. Then butterflies started to tumble in her stomach and she stood up somewhat nervously. She couldn't read Antoine's expression at all. That worried her. It was as though he had disappeared inside himself. No facial expressions or scent of emotions—in fact, no scent at all, which seemed impossible. There was nothing to guide her.

Oh, God! Could my family already be here?

Larry was the only one to notice her brief moment of panic. He gave her shoulder a quick squeeze and smiled encouragingly.

Antoine turned and walked toward the door, pausing by Babette. He and the tiger stared into each other's eyes for a moment and Antoine nodded. Tahira was just slipping on a thick terry-cloth robe over her swimsuit when he turned back to them.

"Babette would appreciate it if you would raise the antelope a bit higher and open the entrance to her compartment so the cubs can watch her pull it into the grass."

Tahira was taken aback at what appeared to have been a direct request from the tiger, but Bruce nodded as though it was commonplace.

"I wondered about that. She's been off her feet for a bit and probably wants some exercise. We'll take care of it. C'mon, Matty." The pair walked off, with Larry following in their wake.

Antoine turned back to her with that same blank expression. "Would you prefer to change first? There are some people upstairs who would like to speak with you."

It confirmed her worst fears. Her mouth felt like sand and her skin was flushed again. "I don't have anything here that my kabile would consider suitable clothing. My grandfather would kill me for certain for wearing a swimming suit where people could see me, but the clothes I had on earlier aren't much better. He's a traditionalist."

The comment raised his eyebrows just a bit. "It's not your family that's arrived." He looked her up and down for a long moment and pursed his lips. "But you have a point. Ahmad is also a bit of a traditionalist. Let us see if we can find you something suitable in my sister's room. We'll take the back stairs so we don't run into anyone by accident before I've prepared you. But we must hurry, *mon chat du feu*. Time is running short."

He walked away before she could ask the questions still trembling on her lips.

Who is this "Ahmad"? I don't know anyone by that name. What sort of preparation is required to meet him, what in the heck does "mon shot do few" mean, and what about—?

She realized that she had started to follow Antoine through the doorway hidden behind a tapestry of a giant polar bear without asking a single question. The realization made her stop cold and remain frozen in place. He cocked his head questioningly when she failed to follow.

Tahira started to tick off reasons for staying put in her head. *Let's see . . . leaving the group . . . with a guy who looks pissed off . . . through a secret door . . . to climb an unlit staircase to who-knows-where. This is starting to feel like one of those bad horror movies where you want to beat the heroine senseless for ignoring the obvious.*

But she *wanted* to follow, wanted to know where the staircase went, and wanted to meet this Ahmad. And then she understood what was wrong. Her defense class training was conflicting with what Grammy had told her on their last hunt together. One part of her brain screamed caution, drilled into her for years before she came into her animal form. *Beware of following strangers into enclosed places. There's safety in numbers. Always stay in brightly lit areas.*

But Grammy's advice made sense, too. *Hayalet are ghosts. We're one with the dark. There can be no stealth in a group, so seek the shadows and solitude. Explore new places, for you are the hunter. The game will not come to you, so always be prepared to follow and strike. Be the master of your surroundings.*

She was feeling out of control, and had been ever since Rabi disappeared.

Reacting in panic made me careless and got me captured. Since then, I've been unsure of myself and depressed, so I've been letting others lead. I've been following along like a scared rabbit, when I should be kicking butt and taking names.

All that was about to change.

Tahira closed her eyes and let her ears and nose flood her brain with information, as though she were stalking prey in the pitch dark. The squeak of pulleys behind told her that Matty and Bruce had begun to raise the antelope carcass higher. The snarls and growls of the cubs were a lie, for their scent was joy and contentment. She searched outward farther and felt Antoine's massive wall of power press on her from the doorway. She tried to find something . . . anything to give her a hint about his mood. But there was no scent other than that which lingered on her own skin. At odd moments, she could still taste brandy and chocolate.

When she opened her eyes, Antoine hadn't moved. Apparently, he'd figured out that she was working through something and was waiting—if not *patiently*, then silently.

He was the linchpin to all of this. Every instinct she had screamed it at her. He had offered help and she would be a fool not to take every advantage she could. She needed information, at the least, and probably assistance, too. But she would get neither by remaining in the basement, swimming and playing with cubs.

She strode forward confidently. A sweeping look around as she walked revealed every potential trap, every weapon that could be used in a fight if it came to it.

"Is there a problem?" he asked quietly as she passed him to enter the stairwell.

"Not anymore." Her deep near-snarl was met with the shadow of a smile.

When he closed the door behind him, he flicked a wall switch and the stairwell was flooded with light from a series of fixtures. She looked up to a small door at the top of a long flight of stairs. Since there were no other landings or hallways, she presumed that was their goal. She continued to climb the stairs while he followed smoothly.

"When you get to the door, turn left. Fiona's bedroom is first on the right."

She slowed and glanced over her shoulder, keeping herself steady with one hand on the rail. "Fiona is your sister? Is this her house?"

"Yes, no, and . . . yes. Fiona is my sister, and this is my sister's house. But it's not Fiona's. The house belongs to my older sister, Amber, and her husband, Charles."

Tahira opened the door when she reached the top of the stairs. Her calves were protesting just a bit. "Amber's a pretty name," she said as Antoine turned off the light and closed the door to the stairs.

He shrugged. "I preferred it when she was called Yvette. It suited her better. But Charles requested Amber."

When she neared the bedroom on the right, Antoine reached past her to open the door. His sweater-clad shoulder brushed her robe, but it felt like skin against skin. His aura seemed to slide along hers like satin, raising enough goosebumps to want to make her rub her arm to warm it.

He put a light hand on the small of her back as she entered the room. It turned her legs to jelly and forcibly reminded her of the feeling of his arms tight around her. With her heart pounding loud enough that it should echo in the huge room, she tried to think of something to say that didn't sound idiotic or incredibly forward.

"So, she changed her name just for him? That's sweet. What did your parents think of that? Mine would scream bloody murder if I changed my name." Her mouth felt dry and her throat tight as he stepped farther into the room and closed the door with a click that seemed far too loud.

She should move, get out of his way so he could show her the closet—but she seemed to be frozen in place, waiting for . . . something.

His soft voice right next to her ear made her shiver and nearly lose her balance. "Did you know that your hair has two different scents, *mon chat du feu*? It smells both of sandalwood where it is dark, and toasted cinnamon."

"Wha . . . uhm . . . what does that mean?" Her voice cracked and then trailed into a whisper as he slid his hands down the arms of the robe.

"I do not know. Perhaps it is because—"

She shook her head slightly and felt his nose right next to her ear. He leaned even closer, until his breath pushed against her eardrum with wet heat. "No, that's not what I was trying to ask. What does 'mon shot do few' mean?"

He moved away from her ear just a bit. "*Mon chat du feu?* It is a French phrase. Why do you ask?"

"Because you keep saying it to me. But I don't know what it means."

He paused long enough that she wasn't sure he was going to answer. When he did, he had stepped back a pace and his voice sounded worried. "I see. It means 'my fire cat.' When you were putting logs on the fire, the coals made your hair glow and the strands smell of smoke." She turned around to see his expression. He was smiling slightly, but it didn't match the concerned expression in his eyes. "Does it bother you? I thought you might prefer it to the rather clichéd *mon cherie* or even that which many of my friends use—*mon petit chou*."

"And what does *that* mean?"

He chuckled, and the sound seemed to wash over her like warm water. Even the roots of her hairs tingled when he laughed like that. "It means, 'my little cabbage.' "

When she opened her mouth in surprised amusement, he shrugged gracefully. "We are a very down-to-earth people in France. So, too, are our endearments. A very nice or obliging person is a cabbage. It's similar to 'my dear' or 'my friend' in America."

He stepped around her and walked toward an ornate wardrobe with his hands clasped behind his back. "It's strange. I remembered thinking *mon chat du feu* would suit you, but I didn't realize I was saying it out loud."

Once again, his voice and scent betrayed nothing. But she noticed his knuckles were white where one hand gripped the other before he unclasped them to open the cabinet doors. "In any event, come look through Fiona's outfits to see if there is anything that suits you. I will leave you to dress and then we can go downstairs together."

She was already looking in the wardrobe, moving hangers aside, and pulling several possible outfits into the light, so she almost didn't hear him. But when the lamps from the hallway lit up the floor near her feet, all of the questions sprang again to her mind, still unasked and unanswered. "No! Wait! Don't leave."

ANTOINE PAUSED IN the doorway. He was annoyed and concerned that his hand was shaking ever so slightly. There were too many things to deal with today without becoming attracted to this young Hayalet. It was more of a struggle than he liked to keep his voice bland, but it was necessary if he were to avoid the circumstances in his vision. "No? I would have thought you would prefer to try on clothing without an audience."

Her arms were full of hangers of clothing. Her frustrated expression matched the hot metal scent rising from her. She pointed with a free finger to the trifold silk divider wall in the corner. "I can change behind that. But . . . well, you know this Ahmad. I haven't a clue what he'll find acceptable. Besides, I'd like to ask you a few questions."

Antoine sighed, closed the door, and took a seat at Fiona's desk. She was entitled to as many answers as he could afford to give, but the questions she'd asked thus far had been more than a little uncomfortable. When was the last time he'd called a woman by an endearment? Even one he was *dating*? And to do it completely unconsciously—*merde*! But he had offered to prepare her to meet Ahmad, and he would honor his word. He would certainly give Gran—or, rather, Giselle no more reason to question his judgment or dedication to his duty. He was still completely befuddled by her accusations, especially considering how *very* hard he worked to learn the details of the various motions that came before the council. He would have to find some way to convince her not to complete the challenge, because it was unlikely she could defeat him in battle. But killing her would *destroy* him inside, and his sisters would never forgive him for her loss.

Tahira stepped behind the screen. She hung the hangers on a wall hook that was just outside the screen's protection. She flipped through the outfits several times before selecting a white, ankle-length wrap-around skirt that he'd seen Fiona wear several times, along with a pale blue ruffled shirt. She pulled them behind the screen with her. He heard the whisper of cloth stretching and moving, and realized that he could see her silhouette through the screen, backlit by the light seeping from behind the lace draperies. He cleared his throat and stared at the carvings on the bed posters, trying desperately not to imagine the image that would match the nicely curved shadow.

Perhaps talking would help. "So, you have questions?"

"Bunches. But I don't know where to start."

Antoine started to open his mouth to reply when she tossed the still-damp suit over the top of the screen and continued speaking. "Let's start with—how did you just happen to show up at a German police station looking for a tiger on the same day that I happened to have been taken to one?"

That's right! She hadn't been in the room when he'd explained the day to Matty and Margo. Naturally, she would be suspicious of his motives. He certainly would be.

For a few minutes, he explained how the day transpired—from Simon's disappearance to his visit to the woods, scenting her and finding out she was still alive.

"So," she said, stepping from around the screen and doing a quick pirouette. "It was just good luck on my part that your day sucked?"

He smiled a bit, but it was filled with sorrow. "You might say that. Simon was one of my favorites, and I'm very sad about his death. He was young and talented, and his loss will upset the whole troupe when they learn of it. But I'm certainly glad that I arrived so the Kommissar didn't discover a naked young woman with streaked hair in a cage in his basement."

Her expression was rueful and her scent was awash with embarrassment. "Oh yeah. That would have been a terrific image. Especially with one black eye from being kicked right where the guard kicked the tiger." She pointed to the outfit. "Yes? No?"

Antoine snorted and leaned back in the chair, crossing his arms over his chest. "He's lucky it wasn't me in the cage. I would have taken his foot off—at the *knee*. Fortunately for him, German food gives me indigestion."

She exploded with laughter that carried the sweet, tangy odor of happiness. "Yeah, they all smelled like cabbage, and that gives me gas."

He looked Tahira up and down slowly, admiring the play of strong muscles that flexed under the cloth. How sleek and dangerous she looked in her animal form, and how lovely that the image carried over to her human side. "Skirt yes, but not the shirt. The shoulders sit wrong. Fiona has very long arms."

Tahira smirked, held out her arms and wiggled her fingers, showing that the sleeves extended well past the unpolished nails. "Ya think? What kind of cats are you guys, anyway—cheetahs? I thought tigers were the biggest cats. And trust me, I *wanted* to take off the cop's foot. But then they would have just up and shot me."

Putting his boots up on the desk, he watched her lithe form disappear behind the screen once more. "Definitely a point. They weren't exactly the poster children for quiet restraint." This time he didn't turn away from the exquisitely curved shadow as she removed the top, but he noticed that she was missing a few accessories, so he stepped to the wardrobe and rummaged through the drawers below the closet area. He selected several possible items and tossed them over the top of the screen. He could see her pick them up, and then turn toward him with hands on hips.

"Hey! Can you see through this thing? How did you know I'm not wearing a bra?"

"Not at all," he lied smoothly, grateful that Fiona had left some of her Wolven cologne in her room for him to use. As head of the Sazi police force, Fiona had access to the secret cologne that masked the scent of emotions to other shapeshifter noses. Normally, it was forbidden for council members to use it, but he decided it wise to partake while the challenge might still be averted. "But you arrived in a bathing suit. Even if you had been wearing underclothes, they would be wet. Yes?"

The shadow tilted its head and shrugged. "Oh. Forgot about that. Well, I'm not too big on wearing other people's undies, but they still have tags on . . . so, okay, thanks. And you didn't answer—what kind of cat are you and your sisters?"

"Cats," replied Antoine, "Plural. Fiona and I are twins, and we're half lion and half cougar. My sisters Amber and Aspen are also twins, and they are half lion, half bobcat. The traits of our fathers seemed to determine the type of cat we turn on the moon. From our mother, who was a lioness, we inherited size and strength. So I suppose the answer is that I'm a cougar; but a *really* large one. And I can roar like either a lion or cougar depending on my needs."

"But you're French. Are there cougars in France?"

"Again, my *father* was the cougar. He was American. Mama was French. Our family arrived in France long, long ago from what is now Algeria. Our estate in Strasbourg has been in the family for centuries."

"So you're pretty rich then, huh? Matty said downstairs that you're some sort of councilman. Does that mean you've got pull with your people? Do you have any resources that can help me find my brother?"

Antoine took a deep breath. Here was the question he

had been dreading, and he still wasn't sure how to answer it. He still disagreed with Ahmad and Giselle about this, but perhaps there was a way to spin the discussion to get the responses they needed.

After a long moment, he finally said, "I am indeed the representative for the werecats on our council. I'm hardly rich through family connections, though. The estate was quite run-down when it was deeded to me. It's why I started the show. The upkeep is a tremendous financial burden, but I get by. Whether I have pull to help you depends on what you need, and whether you would be willing to help *me* in return."

She peeked her head around the corner of the screen, eyes narrowed and dark with suspicion. Her nostrils were flared, seeking some sign of his intent. "How would I be able to help *you*? I'm just an ordinary shifter from California and am in no position of authority in the kabile. Hell, even my grandfather thinks I'd be better off dead."

Now came the delicate stage. Antoine steepled his fingers over his chest. "What you have to offer isn't within your family, but within *yourself,* Tahira."

Her expression stilled and her eyes glittered with a growing anger. She ducked back behind the screen and yanked another outfit from its hanger. The movements pushed the burned caramel scent over the screen. "I see. It's like that. I'd read that about you."

Antoine furrowed his brow because he didn't understand her comments. Her actions behind the screen were quick and sharp as she buttoned and hooked a new outfit into place. He heard jingling of metal, like tiny bells. "I'm not sure you understand what I'm trying—"

"No, no," she replied with fire edging her words. "I understand *perfectly*. Is this more what you had in mind?"

She stepped out from behind the screen and Antoine gasped. It was the outfit from his vision in the tunnel! But how could it be? His feet dropped from the desk with a solid thump that rattled his jaw. He stood and realized his mouth was open. How she had found a belly dancer's outfit in his sister's closet was a mystery, but there was no question about the purpose of the outfit. Thin, nearly transparent black netting heavily embroidered with a gold and red flower pattern clung low on her hips. The red beading caught the light from the window until it was the exact color of her hair stripes. The top was a halter—and tight. It pushed and raised her chest to its full potential. The fringe on the arm coverings, top, and veil swayed as she walked closer.

She was easily the most sensuous woman he'd ever seen in his life.

"So, I suppose you'll want me to dance for you and then have a quick roll in the hay? Is that the price for helping me find my brother? Is that why this outfit was conveniently in the wardrobe?" Her voice was terse, each word spit with venom. "I'm quite good at dancing the karshilama."

Antoine shook his head. He was trying not to be distracted by the outfit, while still trying to decipher what she was implying. When it finally hit him, it was between the eyes, and all he could think to do was let out a vicious roar that vibrated his chest. He raised his leg sideways and kicked the nearest object, which happened to be Fiona's favorite mahogany desk. The massive rolltop slid across the floor and crashed into the opposite wall hard enough to turn it into splinters. Another item to pay for on this visit, in more ways than one.

He was suddenly angry beyond measure, but part of his brain didn't understand the ferocity of the fury. His reputation had been questioned before, but it was different this time. To have her think of him as—

"*Merde! Putain!* Surely my visions can't have degraded to something so absolutely frivolous! This is not about *sex*, Tahira! The future of our kind is at stake. This is not a fucking *game*!"

His anger and the utter destruction of the desk cut through her attitude like a knife. Suddenly, her face was unsure, confused, and more than a little frightened. He stepped toward her and she backed away from him. "But you said—"

He fought against his own pounding heart, let out a harsh breath, and ran his fingers through his hair until he was calm enough to speak. "Yes, I know what I said, and I understand how you could take my comment as you did. But do you actually *believe* what they say about me in the press? Do you truly think that I'm some sort of a rake and a rogue who beds a different girl each night and has left a dozen women crying at the altar?"

All he could see of her face were her eyes and forehead above the veil; her confusion at his outburst was obvious. "I . . . I mean—"

He sat down on the bed and pressed fingers to his temples to try to relieve some of the pressure behind his eyes. He didn't quite know why, but it was suddenly very important to him that she understand. He lowered his hands and inhaled slowly. "Tahira, I haven't had an actual date in more than a year. I don't have the time! My *publicist* arranges my escorts to events. Sometimes they're starlets, sometimes up-and-coming singers— whoever will be helpful to get my name in the papers. But we usually leave in separate vehicles, and I've seldom asked one for a second date, much less invited them to *marry* me."

He stared into her eyes until he was certain by sight

and scent that he had her full attention. "Do you understand? If and when I wish to date or sleep with you, it won't be by coercion or by trickery. I will simply ask you." He stood up and took a deep breath. "But for what it's worth, I am glad you put on that outfit, because it makes me realize that there's more to our chance encounter than meets the eye."

He stepped toward her and lifted up her arm so the fringe would swing. "You, and that outfit, have been the stars of several visions of mine lately. I don't know why, or how, but it's time I began to explore it before we all die because of my stubbornness."

The eyes above the veil were wide and showing too much white. "You mentioned earlier you were a *ruhsal*. What things have you seen of me? Have you seen Rabi in any of them?"

Antoine lowered her arm but kept hold of her hand. He frowned. It wouldn't be appropriate to tell her that he saw himself having sex with her after just telling her it *wasn't* about sex. "I certainly hope he wasn't one of the people in my visions, because they haven't been pleasant. I've been trying to suppress them for months now, because the few that have concluded ended badly—*very* badly. One of the visions was in the van. It's why we wrecked."

"But with the veil, how would you know it was *me*?"

He tried to think of a way to say it without giving away everything. "Even with the veil, there is no mistaking that you were part of that vision." His gaze flicked over her, taking in every detail. "The amazing hair, your lips that taste of cherry jam and sandalwood, the hair, the clothing, and your . . . *exquisite* body—they were all in the vision. It could be no one else. I'm just hoping that you're part of the solution that I must find to stop the snake, rather than one of those in danger."

She reached up with her free hand to unbutton the veil from the headdress and he noticed she was blushing furiously. "Sorry. It's hard to breathe with this thing on. What snake?"

"I don't know," he replied, shaking his head and studiously ignoring her discomfort at his compliments. While all true, he had been a bit overenthusiastic. "But there's something going on. Your brother's disappearance, your capture, our being in Stuttgart. They're connected. I just don't know how. Perhaps it's about your gift. Maybe that's the key."

"My *gift*? I don't have one. I'm just a normal everyday Hayalet. Nothing special."

He squeezed her hand and turned, leading her back to the bed. He sat down and patted the spot next to him. "It appears you *do* have a gift. It's very rare, nearly a myth. Giselle is a sensitive, a type of—what did you call it—a *ruhsal*? We Sazi call them *seers*. She believes that you are a power well. The man downstairs, Ahmad al-Narmer, is the representative for the snakes of the Sazi. He is also one of the few people who have ever been in contact with a power well."

Tahira held up a hand and reared back a bit in surprise. "Wait. You say his name is Ahmad al-*Narmer*? That's not possible. 'Al' means 'of' and there is no such place as Narmer. That was the name of an Egyptian pharaoh, like the Scorpion King."

Antoine nodded and he tried to convey both amusement and warning in a small smile. "All true. But his name is not my story to tell, and you might change your mind about asking after you meet him. Just know that he and his father before him have held their seats on the council since Babylon was the seat of civilization. From what I've gathered, Ahmad was born somewhat over a millennium ago."

The reaction was fairly common, but he always got a small amount of amusement to see the slack jaw and wide, slightly panicked eyes.

"I'm the youngest of our council, a mere cub. The owner of this house is so ancient that he was once worshipped as a god by his people. When I spoke with Ahmad earlier, he told me he believes you have the ability to pull magical energy from powerful shifters. It's why when I held you in form, you continued to pull from me and I couldn't break free. He feels that without training, you're a danger to yourself and others."

"But . . . but this has never happened to me before. Why would the first time I pulled power be with you?"

He shrugged. "Stress can bring out new talents. Or perhaps you simply haven't encountered any other alpha shifters until now."

She shook her head and the scent of frustration fought with a dozen other emotions for prominence. "No, that's not true. Both Grandfather and Rabi are—" She let out a small laugh that was filled with realization. "Hold on! Maybe that's the answer Rabi and I were looking for. It's why they trained us separately. Grammy didn't have potential to be a *sahip*, and the first time I met Grandfather, I hugged him and then felt dizzy and hot. He looked worried and never hugged me again. But Grammy never explained why. She just started to train me personally and talk about lots of metaphysical stuff."

"So," Antoine said with a sigh, "it appears that your people at least understood that you had some unique ability that required special training. Perhaps they wanted to learn the extent of it before they told you. Unfortunately, we don't have that kind of time."

*   *   *

TAHIRA PULLED HER hand away, stood, and walked toward the divider screen, holding herself to keep from shaking. "No, we don't. I didn't . . . well, I didn't tell you everything that Grammy said when she told me to follow Rabi."

"Indeed? She had a vision of her own?"

Stepping behind the screen helped her focus. She wanted desperately to lie to Antoine, but she just couldn't. It was starting to not matter about the Hayalet versus the Sazi, or the cats versus the snakes. Her brother's life, and the lives of the people she had met in this house, were all on the line.

She slipped off the belly dancer outfit and put on the undergarments that Antoine provided. They fit reasonably well, although the underwire on the bra would make her miserable if she had to remain in it too long. She took a deep breath and let it out slow as she hooked the bra. "After I'd been looking for Rabi for nearly a day, Grammy sought me out. She pulled me into a small storage hut and told me to stay silent. She kept her voice very low so that nobody would hear her, but it was really hard to understand what she was saying. Besides, I was so freaked out with Rabi being missing that I didn't really think much about what she said until we were downstairs earlier."

There was no reply from Antoine, so she kept talking as she pulled the outfit she intended to wear over her head. There was no reason it shouldn't fit and promised to actually look good. "She said that the great war was beginning again—between the Hayalet and the Sazi. But more than that, it would be species against species and if Rabi were to be killed by his captors, even the humans would learn of the Sazi's deceit, and blood and fire would rain down on the world."

The buckle on the ornate jeweled belt to the outfit

wasn't cooperating. Tahira kept her head down while she tried to figure out how to attach the pieces.

Antoine spoke during her pause. "But the Sazi have nothing against the Hayalet. In fact, we've been trying to establish friendly relations, possibly even trade between our people."

Tahira sighed. "I know. That's what gets me. Margo told me when she brought wine up to the bedroom that the Sazi council tries really hard to maintain a balance with the humans, keeping shapeshifters from breaking laws and such. Since I've never heard anything in the press about the possibility of were-animals—well, other than the occasional bat/boy hybrid in the cheesy tabloids—you guys must be doing a pretty good job of it. But someone who knew about our abilities took Rabi. How else would they have come up with a drug that could keep me out of it for a whole month?

"I had to have turned at least once for them. I was in animal form when they captured me. By their scent, I know the captors weren't Hayalet. Until I met you, I didn't know any Sazi. But Grammy said that snakes were involved and insisted they were Sazi. When you said that you had visions of snakes, I decided there must be some sort of connection. But finding Rabi has to be my primary goal. Apparently, his life or death will be the thing that starts the war. And I don't doubt it from the Hayalet perspective. Rabi is the first *sahip* born in two generations. He'll take over the tribe from Grandfather. If he dies, our people *will* respond."

As she finished arranging the outfit on her shoulders, she heard footsteps from the other side of the screen. Antoine was pacing.

"So," he said as she ran fingers through her hair to untangle it from swimming, "if both my visions and your *Grand-mère's* are correct, it is vital that we discover the location of your brother. But after a full month—"

She stepped from behind the screen. His back was turned while he stepped thoughtfully with hands clasped behind his back, and he shook his head in frustration. "The prospects are slim," she agreed. "But our best lead is still the site where you found my scent."

"Which is now covered by a foot of—" He turned and looked up, and she was pleased to see his jaw drop. It was a moment or two before he could find words, and she spun in place to show off the outfit to full advantage.

He let out a slow breath, his eyes heated. "That is . . . I mean . . . you look absolutely *ravishing*."

The mirror agreed with his assessment, and she smiled. The black and cream one-piece, long dress was close in design to a classic Greek toga. A split cape overlapped at the shoulder to create sleeves. Although the jeweled belt was tight around her waist, it was actually elastic and gave a custom-fitted appearance. But it covered everything and was actually quite modest. No excess skin showing anywhere. It would probably even be acceptable to Grandfather when he arrived. She would just have to save it for short appearances, since it was too long. The hem would get filthy on the stone floors.

"Now if I only had shoes."

Antoine smiled. "You're in luck. While I never saw Fiona in that outfit, she did wear the belt on occasion. There are slippers to match." He opened the bottom drawer of a bureau near the shattered remains of the desk and removed a pair of gold slippers with medium heels and jewels in the same pattern as the belt. "My sister is quite tall, so she tends to wear flats when entertaining, and heels when she needs to appear in control."

Tahira sat on the bed and was pleased that the slippers

were stretchy. They fit her wide feet perfectly. They were a bit too long, but the elastic around the top would keep them in place. Upon standing, the skirt just barely brushed the floor. "So," she asked, "am I ready to meet Ahmad?"

"I believe that you are perfectly attired." He checked his watch and swore lightly under his breath. He hadn't realized they'd taken so long. "But we should hurry. It's been over half an hour."

They hurried downstairs, her heels clicking rapidly on the stone. Antoine opened both of the doors with a flourish. But the room was empty, save for Margo typing at the computer. She turned as they entered.

"Where are Ahmad and Giselle?" Antoine asked.

Margo winced at his annoyed tone. "Giselle is in the west wing, hunting for mice to serve Ahmad and his men. I think Ahmad got tired of waiting. He kept checking his watch. Finally he just stood up and left. That was about ten minutes ago. I think he went upstairs to his room."

Antoine let out an annoyed breath. "I explained that it would be a few minutes, and he said he would wait. Margo, could you please go ask him to come down?"

It was obvious Antoine was growing angry, but it certainly wasn't Margo's fault. If anything, it was her own fault for keeping Antoine in the room to talk. She touched his arm, feeling the muscles under the cloth tense. "Why don't we just go upstairs to talk to him? I don't think where we meet is a big deal. Is it?"

He sighed and Tahira noticed that Margo smiled the tiniest bit. "No, I suppose it doesn't matter. But Ahmad can be quite difficult. It's generally best not to bow to his wishes too often. Still, time is of the essence, so you're probably right. Come and let us defang the snake in his den."

When they reached the top of the stairs, Antoine turned left. At the end of the hall, two men stood on either side of a closed door. As she and Antoine approached the door, the guards closed ranks, intentionally blocking their path. Both men reeked of the dusty, pungent smell of snakes. But these were not harmless rat snakes like Larry. They were vipers of some variety—hostile and deadly.

"The councilman is not taking visitors. You will leave now." The tall, thin man with olive skin sneered as he said the words.

Antoine's eyelids narrowed dangerously, but his words were civil, almost polite. "Ahmad and I have business to discuss that has already been arranged. Please step aside." He moved forward, expecting them to move apart. They didn't.

The shorter, stockier man with the slicked-back hair put out a hand and pushed Antoine back. "No one will enter until our esteemed master, leader of the snakes, instructs otherwise."

Antoine frowned for a moment and clenched his hands into fists. But then one corner of his mouth turned up. "Are you quite certain that you would challenge the leader of the *cats* for this small thing? I would think you'd accumulated enough *air time* already this month."

Tahira didn't know what he meant, but was certain it was a threat. A flicker of *something* flowed through the eyes of the men, and the sharp ammonia scent of panic filled the air in a burst. But it was short-lived. Apparently they decided that he couldn't live up to his words. The three men stared at each other, Antoine with a smile, and the two guards with growing defiance.

He placed an arm around Tahira's shoulders and pulled her backward a bit. "You might wish to stand back, *mon chat du feu.*"

She backed up a pace and could only stare open-mouthed as the events unfolded almost too quickly to follow. She felt a flare of heat first, like walking too close to a bonfire. Then a buzzing filled her ears. Without warning, the guards leapt into the air, slammed through the door like a battering ram and flew upward until they disappeared from sight.

Antoine stalked into the room like a warrior king, past the door hanging from only one hinge and amid a clatter of loose change that rained down from above.

He turned when she didn't immediately follow and held out his hand. "Shall we?"

She raised her brows and ducked her head as she went through the door, narrowly missing getting hit by a ring of keys. She stared up in amazement at the two guards, plastered motionless against the ceiling, glaring daggers down at them. Never in her life had she ever heard about any shifter having this sort of ability, and she realized that she was shaking just a bit.

A voice that was calm and filled with disdain echoed from the other side of the room. "Feeling a bit petulant today, are we?"

Tahira's eyes followed the words, and she was surprised to see a youngish man seated on the couch near the far wall. He was sipping coffee from a china cup and had a shisha tobacco pipe bubbling nearby. The combination of scents was heady and covered any emotion scent the man might have. She knew many men in the village who smoked the water pipe that contained a concoction of loose tobacco leaves, apple molasses, and milk.

Antoine kept his body between her and the other man, but she could see his face. He wasn't Turkish. His facial structure was wrong. It was narrower, more Egyptian. He was darkly handsome with large, expressive eyes, black hair that was combed back from his face, and a slim, narrow neck rising from a slender but muscled body. The eyes were narrowed in anger. As they stepped closer, his scent rose over the bubbling concoctions on the table. He was also a snake, but he smelled like a toxic cloud—a noxious rolling scent that reminded her of creosote plants in the desert. She knew without a doubt that he was far more deadly than the guards, and she had to fight her instinct to either attack him on sight or run for the door.

It was hard to equate the man with the scent. His appearance was of a well-to-do Arab businessman, looking at ease and comfortable in slacks and an open-necked white shirt.

Antoine's voice was likewise calm and at ease. He spread his legs slightly and crossed his arms over his chest, keeping Tahira behind him. "We have an appointment, Ahmad."

The man carefully placed his cup on the saucer and then leaned back into the cushions. He regarded them with an eerie calm. "No, we *had* an appointment forty-seven minutes ago. You are fully aware that I wait no more than fifteen minutes for *anyone*."

Standing still while the power bleeding off both of the men boiled over her was the hardest thing Tahira had ever had to do.

Antoine didn't budge. "You said you would wait. Time was not mentioned."

While the words on both sides were polite, there was an underlying tension that made her skin crawl. They stared silently for long moments. Finally, Ahmad picked up his cup. "I take it this is the girl you spoke of? Come closer, child—into the light."

Tahira felt herself straighten and let out a low growl. "I am *not* a child." She took several steps around Antoine to where she was only a few feet from the coffee table. He might be a millennium old, and could probably wipe the floor with her, but that wasn't the point.

Ahmad had raised the cup to his lips to drink and glanced at her over the rim. His eyes widened, and a shock of scent rose into the air. He sat up too quickly, causing coffee to splatter in his lap. With a vicious oath, he grabbed a small stack of paper napkins from the table and wiped the liquid from his pants. Tahira didn't need animal hearing to note the amused chuckle from Antoine.

After a few seconds, Ahmad collected himself and looked from Tahira to Antoine with mingled surprise and annoyance. His gaze finally settled on Tahira. "It seems I've underestimated your skills at deception, Antoine. I was under the impression that the Hayalet was a mere schoolgirl."

He stepped slowly around the table and circled her once. She stood very still, even though the magic that emanated from him was a hot, biting wave of power. It seared along her bare skin painfully and should have been able to set her gown ablaze. He was doing it intentionally, but he was not going to get the best of her this early on. Her breath was coming in small gasps just from his proximity when he stopped in front of her.

She steadied herself against the onslaught and looked into his eyes. "My name is Tahira Kuric—*Ms.* Kuric to you—and I am proud to be of the Hayalet Kabile."

The corner of his mouth turned up. "I see. May I say, *Ms.* Kuric, that you are most definitely *not* a schoolgirl. No, you are *very much* a woman." Faster than she could react, he picked up her hand and pressed his lips to it.

If his presence was painful, his touch nearly stole a scream from her throat. His power flowed into her, burning in her veins like lava. She couldn't move her hand, as though she'd grabbed a live wire. She felt her heart beating faster and her skin heat to burning. She would have dropped to her knees if Antoine hadn't stepped forward just then and forcibly removed her hand from Ahmad's.

"That's enough, Ahmad." Antoine's voice was a rumble from deep in his chest. He pulled her backward with a hand on each arm, tight against his chest. "She is our *guest*, not prey to toy with."

Ahmad studied Antoine for a long moment, then smiled broadly. "Oh, I wasn't considering her *prey*, Antoine. Very much the opposite. But . . . perhaps another time."

He backed up a few paces and dipped his head, while Antoine led Tahira to a chair. She nearly collapsed into it and struggled to control the feeling that her skin was trying to crawl off her body.

"However," he said as he stepped around the table once more, "I did confirm what I wished to. I fed power into her, and she received it and remained alive. What I just did would have *killed* an ordinary were-animal. She is quite alive, albeit a bit . . . *singed* around the edges. Congratulations. You have indeed discovered one of the first power wells to exist in a thousand years or more." He sat down on the couch one cushion from where he had spilled his coffee and poured another cup from an ornate pot. He waved his hand airily as an invitation to join him. But at the moment, hot fluid didn't really interest her.

She shook her head, causing him to nod. "Wine then, perhaps?"

The wine had previously helped her calm down, but she was annoyed with him. "That would be fine. And in the future, please let me know when you're going to try to cook me from the inside out. I didn't enjoy it." She narrowed her eyes. "If you try that again, I'll be forced to hurt you."

As Antoine sat down on the opposite chair, he winked at her and smiled just a bit. It made her feel better. Ahmad slid two glasses from the overhead rack and opened a decanter. As he poured the first glass, there was a splash and a clink. He picked up the glass and peered into it, extracting a key ring with a shake of his head. He pushed it to the side and removed a third glass. Apparently he was refusing to acknowledge what Antoine had done to his guards other than the initial comment.

After pouring the wine, he returned and handed them each a glass. Tahira was very careful to touch the part of the stem where his fingers *weren't*, which brought a dark smile to his face.

"The problem with power wells," he continued as though he had never stopped talking, "is that power drained is power lost. It is rumored that if a power well were to totally drain a Sazi—or, more precisely, any shapeshifter—that person would never regain his powers. If the person had a talent or gift, it would be lost." He sat back down on the couch and took a sip of coffee.

Tahira's brow furrowed. "So what are you saying? That I'm some sort of energy vampire?" The aching pound in her ears and fire still burning inside from his power made her fear rise and put a shaky edge on her words.

Ahmad leaned back, tapped a manicured fingernail on the rim of his cup, and put his heels on the table. After a moment of thinking, he replied. "I don't believe that's the case. From what I've gathered in the few references in print. There are books on the subject in Charles's library if you wish to read them. It's more that you are a container, a pitcher. You can be filled and then distribute what is inside. But you cannot seek out the power. Hence, a power *well*. If a water well is empty, it remains empty until the rains fill it."

Tahira realized she was shaking her head as he spoke. "But that's not what happened. The two times this has happened, it just . . . well, *happened*. Nobody, with the exception of you, has intentionally tried to give me power. I pulled it out of them."

"What she says is true, Ahmad." Antoine's voice was calm, but she realized it was a lie. While his lack of scent was still frustrating, his body language gave him away. He was worried. "Neither time when my power bled into her was planned."

Ahmad stared at them with amusement. When he spoke his voice was thick and oozing with sarcasm. "I would have thought that even an alpha of your . . . limited experience should understand the nature of our magic, Antoine." Tahira saw Antoine's eyes narrow in anger, but he didn't reply to the dig.

"Think of our power as a fishing net. We can cast it out and snare things—" he glanced upward briefly with a slightly annoyed sound that made Antoine smile darkly, "—or we can draw it back inside ourselves. But always our power *is*. The size of the net we are given was determined at birth. A net sized for panfish won't hold a flounder. A three-day Sazi can throw a net of magic at me, but I will barely feel it. But the magic that you and I naturally exude from our pores is cast without thought. It surrounds us, bleeds from us. It can be painful to other Sazi, and even humans feel it if we are not careful."

As soon as he said the words, Tahira understood. She had thought she was feeling flushed because of the power Ahmad had fed into her. That was part of it, but she realized that she could feel several distinct lines of magic pressing on her, like water pooling on a sponge before it disappeared inside. One line was from Ahmad himself. His power was unique in the prickling, stinging sensation like black flies biting at her skin. Antoine was likewise bleeding power because of his exertion in holding the guards against the ceiling. While he made it look effortless, it wasn't. The guards were not taking their imprisonment lightly. They were actively struggling against his power. Their efforts were making her muscles tight and her temples throb. She needed to get away from these people, run outside in the cold or swim downstairs again.

Ahmad stood and walked around the table. When he stopped in front of her, she forced her attention to his face. His eyes were twin bits of coal, glittering and hard. "But our Hayalet tiger is different. Her net is deeper and wider than any of ours. Her net doesn't have to seek out fish. It merely has to exist, to remain motionless in place. If a fish happens to swim nearby, it will become snared—from the panfish to the marlin and beyond. And like fish, once our magic is netted inside her, we cannot free ourselves easily, and we might lose a fin or two in the process."

Tahira made a half-snarling noise that reflected her edginess. "Will you *please* stop referring to me in the third person? I'm right here! I understand the analogy of the net and fish, I think. But every net has a limit. What happens if too many fish are force-fed into me?"

He raised one eyebrow. "Why, what happens to any net that becomes overstretched? It rips. Only in your case it will be the equivalent to a nuclear explosion, and anyone who happens to be nearby will be reduced to smoldering ash."

Chapter Eight

"ARE YOU SURE you know what you're doing over there?" Margo was rubbing her nose with an expression of distaste as Antoine stirred the steaming fluid in the pot. He ignored her criticism and concentrated on running spice bottles through the steam at various distances. "That concoction is *vile*."

"Only to your decidedly inferior human nose. Trust me, Margo. I've nearly created the perfect combination. Just a bit more anise oil and . . . yes, I think perhaps a bit of Hungarian paprika." He collected a pinch of the red powder between his fingers and carefully rubbed them together to drop small bits of the spice until he was satisfied. He took a deep breath of the resulting brew. "Ah! Now that is *perfect*."

The swinging kitchen door burst open and Tahira raced through with a look of determination on her face. "What's happened in here? Is anyone hurt? It smells like someone is absolutely terrified in this room! I could smell it all the way in the library."

Antoine chuckled at Margo's shocked expression and waved a hand to Tahira with no small amount of satisfaction. "You see, Margo? A satisfied customer." He stirred just a moment longer, and then pulled the pot from the fire to cool. "I'm sorry to have disturbed you, Tahira. But someone I just met swore to me that Chinese hot and sour soup smelled like fear, so I decided to test the theory."

Tahira walked farther into the room and put her nose over the copper pot. She closed her eyes and inhaled deeply. Antoine could see the back of her jaw clench. She had to swallow deeply to keep from salivating on the stove. "This doesn't smell like any hot and sour soup I've ever smelled, and I go to Chinatown a lot. But I'd *pay* you to try this! How does it taste?"

"Sadly, it tastes horrid, but that's not the point. I'm hoping to entice Babette to eat. She's a bit depressed being here without the other cats. She hasn't touched the antelope or the rabbits. I thought perhaps it's because she can't chase the game, so I thought if I sprinkled some of this on the rabbits I hid, she'd eat one or two and then realize she was hungry."

Margo shook her head and sneezed again. "Well, as much as I like you, boss, I can't stand that smell anymore. It smells like rotten meat cooking in bleach. If that's what dinner smells like to Sazis, I'm much happier being human. Give me strawberries and chocolate any day. I think I'll go work on the bills upstairs where I can light a candle or something. You two enjoy yourselves down here."

Tahira dipped her finger in the steaming soup for a second and put it in her mouth hopefully as Margo walked out the door sneezing. She grimaced. "Blegh. It *tastes* like meat in bleach. But it *smells* heavenly. You should figure out a way to bottle this. You'd probably make a fortune selling it to zoos and shelters and stuff."

Antoine sighed. "Sadly, that's exactly why I *can't* bottle it."

She cocked her head and turned against the counter with her hands in her pockets. "Huh? That doesn't make sense."

"It's much like what your kabile said about your hair. It'd draw too much attention. My sister Fiona has managed to make a good living using her nose as a tester of new perfumes. But it's one thing to have a 'perfect nose' like some people have perfect pitch. There are several humans with that ability. It's quite another to explain how I know what *fear* smells like. The press would jump all over a story like that because of my show. They'd hound me until the day I died—and that won't be for a *very* long time. No, even if it works, it will have to remain a secret."

She sighed in an understanding manner. "You're right, but it's really a shame. This stuff could help a lot of cats." She reached out her foot and lightly touched his leg as he knelt down next to the sink. "I think the way you treat your cats, if Babette is any indication, is really terrific. I've heard a lot of horror stories about what tigers and lions have to go through, but Babette seems to be really happy with you."

He dipped his head in acknowledgment as he bent over to look under the cabinet for a sponge. "*Merci*. But my cats are my family, rather than mere *props* I use to entertain, so I treat them as I would a sister, child, or uncle. And, like family, they're more than happy to tell me when they feel they're being mistreated. I've endured more than one scolding by them about staffing. I went through several handlers who didn't understand that the cats are individuals, with different needs and wants, before I found Bruce."

He finally spotted what he was looking for and pulled a new sponge in a plastic wrapper from far back in the corner of the cupboard. It was blue, but the color wouldn't matter. He just needed to get the scent onto the prey.

Tahira seemed to understand what he planned, and

handed him a pair of tongs from a ceramic crock of kitchen utensils. "I wondered about that earlier. Can you really *talk* to your cats—like you're talking to me now? Do they answer?" She opened a few drawers until she found a box of plastic sandwich bags and pulled one out.

Antoine tried to decide how to answer. He dipped the sponge into the pot repeatedly until it was dripping with the savory scent. Then, while Tahira held open the bag, he dropped the sponge inside. It would have to cool for a moment before he could take it downstairs, but hopefully it would help. Babette couldn't afford to get any weaker. The birth had been unusually hard on her, even though she'd had several other litters of cubs.

"That's a bit of a difficult question to answer, I'm afraid. Wild cats don't think like you and I do. They think in images and concepts. While I've been able to see what they were saying in my head since I was a teenager, it took me a number of years to understand what the images meant. They understand pain and anger, hunger and pride. They share happiness and instill fear. But beauty and art are more difficult. Training a cat for a show that humans will find beautiful or artistic takes patience unless the trainer resorts to brute force all the time."

"Well, I'm glad you don't force the cats to do what you want. I think that's terrible."

Antoine crossed his arms over his chest and leaned against the counter next to her. From her scent of indignation and relief, he realized she had gotten the wrong impression. "I didn't say that, *mon chat du feu*. There are indeed times when brute force is necessary. Hierarchy is very important. They must know that I'm the Rex. I certainly don't *harm* my cats, but occasionally I have to flex my muscles, so to speak, just as the cats would do among themselves in the wild." He pressed his fingers against the sponge through the plastic. It was cool enough that it wouldn't burn her tongue. "Why don't you join me downstairs? Babette likes you quite a bit and would probably enjoy seeing you again. We can continue our discussion while she hunts."

He walked to the doorway that led to the staircase and was pleased she followed. Even something as mundane as discussing business seemed a bit more enjoyable when she was around. Perhaps it was wrong to continue to spend time with her, but it had been so very long since a woman had intrigued him enough to make him actually want to spend time with her.

Tahira's scent was now curious, and the sweet, thick scent seemed so very fitting against the musk of her cat. "You don't yell at them or use whips or anything, right?"

He laughed and it echoed off the high ceiling of the stairwell. It was something reporters asked him every time he was interviewed. "Good lord, no! Of course, I have to raise my voice on stage, because the audience can get quite loud and the cats can't hear me speak. But a *whip*? Never! No, if one of the cats misbehaves on stage, I'll simply use magic to hold it off to the side while the other cats complete the set. In training, I quite often change form and wrestle with them until the cat winds up on his or her back. Once I've proved myself dominant, I'll impress what I want of them in their minds. I know it's harder for human trainers to work with them, but I prefer to use the gifts I have available to me."

The door at the bottom of the stairs was closed, so he looked inside the room, using a small reinforced window that reminded him of a grade school classroom. Babette was laying quietly on the sea grass mat with her head between her paws. She was completely ignoring Matty, who was checking her stitches. He used a penlight to look in her ears and eyes. He shook his head sadly and scratched behind her ears. The cubs were climbing on her and pouncing on her tail, but she wasn't encouraging the attention. Yes, she needed some entertainment.

He reached forward with his mind until he could feel the press of fur against his face and Babette's slow breathing. Her head rose as she sensed him, and she turned toward the door. He caught her gaze with his eyes and offered images of pumpkin diving in the pool, chasing antelope, or even playing ball.

Matty moved back quickly when Babette suddenly became animated. She shook her head and her eyes lit up. The cubs bounded after her as she ran toward her enclosure, leaving Matty scratching his head.

Tahira gasped lightly behind Antoine. He turned and found her eyes wide and her breathing shallow and fast. "The moon is rising."

He felt it, too—a pulsating warmth that sank into his skin like water into rich soil. But cool winds of magic tickled above the warmth, causing him to shudder with anticipation. Tahira didn't seem to be enjoying the sensation. She looked suddenly claustrophobic, her eyes flicked around, seeking an exit from the enclosed stairwell.

"What's wrong, *mon chat du feu*? Surely you don't fear your cat, do you? You keep your mind in animal form. I can feel your power press against me. If you're not an alpha, you're very close."

She shook her head and licked her bottom lip nervously. "No, I don't fear the cat. I can't really . . . well, *explain* it."

He stared at her as she grew increasingly fidgety, then held out his hand. "Come here, Tahira. Look through the window and tell me what you see."

She cocked her head curiously but stepped forward.

He moved back behind her and put his hands on her shoulders. "Well," she said, "I see Matty following Babette around. She's holding something in her mouth, and he's trying to get it away from her."

He leaned down so his head was nearly resting on her shoulder to be able to see through the glass. "But you're seeing something else, too. Matty is human; Babette a wild animal. She has new cubs and he's approaching her aggressively to take something from her mouth. Do you find that brave or foolish?"

He felt her stiffen as she tied the question to what she was seeing. "I suppose I find it foolish, now that you mention it."

"And I still see what you *originally* saw—a man comfortable enough with a tiger to feel safe regardless of his actions. He has scars all down his left leg, you know. A wounded lion wasn't completely put under by its keepers, and mauled him. That same cat played with him like a cub when he checked up on it a few weeks later. Injury and death are always in the back of his mind, yet it never affects his decision to heal."

She shrugged and he felt the tension in her muscles increase where he was touching. "So why did you bring it up? What are you trying to tell me?"

"I'm trying to tell you that there's something about shifting forms that has you frightened. It's affecting your decisions. If Matty can feel confident enough in himself to continue to work with wild cats, then why can't you feel confident with the one that shares your skin?"

She tried to pull away, but he didn't let her. The scent of fear and something deeper began to fill his nose. His hands began to massage her too-tight muscles while she tried to find an escape.

"I'm not afraid of my cat." The words were a whisper—and a lie.

His light chuckle made a few strands of long orange hair float into the air. "Your shoulders and scent tell me otherwise, Tahira. You're treating the rising moon like an enemy to be feared, rather than as a partner in something truly wondrous. I can feel the power rising in you, smell your fur as it climbs to the surface to greet the night. When you stormed the kitchen to confront whatever had caused the scent of terror, I learned that you don't fear death or injury. So what is it you *do* fear?"

The moon began to pull on him, race through his body so strongly that he sucked in a sharp breath. Tahira gasped and clenched her hands into fists. Her scent changed to frustration and worry, and he suddenly understood.

"It's the change itself, isn't it? You need to be in control, and the moon takes that from you."

Her heart was pounding now as magic roiled over her, threatening to turn her where she stood. "You don't know what it's like to feel out of control. You're a *sahip*. You can change at will. But, for the record . . . uhm, that's not why my shoulders are tense."

A new scent combined with the thick, sweet sandalwood and cinnamon—embarrassment. Antoine's voice dropped a few notes, both in anticipation of the change, and in reaction to her scent. He let his hands trail slowly down her arms and enjoyed the resulting goosebumps on her skin.

"I see. I'm flattered I have such an effect on you. Of course, you realize that both reactions stem from the same problem. I understand why you feel it's something to be feared from what happened in the bedroom. Perhaps you'd feel better to know that you *can* control both situations." He pulled on one of Tahira's arms, turning her to face him. Her breathing was shallow and her eyes had started to glow lightly from the night magic that filled her. Leaning toward her, he pressed her back against the wall, and made her swallow audibly. She put her hands on his chest, pushing slightly, perhaps intending to keep him from touching her—but the resulting pulse of energy made her nearly moan with pleasure.

"I can't control the change. What happens if I turn?"

Antoine smiled gently. "That would be lovely, but I doubt it will happen. I think you have much more control than you believe. I think you could change at will if you try. But if you do shift, then I will too. I can think of no sweeter sensation than to feel our fur flow to greet the moon as one. Just relax, *mon chat du feu*. Let the moon take us where it will."

He leaned into her, inhaling the deep musky scent of her rising fur, and lightly pressed his lips to hers. The taste and scent combined with sensation as she encircled his neck with her arms and pulled him tight against her. He held his magic inside by sheer will, not wanting to bleed into her again and make this experience a bad one. But . . . *Merde!* The things he wanted to do to her as their jaws moved into an ever more intensely passionate kiss. He could nearly taste his heart in his throat as he pulled back and whispered into her mouth.

"You see? You can control whatever you wish to. Now, I'm going to take the sponge in and see if I can get Babette to play a game or two—enough to make her hungry. I'd very much like it if you joined us. But if you'd like to be alone, I'm confident you can make it back to your room before you shift."

She looked startled as she removed her fingers from where they'd twined around his hair. "I feel it. The moon is sitting right at the edge of my vision. I can almost reach out and touch it, but it's not sucking me inside like it has been. Until today, it's felt like I was being thrown over a cliff in a dream. Yeah, I'd wake up before I hit bottom, but the fall was terrifying." Confidence grew on her face as surprise gave way to happiness. "I think I'd like to join you and play a game. I don't know how you and your cats play, but—"

He raised up the back of his hand and let his fingernails glide over her cheek. "Then please do join us. Nobody will disturb you if you want to change right here. I'll shift after I've used the sponge on the prey."

He opened the door, forcing himself not to glance back. Part of him wanted to watch her change, wanted to see fur transform that lovely body into something powerful and dangerous.

I'm definitely going to have to be careful of that one.

Matty nodded to him as he crossed the room carrying the sandwich bag. "I'm surprised to see you down here after moonrise, mate. What's that thingo you've got?"

Before Antoine could answer, the door opened a second time, and Matty's face flowed from concern to recognition and then worry. "I'm thinking that's Tahira, mate, but if it's some strange tiger, let me know now so I can do the bolt."

"Hi, Matty!" Tahira said, in that deliciously deep growl. "Sorry that I worried you. I didn't even think about walking around in this form."

Babette pranced toward Antoine with her jaw wide around something large and black, but then spotted Tahira and stopped. Her golden eyes narrowed and raised her hackles.

"That's right!" Antoine exclaimed. "She hasn't met you in this form yet." He dropped the plastic bag on the ground and walked over to Tahira. He ran his hands down her face, concentrating on the scent glands between her eyes. Babette was still in defense position, but seemed less concerned when she saw Antoine approach the new tiger without incident. When he walked back to her, he held out his hands so she could sniff them, and pressed the image of Tahira's human form and then the tiger form into her mind.

Babette sniffed his hands delicately and then cautiously padded over to Tahira, keeping her body ready to spring at any moment.

"Just let her sniff you for a moment, Tahira. But be ready to move if she considers you a threat. Matty, don't get in between them."

The Australian was standing stock still. "Wouldn't think of intruding on this introduction, mate."

The tiger cubs were less concerned. They apparently had already recognized their friend from the pool and were racing over to her, despite their mother's wariness. Antoine was pleased to see that Tahira remained cautious. She didn't stop the cubs from grabbing at her tail and pouncing on each other under her legs, but she didn't touch them either. Slowly, Babette walked all the way around her, sniffing. Tahira did make small chuffing noises of greeting and speak in English, as well, further calming the cat.

Finally satisfied, Babette turned away from Tahira and walked back to the black object on the ground. She picked it up in her mouth again and dropped it at Antoine's feet with a thud.

"What in the world—?" Tahira asked. "Is that a *bowling ball*?"

"Yeah," Matty said. "It's her fave toy, a four-and-a-half-kilo size, which is just perfect for them. It's like a yarn ball to a house pet. She and the other cats can go at it for hours, but it's been a long time since she's played with anyone else. You both just missed Giselle. She'd offered to play, but Babette wasn't interested. I think she was waiting to play with *you*, Antoine."

"Just as soon as I finish putting this on the rabbits and antelope, I'll do that." He started to walk away, but discovered that Babette was padding right at his heels, the bowling ball again in her mouth. When he stopped, so did she, and she dropped the ball.

Tahira laughed, but it was closer to a growl. "I don't think she wants to wait until you're ready."

Antoine sighed. "She can be quite persistent."

Matty held out his hand. "I'll do whatever it was you'd planned if you want to start the game. What's in the bag?"

He handed the plastic over to him, briefly pulling it back with a caution. "This sponge is filled with a chemical compound I just created. Make certain you don't get any of it on your skin."

Matty looked at the innocent-looking sponge askance. "Bloody hell! What is the stuff?"

"You might call it liquid fear," Tahira answered. "Trust me, the scent of this stuff is so powerful, it made me run out of the library to see if someone was being attacked in the kitchen. Spill it on your pants, and you might end up dinner."

He stared wide-eyed at the plastic for a moment and then hesitantly opened it. The potent scent nearly made Matty gag, but Babette instantly turned and sniffed, searching with suddenly hungry eyes for the source of the scent. Matty noticed and zipped the bag. "Strewth! I see what you mean, mate. Right, then. You go play ball with Babette on the other side of the room and I'll douse the 'lope with this *charming* blend."

"What does it smell like to you, Matty?" Tahira asked. "Margo thought was rotting meat in bleach."

"Wish I could say it smelled that good," Matty said

with a grimace. "But I've actually smelled rotting meat cooked in bleach, and that had *nothing* on this stew." At Tahira's surprised expression, he shrugged. "Had to build a skeleton of a rabbit for a biology class, but forgot about the project until the night before. The bleach made the bones nice and white, but I'd forgotten about my mum's dinner party that same night. It was a bit of a balls up, that!"

"Well, then," Antoine said, picking up the bowling ball and slipping in the tips of his fingers, "let's get the game started."

Babette was at full attention as he heaved the ball across the floor in a blur. Babette leapt after the toy and batted it to the side before it hit the wall, sending it nearly airborne back toward them with a powerful swipe of her paw. He considered going into the back room and removing his clothes before changing, but the goal was to keep Babette interested.

Ah, well. The clothes can be replaced.

With a cougar screech, he leapt into the air toward the ball. When he landed, he was in cat form. The tattered remains of his clothing fluttered to the floor.

Tahira's hushed voice made him turn his head after he'd swatted the ball back to Babette. "My God! You're *huge*! You can't possibly be a cougar. Even my grandfather isn't as broad across the chest."

He twitched his ears forward in amusement and flicked his tail. "I warned you that I inherited my mother's size." He nearly pushed her out of the way, but she noticed the ball returning and sent it back to Babette with a powerful stroke.

"Hey! That is sort of fun. It's not heavy as I would have expected. Are we playing catch or keep-away?"

His lips pulled back from his teeth. "The only goal is not to break anything. We can play however you like.

But you should know that I'm quite a good footy player, as Matty calls the game."

"No problem," she said, diving into him hard enough to tumble him over before sending the ball back to Babette. "I'm a hockey girl myself, along with a stint as Rabi's tackling dummy for rugby tryouts."

Minutes passed as they continued to increase the difficulty of the game. The cubs moved to the side once they decided the prey was too fast, and it hurt when it squished their paws. It became a race to see whether he or Tahira would first reach the ball to send it back to Babette. Tahira was very skilled, moving quickly and efficiently to cut off the ball before he could swipe at it. The longer they played, the more aggressive they both became, so by the time the scent reached their noses, they'd nearly lost the memory of where the scent of fear had come from.

After a final swipe of the ball, Babette dropped into a slow stalk that made the cubs prick up tiny ears. Tahira joined her, instinctively moving to the side to trap the prey. "Tahira!" Antoine whispered, slapping his paw against her flank. "Let Babette find the prey."

She blinked golden eyes as the words filtered into her head. She stopped and sat down on her haunches. "Sorry," she said quietly. "I got too wrapped up in the game."

"I nearly did as well. I see that Matty made himself scarce, but he seems to have done a very creative job of application of the scent. He's placed individual drops on the floor, as though from the hind foot scent glands of a rabbit."

Tahira nodded. "I know. I can smell where they wander from side to side and double back—just like a real rabbit. He must be really good at tracking."

"He is. I don't worry at all about him completing his

walkabout. He has a natural affinity for the wild." He stared into her gleaming eyes as she watched Babette follow the trail to one of the rabbits in the stream and felt a thrill of excitement pass through him. "What are you doing for dinner tonight, *mon chat du feu?*"

Every muscle in her hind legs tensed as Babette's tail began to flick frantically at the edge of the cattails. The big cat leapt into the plants with a series of splashing grabs before coming up with one of the rabbits. She carried it proudly over to the cubs and they all trotted back to Babette's enclosure to share it.

Tahira was salivating from watching the hunt, and it took her a moment to answer. "I think Giselle was going to broil some steaks from the freezer, along with some vegetables. Why?"

He leaned his face near her ear and breathed in the scent of her adrenaline-laced musk. "I don't believe I'm in the mood for home cooking tonight. *Fast food* is more what I have in mind."

Her gaze turned wicked with humor. "You're thinking we should find a *run-through* for something fresh and warm?"

"Exactly." He licked a slow line along her furred muzzle to the point of her ear and felt her shudder. "I want to hunt with you tonight, Tahira."

Her chuffing growl was close to a chuckle. "Why is it that everything you say sounds like a come-on?"

He turned and deliberately bumped her as he walked toward the door. "Perhaps because it's what you're hoping to hear." He growled in surprise as she leapt over his head and reached the door first.

"Or," she said slyly, "perhaps it's because it *is* a come-on. But I can take anything you can dish out, Antoine, so bring it on."

Chapter Nine

"WE'RE BEING FOLLOWED."

Tahira slowed her steps and let her eyes adjust to the starlight. The moon was hidden behind thick clouds, but at least the snow had finally stopped. The cold, still air burned her lungs as she held her breath. She opened her senses, concentrating on any sound, any scent that would confirm Antoine's statement. The only movement was the twitching of Antoine's tawny ear as he stood equally silent beside her.

"How do you know?" she asked in a low whisper.

He turned his head to her with what was as close to a look of disdain as a cougar could manage. "I know because I can smell them. There are at least two, but possibly more. They're very far away but moving in concert with us, so probably using scopes or binoculars to track us. They're shifters, but they are too far away for me to know what sort of animal."

"Are we in danger?"

"Something is hunting a pair of apex predators in the woods in the middle of the night. They're keeping to the shadows and staying upwind. What do *you* think?"

"Should we turn back? We're not far from the house. I don't *need* to hunt tonight."

Antoine took a step, letting his massive, furred paw

settle into the deep snow. She had never seen a cougar of his size. He was even larger than Rabi in animal form. He let out a low chuffing sound that was close to a chuckle. "No, neither of us *needs* to hunt tonight, but isn't it nice that someone has given us a *reason* to? With any luck, they'll stay in human form. I do so hate trying to get fur out from between my teeth."

A snort of air, combined with a bright citrus scent, told of her amusement, and he shared the joke for a moment, but then turned serious.

"Keep in mind that it's quite possible that someone out there is trying to finish the job they started."

"Finish the—" Tahira's eyes widened as she finally understood what Antoine was implying. Could Rabi's kidnappers have returned? *Oh my. Yes, I would definitely enjoy finding them again, and to hell with fur in my teeth.*

Her voice lowered to a threatening rumble. "What do you want me to do?"

He moved his muzzle so close to her that his whiskers tickled the sensitive hairs inside her ear. His breath was warm and his power played over her fur like a stroking hand. The combination of sensations caused an involuntary shiver deep inside her.

"First we need to draw them closer, force them to come to us. If we keep to the undergrowth, it will still appear that we are hunting, but they won't be able to see us well enough to risk a shot that would put us on defense. Then, we rely on our strengths. My nose is my best feature, and you apparently have excellent ears. With the moon hidden, sight won't be our ally, so stay close. Our goal is to find their position before they know ours."

"Do we try to capture them to ask questions, or—" She wasn't sure whether she should finish the question.

Perhaps the Sazi showed mercy when it came to hunters. Her kabile did not.

Antoine pulled his lips back, showing impressive fangs. "It will depend on the situation. If they are armed, defend yourself any way you must. Have you ever handled a rifle?"

She nodded. "My father occasionally shoots a rifle and shotgun at a club. He fought against the Russians when they tried to slaughter our kabile, and he taught me. I can handle one if it comes to it."

His voice was still hushed, but there was a fierce intensity in his eyes that made her shiver. "No, that's not what I meant. We'll do our best fighting in animal form. But I want you to concentrate as we lead them into our trap. You need to listen for the whisper of metal on metal if they load a shell or another dart. There should be no human hunters in these woods tonight, so any metallic sound will be a threat."

Antoine took another step, and a sudden rush of breaking branches in the undergrowth caused them both to turn. Deer musk, pungent with fear, made Tahira's heart race and she struggled not to follow her first instinct and start the chase.

But Antoine apparently decided to take the opportunity the fleeing prey presented. She heard him murmur, "Perfect timing!" just before he disappeared into the snow-covered brush.

ANTOINE HOPED THAT Tahira would realize his plan as he ran into the forest after the deer. They needed to get far enough away from their pursuers to set their own trap. But for a few moments he allowed himself to revel in the chase. It was the third night of the moon. The animal inside him was desperate to be free of human con-

ventions. His lungs filled with cold air as his paws
found purchase in the snow. His tail moved in unconscious reaction to the balance of his body as he loped
after the prey. The chase felt natural and so *right*. Here
in the woods there was only the snow on his fur, the
rush of wind pressing against his eyes and nose, and the
power of the moon as slivers of light parted the clouds.
Tahira's natural scent was heady, and combined with
wet vegetation and frightened prey, it was nearly
enough to make him forget his purpose. How long had
it been since he hunted with abandon, just given in to
his instinct? Hearing Tahira running beside him, seeing
the powerful muscles play under her orange coat, made
him want to take down the deer, to share meat with another cat who was a worthy hunting companion.

But not tonight. They had other things to consider. It
was becoming a challenge to get deep enough in the forest. The lone stag was old and wily. He tried to double
back more than once. Antoine was pleased that Tahira
pounced quickly, cutting off its escape. She forced the
deer forward into the deeper trees while Antoine kept
watch around them. She kept stride with him easily, not
attempting to overtake the deer. As they neared the
mountain face, Antoine allowed himself to slow. The
snow was deeper here, piled against fallen trees and
large boulders. As they passed a small stream, he dug in
his claws and slid to a stop. It took Tahira a moment to
realize he had split off, but she quickly returned to his
side, letting the deer continue to race into the distance.

"Did you smell something?" she asked in a whisper
right next to his head. Her breath was deliciously hot
against his chilled skin.

Without warning, something changed. He was suddenly, acutely *aware* of her—the sensation of her flank
against his side, the adrenaline musk that drifted on the

breeze, the golden eyes that held his with intelligence and powerful intensity. He couldn't seem to get the memory of their kiss out of his mind—the scent of sandalwood, cherry jam, and thick sweet musk was making his heart race and his head spin.

"*Yes*." The word came out almost without thought, but Tahira took it the wrong way. Her neck fur rose and her head dropped defensively. She was instantly on alert, scanning the surrounding forest for their foes. It made her even more attractive to him, but it also reminded him that they had more pressing business.

He shook his head to clear it of more personal thoughts than he should be thinking right now. "No, what I meant was, this is a good location for the plan I have in mind."

She was staring into the distance intently, and he could barely hear her whispered reply over the rising wind. "Good thing, because they're coming."

Antoine looked around quickly, searching for a place to ambush them. Yes! That would be perfect. The rock ledge was some distance away and about twenty feet above them, but it was nearly hidden behind a massive snow-covered spruce. From any angle other than where he was standing, he would be hidden. "We need to get you out of sight." His eyes took in the details of the small clearing. The running stream would cover small sounds, and the piles of snow might be an excellent hiding place for her. But she wouldn't be able to see. She would have to rely on scent and hearing for her attack.

"If we buried you under the snow near that spruce—" he began, but she interrupted.

"There's no need. Find your place. I'll *isim* and we'll take them by surprise."

Antoine glanced away when the smell of the attackers, there were three of them, reached his nose. He shook his head and whispered, "You didn't explain what that means . . . I . . . Tahira?" When he looked back, she was gone. He could still smell her, but she was nowhere in sight. When he heard her voice next to his ear, he flinched.

"You are the first non-Hayalet who has ever seen the *isim*, and you must swear to keep the secret. We are called the 'ghost tribe' for more than one reason."

"*Merde!* Your people can become *invisible*?"

The low chuffing sound made his heart beat faster. "Not precisely. It's sort of bending light. I can't really explain it very well. It's still new to me. But they're nearly here. We can talk later."

Antoine raised his nose to the breeze and realized she was right. He felt a rush of wind as she used supernatural speed to leap. He heard a small thump behind him and could now very faintly smell sandalwood on the bare spot under a large spruce. Without another word, he focused on the ledge. He would have to make a single leap. It was a longer jump than he'd accomplished in a very long time, and from a cold stand. He couldn't afford to take a running start since the tracks would give away his location. It was the same reason Tahira had leapt to her spot.

Training with his cats had increased his precision in the past few years. It was much easier to show the cats what he expected than to project the image into their mind through his Sazi gift. But he hadn't practiced any distance jumps. It had been more than a year since he'd trained with Fiona at the Wolven range. Still, a pulled muscle or two was a small price to pay.

His ears flattened as he crouched down low, being careful not to leave any impression in the snow. The tracks should just end without any hint of their position. He wiggled his hindquarters, seeking just the right angle. He felt his heartbeat slow and the world disappear from his sight, except for the small rock outcropping.

With a low grunt, he threw himself into the air, pushing off from the earth like a rocket. He spread his front paws and extended his claws as the rock wall quickly approached. But he realized that the jump was going to be short by a fraction. He might be able to grab on to the ledge with his claws and pull himself up, but that would make noise. Plus, the sand and small rocks that would be dislodged in the process would be obvious on the undisturbed field of white below.

With only microseconds left, he turned his head, changing his flight toward the sheer cliff face. He pulled his rear legs under him and twisted so his head was pointing nearly down. With an impact that shook his bones to the core, he careened into the rock wall with all four feet. For a moment, he was suspended against the wall and gravity was pressing against him like lead. But then he pushed off, using his own momentum to propel him forward.

He threw his body sideways once more and landed on the ledge with barely a whisper of sound. Every muscle in his back screamed from the effort. He took a moment to catch his breath and tried to ignore the stab of pain in his hip.

Merde! *I'll heal, but I won't enjoy it much. I'm just glad that playing so many games of pool with Lucas made me think of a bank shot to reach the pocket.*

A rustling of branches below caught his attention, and he flattened himself against the rock, backing up so his head wouldn't be visible from below. Three men wearing black knit masks walked slowly into the clearing. Two were armed. One of the rifles looked like the dart gun that he had seen in the police station. The tallest of the men, a viper in his animal form, was wearing black

goggles and was scanning the area slowly. Even heat
sensors wouldn't detect him through the icy rock, but
Tahira wouldn't be so lucky. Night vision might not spot
her, but she couldn't hide her warmth.

TAHIRA WATCHED THE men slowly move around the
clearing. The man with goggles smelled strangely like
fresh asphalt. He slowly turned his head, and she held
her breath. He must know he was looking for cats, because he spent as much time looking up into the trees as
scanning the forest. Something caught his eye in a
nearby tree and he raised his hand to focus the binoculars. The other men looked to him for a sign, but then he
shook his head and returned to scanning the area. Tahira
looked up and saw an owl, nearly hidden against the tree
bark. She held her breath and froze as the man scanned
right next to the tree where she stood. She suddenly realized that she'd been foolish and nearly swore under
her breath. Even using *isim* wouldn't hide her from
some technology. She hadn't considered heat signa-
tures. She should have stepped behind the snowy branch
right next to her. But it was too late now. If she was spotted, she'd just have to pounce.

But the goggles moved past her without notice. She
heard the men whisper to each other easily, but didn't
understand the language. It wasn't even similar to anything she'd heard recently, but it was obvious that they
were angry and frustrated. Antoine had been correct that
they were shapeshifters. One of them was a cat, but she
couldn't tell what species. The one using goggles was a
snake. His movements were painfully slow and he was
heavily bundled against the cold. The third man—she
had no idea what the third one might be. There was a bit
of canine and something close to a cat, but mostly he

smelled of spoiled meat. She definitely needed to spend more time at the zoo back home.

Assuming I get home.

Tahira looked up to the ledge and searched for a sign from Antoine. She didn't want to attack before he did, but it looked like the men might leave. That wasn't acceptable. But even with her night eyes, she couldn't see him. Had he already jumped and she hadn't noticed?

The man with the goggles pointed for each man to spread out in a different direction. They both nodded and turned away. This was her chance. She tried not to think about getting wounded or getting captured again. With a vicious roar that made all three men turn, she threw her body forward with claws extended. She had never tried to fight in *isim*, but she had heard Rabi say it could be done. The man in the center went down under her weight, screaming as her claws raked through fabric into skin and muscle.

Out of the corners of her eyes, she could see the fear and confusion in the eyes of the other men. They raised their rifles, but couldn't decide where to shoot. All they could see was their companion. A cracking sound and a rush of bitter tasting blood in her mouth caused the snake to scream again as she grabbed on to his arm to force him to drop the knife he had pulled. She dug in her back claws into the hard muscles of his thighs to try to get into better fighting position, but then heard metal on metal as the man on her right slid the bolt of his rifle into place.

The dart missed her by only a fraction as she jumped sideways. But the other man spotted the sudden indentations in the snow and swung his rifle around. A high-pitched scream cut the air, and the man went down in a flurry of snow and tawny fur. Tahira forced her attention from Antoine's fight and pounced on the first man with the dart gun. The snake shifter was bleeding on the ground, moaning and trying to catch his breath. He wouldn't be going anywhere for a moment.

But now they were expecting her, and the cat under her fought back. He was dark skinned behind the black mask, and the whites of his eyes at the sudden attack quickly disappeared. They hardened into cold professionalism. This was a trained fighter.

Antoine's snarls behind her were met with equal noise from another animal, but she didn't dare turn her head to see what kind. A startled yelp was followed by a savage hiss. Antoine was hurt! She could smell his blood and anger and it distracted her.

With lightning fast moves, her opponent used his rifle as a club. He caught her on the side of the head with a vicious blow that cracked the composite stock. Stars erupted in her vision. Her concentration shattered and she was suddenly visible.

The man under her smiled and dropped one arm to fumble in a leg pocket, while the other arm held her neck in a grip of iron. Darts! He was looking for more darts. She pulled back against the supernatural muscles that held her, fought the magic that tried to choke her into submission. Scrambling frantically, she tried to hold down his arm with her claws. With a desperate shake of her head, she freed her neck but noticed something. His glove had ripped off and a familiar scent flooded her brain. Rabi! He had touched Rabi at some time before he dressed tonight, and her brother had been afraid.

Fury combined with terror and the moon took control of her. She'd never felt her animal fill her so intensely or violently. She felt power pour through her skin, sparkling behind her vision in a wave. Thought was a liability. Language was unnecessary. There was only the scent of family and fear, anger and blood. Pain erupted in her side, her leg, her chest, and she let out a roar that bounced off the mountain, echoing into the distance. Animals and birds in the trees and thicket panicked, fleeing from the sound as they would before a fire.

Tahira reached for his throat, but the clothing was protecting it too well, so she opened her mouth, grabbed on to the man's skull and squeezed. She felt her teeth sink through skin and bone as he beat at her and continued to stab something sharp into her side. He twisted and struggled to escape. She felt his body shift to animal form under her, but she didn't let go, even as sharp claws raked her sides and fur tickled her tongue and tried to make her gag. There was no escape for her brother's tormenter.

A sharp cracking sound filled the air and the body stopped thrashing underneath her just before she collapsed into a pool of her own blood.

Chapter Ten

"HOW IS SHE?"

Antoine turned his head as Margo entered the room. He was seated on the edge of the bed, watching her. Tahira's ragged breaths told of more injuries than appeared on the surface. Giselle had done her best, but between the two of them, she had only been able to heal the worst of her wounds.

He looked down at her pale face and felt incredibly proud of her. "She'll heal. But she was stabbed a number of times and will probably have scars."

Margo walked closer and wrapped her arms around her body, smelling worried. "Are you going to tell her?"

He adjusted the blankets to cover Tahira's shoulders and then stood. He looked down at Margo until her gaze rose to meet his. "Tell her *what*? That she killed a man? She knows. It's not that the human side disappears when the animal takes over. We're aware of our actions, but they don't really . . . *matter* in the heat of the moment. Those men were trying to kill us, and she reacted as any animal would. I can't fault her."

He turned and walked toward the window, pulling them open to let in the bright sunshine. He had to flick his sensitive eyes away from the brilliant reflection off the snow. "There's a point in each Sazi life where we have to deal with this, Margo. The Hayalet are no different. Animals don't regret. Only humans do that, and each of us deals with it differently. I'll talk to her if she wants to, but the truth is that there are occasions when even the best of us lose control of our humanity."

Her whisper was warm and concerned. "Even you?"

He nodded. "Yes. As an alpha, I have more control over my thoughts. But the men last night were trained killers. They knew who . . . *what* we are, and were prepared to capture or kill us. I regret not saving any of them, because they might have had the answers we need."

"So you found no trace of the third man?"

He shook his head, took a step, and winced at the pain still radiating from his hip. "He shifted to snake form. All I found were his empty clothes and a single bloody indentation that disappeared into the forest. I'm fairly certain he was a viper. The blood tasted very bitter."

"So now what? Her parents e-mailed again, saying that someone from their tribe would arrive to collect her."

"That will take a few days, but you already know the answer. For the moment, when she wakes, we'll concentrate on finding her some proper clothing, and letting her get some rest. Ahmad said that Charles has a few volumes in the library with information about power wells, so we'll start there." He stepped back to the bed, pressed the back of his hand against her forehead, and was pleased that her fever was down. He ran a gentle finger down her cheek and smiled slightly.

"It's obvious that she can control herself by instinct. She absolutely should not have been able to overpower that man. He was a lion—bigger and stronger and as close to an alpha as I've seen in a long time in that species. He should have been able to break free from her grasp. Somehow she must have been able to use his own power against him. But having the *ability* to use her gift doesn't mean she has control. There has to be conscious intent behind true control."

Margo quietly walked to the door and Antoine followed. She continued to keep her voice low, since Giselle didn't have Amber's abilities to keep Tahira in a magical sleep to heal. "Maybe you could take her into town? The plow drove by earlier, so the roads are probably clear. Fiona's clothes don't really fit her and she's taller than Giselle. It might do her good to get away from the house and do something other than sit around and be reminded of last night."

He pursed his lips and opened the door, holding it for her to precede him. "That's not a bad idea. How is our food stock holding up? Should we do some grocery shopping?"

"The food's okay. The pantry and freezer are stocked, but I know that Matty is hoping to buy some poster paint or black ink. He's done carving both the boomerang and kylie, and is downstairs on the internet looking for appropriate symbols to decorate them."

Antoine closed the door, turning the handle so that the sound didn't wake Tahira. "He'll want chocolate, too. The Tim Tams didn't last long. But I'd prefer to keep the trip to just the two of us, in case she does want to talk. How's Grand—I mean Giselle, by the way? I was surprised that she even helped us last night, consider her recent . . . decision."

Margo put a light hand on his arm, stopping him from descending the staircase. "She doesn't hate you, Antoine. Of *course* she's going to help you when you come home bleeding from a dozen wounds. She's upstairs in her room, resting. Healing takes a lot out of her. I don't know what all has led her to believe that you're not doing your job, but I disagree. I've been talking to her, trying to convince her to reconsider."

Antoine smiled sadly. "Thank you for that. I've been starting to doubt myself, and I appreciate knowing that some people still believe in me. It's easy to get wrapped up in the day to day events of life and not see the big picture, but I've been trying to do both. I *thought* I was succeeding. I'm not entirely convinced that I'm so far out of touch as to have unknowingly injured those I'm supposed to protect."

"I hope you don't believe that dig from Ahmad about us being servants, either." When he raised his brows in suspicion, she shrugged. "Apparently, the guards were talking about it in the basement and Larry overheard."

Antoine thought back to the end of their meeting last night, before he and Tahira decided to go outside and hunt. Yes, perhaps it had been petty to hold the guards against the ceiling for the full meeting, but he certainly did not equate his loyal employees such as Margo, Matty, and Bruce to the life-bound, unpaid slaves of Ahmad. When Ahmad had said that he needed his servants back to prepare him for dinner, maybe he shouldn't have responded. But he took the bait and asked why Ahmad couldn't survive without being surrounded by servants, when he could do just fine. Even now, the response made him furious.

"*Putain!* To say that I believed myself better than him, when in reality I had surrounded myself with servants and fooled myself into believing they were somehow different, and that perhaps *hypocrisy* was one of the reasons why Giselle had challenged me—" He shook his head angrily and placed his hand on the bannister to ease the pressure on his hip.

Margo let out a light laugh. "We're hardly *servants*, at least not as Ahmad defines the term. Yes, we'd probably stay with you even if you couldn't pay us—" She waggled her head a bit. "Well, for a month or so anyway. But

I'm fond of things like, oh, food and electricity. I think you're a terrific boss, but I'd drop you in a second if the gravy train totally derailed. I'm allergic to weather with no roof over my head!"

Antoine chuckled. "And as much as Bruce loves the animals, Larry would say the same. He's very protective of our keeper, and even as a three-day, I wouldn't want to get on his bad side if I somehow made them lose that new condo they bought."

"Oh yeah. That wouldn't go over very well. Matty might stay. He couldn't just leave the cats until you found someone to replace him or got the cats to good homes."

At that moment, Matty raced into the front room, grabbed for the bannister to take the stairs, and missed. He skidded on the stone and nearly lost his footing, but managed not to wind up in a heap against the far wall. He looked up with wide eyes, and the ammonia panic in his scent was nearly enough to make Antoine sneeze.

"Holy dooley! Did you hear the news?"

Margo and Antoine quickly descended the stairs until they were on the main level. "What are you talking about, Matty?" Antoine asked.

"The coppers caught the bloke! He's in lock-up, and what's going to happen if they find out? I mean, it's a good pozzy for you and Tahira—he can't hurt you from there, but Ahmad will be spewin' mad."

Antoine reached out and put a hand on each of Matty's shoulders. "Who are you talking about? Who was arrested?"

"The one who got away! The snake in the woods. The coppers got a call about a rifle shot and drove out there just in time to find the bloke staggering from the woods. He was still carved up and the cops followed the blood trail back to the other two. The dead one at the scene had the same fingerprints as the ones where Simon was killed, and there was a dead lion at the scene. So he's in lock-up. But what happens if he turns? Yeah, it's not the third night anymore, but how much do you know about snakes? Could he turn if he's hurt? And what happens if he heals too fast?"

Antoine realized that his jaw had dropped and his fingers had frozen tight on Matty's shoulders, causing the other man to wince. He released the vet and shook his head in frustration. "*Merde!* This is a complication we didn't need. Of course, you're right that it's good for our purposes that he was caught, but the issues that it raises. *Pauvre con!* We need to—"

"*Do nothing.* It is not your concern." Ahmad appeared as though by magic at the bottom of the stairs, causing Margo to give a small startled yelp.

Antoine was accustomed to Ahmad's lightning movements, but the others had little contact with the councilman. He did do a double-take when he noticed the Egyptian's attire. Antoine couldn't remember a time when Ahmad had been dressed in blue jeans, much less a polo shirt, but Ahmad appeared perfectly at home in both.

"Once again," Ahmad continued, "you forget your place. Perhaps it's because so many in your family have been involved in law enforcement that you feel the need to think in those terms. Perhaps you should consider a change in careers, because we are *administrators*, Antoine. Nothing more. We will contact Wolven. They will handle the situation. If the prisoner is indeed a snake with ties to a crime scene, he will be eliminated before any harm is done. It would certainly not make me, as your servant's colorful phrasing would indicate, 'spewin' mad.' "

Antoine took a step forward until he was within

inches of the cobra. He refused to get into another debate about whether Matty was a servant, but there were other problems. "There is nobody in Europe right now, Ahmad. With Fiona and Raven on forced leave, and Bobby training his replacement, there are no agents in this part of the world." Antoine's voice was growing louder and his movements more broad as his temper rose. "We have a duty—"

Ahmad narrowed his eyes and used one finger to wipe a tiny droplet of spittle from his nose. He glanced at his finger with disdain and took one step closer to Antoine, until their noses nearly touched. "First, if you *ever* spit on me again, you will learn that cobras *spit back*. Second, once again, we have no *duty* other than to advise the authorities. However, I overheard that you will be traveling to town with the girl. If you feel compelled to verify your concerns, then please do stop by the police station. If you confirm his identity by scent, let headquarters know. But be warned," he said, lowering his voice to a deep rumble that rose and fell with dangerous hisses, "if you de-ssside to become persssonally involved, it might not jussst be Gissselle who feels the need to challenge you."

Antoine felt Ahmad's power sear over his skin and the hot scent of anger fill the air. He knew full well what would happen if the snake actually decided to spit at him from such a short distance. If he wasn't fast enough, he could go blind, or even permanently lose the patch of skin that the venom landed on. But he stood his ground and didn't flinch at the hissing and power show, and didn't allow himself to smell of fear.

Backing down was the ultimate sign of weakness to the snakes, which was primarily why he had held Ahmad's guards on the ceiling as long as he did.

His voice was calm but hard when he replied. "Very

well. I will go to the police and verify the identity of the prisoner. Then I'll contact Wolven. But if they can't have someone in Stuttgart before nightfall tomorrow, we will have another discussion about the *duty* of a councilman when it involves the primary rule of all of our kind."

Ahmad's smile was a dangerous baring of teeth as he stepped back a pace. "I sincerely hope we have that opportunity. We haven't had a vigorous *discussion* since I petitioned to have your sister put down. I would be very interested to see how you fare against me now that my powers have reached their peak. Perhaps Giselle will be spared making the choice to fight."

He turned away with a low chuckle, deliberately slamming his shoulder against Antoine's as he walked into the great room. Antoine felt his head drop into a defensive position and a low growl rise from his chest. He turned to follow, intending to finish this rivalry once and for all, but Margo and Matty each grabbed on to an arm.

"Don't let him rile you, mate," Matty said quietly. "You might win, but what if you don't? What would happen to Tahira, and . . . well, *us*, if Ahmad does you in? He's up himself but was acting too bloody confident just now. He's got something up his sleeve. With you gone, Giselle and Larry and the rest of us will just be mozzies for the squashing."

"Please, Antoine," Margo pleaded. "Let it go. Matty's right—Ahmad will always be an ass, but there's more to consider right now."

Antoine glared at the doorway for a moment. They were right. Ahmad's scent had been sweet and cloying, a clear sign he was hiding something. This was just like Ahmad to deliberately provoke him into a trap. Usually he ignored the attempts, taking his frustrations out on furniture, but even that was becoming a liability, perpetuating the image that he was unstable.

No, I'm better than that. This time, I'm going to just walk away.

He relaxed his muscles and took a deep breath. "*Merci, mon amis.* You're quite right. Ahmad is a minor annoyance and I shouldn't let him get the best of me. I'll go upstairs and wake Tahira, and then we'll go into town. Are there, by chance, any vehicles that were spared the storm, or will we have to dig out first?"

"Bruce and Larry went out earlier to do just that and get the rest of their bags," Margo said. "The second van is in the garage, but with any luck, they'll get the SUV started and beat down a path all the way from the road so we don't have to shovel."

Antoine nodded. "Make sure someone checks on them if they don't make it back in an hour or so. Cold weather doesn't agree with our snake friend. I'll wake Tahira and then shower and change." Matty and Margo both started for the great room, but stopped and looked at each other.

"Maybe we'll go to the kitchen by the back way, so we don't run into him." Margo's voice was light, but there was fear in her scent.

Antoine leaned over the banister from his position about halfway up. "I don't believe he'll have the nerve to harm you. He's got an ego like a black hole, but he's not a fool. *Still* . . . try not to spend too much time in any room where there's no back door until I return."

As he approached Tahira's room, he heard movement behind the door and smelled a rush of confusing emotions. But underlying them was her own essence. He concentrated on the warm, inviting mix of sandalwood and musk, and tried to project a positive scent for her to hold on to. It would be a test of his skills to charm her out of all of the fear, anger, and self-loathing that would accompany her memories of last night.

He knocked and opened the door when she answered. She was sitting up in bed, her legs bent, knees tight against her chest. She looked up at him with reddened eyes and he sighed. Crossing the room in a few short steps, he sat down on the edge of the bed, raising one knee onto the mattress to face her. "How are you feeling this morning?"

TAHIRA LET OUT a rush of air that wasn't quite a laugh. "As good as can be expected, I guess. My side hurts, and I feel like a truck hit me." She looked at him for a long moment. Her fingers were trembling and nearly as white as the silk nightgown she had on. Seeing him here—alive, perfect, with concern and warmth radiating from him, was suddenly too much. Without thinking, she launched herself forward, threw her arms around him, and burst into tears.

He rocked backward with the impact, but quickly righted himself. He wrapped his arms around her and held her close while she sobbed against the soft warmth of his chamois shirt that smelled of grass and fur and flesh.

"I'm sorry," she said in a muffled whisper. "Everybody told me that this might happen. Rabi and I even talked about it. But I thought I could control it. It was like I was a prisoner inside my own head. I *wanted* to kill him when I smelled Rabi's scent on him, but I didn't know how it would make me feel."

Antoine stroked her hair and pulled her a little closer. She could hear his heart beat just a bit faster and a sort of sad darkness fill his voice. "The part that's hardest is the *pride* in your kill, isn't it, *mon chat du feu*? You bested the prey, felt the thrill of pleasure as the body went limp. Even now, the memory brings a sort of satisfaction. That's . . . well, it's what causes many of us to lose the fight—not with our enemies, but with ourselves. Not all Sazi die a violent death. Many simply cannot bear what they have become, and they take their own lives. But I didn't know that you had smelled your brother's scent on the man. *Merde!* That would be more than even the best of us could bear during the moon. You have nothing to apologize for. Nothing to be ashamed of."

She leaned back a bit so she could see his face. Looking into his eyes, she realized that they weren't truly golden, but smoldered with a thousand shades of brown and yellow and green that sucked her inside and made her want to tell him everything in her heart. "I think the part that bothers me the most is that I'm *not* ashamed. He kidnapped my brother and attacked me, and I defended myself. But *shouldn't* I feel ashamed? My friends back home would be horrified. Even my parents would, and they were raised in the Hayalet culture. I felt like this incredible outsider in the village, thinking they were terrible and vicious for speaking of death so matter-of-factly, and here I am now, reacting the same. All I can remember is that I wanted to finish with him fast so I could help you in your fight. I heard you yelp and hiss, and my only thought was the man needed to die so I could hurt the man who—"

"Was hurting me?" Antoine smiled slightly and pushed back a few strands of hair that had covered one eye. "That's a bit unusual in a tiger. That's closer to the thought process of a pride or pack animal. One might think you consider me more than an acquaintance."

It was as though time stopped. Her eyes locked with his and got drawn inside them. She could feel a sudden pulse of energy that played over her body like a hand. When he pulled her closer, she leaned into him and reveled in the sensation of his mouth against hers. His tongue tasted of cinnamon mouthwash as it coaxed and teased hers, and his jaw moved with passion. She reached up and tugged at the ponytail holder that kept his hair back. The small moan that escaped him as she ran her fingers through the thick softness made her body clench with desire. She suddenly knew that she needed this—needed to go further than this, and wanted it more desperately than anything before in her life.

Tahira pulled back from the kiss nearly breathless, her heart pounding hard enough for her temples to throb. Without a word, she slid off the bed and walked to the door. She felt apart from herself, light-headed, but absolutely clear and calm as she turned the big, old-fashioned key in the lock.

She'd never felt this bold before, and struggled not to blush as she pulled the nightgown over her head in one quick movement. Antoine let out a strangled sound, and she could see his eyes take in every inch of her. He took deep breaths and closed his eyes for a moment. She could smell his desire in equal parts with fear and worry, but she couldn't decide why he would be frightened.

"We can't do this, Tahira. I won't take advantage of you."

She felt the cat inside push her forward, accept the challenge. She was standing in front of him before he could open his eyes again. "You won't be. I've had a few boyfriends who I've slept with."

He stood up and met her eyes with all the power and majesty of a *sahip* in his prime. "There are other ways to take advantage of someone. I don't think—"

As soon as he said it, she knew the truth. The words came out in a whisper before they were even fully formed in her mind. "Exactly. I don't want to think. Just for a few minutes, I don't want to think about anything—not family or danger or death. I'm not asking for forever. I don't even care if the whole rest of the house hears us, but I've never met a man who I've wanted as much as I want you right now." Even as she said it, she had to fight down the need to reach for his shirt, tear the fabric apart with her bare hands.

He stared at her for a long moment, searching for . . . *something*. His nostrils flared and his face seemed to come to a sudden realization. "Your cat needs claws and teeth," Antoine said softly. She didn't understand the comment.

He moved toward her slightly and leaned down enough to place his nose next to her ear. She felt frozen in place as his breath heated her cheek. He let out a low growl that was unlike any she'd ever heard, but it made her entire body shudder and her knees weaken. He stepped around the back of her and part of her, deep inside, recognized the dance.

He moved aside her hair and once more put his mouth near her neck. Again he ran his nose along her cheek and growled. "You've conquered in battle, tasted the blood of your prey, and now your instinct drives you toward the second strongest need of our kind." A dark smile filled his voice and the thick, rolling scent of musk made her dizzy. "I nearly took you in the woods, you know. Even with the hunters nearly upon us, I wanted to sink my fangs into the fur of your neck, use claws and teeth to battle you—to claim you, and *mate*."

The word was a hiss that made her nipples harden and flush.

He hovered there for a hanging moment as her heart pounded. Heat and power flooded her, tightened her body, and made her wet. Rational thought left her. She wanted . . . more—

She hissed low and her words were a rich, throaty demand that didn't make sense to her: "*Now, if you dare!*"

Without warning, he responded to the challenge, suddenly sinking his teeth into the back of her neck with the vicious power and snarl of his cat namesake, and digging fingernails into her hips hard enough to make her bleed. Her gasp turned into a growl that was both hungry and angry.

She snarled and fought to be free of his teeth, but they held her fast, twisted her neck down nearly to her shoulder. She suddenly realized that he was naked behind her and couldn't imagine when he'd found the time to undress. She grabbed his hands in a frenzy, twisting in his grip. The struggle was making her even more excited, making her pulse pound and her flesh swell. He was feeding a raging wave of desire so desperate to get him inside her that she would kill for the chance. Some little part of her brain couldn't comprehend why she was fighting, but the cat understood and was pleased he was worthy.

He seemed to know just what she needed. He pushed her forward hard and she fell half onto the bed, with her feet still on the floor. He rode her down, never taking his jaws from her neck. She felt him reposition his hips and realized what he was doing, but the cat inside her still fought to be free, turning and moving away from the inevitable. But with a sudden powerful movement that pulled a startled cry from her, he was inside her. He was larger than she imagined, stretching her uncomfortably in width and length, even as wet as she was. But it felt intense and raw and was exactly what she wanted.

He tightened his grip on her hips and drew himself

out slowly, then slammed into her again. It was pleasure and pain, scent and sensation. His growls, teeth, and musk called to her cat, pulled the tiger to the surface without the moon to bring it forth.

She could almost feel thick fur trying to reach the surface in each of them, to touch in the middle and rub like velvet.

The weight of him pressing her into the bed, the sensation of his powerful chest pressed against her back as his hips slammed against her butt—it was too much, too fast. All of her frustration and desire, her fury and fear were rolled into a single mind-numbing sensation as the insides of her eyelids began glowing with golden fire. She buried her face in the comforter to muffle a scream so deep it seemed to tear from her very soul. It ended with a triumphant roar that rattled her chest and stole her breath.

Her climax was white-hot, so intense that she saw white stars erupt in her vision. It seized her entire body as a single force, raising her physically off the bed.

Just as suddenly, it was over. Antoine pulled out of her as she collapsed back down and he released her neck. He rolled her shaking, boneless body over. The powerful scent of musk and blood and her own orgasm was heady and turned her brain to putty.

"That," he said with a small smile that had smears of blood at the corners, "is what your *cat* needed, *mon chat du feu*. You needed the claws and teeth of your hunting partner. And you do not need to stifle yourself—all of the rooms on this floor are soundproofed. Nobody in the house will hear."

She could still feel her neck and hips throbbing with pain, but combined with the powerful contractions still swelling her insides, it felt so amazing that she couldn't even speak. The tiger inside her stretched and lolled contentedly, and would purr if it was able, as though in gratitude for her human half finding a suitable male.

He gently slid his hands under her shoulders and legs and lifted her the rest of the way onto the bed, laying her head on the pillow. He was still fully erect and the look in his eyes was hungry. "Now . . . I believe the *woman* inside you requires still more attention to detail."

He bent down over her and slowly, deliciously, kissed her. She could taste her own blood on his tongue for a moment, but then the lingering flavor of sweet red-hots washed it away. His powerful hands suddenly became gentle as he stroked lightly down her bare skin, making the pulsing between her legs start all over again. He flicked her nipple with his thumb as he squeezed her breast lightly and wrapped his other arm around her to pull her against him.

He turned his kisses to her neck and slowly ran his tongue along the smooth edge of the ear cut when she reached her tenth birthday, as was her tribe's custom. She could finally think enough to speak.

"That was . . . it was *unbelievable*! How did you know that was what—"

He moved back just a bit and smiled, sending the smell of citrus and spice bursting into the air. "You needed? Remember, *mon amante*, I'm a cat too. It's what we both needed. I've been struggling against it since we met, fearing what might happen if I gave in to my attraction for another cat—which I rarely do. There are very few cats who I could take like this and not injure them beyond repair. But there is a time for consideration and a time for action. You showed me your full fury last night, and it excited me beyond . . . well, probably beyond good judgment." He said it with a strong scent of embarrassment and chagrin.

She felt her eyes grow wide. "I did . . . I mean, um, you said you wanted to—"

The embarrassment disappeared and his eyes twinkled with unaired laughter. "We have a saying where I was raised, *Jamais couard n'aura belle amie*—faint heart never won the lady fair. Our bodies want each other, as do our animals, but there is more to it than that. We're more complex than animals, you and I. You've impressed me, both with your intelligence and with your intensity. Brains, beauty, and aggression are heady attractants to an alpha male. Do you remember that I said I would tell you when I wanted to sleep with you?" His gaze was intense and his chest heaved slightly as he ran a slow finger down her face to end on her lips. "Well, I've mated with you, and while we both needed that, now I want to sleep with you—to make love to you, if you'll have me. There is something that I find quite irresistible about you."

There was something so incredibly serious in his golden eyes framed by long, tawny hair. Even his scent had changed ever so subtly to a blend of cinnamon, oranges, and sweet musk. He truly believed the two versions of sex to be different things. Perhaps they were. She felt warmer inside than she did a moment ago, but not as heated on the outside.

She reached up her hand and let her fingers glide over his smooth, bare chest, feeling the prickling of power that tingled her skin. She had to admit that she enjoyed the effect her touch had on him, from the sudden racing of his heart to the sharply inhaled breath. She chuckled nervously, realizing that she hadn't a clue what to expect from becoming involved with a *sahip* this powerful. "Is there a French saying for 'curiosity killed the cat'?"

He smiled and laughed. "*Oui. La curiosite est un vilain defaut.* But it doesn't reference a cat. You've already given in to your initial curiosity. You claimed it, owned it, and survived *mon chat du feu.* If anything terrible was going to happen, it would have happened when we gave into our beasts just now, but we're just fine."

She moved her neck sideways and a dull ache twinged. "Oh, I don't know about that. My neck still hurts."

Antoine held up his arms and she was shocked to see long, bloody scratches that raked them from elbow to fingertips. "As do my arms. But not enough—" he said, and his voice lowered to a husky whisper— "to quell my desire for you. You've had your fun, but I have not, and I *very much* want to hear you roar in pleasure again."

The intensity in his eyes seemed to burn through her defenses, and he noticed the change. His hand started to move again, stroking a teasing line down her skin that made her gasp. He seemed to be able to control his power to pinpoint precision, making her muscles twitch and dance from the lightest touch of his fingers. When he lowered his face to kiss the skin between her breasts, her arms unconsciously reached around him to pull him closer.

She nearly laughed. *Apparently my body doesn't much care what my head thinks about this.*

Heat warmed her body as Antoine allowed his power to bleed outward, but she didn't feel flushed and there was no pain around the edges like in the van.

Tahira moaned as he took her breast into his mouth, rolling the nipple with his tongue while his fingers explored between her legs. When he slid a finger inside her, the magical energy preceded him, pushed against the already sensitive skin enough to make her cry out and arch her back.

"That was a start." Antoine growled the words possessively and slithered his body along hers until they were again face to face. "But I'm feeling a bit lonely."

He reached behind him and took her hand, guided it between his legs and wrapped it around his erection. He lightly kissed her forehead and cheeks and then whispered into her mouth, "Make me believe you want me."

He kissed her deeply and then turned on his side. He pulled her to face him and put a hand on either side of her face, pressing his mouth to hers in another passionate kiss. She needed no further invitation, and slowly began to stroke and squeeze his penis, enjoying the size and length, as well as the nearly burning heat and power that raced through her. His hands and mouth became more urgent as he gave in to his need, and he began to thrust against her hand, causing a thin liquid to coat her palm. She responded in kind—her slick opening ground against his leg, hungry for pressure against the swollen flesh.

With near panic, Antoine moved his mouth to her neck. Nipping and sucking frantically, he pushed her onto her back with a snarl. "Perhaps we'll get more creative next time, but for now, I only want to fuck you until you scream for mercy. I'd suggest you hang on tight."

He nibbled at her lips and then rose to his knees. Grabbing the back of her legs, he wrapped them around his waist and lifted her to meet his powerful thrust into her.

It all happened so quickly that she only had time for a startled yelp before his massive organ filled her again. He started a slow rhythm that increased in speed, causing a sharp, wet slapping sound with each stroke. She grabbed on to his shoulders to keep her head from slamming against the headboard from the sheer force. More power began to bleed off him, stuffing her completely full with everything he had to offer. She grabbed on to his hair and pulled herself upward into a kiss filled with lips and tongue and teeth. Her fingernails dug in the back of his neck and clawed down his shoulders, causing him to moan with passion. He gnawed lightly on her tongue and then pulled back, moving his hands to the back of her thighs. He pulled her legs open wider and raised them until her calves rested on his shoulders. The change in angle caused every tiny movement to constantly rub against her swollen clitoris.

Abruptly, he stopped moving, but she felt him throbbing inside her impatiently. With a chuckle, he pushed in just a fraction deeper, pressing against her cervix. It caused a full body shudder so intense it nearly hurt. His voice was filled with teasing. "Have you had enough? Shall I stop now?"

"I've never . . . I need . . . *please!*" She felt panicked and her breath started to erupt in pants.

"You 'need'?" He pulled out slowly enough to drive her mad and then pushed himself in again. He was toying with her and enjoying it thoroughly. "You need me to stop? Or you need me to make you come so hard you scream?"

It was so hard to think. "I need . . . don't stop." She closed her eyes and nearly sobbed. "*Please* don't stop, Antoine!"

He rearranged her legs against his neck and lightly stroked his hands down her burning thighs. With infinite slowness that made her whimper, he withdrew again and then slammed into her fully. The sudden movement against her swollen flesh hit her brain like a knife. A strangled cry rose from her mouth, and her hands scrambled and dug into his shoulders.

Where the first orgasm was without warning, this one built slowly in her abdomen. Her world narrowed to the sensation of her body moving on the bed, bent nearly double, totally possessed and helpless as Antoine rammed himself in and out of her in a near frenzy that was more fulfilling than any sensation she'd ever imagined. His aroma became a thick, sweet musk that was filled with citrus and spice and the lingering scent of brandy. Her own grew in response until the sandalwood-infused sex smell was nearly a cloud over the bed. Magic became a flame that seared over her skin and flowed through her veins like lava. The heat and pain terrified her, made her want to run away and hide from what was happening to her.

Then he smiled down at her, and it fluttered her heart, not just her body.

Trust me, the smile said. *I'll protect you.*

"Let go," he whispered. "Let the woman master the beast. Let the magic fill us both and make us whole."

And somehow, she knew they could do it. He was just that powerful, and so was she. They could control the fire inside and it wouldn't destroy them. Her fear dissolved and she gave in to a hunger that burned as rich and deep as the moon magic that created them.

Antoine began to breathe fast and hard. Low growls with each breath made her pulse race, and his power slowly pierced her belly like a dull blade. Down and down it seared until it was between her legs, turning her insides to jelly. She realized with a start that he was doing it intentionally, using the energy to bring her to climax.

"Time to scream," he said breathlessly, and sent a wave of golden light to surround her and fill every pore to bursting. Every inch of her skin began to tingle and move as though a dozen people were fondling her simultaneously. Invisible lips kissed her, and the sensation of a mouth sucked on her neck, pulled at each breast and licked at her toes. The power vibrated and swelled inside her, stretching and moving like a caged cat desperate to be free. The pleasure increased until she was helpless and lost inside the fury of it.

She cried out his name over and over like a mantra and then just screamed—frantic, ragged sounds that made her throat hot. She clutched at anything and everything around her as he rode her to the most intense climax of her life. The sheer force created a spasm so strong that he could barely pull out of her and had trouble getting back in. But he let out a lion's roar of raw power and thrust hard, pushing her body against the headboard. She could feel him expand inside her as he filled her completely.

But even then he wasn't done, because he continued to thrust into her with slow, delicious strokes, fully enjoying his own orgasm until he was spent and limp. With each penetration and withdrawal, he pulled on the power inside her, reeling it back inside himself like fishing line until her skin felt cool and damp from the absence of heat. The sensation of pulling, combined with his slowing thrusts, caused another series of mini climaxes that left her breathless and boneless, unable to move or think.

When he finally released her legs and collapsed onto her, her face was damp from tears of pleasure and sheer exhaustion. After a moment, as their hearts slowed together, he pulled out of her and rolled to the side, drawing her against him until she was resting on his broad chest. She wrapped her arms around his waist contentedly, her eyes still closed in the afterglow and wonderful sensation of floating.

"And that," he said a bit breathlessly, "is what the *woman* inside needed."

It took two tries before she could moisten her mouth and work her jaws enough to get words out. "No shit! But I gotta tell you—the tiger is pretty happy about it, too."

Chapter Eleven

"I WANT ANSWERS!" Sargon's fingers dug into Zuberi's dark throat, causing him to cough and gasp and roll his eyes as he fought for breath. "Explain to me why I should not turn you over to Dr. Portes as her next experiment!"

Nasil spoke in his place, taking a moment to lap in the delicious scent of the lion's fear. It was probable that Zuberi would be unable to answer any questions for some time after Sargon was finished with him. "The details are sketchy, my lord. But it appears that the tiger and the councilman became aware that the men Zuberi sent were tracking them. It is probably my fault for not considering the moon's effect on heightening their senses. The kinsman of Zuberi is no great loss, but Juma's death is upsetting."

Sargon abruptly dropped Zuberi to the cave floor in a heap, where he gagged and wheezed through his nearly collapsed windpipe. "Yes, it is. It's unfortunate that we will lose that source of information in the hyena camp. But the more pressing concern is Kareem's capture. We cannot allow his loyalty to us to be discovered. He is known by too many on the council and in Wolven. Any one of them might be sent to eliminate him before the human authorities can try and sentence him for the animal deaths, and then our plan will be undone."

Nasil bent his head in deference to his master. "What would you have me do? Who shall I contact to take care of this?"

He could feel Sargon's eyes burning on him, but held his ground. "I think this is a job best handled by *you*, Nasil. Eliminate Kareem with a single bite before anyone can discover him."

For the first time in a very long while, Nasil raised his eyes to his master's in shock. "I? . . . *Uhm*, my lord, do you feel that *wise*? How can I explain the source of the poison or my presence? Technology is far superior to what it was the last time I killed by bite. If I were to be found out—"

Sargon turned his back. He paced a few steps with staccato movements, and it revealed a surprising frustration to Nasil. Then he turned with pursed lips. "I've considered that and dismissed it. I am not a fool, Nasil. I know the resources that coroners have available today. But this duty is too important to trust to just anyone. Fortunately, the German police will not allow the body to be removed or examined by anyone but their own until after an autopsy, and we have already eliminated all the Wolven agents who speak German. We will have captured the cat, filled and drained her, and then disappeared before that happens."

"But . . . but, my lord—"

Nasil didn't dare dart out his tongue to learn what his master was feeling, but kept his eyes on Sargon, even though he knew that level of attention was a danger.

Sargon let out a slow breath and then flicked his tongue rapidly to catch the air around him. "You can easily explain away your absence, and even if you're found out, they have no way to find us. We will be leaving soon enough, so your discovery as a spy isn't nearly as critical as Kareem's death." He stepped the few feet back and stared coldly at Nasil for a long moment. "However, I am concerned that perhaps your loyalty to me isn't as strong as it once was. You've never before questioned an assignment. Murder is nothing new to you, and you have always been my first and best weapon. Why do you resist this small whim of mine?"

Nasil fought to suppress the flash of fear that cut through him like a knife. Fortunately, the air was still thick with the panic of the lion. When Sargon flicked his tongue a second time, he appeared slightly mollified by the fact that Nasil's scent hadn't changed.

Just to be safe, Nasil dropped to his knees and prostrated in submission, muddying the knees and forearms of the ski pants he wore to keep his body warm. Fortunately, the clothing underneath would remain unstained. "I would not fail you in any assignment you chose to bestow on me, my lord Sargon. But if our sleeper agents do not succeed in capturing the tiger, then we will continue to need the information I have for so long provided about the actions of the council. Also, there is the chance—however small—that the girl is not a true power well. If she dies, then our future opportunities will be limited if I am outed or killed."

He felt a flash of power, and then the thick, golden body of his master's animal form rose above him.

"You raissse valid pointsss, and ssstate your case eloquently, Nasssil. It isss as you sssay—and yet I remain conccccerned. Go forth and eliminate Kareem and then return to my ssside for further inssstructionsss. Awaken the sssleepers to perform the duty they were assigned. Do not reveal yoursssself if you can avoid it, but I will expect your absssolute loyalty if your identity is uncovered. Now go!"

Nasil closed his eyes and felt a sinking feeling in his stomach that only years of intense training kept from his scent. Further discussion was useless. He feared that Sargon's judgment was growing unstable as plan after plan failed. He stood and looked up into the cold, golden eyes of the king cobra towering over him by nearly fifteen feet. Sargon's head was bent just a bit to keep from brushing the cave ceiling far above, and his forked tongue flicked in and out of his mouth angrily.

His master's hood was fully extended, and he opened his mouth to reveal fangs dripping with venom. Nasil didn't flinch or turn his devoted gaze, even when the poison splattered on the rocks next to his feet. Sargon's anger was the stuff of nightmares. Nasil hoped never to be on the receiving end. "Your will be done, my lord."

"Yesss, it will be." The cobra turned like lightning and slithered over to where Zuberi still cowered against the wall. "And now, my inept lion—let us sssee how quickly you can *run*." With a flash of power, he forced Zuberi into his animal form. With an immediate leap sideways, as though expecting an attack, the lion avoided a spray of thick, yellowish venom and raced into the darkness. Sargon started to slither in chase, but then stopped before he reached the edge of the torchlight.

"Before you leave, Nasil, please ask Rachel to prepare herself for my bedchamber. I believe I will be feeling quite *amorous* after this chase."

Nasil didn't even want to think about that image. He'd seen Sargon's version of sex in the past. There had been little left of the woman to take away and dispose of. But the spider seemed a match for him, in more ways than one. Perhaps part of her attraction was that the spiders preyed on their kind. An edge of true danger to his life was something that Sargon had never experienced, as powerful as he had become over the centuries.

Nasil took a deep breath as his master began his chase

of the lion and cautiously stepped to the entrance to the side chamber where their prisoners were held. The thrashing of the shifters against their chains didn't bother him, but the sickly sweet scent of Dr. Portes set his nerves on edge. He stepped into the room, where dozens of battery-operated lanterns brightened the room.

"Dr. Portes? May I speak to you?"

The tiny Guatemalan woman turned from her task of feeding the two men in the cages. They glared at him as he entered, but the spider's power prevented them from speaking. While he didn't believe it wise to keep the tiger and lion healthy and at full strength, the good doctor had convinced Sargon it was vital to the experiments.

"Of course, Nasil. How may I assist you?" The sing-song, echoing trill in her voice that made her sound like a chorus of cicadas made him shudder every time he heard it. He was certain that she used it only with him, because she knew it bothered him. Her smile was malicious.

"Sargon requests the pleasure of your company in his chamber. He will join you after his hunt." Nasil struggled to keep the distaste from his voice and scent. She had too willing of an ear in his master, and he had no question about where the doubts about his loyalty had originated.

It was as though she heard his thoughts. "You've grown soft and contented in your assumed life, Nasil. You've become a danger to our mission. But Sargon will only see your treachery if you're given enough rope."

Nasil nodded his head. "I should have guessed that you were the one who suggested it. Why do you hate me so? We both serve the same master."

She walked toward him, in human form as she did when a spider, with rapid, clipped steps. "Because you're his favorite, but I *intend* to be soon. I cannot kill you without incurring his wrath, so I will simply make certain that you're put in a position to fail."

Nasil's eyes narrowed. "Better than you have tried. You have no concept of my full potential, *spider*."

Her coal-black eyes moved around in the sockets as she focused on him at short range and smiled again. "And you have no concept of *mine*. Thank you for the message. You should hurry to your assignment, Nasil. You wouldn't want to *disappoint* Sargon, now would you?"

He didn't respond. He simply turned on his heel and departed as quickly as he could, determined to prove his loyalty by bringing a quick but painful death to the prisoner inside the German jail. He heard frantic whispers of desperate running in the distance before the cave swallowed the sounds. As he wound his way up to the hidden, secondary exit, he considered his position and that of Zuberi. While chasing the lion was a favorite game of his master's—one that the tall black man considered a challenge—he had never been forced into a chase while injured.

But perhaps, just perhaps, the point was to *catch* him today. Only time would tell. But how long would it be before he was the one racing through the darkness with a devil at his heels?

Chapter Twelve

"TAHIRA?"

Bruce's voice made her look up from the book in her lap. He was sweating profusely and splatters of mud covered his face and gloves. His natural scent of roasted hazelnuts was more intense with the sweat.

"Are you okay in here? It should just be a few more minutes until we've got a path cleared."

"I guess it's pretty icy out there, huh? I can hear the spinning tires from here."

He shrugged and walked farther into the room to stand near the fire. He pulled off the leather gloves and wiped his forehead, then held his palms near the roaring flames. "It's not so much icy as sloppy. It's melted just enough to turn the snow into soup. But it's so blasted deep that we push piles with the bumper, and then the wheels slip off the road and we have to dig out. Man, do I wish that Charles had a plow here."

"Is Larry doing okay out there? I could go out and help."

Bruce shook his head. "Nah, he's driving the SUV with the heater blasting, so he's fine, but my fingers were getting numb, so they sent me in here to warm up for a minute. But with Antoine and Matty both shoveling, it shouldn't be much longer."

Tahira threaded the ribbon between the pages she was

reading and closed the book. She tapped her nails on the cover as she thought of what to say. "You know, I don't know *what* to think about that, so maybe you can give me some advice. I'm not very good at accepting charity. I know I don't have any money or even a passport, but I don't like feeling . . . well, *indebted* to Antoine. I mean, yeah, we—" She broke off with a blush, not sure if anyone knew what happened upstairs. "But . . . is this normal for him? He said that I could buy anything I wanted and he'd put it on his credit card. So is he just, like, massively generous and does that for you guys, too? I mean, I'm flattered that he would be willing to buy me some things that fit. Heck, he didn't even have to let me use his sister's stuff up to now. I don't want to insult him, but—"

If Bruce knew about them having sex, he didn't give any sign. He just sighed and started to sit down on the chair next to hers, but then remembered the mud and perched on the edge of the low table in front of her. He waggled his head and she couldn't sort out any particular emotion from the jumble rising from him. "Well, yes and no. He can be quite generous, but he isn't all that often. He pays us all a good wage, but it's not like he *showers* us with cash. Larry and I still had to get a loan for our new condo. But," he amended, "he did cosign for us when we couldn't qualify, so that was nice. Not many bosses would do that."

Tahira raised her brows a bit. "He doesn't pay you enough to qualify for a loan? *That* doesn't inspire much confidence."

"No, no. It's not like that at all. It's just that Larry and I have been sending a bunch of money to his aunt, who was really sick—the one here in Stuttgart—and some of our personal bills went overdue. Well, actually, a lot of our bills did, and our credit sucked. I was really embarrassed to tell Antoine, but he was super. He didn't even ask what happened. He just offered to cosign so we wouldn't lose the place we had put under contract."

"Oh," she said quietly. "Well, that's different. But I'm trying to figure out whether to consider this a loan with the clothes and all. Should I offer to pay him back, or would that be insulting?"

Bruce nodded without hesitation. "Definitely insulting. When he *does* give a gift, he expects it to be taken freely. If it was a loan, you'd already know. Trust me. He doesn't mince words. All that cat in him, I guess. He's very up front, so you can usually take him at face value. Unless, of course, he's lying through his teeth, which he also does very well, because of the council stuff. It's all confidential and I know some of the issues are really delicate, so he lies about it if pressed. Still, money isn't all that important to him, so I can't imagine that it would be worth the trouble. Nah, he'd just tell you."

"You're certain? Have you been with Antoine long? I remember he said Larry had been with the show for a dozen years, but you don't seem that old."

Bruce laughed and the bright scent of oranges blended with the hazelnut. "Well, I'm older than I look—I'm over thirty, and Larry's nearly forty. I've been with the show since I was a teenager. I grew up in Reno, and when Antoine first started to tour there, I begged my way into a job shlepping meat for the cats. Hey, what kid doesn't want to grow up and join the circus?"

Tahira couldn't help herself from chuckling. "Well, me, for one. The whole 'girl turns into tiger' thing was a bit of a shock, because my folks didn't tell Rabi or me about our background until Rabi turned fourteen. Nobody knew if we would turn, but he started to show some symptoms at my tenth birthday party, and they decided we should know it was a possibility. So, are you like Matty, where you come from a shifting family but didn't turn?"

He pursed his lips and shook his head, leaning down a bit to rest his forearms on his knees. "Nope. Not me. I was just an ordinary human who got the shock of his life one day."

When her jaw dropped and she felt herself rear back in surprise, he continued. "Long story, but I'll make it short. I was just out of high school when they started to advertise the show. I decided that I would show up at the stage door every single day, begging anyone I spotted for a job. I was sort of weird as a teenager. I had posters of tigers and lions plastered all over my bedroom walls, and kept a python as a pet. It was Margo's husband, Dale, who finally took pity on me. He's one of the handlers at Antoine's estate, where they keep the animals until showtime. Of course, I had never actually met Antoine, since he didn't normally arrive until just before showtime, and I wasn't *supposed* to ever be the same room as the cats, because—well, because they're wild animals. But one day I accidentally walked past a back room in the auditorium on my way home when Antoine was training the cats. He trains them in animal form, and I thought it was really cool that this huge cougar was doing tricks without anyone around, and the other tigers were joining in. So I slipped inside and stayed in the shadows to watch. I figured if the cats decided I was lunch, I could just dive out the door and then lock them in."

Tahira nodded as she realized where the story was going. "He changed back while you were watching, didn't he?"

"Man! Did he ever! Max, that's Simon's father, was the dominant tiger, and he and Babette got into it. The cougar tried to jump in between them to stop the fight, but they were determined to tear each other up. Of course, I didn't know that it was a mating thing at the time. They looked out for blood. I was ready to run and find Dale when I heard someone swearing in French. I turned back, and then the cougar just . . . well, *poofed*, and there was this naked blond guy in the ring with these ferocious tigers, snarling and roaring and tearing at each other.

"Before I could yell at the guy to get the hell out of there, the tigers froze in mid-bite and raised up into the air. He used his magic to pull them apart while I watched, and then he scolded them. Max actually *floated* into his cage and the door slammed shut. I just stood there frozen, until I heard a strangled sound behind me and Dale grabbed me by the arm. Naturally, Dale knew all about the Sazi, but he didn't know what to do about me finding out, so he planted me in the men's bathroom and locked the door until he had a chance to talk to Antoine."

"Well at least they didn't kill you. The Hayalet would have."

"You should have seen me trying to climb the walls when Antoine walked into the room after I'd been sitting there for an hour or so, because I thought that was *exactly* what was going to happen. I was totally freaked out! If there had been a window, I would have been so out of there before he showed up. But—" and he smiled a bit at the memory, "he acted like this regular guy, not some sort of weird creature from the *Twilight Zone*. He was dressed in faded jeans and sneakers and a T-shirt with a smart-ass saying, almost the same shit as I was wearing. I figured out later that the clothes were intentional to make me comfortable, but it was pretty cool at the time—this big star treating me like a pal. He plopped down on the floor next to the door, tossed me a beer, and asked me to sit down and tell him exactly what I saw."

"And the rest is history?" she asked. "Is that where you met Larry?"

Bruce nodded and smiled a bit, staring past her out the window. "Yeah. Antoine takes in 'strays,' as Margo calls them. Larry was one, and so was Matty—family members who get kicked out of a Sazi house for being human or weak, or even too aggressive. Even someone new in the area looking for a job can find one with the show. The Sazi are really close-knit. They hand out jobs without question if the person is family, regardless of the species, usually for a short time until the person gets in touch with their animal side or gets their head on straight."

"It was strange—I didn't even think about Larry as a potential partner for a couple of years after we'd been working together. I had a suspicion I was gay, but had never acted on it with anyone. Larry and I were just buds, going out for beers and hanging out watching sports on TV every weekend. But when he told me he was gay, too, I realized why I was spending so much time with him. I already thought it was cool that he was a snake, and I realized that I didn't want him to leave when the time came for him to go home to his family."

But," he said, slapping his palms down on his legs and standing up, "on that note, I'd better get my butt back outside and relieve him. Cold weather exhausts him pretty quick, and even with the heater going, he'll want to lie down and rest for a while."

"Hey," Tahira said, glancing down at the book still in her lap, and sliding her finger down the bookmark to open it again, "for what it's worth, thanks for answering my stupid questions. I guess I'll go ahead and take the clothes he's offering." She shrugged. "I really do need them, and if he says it's a loan, that'll be okay. But I'll presume it's a gift unless he says otherwise."

Bruce pulled his gloves back on and raised the hood on his coat, pulling the cords tight around his face. "No problem. What I've found works best is to treat Antoine like any other person. I will warn you; he can be moody, and he has a quick temper. But you're a cat, too, so you probably know what that's like. He's got a terrific sense of humor, though, and is really sharp. Plus," he said with a wink, "I think he might just like you, if you know what I mean. It's just a suspicion, of course—"

She blushed again, to the roots of her hair, and hoped it wouldn't show too horribly. "Yeah, I think I have the same suspicion. I sort of like him, too."

He nodded strongly. "Good. He doesn't let himself relax very often, and hasn't had a girlfriend in, like, *forever*. I'm hoping that offering to take you shopping is just a way to spend a little time with you, get to know you better. He really is pretty cool, and you seem like you'd suit him. But even if nothing happens, I do know that he'll move heaven and earth to find your brother. He's just that sort of guy." He turned and walked out the door before she could respond to that.

Tahira sighed and looked down at the book again.

It was one of the ones Giselle said had references to a power well. She was determined to learn as much about this *thing* inside her as possible. But the passages in the leather-bound volume were vague and steeped in talk of demons and witches. The pages were so thin she could see through them, and the faded type was hard to read. She found her place once more and tried to pull some sort of understanding from the writings of a priest during the Spanish Inquisition.

I had believed it the chief business of this august group to save from depravity the minds and hearts of man, and I was likewise humbled by the devout prayers of the accused, filled with blessings for our Creator. Might this be a spiritual gift that few possess, as he claimed? Should it be for thee or me to judge this poor, unfortunate, miserable wretch based on the claims of a few, or instead, should the spiritual truth be based on his actions, manners, and dispositions? We imparted the duty to learn the truth to the Lord High Inquisitioner, and find that the accused is damned by his own actions. His touch contains the power to steal the very soul from the weak, and to make weak the powerful. Through debauchery and lechery, or through torture and pain, rather than devotion and prayer, were the powers begun. Sensual delights corrupted those who survived, leaving them to pine away in heart-rending beggary. It leaves no doubt as to the source of this witchery over goodly men and women, and the testimony of the villagers who claimed to witness the accused take the form of a demon familiar can no longer be in doubt. The accused was sentenced to death, and may mercy be shown upon his soul when he reaches the kingdom of Heaven.

Tahira read it over and over, trying to put it in terms she could grasp, and couldn't help but notice the resemblance to her own situation. She pulled power in times of stress and during intimate moments. What would it be like to have been discovered during the Inquisition? How many of the hanged Salem "witches" were actually shifters like her? She sat back in her chair and stared at the words, then flipped to the next marker. The very modern, yellow, sticky-tape flags seemed out of place on the old pages, but she was thankful for the guide.

"Catching up on some light reading?" She jumped when a thick, liquid baritone sounded next to her head. She looked up to see the snake councilman, resting his forearms on her chair back and looking down at her with an amused expression. She should have seen the door open, should have smelled him coming in. But perhaps it was as Antoine said. He was just that stealthy.

"Something like that." Her words were clipped. The scent of him still made her neck hairs stand on end, but she couldn't seem to pull her gaze away from his dark eyes. She couldn't tell where the pupils began or ended, and the fact that he didn't ever seem to blink was unnerving.

He clucked his tongue at her tone, sending a burst of spicy disapproval to blend with the creosote scent. He was breathing just a touch rapidly, as though he had been exerting himself. "We seem to have gotten off on the wrong foot, Ms. Kuric. Admittedly, Antoine and I have a long-standing rivalry, but that certainly doesn't need to include you."

"You're sweating," she said curiously. "I didn't know snakes could do that. Have you been out shoveling with the others?"

His expression changed just slightly and he smiled, softening his whole face. The citrus still smelled spicy, like potpourri on a railroad tie. "Hardly. Snow is best eliminated by sunshine in my opinion, as nature intended. I see no need to travel until the roads are clear. No, I went out for a long run. I find it relieves . . . *aggression* during the moon cycle and keeps me more able to bear the cold."

She furrowed her brows and closed the book. "But I

thought snakes got too cold outside to stay there for long."

"You're apparently interacting with the wrong snakes. I'm perfectly comfortable in the cold. I don't enjoy snow, as some do, but it's excellent to run in, like beach sand. One *can* find pleasure in new experiences if one takes the time to explore the . . . *sensations*."

His voice lowered to a husky whisper that made her shiver and stand up quickly, nearly flinging the rare book into the fireplace. A strange, tickling scent found her nose, but she couldn't identify the emotion. She reached out to bat the book to the side before the fire touched the brittle pages, but Ahmad was faster. He grabbed the book out of the air while she was still moving, and dusted off the cover lightly. "Charles would never forgive me if I frightened you into destroying one of his rare books." He looked at her for a long moment. "I *do* frighten you, don't I?"

She stepped away as quickly as she could while still appearing nonchalant. Her heart was beating too fast, and she had no doubt he could scent her fear. She started scanning the titles of the volumes in the farthest bookcase, hoping he would get the hint that she wanted to get back to her reading. "A bit, I suppose. But snakes and cats are natural enemies."

He stepped up behind her, until the lines of their bodies were touching. She panicked, but there was nowhere to go. She'd placed herself in a corner. Reaching past her, Ahmad slowly returned the book to the empty slot on the shelf. She felt frozen in place as electric heat prickled her skin, even beneath the clothing. He took another book from the shelf and held it in front of her chest. She took it and started to walk away, but found that she couldn't move. Every muscle was suddenly frozen in place.

He slid his arm around her waist and pulled her tight

against him. She couldn't stop him, couldn't move, much like the guards on the ceiling last night. It was a terrifying feeling, and she suddenly felt sorry for them—and nearly as angry with Antoine as Ahmad.

"Very true. But we're also humans, with minds of our own. There's nothing saying we *have* to be enemies." His voice lowered to a soft whisper in her ear, and she felt his tongue rapidly flick against her neck. "You're a very exciting woman, Tahira. I saw your injuries last night, but also smelled the blood of your attackers on your lips as you passed by me. I would be very interested in getting to know you better. You're afraid of me now, but you needn't be. I can be quite charming if given the opportunity, and we snakes are very . . . *flexible*."

She still had her voice, but it sounded thready and slightly panicked in comparison to his now slow and measured words against her ear. "Please let me go. Your power stings my skin. It hurts."

He chuckled—a low, threatening sound that sent a chill up her spine. "Does it? Many women have found the sensation . . . *intoxicating*, even addictive."

"I don't. I know . . . I know I'm not powerful enough to fight your magic, Councilman, but I hope that you'll be honorable and release me."

Ahmad laughed lightly, but the scent wasn't quite citrus this time. Again, it was that strange scent she couldn't place. "Ah, yes. Appealing to my *honor*—the last resort of women everywhere." He did remove his arm, for which she was grateful, but didn't release her from his magical hold. Walking around her as though she were part of the furniture, he turned his back and scanned the titles. He selected several volumes from three shelves. "I believe that these books will give you the answers you seek, Tahira. I do hope that you will begin to call me Ahmad in appreciation for shortening your search."

"I will if you release me and leave me to my reading."

"Indeed?" He stared at her again, and the scent of—could it be *lust*?—was becoming unmistakable. What in the world had she gotten herself into?

"Hmm . . ." Ahmad tapped his finger on his chin and then sighed. "No, I don't believe that trade is acceptable. I believe for what you ask, my price is a bit higher. But don't worry," he said as he slipped his hand around her neck and pulled her closer. His brow furrowed as his fingers skimmed her skin. He stared at her for a moment, and then seemed to change his mind about something. "*Interesting* . . . Yes, I think we might both find this quite enjoyable."

Before she could even draw a breath to reply, his lips closed over hers in a slow kiss that burned through her entire body. Hotter than Antoine's golden flame, his tongue seemed to seep stinging poison into her mouth as his jaw moved, nearly bringing tears to her eyes. She hated that her body was reacting to the stolen kiss as much as it was. The power inside her pulled on his energy, turning the backs of her eyelids a fiery red and causing a warm sensation in her belly. The well opened and tried to fill her with his sparkling power, just as it had with Antoine's. She could hear his heart beating faster as power flowed away from him, and it seemed to excite him even more.

"*Let her go, Ahmad!*" Antoine's voice behind her was livid, a deep rumbling bass that rolled like thunder. His scent matched the furious tone. "Release her this instant or I will tear out your heart with my bare hands."

Ahmad pulled away from the kiss slowly with a smile. He released his hold on her so suddenly that she dropped to her knees and couldn't breathe for a moment. He walked toward Antoine and the red thread of power moved with him, connecting her to him as though she was a fish caught on a hook—or perhaps *he* was the one caught, in a net. He turned around and looked at her with equal parts amazement and concern. "Hmm. Curiouser and curiouser. A *fin* might be the least of my worries."

With what looked like intense effort, he broke the bond, pulling some of his power away from her through her very pores, leaving her cold and shaking on the floor. But it wasn't all gone. There was still enough of his fiery energy flowing through her veins to make her feel insides feel flushed despite the chill on her skin. She got to her feet slowly, turning her head to see what was going to happen with them.

Antoine was only barely holding himself back from attacking Ahmad. His stance was solid, and his muscles were bunched up as though to pounce. "How *dare* you violate a guest in this house! I have every right to claim damages on her behalf!"

Ahmad's voice was cold, a steel dagger that sliced through the air. His anger was a living, breathing thing that surprised her. "Hardly a *violation*. It was a fair trade for something I agreed to do. If you claim damages, I'll do the same. You also violated invited guests in this house—my guards. This is supposed to be neutral territory, and we are expected to act with restraint. If you are exempt from that rule, then so am I. I did no harm, and I believe that both Tahira and I learned something important just now." He turned to her and stared at her. "Don't you feel you learned something that you might not have otherwise discovered?"

She realized what he meant. While he had no right to kiss her, she learned more about her powers in those few moments than in the last five book passages she'd read. "I don't . . . I mean . . . yes. I suppose I did."

Antoine's hands were clenched into fists, his knuckles white and trembling from anger. His chest had puffed out from making his back ramrod straight. "The only place you and your lackeys are ever *invited* is to leave. No more games, Ahmad. We finish this now."

Ahmad's laugh was a triumphant release of dark glee and joy. He shook his arms lightly like a gunfighter before a fast draw. "Oh, yes. Please do attack me. You need only make the first move."

Tahira could feel power ramp up in both of them. It pulsed against her hard enough to make her cry out in agony, causing them both turn sharply. "Stop it! Both of you just *stop it*!"

She stalked across the room, put a hand on each chest and pushed them backward. She could see her skin reddening, blistering just from their nearness. They both noticed and pulled most of the stinging power back inside themselves.

Tahira turned her fury on Antoine first, pointing a finger at his face. "Look, I appreciate you coming in and making Ahmad release me. But it's not your battle to fight. This is as much my fault as his."

Antoine looked startled and she could smell Ahmad's laughter before he even chuckled. "I could have left the room when he walked in. I didn't. I could have bitten his arm when he touched me, and I didn't do that either. So, I'm to blame for being stupid and thinking I could handle the situation."

Then she turned to Ahmad, still keeping the finger pointed. "And as for you—*lie to me*. Right here, right now."

Both of the men cocked their heads, and their confusion was a burst of scent that made her sneeze. "I mean it," she said, shaking her head and pushing air from her nose until she could breathe again. "Say something that's an obvious lie. I need to see what you smell like when you do, while Antoine is here to confirm it. I've never dealt with snakes before now, so I don't have anything to go by."

Antoine crossed his arms over his chest with no small amount of satisfaction, waiting for a reply. He seemed startled when Ahmad smiled.

"Of course. I'd be happy to." Ahmad tapped a finger on his thigh with pursed lips for a moment and then chuckled when he turned to her. "My greatest wish is that I could spend my afternoon watching football on television with my dear friend, Antoine."

The resulting scent was a blend of spice and mold that made her think of curried take-out left too long at the back of a refrigerator. She looked at Antoine. "Is that his normal scent when he lies?"

Antoine nodded. "That's the common scent when any snake lies. But I don't understand why you asked."

"I needed to see if he could do what you do and pull your scent inside. I wanted to know if he was lying to me."

The sudden reactions in both men to her statement were startling. Ahmad's face darkened and he hissed viciously while taking a step toward Antoine, who seemed massively uncomfortable. He looked at anything and everything except Ahmad, and she could see his Adam's apple move as he swallowed nervously.

"He *can't*." Ahmad's words were spit with ferocity, and Antoine's face dropped into studious blankness.

"He can't *what*?" she asked in confusion.

"He *can't* pull his scent inside, and neither can I." He held out an upward palm to Antoine. "I want that bottle in my hand this instant! It's getting poured down the nearest sink. It's forbidden to all of us, and you know it."

Antoine's reply was calm but cold. "At meetings. That was the final vote, and I have abided by it."

Tahira shook her head and held up her hands. "What the hell are you talking about? I'm missing something important here."

Ahmad flicked his eyes toward her. "You spoke of honor earlier. Well, the *most honorable* representative for the cats has been deceiving you, along with the rest of us. Our police force has access to a product that can be applied to the skin to prevent other shifters from knowing their emotions. It's only to be used when the agents are undercover or in danger, and is *forbidden* for council members to use. But apparently Councilman Monier doesn't feel he is subject to that rule, and has managed to find a supply of it—probably through his sister, who is head of the police."

Tahira closed her dropped jaw and tried to think of what to say in reply. It felt like the world had dropped out from under her feet. All she could think of was to turn to Antoine and ask, "Is that true?"

Antoine's eyes flashed as he replied to her, but she could tell the anger was directed at Ahmad. "I have been formally challenged for my council seat and am trapped in the same house with the challenger *and* with the fight official, which is Ahmad, until one of us can leave. It would put me at a distinct disadvantage to have my anger, frustration and . . . *pain* regarding the charges broadcast to every Sazi in this house. I would allow you the same courtesy, Ahmad, under similar circumstances."

Tahira crossed her arms over her chest and glared at him. His face softened at her annoyance, and he stared into her eyes in near panic. "I have never *intentionally* used the cologne in your presence. You have been fully aware of my emotions when we've been in each other's company, save for the few moments after the challenge, in the basement, when I was trying to come to terms with what Giselle accused me of."

She thought back and realized he was right. At every time other than that spent in the basement, she could remember his scent, filled with musk, cinnamon, and grass. She nodded. "Fine. But Ahmad is right. The 'stuff' you used needs to disappear. And you two need to knock off fighting over me." She nodded again at Antoine's surprised expression. "Yeah, that's what I said. I'm a big girl. I've been hit on before, and that's what Ahmad was doing. He wasn't lying about it."

She rolled her eyes and let out a little nervous chuckle. "Admittedly, it was a new and different *kind* of being hit on, like a spider trapping a fly in its web. But he wasn't threatening me or violating me." She waggled her head, amending, "Well, okay, he was *sort of* violating me, 'cause it was a little scary. But he's going to stop it now, isn't he?" She asked the question directly to Ahmad.

He shuddered briefly. "I would appreciate it if you wouldn't compare it to a *spiderweb*. That's not an image I care to consider. I merely wanted to show you that there are choices available to you, Tahira. Perhaps I overreacted to discovering healing teeth marks on your neck, but I'm not accustomed to Antoine beating me to *anything* I want. It annoyed me."

A growl rose in her throat. "But it's my choice and my decision. At this point, I'm not sure what the hell I want—except some clothes that fit." She pulled at the neck of her shirt, which was too tight in the shoulders, and the bra was digging in under her arm. "That much I do know. I think we all need a few minutes to cool off, and the books will still be here when I get back."

Antoine likewise flinched involuntarily. "I don't often agree with Ahmad, but spiders are something I'd rather not bring into the conversation, either." Then his voice softened and his scent was almost painfully embarrassed. "Would you prefer that Margo or Giselle drive you into town instead? The offer to pay for the clothing still stands, and Margo is a signatory on the charge account. I fully understand if you would rather I not accompany you today."

She sighed and dropped her arms to her side. "I don't know what the big deal about spiders is, but whatever. And no, I'm not *that* mad at you. You didn't do anything worse than what Ahmad did. But, you *do* owe me a lunch for it." She turned her gaze to Ahmad. "And so do you. But let's make it clear—not dinner, not *breakfast*. Just a plain ordinary lunch where I don't have to cook or pay for the food."

The two looked at each other with narrowed eyes, but nodded. "Fair enough." Antoine held out his hand. "If it's not already out of gas from our little conversation, the SUV is warm and the driveway's clear to the road. Shall we go?"

TAHIRA PLACED HER hand in his and they walked past Ahmad. Antoine helped her on with a too-large jacket, but at least it would keep her warm until they reached the shops.

It was . . . worrisome that Ahmad knew he'd been using the cologne. He might find some way to use it against him or even more risky—take the supply for his own purposes before they returned.

Worse still was Tahira's annoyance with him. It couldn't be helped. He couldn't tell her about the visions. The one earlier, while he was in the shower after their lovemaking, had been the worst he'd ever experienced. He'd actually felt pain as silver chains wrapped forcibly around him. He'd fallen to the floor of the shower as the metal scorched his skin. Phantom voices seemed to come from the walls themselves—the deep, hissing baritone of a Sazi he couldn't see, a rolling, trilling alto that was nearly unearthly. He'd been forced to watch Tahira scream in agony as something assaulted her. He could smell the cool, mossy scent of wet rocks, the bitter, acrid scent of a powerful snake, a sickly sweet smell that degraded into a scent so foul that it nearly burned his nose. They were all combined with pain and terror, and a hatred so vivid and powerful that it was frightening.

No, he couldn't tell her that he'd finally seen her brother, seen him bound and helpless and dying. She would learn of it soon enough, because she would be with him at the end. Unless he could find a way to prevent it.

Every time he looked at her face, the image of it twisted in agony overlaid her delicate features. It felt like what other Sazi spoke of when they talked of mating. But were-cats didn't mate for life. He'd been with dozens of other cats of all species during his life, and had never felt . . . well, terrified and, at the same time, *jealous* before.

Yes, she was free to be with whomever she wished, but . . . *Ahmad*? He wasn't the snake in Antoine's vision, but he was still a legitimate threat. What *was* it with him and cats? *I don't know if I can handle it another time.*

The cold air cleared his head as they walked toward the SUV. Tahira was still looking at him oddly, probably trying to gauge his emotions when she reached out to open the right-hand door, being only accustomed to American cars. He shook his head, still not trusting himself to speak, and led her to the other side instead.

Opening the door, he held it while she got inside and then shut it, being careful not to bump her leg with the armrest. The vehicle appeared to be a rental, and the thought occurred to him that perhaps they should take the van, since he didn't know the restrictions on who could drive it. He wasn't even sure who rented it. The thought of driving made him reach back abruptly and feel for his wallet. He couldn't remember whether he'd put it there before shoveling. Thankfully, it was firmly in his pocket. It would be embarrassing to get to town only to have to turn around again.

"I've never been in a British-made car before," she said as he slid behind the steering wheel. "It's really weird to see the controls on that side." There was a tentative smile in her voice, as she tried to put the tension behind them.

While it would be easy to gloss over and pretend it had never happened, it wasn't his way. He put his hands on the steering wheel, put the SUV into gear, and started down the beaten path to the road. He took a deep breath and let it out slow before speaking. "I apologize for what just happened. You shouldn't have found out about the cologne like that. And I shouldn't have reacted as I did when I walked in on you two."

Her voice was surprised and the shock of scent made him look at her. "No! I'm *thrilled* that you walked in when you did. I do think Ahmad's original intention was just to tease me—well, and probably to piss you off— but I could tell that he was getting too . . . well, *excited* when his power started to get sucked inside me. It really was scary to not be able to move." She shook her head and shuddered just a bit, and a light tang of fear drifted past the heater vents. "But you shouldn't ever do that to anyone again. I can't imagine what it must feel like to be glued on the ceiling, knowing you could fall down face first any time the person decided to let go."

He tilted his head and shrugged one shoulder in acknowledgment of her concern. "My only defense is that
it is the same method *Ahmad* uses to discipline his people, so it's nothing new to them. And it's a new skill that
I've just acquired. I've been able to hold animals and
lesser Sazi, but this is the first time I've been able to
hold alpha shifters against their will, so it was useful to
show it to Ahmad during the challenge period. He's the
person Giselle chose to determine my worth as leader of
the cats, and he will most likely advise her that I've increased my power."

She glanced out the window as a plow drove by. "I
was wondering about that. What did she accuse you of
doing? Or is that confidential?"

"Not to my knowledge. I'm sure Ahmad's men already know. He would absolutely relish telling them, so
I don't see why you can't." He flicked the turn signal as
they reached the road and looked both ways before entering the road. When he sped up and had shifted into
third, he reached into the pocket of his jacket and removed the envelope of photographs. He'd started to
carry them with him, to remind him of the consequences of action—and inaction.

She took the envelope he held out to her and opened
it, pulling out the damning photographs. Her head was
moving in small shakes, and her brow was furrowed as
she flipped through the thin stack. Her scent was the
thick, syrupy scent of curiosity, mingled with confusion.

"Okay, I'll bite," she finally said with a shrug. "What
am I looking at?"

"Those are were-lions—my mother's tribe. Apparently, due to some motions that I voted on during my
council term, they are now starving because their
land and water have been taken by other competing
predators on the savanna. I allowed it, even though I

wasn't aware of it. Giselle feels that it's enough reason to have a new councilman represent the cats." She opened her mouth to reply, but he held up his hand. "Before you ask, I can't simply step down from the post. I took the seat by conquest, and that's how it has to be taken from me, according to the rules of the Sazi."

Her voice held surprise and she turned a bit in her seat to look at him. "Well, actually I wasn't going to ask that, but—*wow*! The Hayalet allow the sahip to choose his replacement. Then again, nobody has ever *challenged* Grandfather while he's been head of the kabile, so maybe that's true of my people, too. It's never come up. No, what I was going to ask was whether I was the only person who could see the blindingly obvious in these pictures?"

He took his eyes from the road briefly to look at her face. She smelled confident of something, but he couldn't tell what. "Perhaps you are. The only thing that I see are a pride of starving lions, and I know that I've voted on things in the past that probably caused it."

"Well, yeah," she replied. "They *are* lions, and they might well be starving. But they're not *were-lions*. So how can they have anything to do with you? If this is her only proof, it's bogus. I think she and Ahmad are playing you."

Antoine had to close his dropped jaw. "What do you mean? Of *course* they're were-lions. Why would you think otherwise?"

She shook her head and put the photos back in the envelope. "When we get to town, I'll show you. You need to concentrate on driving, because I *hate* icy roads, especially going downhill. The roads might look wet, but the bridges are icy. I'll have to show you what I'm talking about since you apparently didn't notice. Telling you won't do any good. But hey, talk to me about Stuttgart until we get there. What's there to do in town?"

He was having a hard time concentrating on anything except her words. He thought back to the photos, but couldn't imagine what she might have seen in them. Still, if it were true—

She tapped on his shoulder and her scent was amused. "Hello? Earth to Antoine! Are you in there? We just passed the first turn, the one we took from the police station. Of course, I have no idea where we're going, so I'm not much help."

He started when he realized she was right. After checking his mirror, he skidded to a stop on the wet roadway and then moved to the now clear shoulder to back up.

She was staring out the window at the snow-covered hillside and the sun bouncing off the buildings down below in the valley. "This city is really pretty. I like all of the candles in the windows and decorations. I'll bet it's cool-looking at night." She heaved a small sigh. "But of course, that just reminded me it's nearly Christmas, which makes me think of Rabi, which reminds me of the family coming for me, and—damn it! There goes my good mood."

Antoine was annoyed with himself because he'd nearly forgotten about the primary reason for going into town, and had completely forgotten about *her* situation.

He put his arm on the seat back so he could see better as he backed the few hundred feet to the intersection. "I'm not certain if you were still asleep a few minutes before I stopped in your room earlier. Did you hear a conversation I had with Ahmad on the stairway?"

She shrugged. "No, I didn't hear anything outside. It was quiet as . . . well, as a *tomb* in that room. That's why I started to cry."

Turning the wheel slightly as he reached the intersection, he shifted into first gear and started toward the police station.

"Well, there's a strong possibility that the snake you attacked last night was captured by the police as I was taking you back to the house. The radio reported that a wounded man was seen staggering from the woods after a rifle shot, and he was taken into custody. I need to learn if he's Sazi, because our law enforcement will need to get involved if he is."

"What will *your* law enforcement do to him? Will the police give him up to you?"

Antoine laughed. "Hardly! Our law enforcement is closer to MI-5 or the CIA. If he's Sazi, and committed a felony, he'll never make it to trial. If he's innocent, then it's likely that Wolven will do basically what I did for you—either get him out by subterfuge, or find an attorney to negotiate for his release."

"Who decides if he's innocent? Do you have a trial?"

"No. The Wolven agents are granted the power to make that determination in the field. They're the best of our kind, each with a specialized skill. They're highly trained to learn the truth. But the agents are held accountable to the council for those decisions—with their *lives*, so they don't judge people lightly."

"But couldn't an agent use that stuff you did so nobody could tell if they were lying about screwing up?"

Antoine chuckled lightly and felt one corner of his mouth turn up as he eased into the police station parking lot. "Now that *you* know about it, how would you react to another shifter who didn't have any scent? The cologne doesn't pick and choose. It makes the person a blank slate."

She blinked several times and unbuckled her seat belt when they pulled into an open space. "Oh. I suppose I'd consider them pretty much guilty of *something*. Even if it wasn't a lie, there would be something the person didn't want me to know."

"Precisely. Now, I just need to determine where he's being held and get a whiff of him. You should stay here for now."

He saw her back straighten and her eyes narrow suspiciously. "Why? I'll know better than you if it's the guy in the woods. You didn't fight him. I want to know if it's the same man, because he probably knows where Rabi is."

Antoine shook his head. "It's not a matter of whether it's the *right* shifter. The question is *whether* he's a shifter, and I can learn that easily. Then I call Wolven and they'll handle it."

When she crossed her arms over her chest angrily and glared, his sigh sounded tired. "Tahira, what are you going to do if an officer stops you and you're questioned? Even innocent questions like your name or noticing that you're an American could start a chain reaction that we might not be able to fix. You don't have a passport or any other identification with you. What if your parents filed a missing person report and someone recognizes you from a description? Do you understand?"

He heard her heart speed up and her eyes widen as a pair of uniformed officers walked out the door and got in their vehicle. One of them was the man who had kicked her and stopped them on the road. His eyebrows raised when he saw Antoine. He tapped his partner on the arm and said something, but then they both looked down at the radio. Antoine could just make out a request for backup on the other side of town. The driver responded into the radio, and they drove away in a rush.

"Uhm, yeah. I sort of see what you mean. But what about you? Should you even be here?"

Antoine unbuckled his seat belt and shrugged. "It

would make sense for me to be curious about the radio report. Even though my cat was returned—or so they believe—logically, I would want some assurance that my tiger was now safe. They might not tell me anything, but I only need to get a whiff, and I can at least learn where the prisoners are kept so I can tell the agent who arrives."

Tahira started suddenly, and the blasting scent of fear nearly made him sneeze. "Uh-oh," she said. "I think I just screwed up your timing with too much blabbing. The officer who was with you when you found me is right behind you and coming this way."

"*Merde!* Just what we didn't need!" He took a deep breath and fought down his annoyance and surprise. With the first exhale, he had calmed. After two, he found his center—the one that made him a skilled negotiator and diplomat.

He turned his head and nodded to Reiner amiably as he approached, opening the window as the Kommissar neared the vehicle.

"Herr Monier," Reiner said with a nod and then, noticing Tahira in the other seat, nodded to her as well. "I'm actually pleased to see you. You've saved me the trouble of finding the paperwork to learn your phone number."

"Kommissar Reiner," Antoine replied, filling his voice with a light accent. "I heard a report on the radio that you caught the poachers. Our phones are still down at the house, so I thought I would drop by to talk to you on our way to the Christmas Market to shop for gifts."

"Indeed? You will be staying through Christmas?" He blinked in surprise and then his eyes settled back into professional distance. "Our shops are quite famous for their handcrafted gifts. I'm sure you will find what you're looking for. As for the prisoner, I don't know with any certainty that he might have been one of the poachers. I can say that another man in his company, who was dead at the scene, matched with fingerprints collected at the slaughterhouse we found."

Antoine lowered his brows at Reiner's phrasing. Perhaps it was just faulty English, but—"Excuse me, Kommissar. Did you say your prisoner *might have been* one of the poachers? Has he been released?"

Reiner averted his eyes with a frustrated sound that matched the hot metal scent. He mumbled a few swear words under his breath. "I shouldn't answer, Herr Monier, but it will be on the news soon enough, I suppose. The prisoner was found dead in his cell a few moments ago."

Chapter Thirteen

ANTOINE'S DROPPED JAW made the Kommissar continue. "The cause is unknown. The coroner is on the way over to collect him for an autopsy."

He ignored Tahira's hissing breath beside him and kept his cool. He showed a face filled with curiosity. "Were his injuries that severe? I'd heard you discovered him wounded."

Reiner shook his head. "As I say, the cause is unknown. But his wounds had been treated and he was conscious earlier this morning." He glanced up. "Ah. There is the coroner now." He put a finger to his cap and nodded. "You will excuse me, please?"

"Of course, Kommissar. Thank you for your time." He rolled up the window, and tapped his fingers on the steering wheel in frustration.

He watched the van back up to the curb, where the attendants opened the rear doors. An idea occurred to him as the sheet-covered gurney was rolled down the sidewalk past Reiner. "Stay here," he said sharply to Tahira and quickly slid out of the car.

I just need to get close enough for a moment before the doors shut.

He walked as fast as he dared, and reached Reiner as the body was being loaded in the van. The man was indeed a Sazi, the very snake he'd smelled in the woods by the unique scent of acacia fruit blended with the musty, bitter smell of a viper. However, he was surprised to smell a second were-snake, or at least its venom, which he didn't recognize. He had no doubt that an autopsy would reveal a bite had killed the man. But . . . *which* snake?

Kommissar Reiner's stern voice made him jump a bit. "There is something else you require, Herr Monier?"

Antoine blinked for a moment and then lied through his teeth. "Yes, there is, Kommissar. I wondered if perhaps I left a pair of sunglasses in your office when I was last here? They're quite expensive, and I can't seem to locate them."

"A pair of . . . sunglasses." Reiner's scent was both suspicious and disdainful. He narrowed his eyes for a moment, but Antoine didn't react. "No, I do not believe so, Herr Monier. As you can see, I have other duties to attend to. You will excuse me," he said with finality and took the place of one of the van attendants in securing the rear doors.

Antoine walked slowly back to where Tahira sat patiently, watching for any sign that he'd succeeded. He nodded absently and she breathed a sigh of relief.

He opened the door and got in behind the wheel once more. "It was him. But I also learned that another snake killed him. Perhaps Wolven already sent someone. Yet we only have one snake on the payroll and he's a python. I need to contact Fiona." Then he shook his head. "No, that won't help. She's still on leave. I know I can't reach the temporary chief, but—" A smile slowly spread his lips. "I do know who I *can* call."

"Can we maybe shop while you call? It's already after noon and I don't know when the shops close here. Is there a mall or something nearby?"

Antoine nodded. It was a good idea, and he still

wanted to see what Tahira had noticed in the photos. But the police station wasn't the place for that. He backed out of the space, and in a few minutes, they were driving to their next stop. "Actually, we're going to the Königstrasse, which is the pedestrian district where all of the shops are. We'll park in the lot next to the Hall of the Main Station, the local railroad office. There are any number of pavement cafés, so we can get a late lunch while I talk to someone at Wolven. I thought you might like to try Breuninger, which has good women's clothing, as well as a café. It's the largest department store in the city. It's where *Grand-mère* shops while here. Although," he amended, "Margo prefers H&M or Zara because the clothes are trendier. They're well-known European chains, like the Gap. You'll have to decide which you like."

She snorted lightly. "What I like and what the kabile will like are two different things. But if I'm going to get killed anyway, I might as well like how I look when my head goes onto the chopping block."

Antoine dipped his head and glanced at the seat. Good. The cell phone was still in the center console and fully charged. "It is your decision, *mon chat du feu*. Do you have any particular favorite food?" He felt a small fluttering in his stomach that was new and a bit disturbing. "I *believe* I owe you a lunch. Or would you like to try something local?"

She shrugged, but he could smell a touch of citrus, combined with the lighter scent of hope. "Surprise me. I can't eat Mexican, though. I'm allergic to peppers."

"Then we'll avoid paprika as well. Fortunately, Germans aren't terribly fond of spicy food. Although it's a shame that you won't be able to try the excellent *Fleisch Laberln* I found at one restaurant. But it's quite spicy. We should also drop by Merz and Benzing while we're here. It's a decorating store, and they put up a very beautiful display at this time of year. I see no reason why we can't combine business with pleasure."

"So you've been here before?"

Antoine laughed lightly. "Many times. My family's estate is just over the French border in Strasbourg, where the European Union parliament holds sessions. It's been interesting to watch Stuttgart grow from a quiet city to the thriving metropolis it now is. But they try very hard to keep their traditions despite the growth, such as the Christmas Market, and conducting political business in the New Palace."

Moments later, they were parked in a space at the massive complex of the Main Station. Tahira unbuckled her seat belt and was about to open the door when Antoine stopped her with a light hand on her shoulder. "If you would be so kind, could you show me what you noticed in the photos first?"

"Oh! That's right. I'm sorry." She opened the envelope on the floor next to her and extracted the photos, handing him the stack. "Now, tell me what you notice about those."

He sighed. "I've looked at them until I can't stand to anymore, Tahira. Please just tell me what you see."

"They're taken in *daylight*, Antoine. You can see the sun at the edge of the photos, and the shadows are too strong for it to be moonlight."

Flipping through them still didn't give him a clue about what she meant. "Yes, I'm well aware that they're daylight photos. That doesn't help."

She snorted and crossed her arms over her chest. "Well, it sure as hell *should* help! Margo told me when we were drinking wine in your bedroom that you're like Rabi—the first *sahip* lion or cougar born in a long time. True?"

"Yes, that's true. But I don't—" A startling realization came when she said the word "sahip." He was alphic, and so were both Giselle and Ahmad. Suddenly, it all made sense. His voice failed him for a moment, and then was hushed with an equal blending of shock and admiration. "I had to rescue you from the police station—"

She nodded. "Because it was *daylight*! Unless there's some lion pride out there that is full of *sahip* level cats, ones that can stay out until . . . jeez, the sun looks like it's almost *noon*, then these aren't were-lions."

A joyous sound bubbled up out of him like spring water bursting from the earth. He laughed long and hard, feeling relieved and grateful and so many other things. A couple walking nearby looked at him as though he was a crazy man, but he didn't care.

Antoine nearly pulled Tahira out of her seat into a fierce hug that she returned with equal enthusiasm. He held her for a long moment, resting his cheek on her hair, just feeling relaxed and at ease for the first time in—how long had it been? A year, or even more?

"I don't know how to thank you," he whispered against the smoky sweet smell of her hair. "Someone has been filling Giselle's head with lies, and we've grown so accustomed to our abilities as alphas that neither of us could see through them."

He felt her face move a bit from her smile, and she gave him an extra squeeze. The rolling alto of her voice vibrated his chest. "Well, at least I feel I've contributed *something* in exchange for the clothes."

Antoine pulled back just a bit so he could look into her wide, lovely eyes. "Oh, you've done much more than that, *mon amour*—" He brought one hand up under her chin and leaned forward into a slow, heartfelt kiss. The combination of scent and taste and emotion made his heart race and his head spin in a seduction he didn't want to end. He leaned into her. The feel of the bite marks on her neck and the bitter taste of Ahmad's venom made him instinctively deepen the kiss. He tangled his tongue with hers until both of their chests were heaving with passion.

How I wish we were anywhere but sitting in a public parking lot. But we are . . .

Ending the kiss slowly, deliciously, he whispered into her mouth. *"Merci, mon chat du feu, merci beaucoup. Je t'adore!"*

Tahira's sigh was slow and pleased. "Boy, I don't know what you said, but I just love the sound of it."

He smiled. "Allow me to translate, then." Looking into her eyes until he had captured her full attention, he repeated in English, "Thank you, my fire cat—thank you very much. I adore you."

The stunned expression on her face made him chuckle. "Oh . . . I've never had anyone say they *adore* me before." She began to look a bit uncomfortable, so he decided to lighten the moment.

"Well, I expect you'll hear it again before the day is done. I fear it will be much as the previous endearment. I seem to say things to you unconsciously. But shall we go shopping now? I think both of us could stand some fresh air to cool us down, and I do have a call to make."

"Yeah. Fresh air would be a good thing at this point. I'm feeling a little *warm* in here."

Hearing that pleased him more than it should have. While he was certain that somewhere inside he was competing for her hand with Ahmad, it wasn't the competition that made it important to him that she want him in return. Antoine turned his head so she wouldn't see him smile. She would know the scent, but *c'est la vie*.

Removing the keys from the ignition, he grabbed the

cell phone and got out of the car. Tahira also slid out without waiting for him to open the door, so he pointed the key chain and pressed the lock and alarm buttons.

ANTOINE PLACED HIS arm around her shoulders as they started down the sanded brick walkway toward the shops. Snow was piled high against the sides of buildings and around the decorated, barren trees rising from the path in neat rows. But the weather hadn't lowered the enthusiasm of shoppers. People of all sizes and nationalities wandered around, and she found herself humming along with "O Tannenbaum" when she heard it in the distance.

It felt warm and comfortable walking with him beside her. Without conscious thought, she reached around his waist and pulled herself closer. The familiarity startled her. Should it feel this natural? She'd never slept with a man whom she'd only known for—jeez! Had it only been *three days*?—in her entire life, and now there were two of them fighting over her. It was flattering as hell, but considering how difficult it had been to even get a guy to make eye contact with her lately, it was just—

She felt movement next to her and saw Antoine point to one of the stores ahead. A few stray blond hairs had escaped from the braid hanging down his back. It seemed almost white against the black and silver ski jacket he wore, and she felt a tingle as she remembered the sensation of it brushing against her body.

"There is Zara's, if you want to look inside. Take as long as you wish to try on things, and please don't feel that you have to limit your budget to only a few outfits. There's no telling how long we'll be in Germany. We'll need to arrange for paperwork if your family doesn't remember to bring it along."

"Okay, but . . . um, where will you be? Should I pick some things out and then come out and find you?"

His chuckle was filled with warmth. "I won't be far, *mon chat du feu*. But I won't get cell reception inside the store, especially with the mounds of snow and trees outside."

"Well, then, why don't we eat first? You can call and then we can shop together. That way, we won't lose each other. I *really* don't want to get separated."

He nodded in understanding that was tinged with admiration. "That is a valid point, for more than one reason. We should stay in sight of each other until I find out more about who visited the jail before we could arrive."

He turned her around and they backtracked a bit, taking in the sights and sounds of the season. She almost wished she had a camera, but who could she show photos to if she didn't find Rabi? She wouldn't want to remember this place if she never found him.

Antoine must have scented something of her mood, because he stopped, put a finger under her chin and lifted her eyes to meet his. "We *will* find him, Tahira. It's one of the things I'm calling about." Then he tightened his arm and brushed his lips against hers. The gentleness was almost more intoxicating than the desperate passion had been, and she found her legs a bit unsteady when they started to walk again.

"Café Wien has excellent food," he said, and steered her toward the entrance. "And it appears there's a window seat available. That should be perfect to make calls."

Tahira was surprised when Antoine spoke to the host in German. The language seemed to flow off his tongue as easily as French did. She could tell by their body language and facial expressions—if not from the words—

moments before Antoine was helping her off with her jacket and they sat down. She looked out onto a wide, gray flagstone patio. The shade trees edging the area, and the variety of planters and containers that were now piled with snow, were probably lovely in the summer.

"Should I order for you?" he asked when he noticed she was trying to decipher the menu. It was beautifully designed in blues and reds, and she could at least tell which meats were in which dishes by the photos on the page. But the only thing she recognized on the menu was chicken cordon bleu, and it wasn't her favorite.

"That would be nice," she replied with a frustrated sound. "Just something simple, like a beef sandwich. I know I should be hungry, but I'm too wound up right now."

"Sandwiches aren't common here, but I will ask." He gathered the menus and when the waiter arrived, started to order. He paused for a moment, "Would you like wine or beer with lunch? They have some excellent choices here. Or, perhaps some cappuccino or hot tea?"

She looked back to him from where she was watching people wander by with packages. "Hot tea would be great."

The waiter nodded and replied in thickly accented English. "The Chef Klaus has surprised us today with one of his excellent apple strudels. It's just from the oven—for later if you wish. I will ask about the sandwich."

Tahira saw Antoine smile at her sudden excitement. "Oh! That would be great. I just *love* apple strudel. My best friend's mom used to make it all the time."

"It's one of my favorites, as well. Hopefully we'll have room. They serve generous portions here." The waiter scribbled on his pad, collected the menus, and left. Antoine picked up the phone and pressed one of the buttons repeatedly, apparently scrolling for a saved number. When he reached it, he nodded almost unconsciously and moved his thumb over to dial.

While she didn't intend to eavesdrop the conversation, she couldn't help being curious when a man's voice answered the phone strangely. "Okay, yeah—it's here. I'm headed your way."

Antoine got an odd expression and then replied. "Hello? Raven?"

She heard a mumbled "*Shit!* Sorry, no. This is Raven's phone, though. Who's calling?"

His voice grew suspicious and professional. "This is Antoine Monier. Who are you, and why do you have Raven's phone? And where is Raven?"

"Oh! Hey, Antoine—this is Tony. Raven's at the airport, but he forgot his phone at the hotel, so I came back for it. I thought it was him calling, because he said he'd ring it so I could find it."

"*Merde!* Where is he going? I need to talk to him right away."

She heard static and then outdoor sounds from the phone. "Back to Boulder, I think. I didn't ask. What do you need? I'll tell him when I give him the phone."

He let out a frustrated breath. "I'm sorry, Tony. But it's company business. I need to talk to one of the agents personally. Is Ivan perhaps still there?"

Tahira heard a low chuckle that sounded slightly annoyed. "Nope. But guess what? I'm apparently one of guys to talk to now. I just got drafted—goddamn that Lucas, anyway."

Antoine's voice was filled with shock bordering on dread. He lowered his voice to a harsh whisper. "You? An agent? *Merde!* What could he have been thinking?"

"Thanks a lot, buddy," he snarled. "Fuck you very much. I *thought* you had a higher opinion of me. It's bad enough that I've got to play messenger boy and schlep around all these framed photos to give people, but now I've got to take insults? Don't think so. Buh-bye."

Tahira winced when she heard the connection break as he hung up. Antoine closed his fist around the phone and bared his teeth in the semblance of a smile that most certainly wasn't a smile. He closed his eyes for a moment and then took a deep, angry breath. She could hear the plastic of the phone protest as he squeezed it in a white-knuckled grip. His scent was as heated as his mood.

The waiter brought their drinks at that moment, and Antoine started to count under his breath as the young man turned over her cup with a nervous smile at him. She nodded her thanks and dipped the tea bag in the hot water repeatedly while trying to find a way to lighten the moment. "I guess he wasn't too happy to hear from you?"

He took a long draw from his glass of nearly black beer and wiped the foam from his lip. "Tony has a . . . *unique* personality that I'm still trying to figure out."

She shrugged and felt a little embarrassed, but decided to speak her mind, anyway. "Well, frankly, I probably would have reacted the same as him. What you said *was* pretty insulting."

He waggled his head and she smelled dusty embarrassment join the anger. "Perhaps. But he's a fox who has just been placed in charge of guarding the hen house. Putting him in a position of . . . *authority* makes me question several things, including the temporary chief's sanity. Still, he is a new *ruhsal*, as you call us, and we will have to work together. So, you're probably right that I should apologize."

He pressed the redial button and she could hear it ring once, then twice. There was finally a connection on the third ring, but it remained open air with nobody speaking.

"Tony? Are you there?" He sighed when there was no response. "I apologize. I shouldn't have said that."

The voice that came back over the line had lowered several notes and had taken on a thick Italian accent. "You're right. You shouldn't have. You ever even *think* shit like that again and I hear about it—councilman or no, I'll take you out. *Capisce?*"

"You said yourself that it wasn't a good idea." He tried to put a light spin on it, as though teasing.

Tahira heard Tony's voice become a bit mollified, but only a bit. "Yeah, I did. But not because I couldn't *do* the job; because I didn't *want* the job. So, let's start over while I'm driving. Where do you want your photo mailed?"

"Photo? What photo?"

There was a pause on the phone, and then sudden laughter that startled Antoine. "You don't even know? Right—you left before the fallout, didn't you? You weren't at the hotel when Lucas and I got back."

Antoine's expression changed, showing part admiration, part fear and part . . . something else. "I don't know if you'll believe me, Tony, but for what it's worth, thank you for your sacrifice. We're all very grateful that you . . . took care of that problem. Is that the picture? Of the . . . of *her?*"

"Oh, hell no! You wouldn't want a picture of *that!* There wasn't much left after using the whole arsenal to bring her down. But it is what made Lucas decide I was Wolven material. It's my one shining talent. The hindsight might help close some old cases, or so Raven believes, but if you need something dead, I'm your man. So, for what it's worth, you're welcome."

Tahira started at his words and her scent of surprise attracted Antoine's attention. He held the phone away from his ear for a moment and narrowed his eyes at her. "I'd forgotten about your hearing. I'll discuss this with you later, as it might well involve your people, too."

Tony was continuing to talk. She heard a car door slam over the line, and loud whooshing sounds that drowned out his voice for a moment. "—did you get that? That damn plane was right overhead."

"No, I didn't. Say it again."

"I said that the photos are of the snake representative, Ahmad al-Narmer, plastered against the ceiling of the hotel. Apparently, he pissed off Aspen and she fried one of his boys and then left him and his other goons stranded up there for the better part of a day. The best part was that she did it from the comfort of the airplane on her flight home. You've got a damned impressive sis there! But he was being such a bastard to everyone in our pack that Lucas thought he ought to be brought down a notch. Lucas presumed you'd want a framed blow-up, considering your . . . *history*."

Antoine's jaw dropped, and Tahira could feel cool air on her tongue as well. "Ahmad was . . . *held* by Josette—for hours, you say?"

"Josette is Aspen, like Amber used to be Yvette? Then yeah. I wasn't here for the actual event, mind you. I was busy in the warehouse. But Ivan and Raven both saw everything, so you might chat with them for the details." He chuckled darkly. "Boy, they were glowing brighter than New Year's Eve in Times Square trying to get down." His voice lowered to a threatening rumble that was edged with an animal growl. "Still, considering that Maria won't be able to walk for another week or two, I can't say I'm sorry. He deserved it."

Antoine's smile was as dark as the one she was hearing over the wire. "Oh, yes. Please *do* send a copy. Ask Nikoli for my home address in Reno. Are there by any chance digital copies that you could send to me by e-mail? I would *dearly love* to see one today."

Tahira couldn't decide what she thought about the

conversation. Was Ahmad truly as bad as Antoine claimed?

If there are enough people who want him humiliated to have multiple pictures framed—wow!

The waiter arrived with their plates. As requested, a thick sandwich made with roast beef, a tangy-scented white cheese, and crusty bread was placed in front of her. Antoine's plate held a breaded patty of a meat that smelled *wonderful*, covered in a thick, pungent gravy, along with mashed potatoes and broccoli. The scent made her stomach rumble and her mouth water enough that she was sorry she hadn't just let him order for them both. But her sandwich looked quite good, so she took a bite while he finished his conversation, thoroughly enjoying the taste of meat on her tongue. It didn't used to matter as much whether meat was on the menu, but since she'd joined the kabile, vegetables made her a bit nauseous.

As odd as the topic was, she was at least pleased that the conversation had relaxed Antoine a bit. "But on to business. I need you to tell Raven that I need him here in Germany. We've got an issue here in Stuttgart that requires—"

"*Antoine . . . ?* Antoine, it *is* you!" The jovial baritone from the doorway was thick with an accent that didn't sound quite like the German she'd been hearing. It made Tahira turn. Antoine did, as well, and looked at the heavy-set white-haired gentleman with confusion. "Tell Raven to call me back as soon as he cancels his flight. I've got to go."

He hung up without another word and tucked the phone into his pocket as the man brushed past the greeter and walked to their table with more speed than she would have given him credit for.

Antoine threw a haughty French accent over his

words, covering them like a royal, impenetrable cloak. "*Pardonne moi*, bot 'ave we met?"

The man laughed as though Antoine had told him a joke. "I have met you, but you have not met me! And yet we are the dearest of friends—pawns in a larger game." He continued to stare, smiling like a favorite uncle, waiting for a response.

A slow smile came to Antoine's face after a few moments. "Le? Leland Behr?" When the visitor nodded, he stood up and held out his hand. The accent disappeared as though it had never been. "How wonderful to finally meet you! Whatever are you doing in Stuttgart?"

"Melanie and I are here visiting the Christmas Market. But after seeing one of your troupe here earlier, I hoped I might run into you!"

The words stilled the smile on Antoine's face, but he quickly covered his surprise. "A member of my troupe was here earlier, you say? I'm surprised they didn't let me know they saw you. Do you know who it was?"

"No, no. I saw your show while it was in Austria last fall, but I couldn't get the man at the stage door to let me in to see you, and you had to leave before I could write a note to have taken back. But I remember seeing the man there because I asked him for a pen."

"Did you say hello to him today?"

He shook his head and pursed his lips. "No, no. He seemed to be in a hurry, and we were traveling in the opposite direction. But I am so very pleased you're here, because I brought your *bottle* with me! I received your e-mail and sent the wire. I planned to show it to a friend today, who is also very interested in rare cognacs, so he could keep an eye on the market for any other bottles that might surface."

Tahira watched Antoine's face flow from concerned to delighted and back again. Le continued to speak as he struggled with a reply.

"But you haven't introduced me to your lovely companion." He turned to Tahira and held out his hand. "Are you a member of the troupe as well?"

Tahira took his hand and shook it briefly. "No. I just met Antoine here in Stuttgart. My name is Tahira, and I'm from . . . near the border of Iran."

He raised his brows. "You speak English quite well. Your accent is very American."

She smiled sweetly. "I have some family there. It's been helpful to my English."

"Ahem, yes," Antoine said. "Tahira and I were also doing some shopping, but decided to stop for lunch first." He seemed to struggle with what to say next. "Would you like to join us?"

Le reared back a little and waved his hands in front of him. "No, no. Melanie is to meet me here in a few minutes, and your food will be cold. But perhaps we could meet later at the market? I'd like to get the bottle to you safely, for your trip home." He clapped Antoine on the shoulder. "Perhaps if you're in town long enough, we can play a game of chess that will take less than a month to complete!"

Antoine laughed heartily, and it was the confident sound of friendship and camaraderie. It was different from the burst of relief in the SUV, and far richer than the chuckles when he was teasing her. The sound made Tahira realize that she didn't really know much about him, and she suddenly wanted to know more about the human side of him.

"I'd like that. When the storm hit, we couldn't fly out, so I and a few members of the troupe are staying at a friend's house nearby. Are you here for more than the day?"

Le sighed heavily, and it moved his whole chest. "I'm afraid not. We have to go back today, but you should both stay in town long enough for the lighting of the display near Marketplatz at sunset. Perhaps that's where we could meet later?" He moved up the sleeve of his jacket to check a heavy gold wristwatch. "After all, it's nearly three now. Dark comes early this time of year."

Antoine likewise checked his watch, and Tahira twitched slightly in surprise when she saw the distinctive Rolex emblem. "You're quite right. We'll have to hurry just to finish eating and then get our shopping done." He glanced at Tahira with raised brows. "Would that be all right with you, Tahira? Would you mind staying in town for a few more hours to see the Christmas display?"

She had just opened her mouth to respond when a chirping from Antoine's pocket made her look to see if he was going to take the call first. When he ignored the demanding cricket sound and stared at her calmly, she replied, "Actually, I'd like to stay for a bit longer, but then I really do need to get back to my room." She saw Antoine smile just a bit at the wording and Le nodded.

"Fine. Then we'll meet in front of the tree near the turret in an hour? Melanie and I were just going to have coffee, so our time isn't critical. Do you know the tree I mean, Antoine?"

"Perfectly. I've been there many times. But let's make it an hour and a half, so Tahira has time to shop." He held out his hand again. "It's been wonderful to finally meet you, Le. I look forward to putting a face to Melanie's name as well."

Le bowed slightly. It was a gesture of warmth and respect. "I will leave you both to your excellent meal and look forward to delivering your prize to you." He turned and walked back to the host, spoke for a moment, and then was guided farther into the restaurant.

Antoine was already cutting into the breaded meat

patty when she looked back at him. "So, you play chess with him, but you've never met?"

He nodded while chewing and then answered after he'd swallowed. "On the internet and by e-mail. We met in a chat room and discovered we're fairly evenly matched on the board. Since we both travel a great deal, we each set up a board and then correspond with our moves. It passes the time when I'm touring."

"What do you do *besides* touring? You said you don't date much, so what do you do?"

It was another bite of food and a swallow of beer before he said, "Mostly, I read—science fiction, thrillers, mysteries—that sort of thing. But I'm also a *fanatic* for strategy board games, play pool and snooker with friends and, of course, run with the cats." His mouth twisted and a bit of amused scent rose into the air. "Most people think an entertainer spends all day lolling on yachts and attending parties every night. But for a show like mine, nearly every waking hour is spent caring for the cats, training for the next show, or series of shows, and doing mundane activities such as . . . well, reading contracts and approving poster art. Without my personal involvement, I'd have to pay someone to handle those functions. I did try that route early on, but I found the quality of the product . . . *lacking*. I do have high standards for both the cats and myself. I have several employees, but I do much of the work myself."

Tahira nodded and took another bite of her sandwich while staring wistfully at Antoine's plate. After a few moments, she nodded. "Dad says the same thing. Even though business is good, every month is a question of whether people will pay their invoices. I like pool, too, and mysteries. I've never played snooker, though. I've never even seen a table for it."

"They're quite a bit larger, and—" He stopped speaking when the cell phone rang a second time. He shook his head in frustration at the half-full plate of cooling food and pulled the phone from his pocket, checking the display before he answered.

"Raven?"

Tahira could hear the reply easily. Half of the people in the restaurant probably could as well. The man had a voice that carried enough to make Antoine click his thumb to lower the volume. "What's up, Antoine? Tony said I need to cancel my flight and head your way. Dad won't be happy if I'm not in Boulder for Christmas, you know. The pack party is a big deal."

"I'm well aware of that, *mon ami*. But the situation here is critical. I need you in Stuttgart before nightfall tomorrow."

The man named Raven sighed, and it was a sad sound. "Boy, that'll be a trick. I'll have to find a flight in the next few minutes to manage that. Talk to me. What's up? It had *better* be good."

Tahira saw Antoine glance around him and then shake his head almost imperceptibly. "Not here. I'm finishing a late lunch in a crowded restaurant. Stay in a good reception area, and I'll call you back in about thirty."

"Hell, it'll take me *that* long to change the tickets. You're just lucky I have my passport with me. I nearly left it in Boulder when I got called to the meeting in Chicago."

Antoine's reply was light and friendly. "You are always prepared, *mon ami*. It's why you're second to my sister."

"Yeah, yeah. Well, I suppose it'll give us a chance to compare our hair. Are you ready to admit defeat even though it's not the end of the year? Mine is nearly to my butt."

The smirking reply told Tahira quite a bit. "I haven't measured, but mine is close to that. Even in a braid it's to the top of my belt. But yes, I'm ready to finish this. The hair's becoming a nuisance."

"Not me, buddy. The ladies *love* my hair."

"True, but the daily ritual is annoying. I used to be able to shower in five minutes. Now it's an hour before I can put on a shirt and not soak the whole back of it— even with a blow dryer."

"Yeah, well, there is that. But I'm probably going to keep mine. Damn, it's my turn next. I have to go. Call me back in a half."

Tahira heard the connection break as Raven hung up. Antoine pressed the end button on the phone and looked at her pathetically. "Perhaps now I can finish my meal. Necessary as both of those conversations were, schnitzel isn't nearly as good when it's cold." He winked at her and a corner of his mouth turned up. "I notice you've been watching my plate quite hopefully. Would you like to try a bite?"

She barely managed to suppress a whimper and smiled. "Yes, please. It smells just *amazing*. I know it's horrible of me to ask—"

"You didn't. I offered." He cut a bite-sized piece from the untouched side and held out the fork. She reached to take it from his fingers, but he shook his head and pulled back the fork a little. "With your mouth, *mon amour*. It's a silly thing, but I enjoy it." He held out the schnitzel again.

She felt a blush rise to her face. It seemed so innocent, here in a public restaurant. But she knew he meant it to be intimate, and it felt that way. She leaned forward and opened her mouth. He smiled as he fed her the bite and watched her reaction as she chewed.

"Mmmm!" The complex flavor and combination of

textures was amazing. She looked down at her sandwich sadly. "Next time, I've *got* to get that!"

He picked up his plate and held it out to her with raised brows. "Why don't we simply trade? I have to admit your sandwich has been making my mouth water. The roast beef is prepared just the way I like it."

"But I've eaten half of mine, and most of yours is still there!"

"It's still worth it," he replied with a smile. "I want that sandwich."

Without another thought she happily turned her plate over to him and accepted the schnitzel. The entire meal was delicious, and she discovered she was a lot hungrier than she'd thought because she finished the plate at almost the same time that Antoine finished his sandwich. But he seemed equally happy with hers. As he drained the last of his beer, he checked his watch and let out a sigh.

"I'm afraid we're going to have to skip the strudel if you're going to get any shopping done. We only have about forty-five minutes now before we meet Le and Melanie."

They quickly put on their jackets and paid. Antoine steered her through the maze of shoppers until they were in front of a tall white and glass building with a small tasteful sign high above them.

"H&M has a good variety of fashions, so you should be able to find what you like here. If we have time, we can still visit the others on our way to Schlossplatz."

Tahira smiled as she stared through the windows. The clothing was the very latest style and there was an amazing variety. She just adored the layered tops in primary colors over jeans tucked into boots. Or maybe the plaid knee-length skirt with a shawl over a leather jacket. She felt like a kid in a candy shop and she grinned. "No, I think this store will be just fine."

After she had an armful of clothing and was heading for the dressing room, Antoine touched her arm. "I see a shop across the street that has something I need. I shouldn't be more than a minute, but stay in the store until I get back."

She nodded and found a clerk to open one of the rooms. After a few minutes of trying on outfits, boots and jackets, she heard a woman's voice through the door, and a knock.

"I'm sorry," she said through the door. "I don't speak German."

"Ah!" replied the woman in English that was lightly accented with something close to Spanish. "You are American. I am also from that part of the world. Do you need any assistance—different sizes, or perhaps accessories?"

"No, I think I've made my choices." Tahira was just slipping back into her original outfit and wincing at the number of hangers in the keep pile. Yes, Antoine had said to buy what she wanted, but it seemed silly to buy so many things when she didn't even have luggage here.

With a sigh, she pared down the stack to a ski jacket, a simple swing coat, four pairs of pants, a half dozen sweaters and shirts, underthings, and a pair each of boots and sneakers. On her way out the door with a sigh, she couldn't help but impulsively grab one more item from the stack—the plaid skirt that had originally caught her eye. The multicolored fabric would go with several of the sweaters, and the boots, so she didn't feel quite as guilty.

When she exited, she looked for a checkout counter. There were several, but nobody was in sight at any of them. Then she noticed a small Spanish woman with a name tag reading "Bertha" rearranging clothing on a rack, so she walked up to her.

"Hi! Can you help me?"

The woman turned dark, shining eyes to her and smiled brightly. Tahira noticed a strange, sickly sweet odor rising from her, but she couldn't place it. It was *nearly* a shifter smell, but it wasn't. But her voice had been the one through the door a few moments before. "Yes, of course," she said and took the stack of hangers from Tahira's hand. "Are you ready to purchase these?"

Tahira started to say yes, but then remembered that Antoine was paying. "I don't know. My companion is paying and he stepped out of the store. Should I wait?"

Bertha shrugged. "There are no other customers at this moment. I can at least scan and bag the items and then close the register until he returns. Then it is a simple matter to complete the purchase."

"That won't cause you problems if another customer wants to check out before he returns?" Tahira raised her brows in surprise. The stores in California would never do such a thing.

"No. That will not cause difficulties. I can merely ring up the items in another department."

After they got to the checkout, the woman removed the hangers from the clothing and started to sort them into piles. A few moments passed before she said, "Are you and your family in town for long? It is a lovely time of year to visit Germany."

Tahira shook her head and felt a stab of pain in her stomach. "No. I'm not here with my family. I'm out today with a friend."

Bertha cocked her head and looked at her quizzically. "Oh! I'm sorry. It was just that a young man was in earlier with two companions who looked very much like you. I thought perhaps he was a relative."

Tahira felt her heart race for a moment. "Can you

describe this man? Did you notice anything unusual about him?"

She took a deep breath and looked deep in thought, so all Tahira could do was drum her fingers impatiently on the counter and wait.

"Well, he was a bit taller than you, nicely built with thick hair down to his collar. His face was shaped like yours and his eyes were the same hazel, which is unusual in someone with darker skin, I thought."

Tahira found herself leaning forward, taking in every word with increasing excitement. "Did you notice anything strange about him . . . like his *ears*?"

Her eyes lit up. "Ah! Now that you say it, I remember! He looked like he had been in an accident, because the corner of his ear was missing. I noticed because he was wearing an earring—an emerald—and it seemed strange for someone to want to draw attention to that ear."

It was Rabi! Nearly jumping over the counter to grab the woman, Tahira barely kept from screaming the words. "Did you see which way they went? How long ago was he in here? He might be my brother. He was abducted and nobody has seen him in over a month!"

Bertha backed up a step at Tahira's frantic questions. "Only a few moments ago, while you were in the dressing room. I thought you were together." She frowned and tapped a coral-colored nail on the side of the cash register. "But there was something strange about how the young man spoke with his companions. He *did* seem very nervous." She glanced at her watch. "I am ready to go on break. If he was your brother, you might still have time to catch him. I would be happy to take you to where I overheard they were headed next. I *could* give you directions if you'd rather, but it's a difficult street to find unless you know the city very well."

Tahira glanced around frantically, looking for Antoine. *I promised I wouldn't leave, but this might be my only chance!*

She struggled with what to do. Her heart was racing and she ran to the front window, trying to find some sign that Antoine was returning. But then she took a deep breath. She was a big girl, an adult of the Hayalet. Once again, she was growing too reliant on Antoine. Bertha could tell him where she went. "Okay, I'll go with you. But you'll need to tell my companion where I went when you get back from break. His name is Antoine, and he's a tall French man with long blond hair." She rushed back to the counter and impulsively hugged the tiny woman. "Thank you so much for this, Bertha! You don't know what it means to me!"

She felt a pat on her back. The voice was soft and low, and had an odd lilt like a vibrato. "I only hope that I might have some small part in reuniting you with your brother. It's best that you should end up together in the same place."

Chapter Fourteen

WITH QUICK STEPS, Tahira followed Bertha to the front door. She realized when it opened that she'd forgotten her coat in the dressing room, and the sun was getting lower on the horizon. Yes, she could stand the cold, but why if it wasn't necessary? She called out the doorway to Bertha, who was standing with hands on hips, waiting. "I forgot my jacket, Bertha. Don't go anywhere. I'll be right back."

The woman narrowed her eyes a bit but nodded. Tahira raced back to the dressing room, grabbed the oversized coat, and pulled it on while turning. She ran right into Antoine, causing him to drop a large, white plastic bag. She heard a rattling inside the bag as it hit the floor.

"What's the rush, *mon chat du feu*? I said I would be right back."

"Oh, thank heavens, Antoine! I didn't want to leave without letting you know. But the clerk who was checking me out actually saw Rabi here in the store while I was trying on clothes! Obviously, she didn't know it was him, but she described him perfectly. She says she knows where he is going next and offered to take me to him."

Rather than looking delighted, he glanced around him suspiciously and smelled worried. "I saw nobody outside who looked like they might be waiting, Tahira."

Tahira moved past him and headed for the door. "But she promised to wait!" She looked out the window both ways in panic, but Antoine was right—the tiny Latina woman was nowhere to be seen.

Antoine stepped up behind her as she pressed her hands against the window, frantically looking about. The blending of scents from him was nearly enough to make her sneeze. He put his hands on her shoulders and pulled her back a bit as a customer pushed open the door blindly, nearly hitting her in the head.

"I'd very much like to talk to this woman. Might she perhaps have come back inside? If she has truly seen your brother, then she's worth finding."

"She did see him! She even described the earring he always wears in his ear. Rabi was forever leaving it places because the back would slip off when he combed his hair, so he glued the pieces together." Her eyes grew cold and she could smell her own anger. "Now I've lost him again. If something happens to him, I'll never forgive myself. I should have just left the damn coat!"

Antoine guided her to a pair of chairs in the shoe department and sat down next to her. "Did *you* smell him? Are you certain he was here?"

Her expression changed from angry to startled. "What do you mean?"

He took her hand in his and stared at her, trying to will her to listen. "You're fairly new at our lifestyle, so you might not understand that warm air holds scent better than cold air. The heater vents keep scents close to nose level, so if he's been in this room in the last thirty minutes I've been gone, you *should* be able to smell him. My nose is exceptional, so I was able to pick out your scent in the forest at dawn and know that you were still alive. I don't smell any other tigers in this room, but I do smell a strange, sickly sweet scent that concerns me. Do you smell your brother? Walk around if it will help."

Tahira's own suspicions were growing the more he talked. She *didn't* smell Rabi, but hadn't thought about it until Antoine said something. She stood up and walked around the room, letting the scents guide her. She could smell the lingering scent of Bertha, and her and Antoine. But when she started to concentrate on scents, she could pick out a small sick child who had tugged at the bottom of a jacket, and an elderly woman's fragrant scent of pine boughs and bayberries that covered the yarn on an elegant knitted scarf. There were multiple men and women who had touched here and there, but no tigers, no shifters, and most definitely, no Rabi.

"Why would she say that?" she asked, almost to herself. "How could she know—"

Antoine's words were hushed and worried. "She could know if she was one of his *captors*, Tahira. I don't doubt she was going to take you to him. I only question *why*."

She slammed her fists down on the edge of a rack of clothing in frustration. "And once again, I was nearly impulsive enough to get caught! Damn it! What is *wrong* with me?"

He pulled her into his arms and hugged her tight. "There's *nothing* wrong with you. You're not impulsive—you're a *warrior*, so you walk into danger willingly. But the moon is gone, and your skills and gifts in that form wouldn't help you if you got caught. Perhaps you *are* too trusting of strangers, but some days I wish I could return to that level of naiveté. I wish I hadn't been tricked often enough to become cynical."

*   *   *

ANTOINE NOTICED A change in her scent. It went from being sad and worried to angry. He pulled back from the hug and saw her staring at the checkout counter.

"You said you could smell something sweet. Do you think you could *track* that scent? She touched all of the clothes I was buying, along with the hangers."

He pursed his lips, thinking quickly. "It would be difficult considering all of the people outside, but it's certainly possible. Still, I think it would be wise to make certain that she didn't backtrack into the store hoping to follow us."

He looked up and spotted a tall blond woman wearing a name tag reading "Gretchen." "Was that woman over in the shoe department the one you saw?"

She looked over to where he was pointing. "No. Her name was Bertha. She was tiny and from somewhere in South America. I remember she mentioned that she was from the same part of the world as me. But she didn't talk like she was from the U.S. Her accent was Spanish-sounding, but not a sort I've heard before."

Antoine raised a hand and caught the eye of the woman in the shoe department. "Could you help us, please?" he called out in English.

She walked toward them, looking around her curiously and addressed them in stilted English. "*Guten tag!* Is there something with which you need help? There should be an attendant in this department, but I do not see her person."

"My friend was being assisted by the clerk named Bertha. Do you know where she is? She told my friend she was going on break but would return shortly. We would like to pay for our items now."

The clerk narrowed her eyes a bit, crossed her arms over her chest, and tapped a foot in annoyance. "Bertha was not scheduled for break in this moment. I will find her for you to check out. Thank you for this information. I will return in the quickest time."

When the clerk left, Antoine picked up some of the clothing, holding it close to his nose. He inhaled deeply, sorting out the primary scent of the woman from Tahira's own aroma, along with the dozen other people who had handled the fabric. He felt something open inside of him, some dark door in the back of his mind that was shrouded in fear and anger. A strange prickling sensation came over him and the store dimmed from view. Suddenly he was outside, moving forward through the cold, still air. A small, dark-skinned woman with shoulder-length black hair was running quickly across the plaza ahead of him. The scent that was left in her wake was the same as on the fabric. He pressed forward into the vision, keeping her in sight. With a startled look and scent, she stopped and looked around her carefully, staring at each face in the crowd as though they were enemies. She stared right into Antoine's eyes and he fixed her face in his mind. But she passed him by without notice.

The woman backed up a few steps and her glances were now nervous, and a light scent of fear began to flow to him. She turned and started to run again, slamming headlong into a couple carrying overflowing plastic bags that nearly touched the ground.

"Hey! Watch where you're going!" the man shouted in English as she quickly got to her feet again with the grace and speed of . . . a *shifter*. He reached forward and touched the woman. Pain erupted in his hand, and she began to slap at her shoulder as though it had been bitten by angry bees. He saw her mind in the brief moment before she started to run again. He knew without question who . . . and *what* she was. He just didn't know if he was alpha enough to do what would need to be done. But he did know that he would have to hurry if Rabi was going to survive. There would be no time to wait for Raven.

A car drove up beside the woman in a flurry of screeching tires. She got in the car, still watching behind her for the source of the pain in her shoulder, but there was nothing to see.

"Antoine! Are you all right? What's happening?" Tahira's frantic voice invaded the dream. He felt hands shaking him and his own thready breathing. The green Volvo with the woman faded into blackness, and the door slammed shut with a ferocity that echoed through his mind and left him feeling nauseous.

"I'm fine," he said, and his voice sounded distant, as though not completely connected to him.

When he could finally see the store again, Tahira's eyes were concerned and her scent was worried. He realized he was looking up at her. "Are you sure? You took a smell of the sweater and then had a seizure. You froze up and fell over, and you've been shaking and sweating for almost a minute."

As he came more into his own body again, he realized she was right. His skin felt damp and clammy, and there was a fine trembling in his fingers that hadn't been there a moment before. "I saw her," was all he could think of to say, but Tahira immediately seemed to understand.

"You did? Do you know if she's one of the captors? Do you know where they are?" She looked up and saw something. "C'mon, you have to get up. The clerk is coming back."

He peeked around the corner of the register island and saw the russet heels headed their way. As she passed behind a column, he used full Sazi speed to get to his feet. The movement made him a bit dizzy, but not so much that he couldn't appear composed.

Gretchen smiled professionally and dipped her head. She stepped behind the register and pressed a series of keys. "I will be assisting you to buy your items. I'm afraid that Bertha is unavailable at this moment."

Tahira exchanged a look with him that said volumes and then addressed the clerk. "She is? Well, I . . . I want to make sure . . . that is . . . uhm, will she get her commission on the sale?"

The woman nodded strongly. "That is not our way, but yes, I am the manager. I will be most certain she receives credit." She swiftly began scanning tags, carefully folding and bagging the clothes as she progressed. When the last item was being scanned, a loud noise caught their attention outside. An ambulance pulled up in front of the store. Gretchen looked up and moved from behind the register in a rush. "You will excuse me at this moment, yes? I will return in a very quick time."

Antoine listened in as Gretchen reached the glass door and held it open for the attendants. She spoke in low tones, frequently glancing their way, but neither he nor Tahira gave any hint that they were interested or listening.

As they passed by, still talking, he bent close to Tahira's ear. "One of the clerks passed out in the back room and they can't wake her." He continued to listen as they walked to the back of the store, carefully hurrying without attracting undue attention or causing a panic in the milling customers. "Her name is Bertha Kassner and . . . ah!"

He nodded his head with mingled anger and relief. "Our dark-haired friend was an impostor. One of the attendants just commented that they'll need help to lift her. Apparently the real Bertha is a large woman. We need to finish this quickly so I can call Raven back. He needs to make an additional stop before he comes here. But I don't think we'll have time to wait for him."

Less than five minutes later, Gretchen appeared from the back room, looking a little less composed than she had been, and smelling of worry and fear. "I am very sorry for the delay in my presence. Thank you for waiting." She hurriedly finished the transaction, and Antoine passed over his credit card. She was apparently quite stressed, because she didn't ask for his identification and nearly forgot to give him the slip to sign.

As soon as they were outside with their bags again, Tahira whispered to him. "What did you see about the woman? Do you know where she is?"

Antoine took a deep breath. "I believe that she's gone. If I'm correct and my vision was somehow in real time, a green Volvo picked her up near the Schlossplatz. But the air is still, and I can smell her scent. If you concentrate, you should be able to as well."

He watched Tahira close her eyes and flare her nostrils and then slowly turn her head from side to side. She sighed after a moment, and her scent was rife with frustration. "Nope. You've just got a better nose than me. But you really did see her? Why are you worried? What's going to happen?"

He transferred his bag to his other hand and put an arm around Tahira's shoulders. "It's a very long story, and not one for open air. Please trust me when I say that you'll have my wholehearted support in finding your brother and the others as soon as possible."

Her eyes narrowed suspiciously, and a hint of worry filled her scent. "You saw something, didn't you? You said 'others.'"

He kept his face blank, which frustrated her. "Let's go meet Le first, and I'll try to follow her scent. If she is truly gone, then we'll simply pick up the item and return to the house. That's a better place for this discussion."

She pointed a finger at him and smelled vaguely angry. "All right, but when we get there, I want answers."

"I'll tell you what I can. Is that fair?"

She was debating how to respond when he heard a chirping in his pocket. He flipped his wrist up and discovered that more than forty minutes had passed. A glance at the display didn't surprise him. He pressed the button to connect the call. "Sorry, Raven. I got tied up here. Do you have a flight lined up?"

"By the skin of my teeth." His voice sounded weary and frustrated. "I leave in a few hours, and I should make it there by nightfall tomorrow, if the connections happen on time."

Antoine hated to do it, but there was no choice. "Does one of the connections happen to be Washington?"

He heard fumbling fabric and papers for a moment. "Yeah, as a matter of fact, it is. The flight from O'Hare is to Washington and then I catch a puddle-jumper to New York for the flight to Berlin. Why?"

"I'll have to talk with Ahmad about this, and probably find at least one more council member to agree, but I might have someone meet you at the airport with a package to bring with you."

"Aw, hell, Antoine! That'll totally screw things up, and you know it! I only have about thirty minutes of layover for the international flight. I can't *afford* to wait for someone."

Should he tell Raven? What sort of panic could that start?

"Are you there? Give me a damned good reason why I should take a chance on missing the flight."

Antoine walked over to a tree and rested his hand on it. Sitting would be better, but at least he wouldn't fall over. The aftereffects of the strange vision were stronger than usual. He was feeling a bit light-headed, although it could have been the *subject* of the vision that was causing it. He lowered his voice and tucked his chin inside his jacket to further muffle his words. If it were anyone else but Raven, he'd simply tell them that he was a councilman, and to shut their mouth and *do* it. But their friendship, and Raven's position as second of Wolven, demanded some level of honesty.

"*If* the package is necessary, Raven, you'll want to wait for it. If a vision I just had is correct, another spider has been born in this generation, and it's in Stuttgart."

There was silence on the other end, punctuated by distant conversations and loudspeaker announcements of arriving flights. When Raven finally responded, the voice was stunned and slightly panicked. "*Holy shit.* When will you know if it's necessary? Should I call anyone?"

He shook his head, even though Raven wouldn't see it. "No, not yet. But I want to be prepared if we need it. Ahmad is here with me at Charles's house. He doesn't know yet, so I want to talk to him first. We can find a quorum by phone and decide what to do. What time do you arrive in Washington?"

"Let's see." Rustling paper interrupted the dead air again. "It looks like I arrive there at about 5:00 tonight. I won't have cell reception on the plane, but keep calling and leave me a message. Just yes or no will do, and I'll know how to proceed."

"I'm sorry to place this on you, *mon ami*. But if Ahmad and I aren't . . . *here* when you arrive, it's only fair you know why."

His reply was low and concerned, but he kept a note of teasing. "Well, if you aren't . . . *there*, I guess I win the bet, huh?"

Antoine chuckled, but it was filled with regret. "*Absolument*. That will be the least of my worries, *mon ami*. Please hurry, and *bonne chance*."

He hung up and took a deep breath before turning back to Tahira. When he did, the bags were sitting in a pile of slush and her arms were wrapped around her body tightly. With the sun setting behind her, she looked like a little girl who just learned there really were monsters in the closet. Her voice was hushed and serious, mirroring her scent. "I didn't like that conversation, Antoine. I don't understand what's going on, but it sounds like you don't expect us to *survive* until tomorrow afternoon."

He picked up his package and held out his hand, burying the dread deep down inside. "Come with me. Let's meet Le and enjoy the display for a few moments before we have to face what's to come."

Tahira shook her head and stayed frozen in place. The look in her eyes should be able to burn through skin and bone. "Not until I find out what's going on. Who was that woman and what's she want with me and Rabi?"

"Please, *mon chat du feu*—please trust me until we're alone and can talk. Nothing will happen in the next few minutes. I don't believe anything is *going* to happen to your brother until they have you, too, and I don't plan to give them the chance. Gather your things and let's finish the trip and get back to the house so we can talk to people. I'm just hoping there are still people to go back *to*."

When she still didn't move, he clucked his tongue in annoyance and walked over to her. He placed a hand on each shoulder and squeezed. "Tahira, you're better than this! None of what's happening should be a surprise. Your brother is a *sahip*, an alpha male in his prime. Surely you've already realized that whatever captured him is strong enough to hold him. But we now have the advantage, in that *we* know who has him. We'll know what to expect if they make another attempt on you before we're ready, and we are *warriors*, all of us. The Sazi and the Hayalet will take the battle to them, and even Ahmad, for all of his ego and puffing, is a powerful, skilled fighter. We are a force to fear."

She blinked repeatedly as she processed what he was saying and stared at him for a long moment. Then she nodded, and her scent grew confident and her eyes clear. "You're right. We have more information than we did, and there are several of us to stand against them. If you'll fight alongside me to save my brother, I'll find some way to repay you. I promise."

There was a sudden stabbing in his chest that shouldn't have been there—*wouldn't* be there for anyone else—and he hated knowing what could happen if his visions became reality. Whatever it took, no matter the cost, he would keep her safe from that fate. He gave her a brief nod and winked. "I'll hold you to that. Now, let's find Le and start the dance."

Chapter Fifteen

ANTOINE WAS AS good as his word. They had quickly walked to the plaza at Schlossplatz and, using his nose, instantly found Le and Melanie. They made the appropriate platitudes, collected a wooden box that he didn't even look in, and gazed at the lovely display for a moment. It felt so very surreal to see all the lights and conifer boughs and banners that spoke of peace and love, while they were on their way to plan a war.

Now, sitting in the SUV beside him as they sped along the winding, icy road, she tried to decide what she could possibly do to help Rabi, even if they found him. Antoine had been right—the moon was gone, and she couldn't change at will as an alpha could. She knew some martial arts, but what good would that do against something that frightened a powerful *sahip*?

"When we get there," Antoine said, startling her out of her musings, "I want you to stay in the library. There's only one entrance and no windows, so it's easily defensible. Keep Giselle or Larry with you while I talk to Ahmad. I don't want you alone at any time until this is done."

"Can you at least tell me what sort of shifter we're looking for? I've never smelled anything like her."

Antoine took a deep breath, and his fingers fidgeted on the steering wheel. He was controlling himself, but she could nearly taste his frantic heartbeat, and the steely determination in the car was overwhelming.

"Do you know the legends of your people? Have they ever spoke of an ancient being that preyed on our kind?"

"Well," she said, desperately trying to remember the fables that Grammy had told her and Rabi when they were children. "She said there were once great snakes that towered as high as the mountains. They battled with our people and they were defeated, never to return. I think there were also some legends about tigers disappearing with no trace, and one legendary warrior *sahip* who defeated the mysterious shifter that had killed our people with a web of deceit. But he was killed in the process, so whatever it was became sort of a bogeyman for children."

She saw him nod in the light from the dashboard. His jaw tightened as he clenched his teeth. "So, they had made it that far east. Very well. Tahira, what would you say if I told you that the woman you met was a were-spider, a being that lived on the essence of other shifters?"

She raised her eyebrows. "Uhm, I'd probably say you had some really good drugs."

"Well, it's true. Originally, nature created balance. Even we who were on top of the food chain, who preyed on humans and animals, could be preyed upon—like a mongoose that kills a cobra, or a praying mantis that feeds on a deadly black widow. Unfortunately, the spiders were too efficient, and the shifters were all dying. They made species after species extinct, including all of the humans in their territory. Because they could not grasp discretion in their choice of prey, it was decided they were too great a threat to exist. Two of our greatest warriors eliminated the were-spiders. Or, at least, they *thought* they eliminated them. But like the other shifters, they bred with humans, and now we are faced with those long dormant recessive genes coming to the surface. Once again, the were-spiders live, and every living being on earth is at risk if they can manage to breed a sufficient population."

"So this shifter is like a *real* spider? One that makes webs and can crawl up walls and stuff?"

Antoine flicked on his blinker and turned the wheel hard enough to send the rear end skidding to the side, nearly hitting a tree. He stomped on the gas once more and powered out of the slide onto the driveway, while Tahira clutched at the armrest and tried to get her heart to slow down.

When he spoke, his voice was cold enough to drip frost. "Yes, and 'stuff.' I've heard the webs are so strong that even the most powerful Sazi can't escape once trapped. There is also the venom to consider. As I understand the process, the spiders wrap their prey in webbing and then inject a venom that will liquify the organs and tissue of the person. Unfortunately, the person is still alive while it's happening. I try not to think about that too much."

Tahira felt her brow lower in confusion until her long eyelashes touched the hairs. The entire conversation seemed so surreal it felt like a joke. But she knew that Antoine wasn't kidding. His scent held no humor. "So why does she want *Rabi*, or me?"

"Since you smelled him still alive but afraid, from the scent on the lion's hand, my best guess is that the spider has learned your talent, and has discovered some way to use that power to breed. Or, perhaps it's a vendetta specifically against your people. You might be only the first to be captured. It's possible we'll never know for certain."

Tahira clenched her jaw as the back end of the SUV

fishtailed again when he made the final turn to where the porch light blazed. "But what about the prisoner killed? Didn't you say it was snake venom? Could it have been spider instead?"

"No. I'd stake my reputation that it was a snake. But that's not to say that the spider couldn't have injected the venom with a *needle*. I didn't examine the body, after all."

He unbuckled his seat belt and quickly reached behind the seat to remove the shopping bags. She got out of her side and waited to go in with him. He started to stalk through the snow, but then stopped and turned to her. "Tahira, you need to know that I've told you far more than I plan to tell any other person in the house, save Ahmad. I just . . . *couldn't* let you step into the unknown without some knowledge. But please, if nothing has happened, *please* don't reveal anything I've said. I won't be able to think, much less plan a strategy, if the entire house reeks of fear."

"But what about Giselle and Larry? Won't they know I'm afraid? I can't change that. The thought of Rabi, hanging like a fly in a web—I mean, I can even smell it *myself*!"

His look was haunted when he reached up to touch her face with the back of his hand. The bag of clothing bumped against her shoulder, but she didn't care. There was something in the look that made her legs turn rubbery and her body clench despite the terror that still raced through her.

"You can tell them there was another attempt, but you don't know who the woman was. That much is true. But my vision might have been of a different time, or a different woman from the one you saw. It's highly unlikely but possible that all spiders have a single scent. We know little about them. For now, spend your time researching the books that Ahmad found for you. Find out anything we might be able to use, or block, if you do happen to get captured."

"And what will you be doing?" she asked, as he lowered his hand to his side.

One deep breath was followed by another, and then by a shake of his head. A trick of the yellow lamp near the door made his pupils glow an amber that lit up his whole face. His indecision was nearly an emotion of its own, and she couldn't think past the scents for a moment. Perhaps it was because the moon was still nearly full, but his essence seemed to surround her, steal the breath from her lungs.

"If nothing has happened inside, I plan to speak privately with Ahmad and explain what I've seen. We don't like each other, but he does respect my seer abilities and might listen to a plea for action. After we've made a decision how to proceed, I plan to spend the rest of the night guarding you. If you'd rather not share my bed, then I'll sleep on the love seat, but we should stay in the same room. It's too risky not to guard you, because it's obvious they're getting desperate."

They had just turned to walk to the front door when it opened in a rush. Matty came racing out, flew off the icy stone sidewalk, and landed on his back in the snow. They ran over to him as quickly as they could, but he was already getting up and brushing snow off his pants.

"They're gone, Antoine! Something took them!"

Antoine started to mutter in French under his breath, and she didn't think they were endearing comments. "Who's missing, Matty, and who came for them?"

Tahira reached out her hand to help him pull his legs out of the deep pile of snow, and they followed him inside.

"Giselle, Bruce, and Larry are all gone. Bloody hell! It just happened so damned *fast*. I was sitting in front of the fire. Margo was helping Giselle get dinner ready, and Larry had just come upstairs with Bruce. We heard a pan drop and then a scream that was cut short. We all raced in there and saw a pair of lions pulling Giselle out the door. She was unconscious, and Margo was knocked out, too. Larry jumped on one of the lions and tried to pull her away, but a tiny, dark-skinned sheila picked him up like he was one of Babette's cubs and squashed him up against the wall by his neck."

Antoine had already dropped the bags near the staircase, and was moving from room to room, his nostrils flared. Power began to roil around him, making the air feel heavy. When he entered the kitchen, he went immediately to the spot where the struggle had taken place. Broken dishes and copper-bottomed pots were strewn across the floor and the scent of anger and fear hung in the room like a cloud. "*Merde!* Where was Ahmad during all this?"

"He and his men were in their room, so I figured they hadn't heard it happen. I ran to get him and he came flying down the stairs, but by the time we got back to the kitchen, they'd all left, and Bruce was gone, too. Ahmad and his men are outside now, tracking them. He was mad as a cut . . . well, *snake*. I grabbed my jacket and went out too, but the tracks just *stopped* when we got to the trees, so Ahmad told me to come back and tend to Margo and they'd go on. Margo was already waking up when I got back, so I gave her a quick look over. She didn't seem to be in any danger, so I put her upstairs in her room to rest."

Antoine's head moved from side to side, pulling in the various scents. He nodded, mostly to himself. But Tahira could already smell the tell-tale sweet, decaying odor that reminded her forcibly of the rancid bottom of a Dumpster. Bertha, or whatever her name was, had been here.

His voice was cold but calm. "It will be harder to track them if they're moving through the trees, but it can be—"

They all turned as the back door opened and Ahmad walked in with a snarl and a hiss that made Tahira shudder. "We lost them. They took to the treetops and then just seemed to vanish. Even their scent disappeared. We couldn't follow fast enough because the snow had drifted and my men soon tired." He turned to the pair of pale, shallow-breathing guards behind him and fixed them with an annoyed glare. "We will need to discuss a training ritual for you both that includes cold weather endurance and tracking. Your performance out there was dismal."

Watching their reactions was like watching molasses pour in the cold. It was startling to see the difference from their normal, nearly blurred movements. She could watch each blink of their eyes, like flowers slowly opening their petals.

Antoine's fists were clenched and he snarled lightly. "We should have come straight back without making that last stop. We might have been able to prevent this."

Ahmad raised his eyebrows and dropped his head. "You *knew* someone was going to attack us?"

Tahira shook her head and answered before he could speak. "No, we *didn't* know. But someone tried to grab me from one of the stores, and ran when Antoine came in."

"We stayed in town specifically to *avoid* them learning where we were staying," Antoine said angrily. "But apparently they already knew. Ahmad, we need to talk immediately. I've instructed Raven to fly here as fast as he can, but we must make plans."

He started to turn and walk through the doorway, expecting that Ahmad would follow as he commanded. Tahira touched him on the arm as he went past. "Library?"

He nodded once sharply. "We're *all* going to the library. It doesn't matter if people hear at this point. Ahmad and I will be able to protect you and the others," he said, and reached for her hand. "Ahmad, post your men in the great room near the fire. They can see the library doors from there, and they need to warm up before they're of any use to us."

"You're making many presumptions, Antoine. You do not command my men. I think that we need—"

Antoine's voice and scent were calm, and his golden eyes were unblinking as he stared at Ahmad. "I *think* you need to listen to what I have to say if you want to survive until morning. We have to put aside our differences. For once, Ahmad, be a councilman for *all* of the Sazi." He turned and pulled Tahira out the swinging door, throwing his final words over his shoulder. "But if you don't feel you can cooperate so that the people in our care survive, then at least have the dignity to leave this house so I can make plans without your interference."

The thick scents of anger and frustration from the exhausted cobra were followed by a searing rage of power that followed them out the door. Antoine ignored Ahmad's bellow for them to return this instant and, instead, guided Tahira and Matty to the library, after first carefully sniffing around the room and picking up one of the plastic shopping bags from the staircase.

He turned to the stocky Australian. "Matty, could you go downstairs and get Babette and the cubs, please? Bring them here to the library. We need to all stay in one place for the time being."

Tahira cocked her head a bit as Matty quickly went to his task. She started walking toward the leather-bound books still on the table where Ahmad had placed them. "Do you really think we need her to protect us?"

Antoine's voice and scent were still calm, which seemed strange to her. "No, she needs *me* to protect *her*.

I'm her Rex, so just as I plan to protect you, Matty, and Margo, I will protect my cats. I can't do that if we're all in different places."

She picked up the book on top of the stack and turned to stare at him. His features seemed chiseled in stone, and the play of light from the fireplace highlighted every angle. He slowly removed a box from the shopping bag and began taking off the outer wrapper. "Are you okay? You seem . . . *odd.*"

ANTOINE SMOOTHED HIS hand over the black box and shifted the lid back and forth until it pulled away from the bottom half. *Terrace* was, by far, his favorite strategy board game, and he needed to step away from the emotions that were clouding his judgment—from fear and anger that his friends and family had been taken to a self-righteous satisfaction that Giselle could no longer stab at him with her accusations. Memories of happy times, playing this very game with Larry as Giselle stitched on a quilt in the corner of their main trailer, fought with the scent of terror and pain that lingered in the kitchen.

He jumped when he felt Tahira's hand on his arm. "Antoine? Are you okay?"

He nodded, afraid to speak, afraid he might say things that should never reach air. He sat down, his back still to her, and started to open the individual packages of black and white dome-shaped pieces. As he was pulling the square, three-dimensional board from the box, he felt strong arms slip around his shoulders, and the scent of smoked cinnamon and sandalwood filled the air next to his neck.

She wouldn't remove her arms when he reached up to pull away, but instead tightened them, pressing her chest tightly against his back. Yes, she was no match for him in strength, and he could easily pull away. But it would probably hurt her. He took a frustrated breath. "If you're trying to distract me, Tahira, this isn't the time for it. I need to concentrate and we need to get some answers— *any* answers—from the books you should be reading."

Her voice was strong and solid, an anchor in the swirling tide of emotions. "*Yes*, you need to concentrate. But you can't do that if you're spending all your time beating yourself up about this. There's something deeper going on with you than just the danger from the spider, or just me. I really think you need to talk about it before you go out there to save the others and wind up getting killed because you think you *deserve* it."

Antoine unconsciously raised his hand and began to stroke her hair. He found himself leaning into the softness of her cheek against his jaw. He opened his mouth to repeat that he was fine, and to thank her for her concern, but it was not what came out. "Today in the store was the first time since I was five years old that a vision was in real time. I've fought for my whole life to keep the visions under control, burying them in the darkest depths of my mind so they didn't make me go mad like my sister—or my mother."

She brushed her hands over his chest and squeezed. It was a comforting gesture rather than a sexual one. "What happened when you were five that was so terrible that you *had* to bury them?"

"I watched my world end, and I couldn't shut my eyes or hide from it. The vision *made* me see, made me watch my mother drown my sisters and brothers in the bathtub. It made me see my twin, Fiona, screaming in fear while I deserted her to hide in the ductwork behind a furnace grate."

There was a long pause and he could feel her face

muscles working as she tried to grasp the image. "Antoine . . . you . . . you were a *child*. How could you be
expected to do anything else but try to survive? I can't
imagine how horrible that must have been. I . . . don't
know what to say."

A puff of breath that wasn't quite a chuckle moved
her arms on his chest. "There's nothing *to* say. Until
just days ago, I thought I knew the villains in my
world. My oldest sister, Josette, called the men who
came to kill my mother, and I hated her for it. I hated
Ahmad for his role in my mother's madness. I hated
the entire concept of a Sazi *law* that would murder a
woman in front of her children. And mostly, I *despise*
this thing that hides inside me that makes me watch
people in pain when I don't know when or where it
will happen, and there's nothing I can do to stop it.
Grand-mère, Bruce, your brother and . . . *you*. All a
seer can do is watch and pray and try not to think too
much about it."

Tahira shook her head in tiny little movements and
sighed. "The horse is riding you." When he turned his
head in confusion, she pulled back from him and
stepped around to the front of the chair. Crossing her
arms over her chest, she leaned against the edge of the
table and stared at him. "Look, I might not know much
about how to be a good tiger yet, but I've really got a
handle on psychoses after spending my whole life in
California. You're concentrating so much on one tree
that you can't see there's a whole forest around you. The
bad things that you've seen have made you skittish, like
getting thrown from a horse."

"It's not the same thi—"

She held up her hand and raised her eyebrows. "Yes.
It is the same. You get *visions*, Antoine! You're a *ruhsal*,

a seer, a psychic. No matter what you call it, do you have any concept of how *amazing* that is? The rest of us are plodding along in the world, whispering little prayers each time we turn a corner, while you have this amazing horse to ride that tells you what's around the bend."

He snorted in derision. "Yes, it's *quite* amazing to see people you care about being chained down and tortured, or drowned by their own mother's hand, while I can do *nothing*! Do you grasp that at all? If I know that a person is going to die a horrible, painful death—but only if they happen to take a trip they haven't even considered, or if they happen to be on a particular road *someday*—how can I tell them? I might as well say, 'Oh, but don't worry about it, and have a nice day!' You can't possibly understand what it's like."

Her face had gone serious, but her eyes were calm and her tone warm. "No, you're right. I don't know what it's like. But neither do *you*."

"*Pardonne moi?*"

Tahira scooted between the chair and table, and straddled his knees. She took his hands in hers and used every trick of her body to grab his attention. It did, and he couldn't understand why. "You've been bareback riding a wild horse your whole life, Antoine, and the horse is running away with you. I know the visions have been coming more and more often since I showed up. I can see it in your eyes—a haunted look where you can't bear to even glance at the person who was just in the vision. But people have figured out ways to control horses. There are bridles and saddles, and once the horse is forced to go where *you* want to go, it becomes a tool rather than a threat. That's something my grandmother told me about her gift. She said it was like being buffeted in a storm. Everything was too much, too fast to keep her footing. But when she started to enter the storm on her own terms, make the images *work* for her, make the storms come on her command—"

Antoine shook his head and pulled his hands free. "They can't be controlled, Tahira. That's the problem."

She smiled just a bit, and it was understanding and patient and kind. "If you've been fighting them since you were five, you've never *tried* . . . that is, until you decided to smell the sweater at the same time you wanted to track the woman. While it surprised you, you *did* take control of that vision. You watched and followed and even touched her. That was a *saddle*, Antoine. It's no different from my power well thingy. Granted, I don't understand it yet, but we did control it somewhat that once. It means it *can* be controlled. But before you can let yourself control it, you have to free the visions from the chains you have them held down with. They aren't meant to torment you. They're meant for you to *use*. If you know that a person is going to get chained down and tortured—and no, I'm not stupid; I know you mean me—then try to figure out the when and the where. Take control of it. Find that image again and examine it. Don't focus on the screams or the fear. Focus on the room. Where is it? What are the ways to escape or rescue them?"

He felt a strange realization prickling at his mind. He opened his mouth to speak, but she interrupted him.

"It's okay to want to plan a strategy to find them. I want to, too. But the visions are a *form* of strategy—another tool to use to find Giselle, my brother, and the others."

He reached out to touch her cheek, to say . . . *something*, when he heard slow, punctuated claps behind them and turned to see Ahmad, leaning against the doorjamb, taking in the scene with condescension. Matty was close behind, holding Babette's leash and carrying a squirming cub under each arm. He looked uncomfortable, and hurried past the other man to set the cubs on the floor in the corner. Then he sat down beside Babette and tried very hard to look invisible.

"*Bravo*," Ahmad said with sarcasm dripping from each word. "A very poignant and moving speech, Tahira. Unfortunately, your words fall on deaf ears. A dozen people have told Antoine the same thing, but he chooses to hide behind his wall of torment and play the martyr." He held up the back of his hand to his forehead. "O, woe is me! My childhood was dreadful and I might end up as mad as my sister. I simply *cannot* be expected to use my talent to save those in need, or be useful, or *lead*." The melodramatic words ended with the cold, hard weight of iron.

He glided across the room with a scornful chuckle and a scent that dripped hate, and then sat down in the easy chair by the far wall so he could watch everyone in the room. "I see I've lost the battle for your hand by default, Tahira. Pity. But I wonder if Antoine has let you in on his little secret yet." He smiled evilly at Antoine. "If I can't win, then perhaps you shouldn't either."

What is he talking about? What secret?

Tahira frowned and stood up so she could see them both. With her hair loose and wild around her shoulders, she did look like a warrior, and Antoine suddenly realized that he would do almost anything to prevent her death. "You aren't going to win any points with me by slamming Antoine."

Ahmad shrugged. "Whether the information is good or bad is up to you. I told you earlier that I was remiss in not giving Antoine enough credit for deception. I admit it never would have occurred to me to bed a captive to make her *want* to stay in prison." He noticed her confused expression and gave a look of false shock. But his scent was still a dark glee as thick and vile as tar. "Chains have always worked for me in the past, but I might have to rethink my strategy. Your method seems to have certain *advantages*."

Antoine lowered his head and felt small hairs rising on the back of his neck. "What are you talking about, Ahmad? Just say it and be done with it. I have nothing to hide."

All emotion dropped from the snake's face until it was a cold, unreadable mask. "You think not? Very well. Did you or did you not have direct orders to hold Tahira a prisoner in this house until further instructed, and deny her family entry if they arrived?"

"*What?!*" Tahira's voice was filled with such hurt and anger that he couldn't look at her immediately. But he could feel her eyes bearing down on him and her scent was a wall of emotion that pressed against him with the weight of the ocean. Instead, he kept his attention focused on Ahmad. The slow smile that came to his face unnerved the cobra.

He flicked his eyes toward Tahira, who was waiting for a response with pained disbelief on her face. "Ahmad is absolutely correct. Those were my orders."

She reached out fast and hard, but he caught her hand before she could complete a slap across his face. "I can't believe . . . I *trusted* you! You . . . *bastard*! If one of your precious people hadn't been captured, would you have—"

Antoine growled low in his chest and glared daggers at Ahmad's smug expression. "Tahira, I haven't lied to you. You can smell it. What I was *trying* to say is that I was *instructed* to hold you captive, and have been disobeying those orders—at great personal risk to myself, I might add." He loosened his grip on her hand and locked his gaze with her flashing eyes. "Please believe me when I say that I don't believe all orders are meant to be followed. Sometimes, you have to trust your *instincts*."

Tahira's back straightened and she got an odd expression on her face. The confusion in her scent was being replaced with something completely different. It was a combination of odors that made Ahmad hiss low. He couldn't help but smile.

Tahira had just opened her mouth to reply, when the doors burst open at that moment, and Ahmad's two guards came rushing in. One of them was still wearing his winter jacket and gloves.

Ahmad stood in a flash. "What has happened?"

The tall, thin guard whom Antoine knew as Hakeem sneered. "Nothing has happened . . . yet, *my lord*." With lightning speed, the other guard, Bahir, threw his arm toward Ahmad and the cobra immediately froze with a startled expression. He slumped to the floor with glazed eyes. While Antoine was watching a trio of darts that reeked of some horrid, bitter scent hit Ahmad's leg, Hakeem threw himself forward toward Antoine. He turned and moved, but looking at Ahmad had cost him precious seconds. A metallic rattle filled the air and then searing burns on his arms, neck, and chest tore a roar of pain from his throat as shiny chains were wrapped around his body and locked together with a padlock. Now he understood the reason for the gloves. The chains were silver and were burning his skin wherever it wasn't covered by clothing.

Bahir kicked Antoine in the face, causing pain to blossom in his mind and the rich copper scent of blood to fill the air. A nearly deafening cougar snarl was cut short when a second kick caught him in the stomach. As he wrestled against massive links as big around as his thumb, the pair raced to grab Tahira. But she didn't plan to be taken that easily. She jumped over the table with blinding speed and ran to the center of the room where there was more space to fight. Babette moved to her side protectively and roared loud and long.

Matty was also moving. He picked up the kylie and boomerang he'd carved, along with a spray can of some sort, and held them up threateningly. He might be human, but he had been raised with snakes. He knew their tricks.

With both Ahmad and Antoine out of the way, the two traitors felt no need to hurry, and apparently didn't have a high opinion of either Tahira or Matty. They did shy away from Babette, moving so that there was furniture between them and her. It gave Antoine an idea.

He stopped struggling against the chains and concentrated for a moment. It took agonizing seconds to ignore the skin that was crisping under the silver. He just had time to scream, "This is going to hurt, Tahira!" before he threw a blast of power that shot across the room and hit her in the chest. The effort left him heaving for breath and caused the chains to dig in deeper.

Luckily, Tahira remembered him saying the same thing in the van when the police were behind them and leapt backward behind Babette just before she dropped to the floor with a scream. Babette had seen people shifting form too many times to be startled by it, but Antoine reached outward again, felt for her mind, and pressed the impressions of *protect* and *fight* with images of her cubs, Tahira, and Matty. She flicked her emerald eyes to him, and then to the cubs, huddled together in the corner. She snarled once and then roared again. With a powerful leap, she vaulted the furniture and grabbed Hakeem by the arm while her extended claws raked down his chest with a thick, wet sound. The air was filled with his screaming.

Ahmad always surrounded himself with lesser alphas, but they could still shift form at will. Bahir changed to a snake in a burst. He opened his mouth with fangs extended, intending to inject deadly venom in Babette's neck, but a whooshing sound was followed by a hard crack and he was suddenly flailing on the floor.

It took Antoine a moment to recognize the chunk of wood that clattered to the floor in front of the fireplace. Matty had actually used his kylie to take down an opponent! Both Tahira and Matty pressed the small advantage as Hakeem continued wrestling with Babette. Tahira pounced on the snake and bit down again and again as he hissed and desperately tried to sink his fangs through her thick mane.

Matty yelled for Tahira to hold Bahir still, and she pulled backward and wedged the cobra's body between the couch and table. The snake hissed and spit a long string of venom, which Matty barely avoided, but while the mouth was open, he sprayed a long stream of product from the can. The cobra gagged and shuddered and began to twitch.

"Wasp spray, mate!" Matty said to Antoine as he quickly backed up. "My cousins hated the stuff when my mum doused them for biting me."

Antoine didn't have time to warn Matty before Hakeem broke free Babette's grasp with a wash of blood and flesh. He did have enough time to throw a shield of magic up so that when Hakeem hit Matty hard on the back of the head, Matty went down in a heap but would survive. Hakeem raced forward and picked Babette up from the floor and threw her against the bookshelves hard enough for the entire wall to shudder. Antoine protected her, too, by softening the blow with a cushion of energy. Books rained down on her and the cubs as she shook her head and tried to right herself. But Hakeem had grabbed another two darts from a pocket and was coming up behind Tahira. Antoine was quickly growing tired, but he had to warn her.

"He's got darts!" Antoine shouted, and she moved in a blur. He struggled harder and harder, ignoring the blinding pain and scent of charred flesh as the chains cut through his clothing and skin. He began to feel the metal stretch, and he let out a roar of frustration and anger.

But Hakeem was expecting Tahira to move as she did, and managed to sink both of the darts into her side as she passed by.

"Antoine!" she screamed as she hit the floor, and then she was limp.

Bahir slithered over to Antoine and extended his hood with glittering eyes. "I ssshould kill you now, but time is sssshort." Antoine glared at the snake but didn't move. He wouldn't show fear, even as Bahir sunk fangs into his thigh repeatedly. But as the snake turned into a man once more, he threw a blast of power that caught Babette in the chest and toppled her again.

As he had seen in his vision, Antoine could only watch helplessly as the two men dragged Tahira from the room. He didn't dare continue to force power into her to keep her in form while unconscious. It might start a power drain that he wouldn't be able to stop, and he needed every bit of energy he had. He could feel the men nearly drop her still form as she changed back to human, but then they continued on into the snowy night.

While they were still connected, Antoine steeled his will and flung the door open in his mind. He tried to connect a vision with her, but all he could see was a wall of rock and a creek that flowed out of it. Then a horrible pressure on his chest made him nearly pass out before air filled his lungs again. Torches burned in a massive cave that felt somehow familiar, but he'd never seen it before. There were whispers in the darkness that grew into chants in a language he'd never heard before. A guard walking by suddenly became alert and peered into the shadows where he stood, searching for a threat. Then he shuddered and backed away, moving closer to the orange circle of light on the floor.

"Hang on, mate!" Matty's voice seemed to come from a great distance. But to his great surprise, he opened his eyes and found his friend holding a pair of bolt cutters to snap the chain, the vision didn't disappear. It became superimposed over the reality of the library. He could still smell the pungent trickle of fear and pain from the torchlit chamber, and see figures moving in shadows no matter where he turned his head.

Babette was lying against his side and nuzzling his cheek, chuffing nervously. As Matty unwound the long length of chain from his body, he winced at what he saw. Antoine couldn't disagree with the reaction. As the metal pulled away from him, the outer layer of skin, still black and smoking, went with it. The raw, bloody stripes that crisscrossed his body were painful, but he'd endured worse. He sat up to make it easier for his friend to remove the chain, and once his arms were free, he helped the process along.

It was disconcerting to have his brain try to process the scents from the dank, smoky cave in the warm, brightly lit room, but after some concentrating, he could determine which scents and sounds were from which location, if only by distance. But it was the least of his worries at the moment.

As soon as the last of the chains fell onto the floor, he was up and racing over to where Ahmad lay. Whatever the drugs were, they hadn't killed him, but he was having a hard time metabolizing them. Antoine pulled the darts from Ahmad's thigh. Ahmad's powerful muscles went from being still and cool to twitching wildly enough that Antoine had to hold his arm on the floor to keep him from hurting himself.

"Can you follow my finger?" he asked and slowly moved it from side to side past the dark eyes. "Do you have any idea what was in the darts?"

Ahmad tracked the finger adequately, but with his dark irises, it was difficult to tell if his pupils were dilated. He was able to move his jaw enough to hoarsely whisper the word "venom."

While it was no surprise, it was a worry. Without a healer, it would take Ahmad days to recover—*unless* . . .

He slowly rose to his feet, wincing as the burned tissue stretched and the cobra venom in his leg stung with force. But if he was lucky, Fiona had more than one specialty Wolven drug in her bag of tricks. He just had to find it upstairs.

But before he could get to the door, Matty was in front of him. "Whoa, whoa, mate! You're stark raving mad if you think I'm going to let you move around until those burns heal. Now you sit your arse right back down. You're in worse shape than either Ahmad or Babette, and in no condition to—"

He placed his hand on his friend's shoulder, seeing it through the image of rock and fire. The image of the cave was unmoving. Nobody was in sight and only the flickering torches and scent of fear and pain made him realize it was really happening in some other place. Bits of black skin were slowly giving way to puckered, brilliant pink new skin on the thin flesh of his wrist, but he knew that the chest and arm wounds would be there for days. They might even wind up scarring, as weak as he'd made himself from throwing power around. "Matty, I'm fine. But there might be a drug upstairs that will speed up Ahmad's healing. I have to check. Fiona would have hidden it, so I'll have to go by smell. It wouldn't do you any good to go in my place. Just keep an eye on Ahmad and yell for me if he gets any worse."

Matty growled, sounding very much like the animals he tended. His worry, fear, and anger were nearly glowing in the air around him. "Yeah, right. Antoine, that is so patently untrue that I'm not going to even bother to comment. If you're not back in five minutes, I'm coming up to get you."

Antoine let out a short snort of air. "If I'm not back in five, you'll *need* to. I'll poke my head in Margo's room, too. I'm hoping she's all right. I worry that she didn't come down during the battle. It was violent enough to shake the walls. Did you shut her door?"

Matty frowned, and his worried scent increased. "No, I didn't. I wanted to be able to hear if she called out. Yeah, dead-set sure—you'd better check on her. I can't imagine that those blokes would consider her a threat, but considering the things they did for *laughs* around here—I nearly felt sorry for the mice, and I hate squeakers."

Antoine walked out to the entryway and looked up the staircase. It hadn't seemed nearly so far up earlier, but he'd had both legs working properly. He took a deep breath and closed his eyes. The vision overlay wasn't too bad until he looked down. That was a little too much for his equilibrium to handle, and the dizziness wasn't worth dealing with.

At the top of the stairs, he debated whether to check on Margo first or to search for the drug. Friendship won out and he walked nervously down the hall to where the massive oak door was standing wide open. "Margo?" he called out lightly, not completely hiding his own fear. She'd been his assistant for nearly ten years, and a good friend besides. There was no answer.

He poked his head inside the door, fearing the worst. But she was on the bed, under the comforter, and she was most definitely alive. The wave of relief quickly passed as the cave started to flow with activity. Tahira was being carried in by four men, one holding each limb. She kicked and flailed viciously, and the scent from the men was frustration and barely contained fury. She very nearly managed to get away after a few well-timed blows, but then froze so quickly and completely that he knew someone was holding her with magic. The men let go as she glided through the air to disappear inside the chamber entrance. No matter how hard he pushed forward in the vision, he couldn't seem to follow inside.

It's time to end this.

Antoine walked over to the bed and sniffed Margo's face and breath. Her sweat smelled very similar to the bitter venom that had hit Ahmad. Her breathing was shallow, but her heartbeat was steady. Considering it had been nearly an hour since the original attack, her condition was probably as bad as it was going to get. He quickly smelled around until he found the bite mark. It was on her shoulder, under her shirt. Fortunately, the bite itself didn't seem to be causing her any distress, so the venom must have some sort of paralysis agent without being toxic.

To be safe, he let a bit of his magic flow into her and was pleased that her breathing became stronger and the sweating stopped. It was all he could afford to do for the time being. He wasn't a healer and needed every bit of his power for what was to come.

He sprinted down to Fiona's room and started to search for his sister's backup supply of chemicals. He knew she would keep some in the house because of the security normally present. He found himself wondering how Ahmad could have been blind to his own men being traitors. He was careful to the point of being paranoid, so the deception must have been long-standing. He pulled out drawer after drawer in the bureau, flipped the mattress off the bed, and opened wide every door in the place. But the kit was nowhere to be found. Could it be in a safe or in a different room?

"No," he said out loud to the empty room. "She'd keep it nearby. It has to be within reach of the bed." The bed was the most inconvenient location in the room, the most indefensible, so that is where Fiona would want the most protection. He sat down on the edge of the empty bed frame and looked around more carefully. Fiona was amazingly fast for her size, but sleep would dull the senses if an attacker came at night.

Ahmad was right. He did think more like an agent than an administrator. But that mind-set would be valuable to them both today. Fiona wouldn't trust something as simplistic as taping it to the bottom of furniture. There wasn't much in the room, anyway, and the decor was subject to change by the owners.

"So, that means—" he whispered, and turned to the stone walls. The reddish tan laced with white limestone deposits of the cave gave a strange, fuzzy hue to the gray stone in front of him. He carefully scanned the wall, searching for anything out of place. He found what he was looking for under the large framed print of wolves running under the moon that had been painted by Star, a famous artist and one of Charles's daughters. One of the massive stone blocks was loose. It took some wiggling and two chipped nails before the stone slid out on tracks inside the wall. It was quite clever, really. He looked inside the hole and was surprised that it had obviously been built when the castle was. The stone had been hollowed out somewhat, and there was a black nylon case stuffed in the opening.

He set the stone on the floor, being careful not to break off any edges, and opened the case. Inside, in carefully padded pockets, were a variety of small vials of viscous fluids. Each one was labeled with a different code—obviously ones she had developed to prevent theft. But he did know how his sister thought, so when he spotted two labels with RBT-01 and RBT-02, he knew he had found the right compounds.

Next to the special cologne that Wolven chemist Robart Mbutu had developed, the chemical cocktail that was affectionately named *Rabbet* was the most widely used by the agents. While he didn't know the exact ingredients, he did know the effect. He took a deep breath and pulled out the tight plastic stopper from the glass test tube and threw the contents down his throat, praying that none of it would land on his tongue. The taste was hideous. He quickly moved to lean against the wall, bracing one hand on the corner so he wouldn't fall over.

Antoine started to shake all over as the powerful Rabbet stimulants coursed through his body like an instant adrenaline high. He watched as his Sazi metabolism began to speed up until his fingers and eyes were twitching like a rabbit's nose when frightened, and his chipped nails actually filled in and started to grow as he stared. Healing was intensified not by actually fixing the wounds, but by putting his Sazi body's natural ability into hyperdrive, forcing along the already fast mending process. His breathing was so rapid it was as though he was absorbing air through his skin, and his heart was fluttering so fast that he could feel the blood vibrating in his veins.

But he hadn't considered the consequences on his vision. He saw the image in front of his eyes fast forward and knew that it was the future rather than the present. But he was also transported inside the torchlit chamber.

Like in an earlier vision, Tahira was naked and bound to a massive boulder by silver manacles with spiked chains driven far into the stone. She struggled violently against the shackles as the small spider-shifter read from a book with a leather cover dyed a whitish-green that reminded him of mold.

The words she spoke were in a tongue so ancient that they weren't quite language. He heard hissing and snarling in the background and looked up. For the first time, he could move about in the vision, doing what Tahira had suggested. Giselle was also chained down, but had been blindfolded and had a silver collar chain in addition to the wrist and ankle bindings. He reached out to touch her, but his hand slipped through her like a hologram.

A tall, olive-skinned man was behind bars, as well as in chains. His features matched Tahira's, and looking carefully, Antoine could just see a single emerald stud in his ear underneath the unkempt hair. He was screaming and pulling at the shackles, staring frantically at Tahira. His eyes were wet, and his expression was enough to tear at Antoine's stomach, but no sound was coming out of the man's mouth.

There was still time—he could feel it. He could still save her if he hurried. He tucked the case back in the stone and pushed it back into the wall until it was flush with the others. After he replaced the painting, he considered whether he should check to see if there were any more useful items on this floor, but Matty's voice stopped him at the doorway.

"You'd better say something up there, mate, or I'm coming up! Babette's looking at Ahmad really strangely, and I don't know if it's good or bad."

Merde! That wasn't a good sign. Babette was always the first one to know when there were problems with the other cats. He took a deep breath and ran down the stairs, intentionally staring at the front door and not looking at his feet. When he reached the ground level, Matty stared at him in shock.

"Fuckin' oath, Antoine! What in the hell sort of witches' brew did you find? All of those burns—they're just *gone*!"

Antoine looked down and realized Matty was right. The burns had faded to long lines of new skin, pink and shiny. "Let's see if we can put Ahmad back on his feet, too."

They hurried inside the library. Matty had been correct that Babette was standing over Ahmad, nudging him with her nose. He pressed his mind into hers and she looked up and snarled in greeting and then bounded to stand by the fireplace. Antoine took her place. Ahmad was worse by far in the last few minutes. His eyes were nearly glazed, but there was recognition deep inside them. It was quite possible that even the Rabbet wouldn't be enough, but it was worth a try.

"Ahmad, can you hear me? Can you swallow at all?"

He saw the man's tongue press against the roof of his open mouth as he tried to get his throat muscles to respond. Finally, after several agonizing moments, he managed to swallow and relaxed back in relief that closed his eyes and flooded his scent enough to cover the bitter scent of the venom.

Antoine held the vial so Ahmad could see it. Distrust rose to the surface and if Ahmad could have frowned, he would have. Antoine asked, "Have you ever had a Rabbet? I know you've read the report on how it works." He turned the tube so Ahmad could see the lettering in Fiona's strange blend of calligraphy and cursive. "You might recover from this on your own, but you might not. I'll leave that choice up to you because I have no idea what the Rabbet will do to the venom. It might well kill you quicker."

Ahmad's eyes went steely with determination and he nodded, but just barely. But his scent was clear. The hot metal scent of determination was enough to make Antoine slip an arm under his neck to raise him up enough so he didn't choke. He flicked the vial lid off with his thumb and opened Ahmad's mouth a bit wider. "I'll try to make sure that you don't hurt yourself while it's taking effect."

The were-cobra took a deep breath and blinked his eyes. While it would be easier to pour it down slowly so that he didn't have to work at getting it all down, the taste was likely to make him gag, and his throat might seize. "Bottom's up!" he said with false humor and poured the entire contents directly down Ahmad's throat.

The reaction was much as Antoine had expected. Ahmad tried to gag, and Antoine massaged his throat to get him to swallow it all into his system. He ignored the scene still playing out, ghosted in front of him, concentrating instead on physical sensations to keep him grounded.

Placing Ahmad back down on the floor, Antoine used brute strength to keep him steady as his body began to speed up. It was like riding an insane bucking bronco or a rabid bull. Foam flecked on his mouth and every drop that touched Antoine burned and instantly scarred his skin, making him wince. Ahmad's muscles soon began to convulse as his system tried to rid itself of the poison. As he strained his muscles enough to hurt, Antoine finally resorted to using magic energy to help hold the cobra to the floor. He could see Matty pacing in the background, his eyes wide and panicked. But he didn't offer to help, knowing that he might wind up with broken ribs or worse.

Babette wasn't worried in the least, and it almost made him smile. She had flopped down by the fireplace and her cubs were happily nursing while she cleaned herself with long strokes of her tongue. Her Rex was wrestling with a rabid cobra against the wall, and that was just fine.

It took a few moments for him to realize that Ahmad had stopped struggling. He leaned back tentatively, taking some of his weight from the lightly twitching arms, just as he heard the snake's hoarse but clear voice.

"*That* was an experience I should not like to ever repeat. You can let me up now. I think I can stand."

Matty let out a low whistle. "Holy dooley! That drug is bloody is amazing! Could it help Margo heal?"

Antoine shook his head as he moved back, giving Ahmad room to stand. "No," he told Matty strongly. "This would kill a human. It would probably kill an ordinary Sazi. Only alphas are allowed near this stuff." He put a light note of teasing in his voice and said to Ahmad, "Aren't you glad now that you voted to approve funding the research on Rabbet?"

Ahmad's hand, bearing a large gold and ruby ring, appeared on the back of the chair, and muscles strained as he pulled himself to his feet. He continued to lean heavily on the leather upholstery as he spoke. "I can't imagine *ever* being tired enough to consider it worth the price to use this on a mission. But for healing purposes, it's an excellent product. I presume that I'll wind up with a massive headache tomorrow?"

"Or worse. But you'll recover. Now, I have to start finding weapons to go and save my people. Obviously, you should probably stay here until—"

Ahmad took a tentative step and found his legs would bear his weight. He stood up and took another step, forcing his spine straight. His face was cold, and fury blended with determination in his scent. "Oh, no. I fully intend to go along with you. My most trusted guards have defected and tried to kill me. I want to know who managed to secure their loyalty, and then I want to see all of their heads rolling on the ground, loose of their bodies."

"What you didn't bother to find out, Ahmad, is that our foe is another *spider*. I scented it when it tried to capture Tahira, and touched it within a vision. I'm still having a vision, probably because of the Rabbet. I can see all of the people taken, superimposed over this room. Presently, you're standing inside a stalagmite. It's really quite an interesting image."

Ahmad staggered a bit as he realized what Antoine was implying, but remained standing despite the shock on his face and in his scent. "I find it difficult to believe that my snakes would work for a spider. I thought at least *that* would be beneath them. But unless we have more than one enemy—which is a possibility to consider— then I'm forced to accept it. Therefore, we need weapons. We're in a castle belonging to an ancient swordsman. Surely Charles has suitable weapons somewhere about?"

"The broadswords over the mantel were purchased in Chicago. Apparently, Charles thought we might need them and brought them here. They're quite sharp."

"Yes," Ahmad said, nodding. "I remember you purchased them yourself and had them sharpened. We didn't need them then; it is almost fate that we have them now, when we do. I've spent many years behind a blade, but would feel better if I were stronger. I presume that by the time we arrive . . . wherever we're going, the Rabbet will have me back at full strength?"

"It *should*, but I make no promises."

Matty held up his hand behind Ahmad. "I'd like to go along if you think you need a strong arm."

Ahmad shook his head, surprising Antoine with the response. "No, you need to stay here and watch over the woman while she's unconscious. The tiger will eventually need food, and it might not be wise to leave that particular combination in the house if we don't return. It would also be best to keep someone here at the house for when Raven arrives. Once again, if we don't return—"

Matty nodded with quick little movements that made Antoine know that he had truly grasped the situation. "Yeah, I see your point. In fact, I should get downstairs and get something warming for her for dinner, before she considers *me* on the menu."

Ahmad looked at Antoine and raised his brows as Matty darted past them to go down the back stairs. "And now, I need to go upstairs and dress for the weather. It might take a few minutes. Afterward, how would you suggest we proceed?"

"Afterward," said Antoine with fire in his voice and a cold smile on his face, "we go to *war*."

Chapter Sixteen

NASIL WAS OUT of breath as he approached Sargon, who was reclining almost lazily against the pillows in the main chamber. "Dr. Portes is nearly ready to begin. Taking the other cat from the house was very useful."

Sargon watched him carefully, and he couldn't decide what his scent was. "Yes, it was a successful operation. I wondered if you would agree with my decision."

He bowed low. "I'm pleased you value my opinion, but your word is law. My agreement or disagreement does not change that. But I am concerned that we've not heard from the sleepers that they're on their way with the girl."

The dark face showed the first sign of annoyance. "No, we have not. Loyalty that can be bought can be outbid as well. Unlike you, they have not proven their loyalty in a very long time."

"I'm pleased you were satisfied with my effort. I have to admit that I hadn't had a sufficient challenge in some time. The fools in the police station had no clue that anyone had even been in the jail."

"Where on the body did you bite him? Will they discover it quickly?"

Nasil chuckled. "I doubt they will discover it at all. I bit him in one of the healing wounds from his battle with the girl the other night. Then I used power to heal over the wound without affecting the poison. They'll discover the venom but have no idea where it originated."

Sargon graced him with a rare smile of warmth. "It's quite remarkable what you can do when you put your mind to it, Nasil. I hope you'll be as expedient on the prisoners in the other room after their power has been taken. While I do enjoy the sound of screams, I find *whimpering* distasteful, and that seems to be common lately."

"Was Zuberi reduced to whimpering? I haven't seen him since your last chase."

Sargon sighed and readjusted himself on the pillow. "Sadly, I wounded his throat too much for him to be good prey afterward. I believe he drowned in his own blood shortly after the first strike."

Dr. Portes walked in the room wearing a sleek black spandex outfit that hugged every curve. She dropped to her knees in front of Sargon's legs and then bit the finger he used to touch her lips, causing him to inhale sharply and then smile as the tiny wound started to swell.

"My lord, all is in readiness," she trilled in fear. "We only wait for the girl to complete the ritual. I believe she is truly the one. I felt her depth as we touched, and I'm sorry I was not able to bring her from the city."

Nasil's voice was steady, but there was more than a bit of satisfaction in watching her squirm. "*I'm* sorry that you didn't deign to inform me of your plan. I was already in town and could have assisted."

Sargon's eyes were beginning to bleed as red fire caught the light. "He is correct, Rachel. With Nasil's assistance, we would not have been forced to expose our hand by attacking the others at the house. The old cat will be useful, but I'm not confident that our sleepers are powerful enough to overcome the Monier cub.

You're fortunate that you're the only one capable of reading the old text to perform the ritual, but that good fortune will end rather abruptly if we have no power well to perform the ritual *with*."

She looked up at him and widened her eyes, then brushed her chest slowly along his leg sensuously. "I'm certain that you can think of *some* way that I may make amends for my failure, my lord."

"If the ritual goes well and I gain the power I seek, you will be forgiven. I will probably even gift you with the lesser beings we captured for our shared entertainment. But if the power well is lost, then *you* will be the entertainment. I can assure you that you haven't seen my full abilities in our games."

Nasil felt his heart beat just a bit faster but quashed any emotion in reaction to the image that popped into his mind. "My lord, shall I go outside and find the sleepers and the girl? It might be that the trail we used earlier has become impassible in the snow. They're barely alphas, so the cold could also affect them."

Sargon sighed deeply and then nodded. "That would be best, Nasil. If you discover that the girl has escaped *again*, then make certain that everybody in the house is eliminated. We will have to continue our search if we fail here, and that would be easier without being tracked."

He held out his other hand and Nasil dropped to his knees beside Dr. Portes and kissed the cool, bitter skin fervently before speaking. "Your will be done, my lord."

Chapter Seventeen

"AHMAD! ARE YOU nearly ready?" Antoine knocked once again on the locked door to his room, watching the torchlight from the vision flicker on the wood. He was growing more accustomed to the dual images, but movement in either reality was still disconcerting. "If you don't open this soon, I'll have to break it down to see if you're dead."

He heard a small thump behind the wood that concerned him, but moments later the door opened. A chilly blast from the window hit him square in the face and made him shiver. "What in the world are you doing in here?"

Ahmad still seemed to be breathing a bit heavily, and Antoine could hear his heart racing from the Rabbet. "There's such a thing as being *too* warm, which is a concept I'd never imagined. Unfortunately, this drug has sped up my metabolism to the point that I'm actually flushed for the first time in my life. When winter wind feels *good* to a snake, especially an alpha of my caliber, it's time to consider a different formula for our agents."

He pulled on a heavy woolen coat and then nearly stripped it off again in frustration. He blew out a blast of hot air that smelled heavily of creosote and the Rabbet drug. After a moment, he stood next to the window and closed his eyes to the icy breeze as sweat painted his brow.

"You don't have to go, you know. You're looking a bit pale." Antoine was growing concerned. The drug had made him feel nearly at his peak of strength, but what would happen if Ahmad couldn't carry his own weight in a battle?

By the time Ahmad turned to him, his voice had dropped into snide tones. "I didn't ask for your opinion of my condition. If you'll hand me my weapon, we'll be off. Once I'm outside, this miserable layer of clothing will be acceptable."

Matty met them at the bottom of the stairs and put a hand solidly on Antoine's shoulder while Ahmad easily sliced the nearly five-foot sword through the air with one hand. The resulting whistle pleased him. He pursed his lips and nodded with the slightest scent of approval as a nearly transparent sliver of skin was carved from the surface of his thumb when he slowly ran it across the sharpened edge.

"I'm sorry I can't go with you, mate," Matty said with mingled relief and annoyance. "But I'll save a slab to share when you get back."

Antoine chuckled darkly. "If we *make* it back, I think I'll want something stronger than beer. Rare or not, I think that the cognac might be opened."

Ahmad was at the door, holding it open behind him. His voice was nearly back to its arrogant best. "If you're quite done with your camaraderie and *male bonding*, I'd like to leave. I want this sword bloodied before dawn."

The tracks were easy to follow. Tahira's limp body had forced the men to walk instead of taking to the tree-tops. That meant they were to deliver her in good condition, which was useful knowledge. Antoine pointed toward the mountain. "We go that way."

Ahmad stopped and gave him a look of condescension. "The tracks go in the opposite direction, Antoine."

He started toward the distant hill, speaking over his shoulder. "And my vision says that this is the way. Maybe the tracks double back or disappear again to lead us off course while they complete the ritual."

"What ritual?" Ahmad's voice was curious now. The wind was too strong in their faces to get any scent from him.

"In my vision, I saw Tahira and the others chained down with the same silver that tied me. The spider is reading from a book in a sing-song way and power begins to flow into Tahira like water."

"Or like fish in a net," Ahmad said in a nearly hushed but angry tone. "You do realize that my only goal is to seek vengeance on my guards, not to free all of your people."

A small smile curled up one corner of Antoine's lip, but he didn't look at Ahmad. "I don't think you'll let her die, even if she doesn't choose either one of us."

He shrugged under the heavy weight of the coat that made his long neck seem pencil thin. "If it's a choice between her life or mine, I will choose mine."

Antoine didn't comment, but he noticed the distinct scent of a lie before it drifted away into the night.

The snow was piled deep in the bare spaces between the trees, and they were going more slowly than Antoine would like. A burst of activity in the cave vision that swam in front of the darkness made him stop and then hurry forward. Tahira had arrived, and she was fighting her captors the same way as he saw in his earlier vision. But as the vision had showed him, it was to no avail. A violent power grabbed her like a fist and she floated onto the rock and remained motionless until the shackles were on her arms and legs.

"I'm so very happy to see you again," said the spider shifter, still in her human form. "You see? I would have taken you to see your brother, just as I claimed." Tahira turned her head up and back, and saw the man in the cage.

"Rabi! Oh my God! Rabi, are you all right?"

He opened his mouth, but no words came out.

"I'm afraid he won't be able to speak until I allow him to," the woman said. "His yelling was growing quite annoying. I'm very much looking forward to draining him first." She regarded Tahira curiously. "I wonder how you'll react when the ritual has pulled all of his life force into you. Will you break, knowing you're the cause of his death? Or will you fight harder, raising him to the level of a martyr?" She shrugged. "Either way, I'll be interested to watch."

The snow was nearly waist high as Antoine pushed his way through to the cliff face, followed quickly by Ahmad, who hadn't even asked why they were hurrying.

In the cave, Giselle's voice rang out from the far corner. He couldn't quite catch her scent, but her voice was cold and haughty. "Your kind has never bested the Sazi or the Hayalet people, spider—at least not in *fair* combat. You skulk in the corners, hiding in the shadows to ambush your prey. If you had any true courage, you would unchain me and face me one on one. But then, I suppose we already know that you're a coward. Requiring silver shackles on a woman of my age speaks quite clearly of your abilities."

The woman turned with fury etched on her face. "Silence, old cat! I could hunt you and eat you alive before you could make a single move to defend yourself."

Giselle laughed lightly, and it sounded like crystal bells tinkling. The sound made the tiny, dark-haired woman clench her fists and jaw simultaneously. "I highly doubt that. But I'm not concerned, since I'll be the one living to tell the tale of your failure in battle."

Antoine was startled, because the thick, sarcastic tones didn't sound like Giselle at all. But after a moment, he realized what she was doing. She was being faithful to her oath. She would die to protect the others, and was ensuring that she would be the first one chosen to be drained. Regardless of their disagreements, she was his *Grand-mère*. She was Giselle, leader of the lynxes, and she deserved a better fate than that. He raised his long legs high out of the snow and bounded across the landscape fast enough to leave Ahmad struggling to catch up.

He slowed as he neared the mountainside, and gathered as much moonlight as he could into his eyes, searching the darkness for a portion of the cliff that had matched the vision.

"Very well done." A voice from the darkness seemed somewhat familiar, but he couldn't quite place where he'd heard it. It was a warm rolling hiss with ominous edges, and he saw Ahmad stiffen beside him.

A figure glided out from the shadows with remarkable grace and stopped just out of view of even Antoine's sensitive eyes. "Of course," he said, "I wouldn't have expected any less. Normally, I would have simply killed you both before you reached this far, but I find myself in a bit of a quandary. I'm in need of your help, so killing you would be counterproductive."

"Ssshow yourself!" Ahmad's voice was a vicious hiss that was filled with warning. He held the sword and was gripping it with white knuckles while his power flared enough to press against Antoine uncomfortably. Antoine brought his own power to bear in response to the threat.

The laugh was both light and low. It was a pleased sound, like a teacher whose student had done well. "It sounds like I don't need to. But stay your blade unless you do wish to die here in the snow. You know I'll win."

Ahmad's eyes narrowed. The sword stayed where it was. "That was long ago, in another life. I don't share your . . . *confidence*."

The figure stepped out from the trees into the brightly lit field of undisturbed white. Antoine gasped when he saw who it was and started to walk forward, but Ahmad slammed an arm against his chest and stepped slightly in front of him with the blade out. Antoine felt a sinking feeling in the pit of his stomach as he asked, "Larry?"

"No, Antoine," Ahmad said. "I should have seen it earlier, but I was blinded by time and ego. The man standing before you is named *Nasil*—Ea-Nasil, the Tormentor of Akkade. We've found our *true* traitor."

Chapter Eighteen

LARRY, NOW *NASIL*, raised his eyebrows and pursed his lips in satisfaction. His entire bearing was different from the man Antoine had come to know over more than a dozen years, and his scent was even different. Gone was the warm, caring, slightly overweight man who smelled of fresh pecans and helped feed his cats. The man before them was slender and confident, self-assured. His scent was the thick, bitter scent of a viper, and his body was loose and ready, as though he expected to fight, and expected to *win*.

"I'm flattered that you remember my name *and* title. It's been a very long time, Prince Rimush. *Ahmad* suits you better."

Ahmad didn't move, but the arm on Antoine's chest was trembling just a little. From his scent, it was in anger rather than fear. Disdain and hate in his scent were strong enough to choke on as he spit the words across the snow. "How could I forget you when I'm reminded by the scars I see in the mirror every morning?"

Nasil shrugged and took a step closer. Even burdened by the weight of snow, he seemed to move effortlessly. Ahmad held his ground and raised the blade to a slightly different angle. "They made you strong. You survived where your brothers did not."

Ahmad snorted. "I might have known that it would be

someone like you who would steal my guards away with threats and empty promises. You've come into your own quite well to have a were-spider as a lackey. Or are *you* the lackey of the spider?"

Nasil burst out laughing, and it was so similar to Larry's laugh that it made Antoine wince. "Hardly, Ahmad. While I appreciate your so high opinion of me, I am as I always was—loyal in service to my lord."

Ahmad faltered, and the blade dropped from his suddenly limp hand. He clutched at Antoine's jacket to keep from falling.

"What am I missing here, Ahmad? Larry? What's happening?" Antoine held his blade a bit higher and put his other arm under Ahmad's for support.

"*He's dead!*" Ahmad whispered the words so passionately that they should be true just by the saying of them. His frantic eyes stared at Nasil, and his tongue flicked out over and over. He picked up the sword from the hole in the snow, being careful to watch the other man's every movement.

Nasil's tone was chiding after he tsked and shook his head. "*Ahmad . . .* surely you didn't believe that two lesser guards of the youngest prince could somehow manage to kill him? Sargon of Akkade is the most powerful king the world has ever known. But if it helps any, your father *was* impressed by your cleverness in planning the attempt on his life. He ceded you the throne as a prize, and we sought other adventures."

"*Putain!*" hissed Antoine in anger and frustration, startling them both. He didn't care who he needed to fight. Tahira was in danger, as were the others, and the conversation was going nowhere useful. "You're welcome to reminisce and trade insults until you're both frozen solid, but I will be finding a way into the cave to save my people. If this is an attempt to stall us from facing the spider, then attack and be done with it, Larry. Only death will stop me from saving Tahira, Giselle, and the others."

He turned to walk toward the cliff, the vision from the past repeating in the present. He clutched the sword in tight fingers, and made sure of his balance as he stepped, in case he was attacked. What he didn't expect was that Larry, or Nasil, would simply move in front of him so quickly that he couldn't draw a full breath.

"The spider is now the least of our worries, Antoine," Ahmad said quietly, placing a firm hand on his shoulder. "I don't normally urge caution in battle, as you well know. But while most asps are slow moving, Nasil has the blood of a black mamba flowing through his veins as well. It's only from constant attacks that I was able to increase my speed enough to keep ahead of his teeth. You would be dead before you hit the ground if he wanted you that way. He was my father's primary enforcer and that he's still living is a testament to his skill."

Nasil acknowledged it with a graceful shrug. "Quite true. But as I said, killing you would be counterproductive to my goal."

"You killed the man in the jail." Antoine's voice was filled with fury. "So apparently, life means little to you. I'll wager that you don't have an aunt in Stuttgart, either. You've lied to me, hidden your abilities, and probably spied on my council activities for your *lord*." His eyes narrowed, and it was only through sheer force of will that he didn't pounce and cut off the head of the man who betrayed him, and Tahira, and mostly . . . "I just can't understand how you could lie to Bruce. He's never done a thing to deserve this. He's loved you every day of the past twelve years."

Ahmad's voice was cold with hatred and some other

emotion that might have been pain. "He has no morals, Antoine, no conscience, no heart with which to grasp another's suffering."

Nasil sighed and crossed his arms over his chest, looking once again like the Larry Antoine *thought* he knew so well. "And *that* is where I made my mistake. Ahmad knows that I was never a lover of men. Finely curved women were my taste for centuries. But I played the part of a homosexual when my lord Sargon commanded it, and infiltrated your troupe by attaching myself to the one person who desperately craved attention. Twelve years, when you've lived for countless centuries, is a small price to rule the world. No, I have no aunt in Stuttgart. She was sacrificed to the greater cause several months ago." He let out a small, pained laugh that felt wet and heavy. "But I didn't expect to enjoy myself. I didn't plan to admire the way you treat your people. It actually *bothered* me to feed the information to Giselle that would force her to challenge you." His voice lowered to a soft warmth. "Most of all, I didn't expect to fall in *love*. And now, because of that, I need your help."

Antoine and Ahmad both let out bitter laughs, nearly simultaneously. Antoine pointed his sword directly at Nasil's neck. "Why would I help *you* after you've just admitted that our entire relationship has been a lie?" Antoine couldn't afford to continue this. The ritual was starting in earnest, and he could see a light glow form over Tahira's body as the chanting grew in force and volume.

Nasil's scent was a blend of determination and anger. "You'll help me because I can get you inside the cave unseen. I can give you the positions of all of the guards and their weak points. Sargon took Bruce and plans to torture and eat him—most likely at the insistence of Dr. Rachel Portes, who, as you saw in your vision, is indeed a were-spider. We've come to loathe each over the years and she wants to hurt me with Bruce's death. As loyal a servant as I've been to Lord Sargon for these many years, I'm actually willing to go against him to save a mere human companion. You and the young prince *might* actually be a match for him—at least long enough to weaken him. But most of all, you'll help me because if he manages to use Tahira's abilities, he will be unstoppable. The Sazi council, even the great Charles Wingate, would be nothing more than cannon fodder."

Antoine couldn't help but remember the first vision in the tunnel. "And the world would burn to ash." He nearly whispered the words, but Nasil nodded.

"Indeed. I'll even sweeten the deal. I'll slay the spider and free the others while you distract Sargon. Perhaps with the help of the cats, Sargon might be brought down at last."

"And what do *you* get out of it?"

Nasil smiled, and his scent was filled with a dozen different emotions that all fought for dominance. "I'll avoid getting tortured for helping you. I'll get my freedom from an eternity of slavery—and I'll get Bruce back. I don't need anything else."

Antoine let out a snort of derision. "Do you really believe that Bruce would have anything to do with you after this? If anyone dies here today, he'll hold you responsible. Even if we *survive*, he'll never forgive you."

"If he doesn't *remember*, he will," Ahmad said thoughtfully. As Nasil once again gave a pleased expression to the cobra, Ahmad continued. "Nasil is one of the very few who can make a person black out and not remember short periods of time. Very likely, Bruce has been Nasil's alibi for any number of events that might otherwise have raised suspicion."

Nasil nodded and smelled pleased. "Just as the police

didn't remember me walking in and killing their prisoner while Bruce was asleep in the car. I returned and woke him up after digging out the SUV. He didn't remember falling asleep, or me leaving." He raised his arm to his face and checked his watch. "But we're nearly out of time. If you both want to do this, it needs to be now. If you don't, I can't afford for you to interfere, so I'll have to eliminate you."

Antoine pushed his way into the vision again, while Ahmad ground his teeth, smelling of hate so strong it could kill on contact. But mingled in the scent were anger, a dark glee, and indecision.

Once more, he tried to manipulate the vision, moving backward through the shadows until he could see the cliff face once more. With sudden intensity, he saw more than he intended—Nasil leading them around the edge of a boulder and pulling away brush from the rock to reveal a small opening where the stream he and Tahira had fought near originated. "I don't trust you, but I do trust my visions. I'll know immediately if you're leading us wrong, and then we'll see if you're able to eliminate me."

"As much as I would relish the challenge, I might actually regret killing you. So let's not go there." He turned his back on them and walked away, expecting that they would follow.

Antoine turned to Ahmad. "Tell me everything you know about your father and how he fights. Any weaknesses that he might have would be especially useful right now."

Ahmad let out a harsh, angry breath. "I thought I knew the one he had. I spent nearly two millennia planning his murder, to avenge the thousands he slaughtered. I believed I'd succeeded a few hundred years before you were born." He stared at Antoine's suddenly shocked expression. "Yes, you heard right. I've been alive for longer than most of the council believes, save Charles. And yes, we *do* need to talk or we'll both die a very slow and painful death."

TAHIRA WAS STARTING to feel strange. The more the woman read the words from the moldy book she was holding, the more light-headed she was getting. She'd finally found Rabi, so that was something. But she'd also just argued with the one man who might help them, and she couldn't be sure that he would come.

I shouldn't need saving. There must be a way out of this.

She looked around the room carefully. The manacles that held her had already burned the first few layers of her skin, providing some protection against further damage. But the pain was incredible, and it made her wonder again about Antoine. He'd fought so hard against the chains, using his power to change her. It must have weakened him a lot to do that. She vaguely remembered changing back to human form after the men took her from the house. Did that mean Antoine was already dead? Just the thought of it made her sick to her stomach and a pain filled her chest. Ahmad had been right. She'd made her choice, even though it didn't matter anymore.

Stop it, Tahira! You can't get sucked into feeling defeated!

The memory of Rabi shaking her behind a tree on their last run came flashing back to her. Their grandfather considered her a waste of fur, nobody in the village would talk to her, and she wasn't learning as quickly as Grammy wanted.

"Really, Rabi, I mean it. I think it's just time I went home. You're going to be the new *sahip*, but I'm just a nobody. I'll never be able to do what Grammy expects from me, whatever the hell that *is*, and I'm not willing to get married and have kids just to impress the people here. I can finish college back home and then move somewhere that tigers are common. Maybe I can teach English to kids in China or something."

Rabi had sighed and pounded his forehead on the bark of the tree. "Tahira, you're *not* a nobody! You're the smartest person in our family by far, you can *isim* better than anyone in the village and hold it longer, and you've learned how to defend yourself with teeth and claws. Maybe you can't run as fast as me, but you're more than a match for half the men in the village. That's why they don't like you—you're *too* good."

The words froze in her mind. *You can* isim *better than anyone in the village and hold it longer—*

No, she couldn't escape, but what if the spider *thought* she had? She tucked that idea in the back of her mind, because there was no way to use it presently. Bertha, or whatever her name was, needed to be distracted, and right now, her entire focus was on whatever she was reading. The words were coarse and guttural, filled with too many sounds that didn't have vowels. But whatever she was doing was beginning to have an effect. She had to blink more than once to be sure she was seeing what her eyes told her, but it didn't appear to be an illusion. She was actually *glowing*. A pale orange light was seeping from her skin and was beginning to swirl around the boulder as though caught in unseen breezes.

She began to feel warm. Heat began to swell inside her as it had when she was pulling power from Antoine. It didn't sting like Ahmad's power, but it was definitely magical energy and it was joining the swirling orange light and making the color move around faster.

Giselle gasped and it made Tahira twist her head to

look at her. Like something out of a dream, or closer to
a *nightmare*, Giselle began to . . . thin. It was as though
the faster the orange light swirled, the thinner she became. By the time Tahira realized what the circle of
light must be, Antoine's *Grand-mère* had been reduced
to a shadow of her former self, looking for all the world
like a concentration camp victim in Holocaust photos.

"You see what your sharp tongue has gotten you, old
cat?" Bertha stalked toward Giselle and pulled the
blindfold from her eyes. "I chose *you* to start the ritual,
instead of the tiger male. You will beg for mercy before
I'm done with you. I can start or stop the ritual at will."
She smiled at Giselle and it was filled with malice.
"Rghnl olpnst nbwiq!"

Tahira gasped as everything froze around her, causing
a lunge in her stomach that felt like like hitting an air
pocket in flight. She felt like she was trapped in gelatin.
The power surrounded her, filled her, and was solid
enough that she should have been able to grasp it in her
hands. This wasn't like the other times when her skin
felt heated and threatened to crawl off her body.

Giselle stared up at the woman with proud eyes that
were sunken deep in a skeleton-like face. "There is
nothing you could do to me that would make me beg to
the likes of you."

"Oh, I see it quite differently." She put on a heavy
canvas glove and then reached out. She pulled at the
neck collar Giselle wore until the bite of silver turned
Giselle's neck to a smoking, charred mass that made the
old lynx nearly pass out. "I am Rachel Portes, heir to the
glorious spider empire, and you will soon learn that begging is the least of what you'll be willing to do."

"Leave her alone!" Tahira screamed the words loud
enough to echo through the chamber. Rachel turned to
watch her struggle against her chains. They bent and

stretched but held her firmly against the rock. "It's me you want! You don't need the others. Just kill me and be done with it!"

Rachel looked amused, but Tahira couldn't smell a damned thing through the haze of power. "But I don't want to kill you, Tahira. Lord Sargon intends that you will live to serve him. You are the power well he has sought for centuries." She raised her hand and turned in a slow circle. "All of these shifters will give their lives to fill you and then Sargon will pull the power from you to increase his might." Rachel walked right to the edge of the circle and peered down at Tahira's stunned face with glittering silver pupils that seemed to swallow the whites. "Of course, *how* he pulls it from you is the thing you should fear. You need only be *alive* to serve him. There are many things worse than death, as you will soon learn. *Krhlow plihep!*"

The dance of light started above her again, and Giselle let out a small sound that was not quite a whimper, but her eyes remained steady and angry. Tahira raised her shoulders and pulled her arms inward hard, straining every muscle she had. Her shoulders began to hurt and then burn. But this was the butterfly machine from hell. The chains wouldn't give. The rock wouldn't budge. She fell back against the cool stone, panting for breath, watching in horror as life drained from Giselle's tiny form and joined the swirling light above her.

"Dr. Portes? Please stop the ritual for a moment." Tahira looked up at the same moment Rachel did. A strange, trilling hiss of annoyance was directed at the man still standing just past the doorway, hidden in the shadows. Tahira couldn't quite place the voice, but it sounded slightly familiar.

"If Lord Sargon wishes this experiment to succeed, then I must remain undisturbed."

"One disturbance won't harm the experiment. We both know it will succeed. Now, stop the ritual or I will do it myself."

Rachel smirked at the shadow in the doorway. "Only one who knows the proper incantations can make the power dance on command."

There was a deep sigh that spoke of frustration and annoyance. "If you insist on making a fool of yourself, then perhaps you've outlived your usefulness. *Rghnl olpnst nbwiq!*"

Rachel's mouth opened in shock, but then her face settled into a livid hate. The man stepped into the room and Tahira gasped at the familiar face. "Larry! Get out of here. You don't know what this woman is capable of!"

Rachel laughed with equal parts bitterness and amusement. "Oh no. He knows, Tahira. But that's right—you're still under the impression that 'Larry' is a close and trusted friend." She smiled wickedly. "He's not. Nasil belongs to Lord Sargon, just as I do. He betrayed you all so Sargon could rule the world."

Tahira stared at Larry, waiting for him to deny it, to come and unchain them. But he merely sighed and wouldn't meet her eyes.

He stepped farther into the room with his hands behind his back. He moved gracefully, with the smooth, powerful steps of a dancer. Power beat at the edges of the orange circle like waves buffeting a wall. He was totally unlike sweet, slow Larry the rat snake. He looked down on her, naked and helpless on the rock, and shook his head. Dr. Portes stepped to his side and grinned at Tahira's suddenly frightened face.

It was all a trick! Bruce, Giselle—he knew. He helped!

"It's an interesting thing about betrayal," he said quietly, with an odd lilt to his voice. "Once you get past it the first time—"

A scuffle from outside the chamber made Rachel look up, but Larry, or whoever he really was, didn't. A man's cry was cut short with a wet, thick sound that ended with a thump, and Rachel started to move behind Larry to go investigate. But he grabbed her arm and spun around sharply. Tahira saw the flash of a blade just before it sank into the woman's small form.

"It's quite easy to do again." He pulled the blade up and blood began to flow freely from a gaping wound in Rachel's stomach.

But she wasn't killed that easily. She yanked back out of reach and changed form in a blur that seemed to vibrate the air. Tahira screamed as she finally saw Rachel's animal form. The spider was nearly as high as the boulder she was tied to and as wide as a car. She was still dripping fluid from her stomach that was thick and yellow.

"So," she said, with an eerie sing-song voice that made Tahira's skin crawl, "you've finally decided to replace me in Lord Sargon's favor. But I won't be as easy to eliminate as you think."

Another blur of movement and a massive snake appeared with golden eyes and a narrow nose that ended in a point. It rose above her to the ceiling and was the same thickness as Larry's chest had been. U-shaped black markings stood out in sharp relief against the tan and white scales. A forked tongue nearly as dense as her arm flicked from his mouth, and when his jaws opened and he hissed, she could smell the distinctive bitter odor of a viper. Despite the orange press of power against her face, the thick, deadly scent told her that Larry had been lying about more than she'd ever imagined. But who had he been lying *to*?

* * *

WATER AND ROCK pressed against Antoine's chest as he struggled through the opening into the cave. Ahmad had gone in ahead of him and his thinner body had easily moved through the underground stream. But Antoine's rib cage was now stuck fast, wedged in between the solid stone walls. He couldn't even move his arms backward enough to chip at the stone with the sword. He raised his head, but there was no air pocket to get another breath. The icy torrent pushed against him and his muscles began to shake as his chest burned from lack of oxygen. Perhaps if he shifted he could swim through.

But can I shift without taking a breath?

It's something he'd never tried before, and he was afraid to find out the answer. But the vision was continuing in front of his eyes, like a motion picture playing against the murky water. Giselle's skin looked like parchment. It was stretched taut over her skull, and she was breathing so shallowly he wasn't positive she was still alive. Tahira fought like a wildcat against her chains, to no avail. He watched as Nasil entered the room and was at least gratified when Nasil stabbed a long knife into the spider's chest. Perhaps he really would save the rest, even if Antoine didn't survive.

His eyelids were growing heavy as the pressure in his chest increased. Eventually he would pass out and draw water into his lungs. Could a Sazi survive drowning? He just didn't know. As white spots and flowers replaced the vision in front of him, he heard a muffled voice.

"Grab hold of the hilt!" The annoyed baritone seemed to come from a long way away, but when he felt something hard and metal bump against his hands, he released his own sword and grabbed on to the grip of the matching one firmly. He felt a tug that tore at his shoulder muscles, and then he slowly but steadily slid through the opening. Unforgiving rock ripped painfully at his skin, but he would heal. When he finally saw light above him, he raised his head frantically and pulled cool air into his lungs, coughing and gasping until he could breathe normally.

Ahmad was glaring at him and wiping blood on his soaking pants. It occurred to Antoine that if he had been holding the *hilt* of the sword, then Ahmad had been pulling him through while holding the blade.

"Thank you," he said quietly so that nobody would hear. Pulling himself from the stream, he noticed a familiar scent and glanced over to see the decapitated head of Hakeem staring at him with wide, startled eyes.

Well, he managed his goal—he's had his vengeance.

He didn't have to wonder for long whether his fellow councilman would continue the battle despite killing the guard.

"Can you still reach your sword?" Ahmad hissed angrily. "We'll be at a disadvantage if you can't."

Antoine turned around and ducked his head back under the water, reaching back to see if the sword was still there, or if it had been carried away by the rush of water. He used his feet to push him even farther back and could finally touch the hilt with his fingertips. He clawed at the handle to draw it closer, but it shifted and sank a bit farther down.

"Oath of my mother!" Ahmad muttered almost too softly for him to hear. Antoine felt hands grab his ankles, and then he was shoved hard into the rock tunnel once more, nearly stealing the breath from his lungs. But it was enough, because he was able to grasp the leather grip of the sword. He kicked one foot as a signal that he hoped Ahmad would understand, and was relieved when he was pulled back out of the water.

"You're worse than useless so far," Ahmad said with an annoyed shake of his head. "Hopefully you'll do better on dry land." He gripped the leather bindings of the sword carefully, but with a surprised expression he noticed that the deep cuts in his palms had already healed. He flexed his hands experimentally and chuckled softly. "I take back what I said about the Rabbet. With this level of healing ability, we might just walk out of here under our own power."

"That's the plan," Antoine replied as he secured the rubber band around his wet, disheveled hair. "I see you've already taken care of the first guard. Where is Bahir?"

"The coward ran deeper into the cave. I suppose we must expect that he'll raise an alarm."

Antoine motioned as the sound of furious fighting and crashing glass in the chamber in front of them grew in intensity. "If nobody has come to investigate whatever is happening in there, then I think we're safe for a time."

Before they could move out of the way, the battle came to them. Antoine could tell by the scents of the snake and spider that were grappling that Nasil had been true to his word. But as he tried to get past them to get to Tahira, the spider made a break for the cave again. A trilling sound spewed from her mouth. "*Krhlow plihep!*"

Nasil quickly slithered after her, ignoring both him and Ahmad. Antoine started to follow, but Ahmad pushed him away with a sharp hand to the chest. "We don't have time. Nasil is perfectly capable of dispatching that . . . *thing*. We have to concentrate on my father. He cannot be allowed to leave here. If the ceremony is interrupted, he'll know and will disappear. We have to find him and engage him before that happens."

Antoine frowned. "But Tahira—"

"Will survive if we kill Sargon. But if we choose to save Tahira, he'll get away, and then he'll simply hunt her until he captures her again. No, this must end now."

He glanced at the doorway with rising panic. The vision had deserted him, perhaps because he was now living it. Since he hadn't seen Nasil attack the spider, maybe the future was wavering, waiting for his next act. He nodded at Ahmad. "Very well. We find Sargon and kill him."

Ahmad actually smiled. "You make it sound so simple. I hope your confidence and enthusiasm hold when he ambushes us. That's his preferred method of attack. Remember, as we discussed, our goal is to keep stabbing and cutting at him to wear him down and force him to use some of his power to heal. Concentrate on using your power only to *divert* his strikes. Don't wear *yourself* down trying to hold him or attack with magic. He will attack *us* with magic, and you'll need to use your power as a shield." He turned to walk into the darkness but then snapped his fingers and said over his shoulder, "Oh, and he's very accurate with his venom spits, so keep moving, even if it means you miss a cut, but then quickly slash before he can spit a second time."

It had been a long time since he'd battled anyone with swords. He was adequate with a blade, but certainly not at Ahmad's level. "Is there a chance that we can defeat him using that method?"

The cobra's face was amused. "Hardly. No, our goal is to hopefully wear him down until Nasil can release the others. If we can use some of our power to change Tahira and her brother, then we might stand a chance with a multiposition attack."

A rolling, malevolent bass from the darkness made both of them turn with swords extended. "Thank you for explaining your plan, my son. I see that my disappointment in you wasn't misplaced."

A rasping sound of something hard slithering over the stone came closer and closer. Antoine could smell him now, and the bitter odor was so strong that it nearly made him choke. Glowing red eyes blinked in the darkness and remained still for a long moment. He flexed his fingers on the wet leather grip and added his other hand, steadying his stance for either a thrust or a cut.

He felt power press on him that was stronger than he'd ever experienced. It seared his skin and burned through his chest. And Sargon wasn't even attacking yet. The torch caught the bright yellow of Sargon's belly as he rose up and up until his head was far overhead, against the ceiling. His tail disappeared into the darkness, leaving no clue as to his true size.

Although Antoine was concentrating on Sargon's movements, he heard a small clatter of rocks behind and then the pad of soft paws.

They intend to trap us between attacks.

"Ahmad! Change of plans!" Antoine dropped the sword and leapt into the air, not waiting to see what Ahmad would do in response. When he landed, he had changed to cat form and he shook the tattered remains of his clothing from his fur. With a second leap before his heart could beat again, he found the location of the lion by scent, and slammed into the cat with teeth and claws bared.

They tumbled from the ledge where the lion had lain in wait, and hit the cave floor with a bone-jarring crash. He heard vicious hisses in the distance and knew that Ahmad had also decided in favor of animal form for their battle.

Antoine raked his claws down the lion's side and as it turned away, he closed his jaws around the neck. He squeezed down, feeling his teeth sink through fur and flesh. The scent of fresh blood filled his nose and spurred him on. The lion was thrashing in pain, trying to get purchase on the rocks to break free.

He heard the noise just before a second lion struck him in the side. He lost his grip for a moment, but then once again closed his jaws around the first lion. He ignored the pain as fangs sank in his back; the Rabbet was making his system work so fast that he healed as quickly as he was wounded. It wasn't worth wasting his power to stop the second lion.

Instead, he clamped down harder on his opponent's neck and then twisted and pulled sharply. He heard a crack and then the full, limp weight of the lion pulled his head to the floor. He turned in midair and leapt on the second lion. It tried to break free and escape, but Antoine was faster. He grabbed it around the sides and dug his claws in the soft belly while his jaws once again claimed the neck, this time from the top. It was over in moments and two bodies were lying at his feet.

TAHIRA LIFTED HER head as the triumphant roar of a familiar cat washed over the sound of Larry and Rachel's battle. Elation filled her, despite the circumstances. He was alive!

But there was still the man Rachel had called Sargon to deal with. She had to get out of here to help Antoine. But she couldn't figure out any way to get out of the chains, unless Larry managed to win. But they seemed equally matched, and neither was wearing down. They were both carefully avoiding the rock where Tahira was chained. At one point, Rachel had stepped within the circle of light, and Tahira felt a stinging flow of power that felt even more toxic than Ahmad's.

Maybe that's the key!

As soon as Rachel had pressed another attack and her

back was turned, Tahira raised and turned her head to look at her brother. *"Rabi! Isim!"* She whispered the words very carefully, hoping he would hear. His ears were at least equal to hers. She concentrated, closed her eyes and willed the edges of light and motion to blur until she disappeared from sight. When she looked down, only the manacles remained visible. But the angles were wrong. They would reveal that she was still there, so she moved her body, stretching and straining her muscles to bend until the silver chains appeared to be empty and loose. She might be able to hold the *isim*, but she didn't know if she could keep her muscles from twitching the tight bindings for very long. Rachel had to notice soon.

She looked over into the cage and saw Rabi smile. He'd figured out her plan and she saw him fade into nothingness. It would take her eyes a moment to find him while he was ghosting. But then the strangest thing happened. The manacles dropped to the floor of the cage with a sharp clang that caught the attention of both Rachel and Larry. She wasn't sure how Rabi had managed to make the chains appear so loose, and she couldn't see him yet.

"No!" Rachel screamed the word and frantically turned her body in circles, desperately looking for her prisoners. She leapt onto the wall to avoid Larry's strike and skittered onto the ceiling as she took in the empty manacles. She raced forward and back onto the floor, keeping the orange circle between her and the giant snake. Unblinking, multifaceted eyes stared at her without notice, and the spider moved her body left and right, close enough that Tahira could smell that she was increasingly desperate and panic-stricken.

Two things happened at once, and Tahira couldn't move out of the way. Larry had decided to brave the circle of power. He threw himself into the orange light in a head-on attack on Rachel. But instead of backing up, Rachel fell forward into the light as though shoved.

Unimaginable power poured into Tahira like boiling oil. It coated her, filled her until she felt made of light. Even invisible, her body began to glow with the light of a thousand candles. Tahira screamed over and over, as fast as she could draw breath. Larry took no notice of her screams. He opened his mouth wide, revealing a startlingly pink maw. Tahira could only watch, helpless and in agony as Larry closed his mouth over Rachel's body, driving twin fangs deep into her back. Rachel struggled and pulled to free herself, but Larry held on tight, and she was hampered by the fact that two of her legs seemed to be frozen in place. As hard as she tried to move, the legs remained in the circle, even after Larry's strike pulled them through the circle and beyond.

Again and again, Larry's jaws moved as he pulled her deeper inside his mouth, forcing more venom into the spider with each bite. It wasn't until she was completely limp and her narrow black legs had started to curl under that he released her.

Tahira couldn't move from the fury of power that soared around her, but some part of her brain that wasn't on fire recognized a voice next to her ear. "Hang on, sis. I'll get you out of this." She shrieked as hands touched her, adding to the agony.

She heard a commanding baritone that had hints of Larry's soft tenor. "*Rghnl olpnst nbwiq! Hoplez re-quay!*"

The circle of power dissolved as though it had never been, and she released her *isim* when she saw Larry approaching with a ring of keys. Her heart was still vibrating painfully with unspent energy, and the surface of her skin was red and raw. But the flow into her had stopped, which provided a little relief.

Rabi was standing next to her, looking worried. He smelled equally of love and concern, but there was more than a little embarrassment there, too. He winced at the crackling sound as he carefully peeled the manacles away from the charred skin on her wrists, while Larry attended to her legs. Their own fingers were smoking by the time the silver had dropped against the rock.

Her voice sounded breathy and hoarse from screaming, but she had to know. "Who released you, Rabi? How did you get out?"

"You're not going to believe this, Tahira. I can *truly* ghost, like the legendary Khalid! Like from the old fables!" He smiled ruefully. "I told you that you were the smart one in the family. If it had occurred to me to *isim*, I could have walked out of here a month ago!"

She smiled at him and squeezed his hand proudly. "You're going to be a wonderful *sahip* for our people, Rabi. I always knew you were special!"

Larry cleared his throat and they both turned to him. "As touching as this family reunion is, Ahmad and Antoine aren't faring too well in the next room. Go! I'll free Giselle."

As though on command, a cat's scream of pain filled the room.

She called out and was halfway to the doorway before she even registered the movement. "*Antoine!*"

Chapter Nineteen

ANTOINE WAS FORCED to change back to human form as the venom from Sargon's bite flooded his body. Fortunately, the Rabbet was still working to heal him, but he wouldn't be able to run on all fours until the poison was overcome and pushed out of his system.

Ahmad was still twined around the larger cobra, desperately trying to keep him still so Antoine could attack. They hissed and struck at each other, avoiding each other's fangs with movements so quick that Antoine could barely follow the fight.

He sprinted over to where the swords still lay, holding his injured arm against his body. The pain was terrible and his entire body trembled as the venom destroyed nerve endings. But he couldn't stop now. They had to finish this or die trying. He prayed that Tahira was alive. Her scream had torn at his heart and made him panic. The distraction had nearly cost him his life when Sargon struck.

He grabbed both blades and dropped one at the edge of the battle in case he lost the first. He raced forward, sword low with the blade edge up. He needed to thrust hard and then slice either up or down to wound Sargon the most. At least it would be easy to know which snake to cut. Antoine had always assumed that Ahmad was a full-blooded king cobra due to his markings, but now he realized, when the two snakes were together, that Ahmad must have some other breed mixed in. His back was paler than the inky blackness of his father.

Antoine leapt high into the air as the great king's tail lashed out. With a powerful thrust he sank the sword into Sargon's bright yellow chest and used his momentum and gravity to drag the blade down through his rib bones as he fell.

Sargon reared his head back in agony and Ahmad struck, driving his fangs into his father's throat. Using his hood like a weapon, Sargon slammed Ahmad's mouth away, and his tail grabbed Antoine around the chest before he could regain his footing in the tangle of scaly coils. Sargon's eyes bled red until they glowed and Ahmad was suddenly sailing through the air, pushed away by a wave of magic so great that it superheated the air and singed Antoine's hair, making it frizzy and foul smelling.

As the coils constricted with each breath, Antoine realized that Sargon's goal was to crush and then eat him. But he was no mouse, no rabbit to swallow whole. He called up power inside him and expanded it in an outward wave that forced the coil open. He slipped to the floor and backed up. But he was nearly spent, and Ahmad had turned back to human from slamming against the cave wall. He was lying still and Antoine couldn't tell if he was breathing.

He was worried that he was weakening so quickly because it didn't appear that Sargon was in the least. He picked up the second sword. This would be his final stand.

Sargon's tongue flicked out, and his whole upper body waved back and forth as the massive hood extended with a snap. "You're frightened, as you should be, Councilman Monier." His mouth opened just a bit in what might have been a smile at Antoine's brief moment of surprise. "Oh, yes. I'm well aware who you are, since Nasil has been in your employ for nearly a dozen years. It's interesting that you've taken on so many abilities of both your mother and sister. Perhaps I was wrong to try to claim the girl instead of you. But that doesn't matter now, since I have the power well. You and my . . . *child* will die here and then I will—"

"Rule the world?" Antoine asked snidely. "I don't think so. There are still the other council members to face, along with Wolven agents who are every bit your equal."

"Oh, I *will* rule the world, young cat, but not in the way you're thinking. My plan is even greater than you can imagine. I will free the snakes of the world, once again create a true civilization—one that hasn't existed since the kingdom I was forced to dissolve. The precious *council* decided that no shifter should rule over humans. We should hide in the shadows, let the lesser race populate and thrive. But no more. Once *she* awakens, we will lead the earth into the glory of a new age. And there is nothing you or my feckless son can do to prevent it."

She? What could he be referring to? But there was no time to consider it, because Antoine suddenly felt a powerful running shake the ground under him, and then a pair of orange and black forms sailed over his head with twin roars that were both vicious and heartening. Sandalwood and cherries filled the air, covering the bitter scent of venom for a brief moment.

"Maybe they can't. But *we* can!" Tahira said as she and her brother both slammed into the cobra with claws and fangs extended. Blood erupted in thick lines that coated Antoine and stung his eyes. Sargon thrashed and slapped at the tigers with his tail and tried to shake them off, since he couldn't reach them to bite them.

Antoine jumped as he felt a hand on his bare shoulder and turned to find Nasil staring at the battle with cold eyes. He smiled evilly and then whispered, *"Krhlow plihep!"*

Snake and tigers all reacted as though struck by a wrecking ball. The air began to glow with the power of the sun. Tahira reared back and shrieked in agony, hanging on to the snake only by her claws. Sargon raised his head to the sky and hissed and thrashed as though he were being cut apart.

"Tahira!" Antoine couldn't decide whether to attack Sargon now, try to help Ahmad while he was distracted, or gather Tahira to him to ease her pain.

Nasil made the decision for him. He pushed Antoine forward almost viciously with a strong hand on his back. "It's yours for the taking and it will destroy him! Go to Tahira and help her slay this demon."

Antoine didn't know what he meant, but he moved forward, anyway. He heard Nasil's voice call out from behind. "Tahira! You have the ability to *choose* to end this! That which is taken must be given. Only love is stronger than hate, so make your choice!"

SHE COULDN'T SEE through the fire that burned in her vision. Somehow the well inside her had opened once more, and unimaginable magic made her skin swell and seared across her mind. Her very fur was glowing, and she couldn't help but remember the old William Blake poem.

"Tyger! Tyger! burning bright, in the forest of the night!" She thought she was saying the line in her head, but the sound of the words filled the room until it was painful to her ears, like a scream that was pulled from her very soul. Somewhere in the distance, she heard

Antoine yell, and Larry's voice telling her to choose. But choose *what*?

Again, the words whispered into her mind, *What the hand dare seize the fire?* She turned her head, as though in slow motion, and saw Antoine slashing his way across the snake's dense body. His panic was so real, and so painfully endearing that she knew, absolutely knew what Larry meant. Sargon had planned to drain her, but she was draining him instead.

The power flowed through her veins, turning her skin, muscle, and bones into the living embodiment of magic. Without a second thought, she willed herself human again and flung herself into Antoine's arms. He grabbed her and held her tight against him with something close to a sob. She pushed power into him in a fiery burst that arched his back and pulled a cry of agony from his lips. She pulled his face down and covered those lips with hers, fed the fire into him wherever their skin touched. He tried to pull away from the kiss, but she held him tight, willed him to accept the fire and love inside her.

She filled him until he was a glowing star, golden and pure with a light that rivaled the harvest moon.

But there was still more to give. The fire was still strong enough to burn, so she reached out and found the others who owned a piece of her heart. Rabi was filled until he resembled her—a neon sculpture of fur and muscle. Even Ahmad, for all of his faults, had showed himself honorable and worthy. She went to him, raised him up and held him close, even though she never moved from Antoine's embrace. He woke as she filled him with fire. He welcomed the power, pulled on it greedily until he was fat and lush with it. She felt Antoine pull away from her, hand her back to Nasil. She looked past the eyes of a traitor and into *Larry's* eyes, silently asking if he wanted to share the fire, but he shook his head.

"There's another more deserving. Reach out and see if she can be saved."

Giselle! She whispered the word and felt the old healer faintly in the next room. She was barely hanging on. I'll heal you.

She felt the old cat's words in her mind. No, child. My time is over. Too much was taken and the venom from the spider was too strong.

She started to run, to find her and save her. Grabbing the corner of the doorway into the other chamber, she swung in, but Giselle wasn't there. She realized almost belatedly that tears were streaming down her cheeks. Where are you, Giselle? You'll be fine. I have more power than I know what to do with. I'll give your magic back to you. Hold on for me.

Tahira, please listen. I can think of no one more fitting to inherit my power than you. You must help them. You must use my power to save your people—and mine—from Sargon's menace. Tell Antoine for me that I'm very proud of him. He is a . . . great leader of our people . . . more than I ever could have been. Take ca . . . care of hi—

"GISELLE!" Tahira dropped to her hands and knees as she felt Giselle slip away. She vaguely felt sharp stones ripping at her skin. She cried wordlessly from the sudden emptiness in her mind.

But then there was an audible pop, and sound flooded her brain. Antoine's scream of anger and pain told Tahira that he knew Giselle had died. There was nothing more she could do—at least not for Giselle. She turned and ran back across the cool stone. Even with the three men sharing the excess power, Sargon was slowly but steadily winning. She watched as Antoine threw Rabi away from a frighteningly fast strike, and Sargon's fangs buried themselves in Antoine's shoulder instead.

She rushed forward but was pulled to the side by Larry and held in a grip of iron.

"Nasil!" Sargon's voice boomed through the chamber. "Kill these fleas that attack me and bring the girl to me!"

Tahira struggled in his grip, stared into his cold, hard eyes and pleaded. "Larry, please! I have to get to them! *Please* don't let them die!"

Nasil looked from her to Sargon and back again. His voice rang out over the sound of snarls and hisses. It was filled with something like sorrow, but his scent was determined. "I'm sorry, my lord. But as you said—you can't trust those who can be bought, and there are things more valuable than money. You've been . . . *outbid*." He pulled Tahira close to him and whispered, "Use it well." Then he pushed his own power into her until she screamed. He was nearly as powerful as Sargon himself, and her vision began to sparkle and burn with blue-tinged fire.

She vaguely heard the words, *"Rghnl olpnst nbwiq! Hoplez requay!"* and then she was standing alone at the edge of the battle. Only Rabi was still in animal form, and he was tearing mouthfuls of flesh from the snake's neck, while Ahmad and Antoine hacked at Sargon desperately with magic and blades. They were all bloodied, and the scent of their pain and fear angered her.

She felt the power swirl inside her until it was a tight ball in her chest. It hovered there, making her skin feel so tight it felt like it could tear apart. Her lungs couldn't expand for air and her heart couldn't beat. But she didn't need them. She could not only use the power, she *was* the power.

With a roar of animal rage that transcended any humanity inside her, Tahira launched herself forward, turning in midair to a shining tiger with a coat of pure flame. As though the snake was dry tinder, Sargon erupted in a blaze of orange and blue so intense that Antoine, Rabi, and Ahmad were forced to move away from the fury of it.

She held on with her teeth like a thing possessed, as he fought and struggled to rid himself of the thing he had created—the animal, and the woman, that would be the instrument of his doom. The toxic fumes as he burned made her dizzy, and she felt her blood flowing freely as he savagely beat her body into a sharp stalactite and bit her in a frenzy. She dug in her claws and increased the fire, letting her hatred for his acts against Antoine and Larry, Rabi and *Giselle* fill her with the need for vengeance.

Finally, with a scream that she feared would haunt her until the day she died, Sargon of Akkade crumbled into a hot ash that rained down on her head as she dropped to the cool stone. It coated her skin and burned away the pain in her heart.

Chapter Twenty

REDDISH DUST ROSE in a cloud around the Jeep as Antoine braked to a stop under a lone tree at the edge of a tiny village a few miles from the Iranian border. The cold wind reminded Antoine of the holiday season, even if the surroundings didn't. It would be the first Christmas in his life that his *Grand-mère* wouldn't be—

He ran his fingers through his newly cut collar-length hair, and pulled off his sunglasses to look at the gorgeous woman in the seat beside him. "Are you *certain* that I'm invited to this, Tahira? We don't need to start a war just because I'm curious. I didn't even have time to buy a suitable tribute." He'd considered bringing the cognac, since they'd been too tired and wounded to open the bottle after Sargon's death. But there hadn't been time.

Tahira smiled and pulled the scarf from her striped hair, shaking it until it lay in loose, luxurious waves around her shoulders. "Rabi called me personally and said I was supposed to bring you. He wouldn't be taking over the kabile at all this early if we hadn't defeated Sargon. You helped, so he wants you there. Don't worry about a gift. He doesn't care." She touched his hair and smiled. "I still can't get used to the short hair. It just looks so different."

Antoine smirked and put the sunglasses on top of his

head, tucking the ends behind his ears. "Well, I'd already lost the bet after half of it singed off from the firestorm in the cave. I was lucky I didn't lose it *all*. And as for Rabi, he's taking over the kabile because you turned him into a full-blown *sahip* with your little power play."

She opened the Jeep door and swung her skirt-clad legs out, carefully checking the ground before she put a foot on the sand. He wasn't sure why, but it seemed to be important to her.

She shrugged. "I wouldn't have had to fill him if *you'd* just taken it all like you were supposed to."

He walked around the back of the Jeep and held out his hand to help her out. "I would have been the one who burned to ash if you had pushed any more power into me. As it is, the cats in Reno are nervous when I'm on stage with them."

"Are they? I didn't know that. It's been almost two weeks. Do you think they'll get over it?"

He held out his arm and she tucked her hand through the crook. "I certainly hope so. But we're a bit worried about the Midwest tour. Margo was able to change a few of the venues, but . . ."

She got a look of disbelief and smelled of annoyance. "You're making her *work*? Antoine! She just barely survived the spider's venom. If Raven hadn't shown up when he did, she might not have made it."

He let out a frustrated breath. "No, she's *insisting* on working. I've tried to keep her down, and so has Dale. She keeps sneaking into the office, and I don't have the heart to take away her keys. She says she has nightmares if she doesn't keep busy, and after I found out that Rachel had taken Bruce away in spider form, I understand why."

They started to walk toward a small gathering of people. Tahira kept her voice low, and a frustrated scent began to rise from her. "I didn't know that either. God, it feels like we haven't talked in months, Antoine. I know it's only been a couple of weeks, but so much has happened and you've been so busy. Have you heard from them?"

"Bruce and. . . . *Nasil*? No. We searched for them after you killed Sargon, but they'd disappeared. Nasil called Matty to tell him where we were and that we were okay, and—"

"I know," she completed. "And then they left town. I meant *since then*. Do you think he made Bruce forget, or did he leave with him knowing?"

Antoine shook his head. It was a question he'd been asking himself since it had happened. "I don't know. I have to admit I was surprised that he gave his power to you to help us."

"And to save his own butt."

"Yes, that too. But there was still some little part of *Larry* that was there at the end. He said he might regret killing us, so . . . maybe. I don't know that Bruce would leave him after he played the hero. Maybe they'll show up someday. But for now, I'll have to find someone to replace them in the show. With the emergency council meetings and planning *Grand-mere*'s memorial, I'm afraid that life has been frantic."

"Please let me know when the memorial service is. I definitely want to be there. I can't believe we couldn't find her body in the cave to have a proper funeral."

"Cats often disappear when it's their time," Antoine said with a sigh. "The cave was quite large and we didn't have much time. I'm hoping the Wolven agents will be able to find her and bring her home."

Tahira nodded sadly, but then her mood changed. She raised her hand and waved to someone in the crowd with a bright smile. It was nice to see her smile. He'd forgotten just how lovely she was when she was happy. Had it really been *two weeks* since that night? It felt like only a day or two had passed. He felt her tug away and gasp in surprise and joy as a dark-haired man with vivid blue eyes swaggered up to them.

"Matty!" She ran forward and leapt into his arms, hugging him tight.

He held her with one arm and put out his other hand to shake Antoine's. "G'day, mates! Thanks heaps for inviting me, Tahira. I wouldn't miss this for all the Tim Tams in Sydney!"

"Thank you *so* much for changing your flight. I was worried that you'd already left for the walkabout. Did you get everything carved and painted and stuff? We haven't talked since Germany."

He looked at her ruefully. "Yeah, not much else to do while you're waiting for word on whether your best mates are still alive. I got loads done while you were all out saving the world. Everything's ace now. But I have to admit that I'm nervous. I haven't spent much time in the bush. I wish I had a bit more time before the corroboree to practice closer to . . . well, to a *city*. But, I decided that it was worth trying, even if I fail. I think that Gramps would have wanted that."

"Promise me you'll let me know how it goes!" She smiled when he winked and nodded.

Antoine saw movement from the corner of his eye and jumped out of the way just in time to avoid being hit by a sleek black SUV with a Mercedes emblem. It stopped right next to their Jeep, and he was surprised to see Ahmad emerge from the driver's seat. He was alone, without any guards. He was dressed in flowing robes over loose white pants. The patterned head cloth and black ogal of a desert sheikh was much more fitting of the location than Antoine's own khaki-colored suit pants and white dress shirt.

Once again, Tahira smiled and walked over to him. "Thank you for coming, Ahmad. Rabi will be so happy you're here."

He grinned teasingly. "Only Rabi? What about *you*?"

She laughed lightly and put her hands on his shoulders. To Antoine's shock, she leaned in and pressed her lips against his gently. Antoine struggled not to growl when Ahmad slid his arms around her and pulled her into a deep, passionate kiss. She stiffened for a moment and then melted into his arms, returning the kiss. Emotions filled the air that had little to do with the occasion of Rabi's installation, and Antoine felt a dull weight like lead in the pit of his stomach.

Matty raised his eyebrows and let out a low whistle but didn't say a word.

Ahmad pulled back slowly, just as he had done in the library. His eyes had lost some of the cold arrogance that normally surrounded him like a cloud, and he stared at her warmly. "Your outfit is quite lovely, Tahira. It's not as . . . *revealing* as the dress you wore to dinner on Friday, but probably more suited to the occasion."

The lead in Antoine's stomach turned to a sharp blade that cut into his chest. *Dinner*? He unconsciously reached into his pocket and touched Tahira's Christmas gift. He'd been waiting for the right time, but the thought that he'd already waited too long had never occurred to him.

She let out a laugh and pulled away to straighten her dress. "God! Could you imagine the look on my grandparents' faces if I wore *that* here?"

Matty walked over and held out his hand to Ahmad, allowing Antoine the opportunity to take Tahira's arm and lead her a short distance away. He tried to keep his voice calm, but he knew there was no way to stem the scent of anger and jealousy.

"You had *dinner* with Ahmad? You didn't mention that to me."

She regarded him with the tiniest bit of insult on her face, and her scent was hot metal frustration and annoyance. "Well, first, it's none of your business, but yes—we've had dinner a few times since I got back to California. And second, you haven't exactly been around *to* tell."

Antoine felt a rush of air and then Ahmad's snide voice in his ear. "I would have thought you learned that particular lesson. You can lose as much by *inaction* as by malice."

Angry power raced through his body and Antoine turned and grabbed the front of Ahmad's robes with a snarl that made the cobra hiss. "Be very careful what you start here, Antoine. I'm not certain that you fully grasp what powers I gained from my father's death. I promised Charles I would use restraint, but—"

Antoine's eyes narrowed. "Yes, he informed me that you can now kill by touch, though I don't understand why, if Sargon had such a power, he didn't use it. However, I watched what you did to Bahir when you found him hidden in the shadows, and noticed that your back is fully black now. At the time, I didn't understand what that meant, but now I do. Perhaps you don't fully grasp what *I* gained from Sargon, though. I was also forced by Charles to promise to use caution. Does the cat now have a poison bite, Ahmad? Can I too kill by touch? Shall we dance and discover who is more powerful?"

He saw the indecision in Ahmad's eyes, the moment that Ahmad began to wonder about him. In truth, even *he* didn't know what he'd gained from Sargon, nor did he plan to test any new skills without supervision by

Wolven members. But Ahmad didn't have to know that. After a moment, the snake's eyes cleared and that insufferable smile curled his mouth again.

"My father *enjoyed* fighting, just as I do. Remember that he hadn't ever been beaten in battle in thousands of years. By the time he realized that he might be in danger, Tahira had already taken the power to kill from him. If I choose to believe you—that I'm not the only recipient of his great power—then I feel it's only fair to advise you that *I* know how to use that power after years of watching him. I have the skill to make the power my servant—do *you*?"

Tahira put a firm hand on both of their chests and pushed them apart. She gasped and then pulled suddenly reddened hands away. "Stop it, both of you! Ahmad, will you and Matty *please* go see if you can find our seats?"

"Right then. Even *I* can take a hint that wide. Let's go grab a throw-down and gander at what they've put on the barbie, Ahmad," Matty said, and swept his hand to offer Ahmad the lead. With a wicked smile, Ahmad bowed slightly to Tahira and preceded Matty toward a low platform of stone that was set up in the middle of the square.

Tahira put her hands on her hips and lowered her head in a defensive stance. "Antoine, what do you think you're doing? This is supposed to be a tribute to my brother and hopefully a peaceful event that will show the kabile that Sazi can be warm and kind and respectful, instead of . . . well, trying to rip each other to shreds."

He clenched his hands into tight fists and fought down the bile that was rising into his throat at the thought of Tahira with . . . *Ahmad.* "I don't want you to . . . I mean, you *can't*—" He shut his mouth when he saw her eyes narrowing, as though she knew what was going to come out of his mouth next.

Instead, he stalked back to the Jeep and opened the rear door, just for something to do. He closed his eyes and slammed his palm down on the carpeting in frustration. Ahmad was right. He'd been so occupied with his own life since they returned that he'd neglected her. He had no claim on her, and he shouldn't be surprised that Ahmad had swooped in.

She stepped up behind him and put a light hand on his arm. "Did you know that since Sargon bit me, I'm more sensitive to poisonous bites? I swell up like I'm allergic, and everything that *does* bite seems to be attracted to me."

He turned and looked at her, shaking his head. He hadn't known, but realized he should have. She raised the sleeve of her dress to reveal an angry, swollen red mark on her forearm. "A wasp dive-bombed me at breakfast and this is what it looks like now. It'll heal, but it's painful. Now, look over there." He followed her pointing arm to a small black object half-buried in the sand where they had been standing. "That's a scorpion. Ahmad killed it while he was taunting you because it was about to climb up my leg. *Ahmad* knows about the insects because he's been around to hear me talk about it."

He felt another stab in his chest that left him stunned. The press of the box in his pocket seemed to dig into his skin. His voice sounded flat and hollow. "So you're saying that you've chosen to be with Ahmad?"

Her scent was a wash of pain and frustration that masked the sweet cherries, sandalwood, and cinnamon as she quietly said, "No, Antoine. I'm saying that I wish *you* had been the person to notice the scorpion and know why it should be killed."

As her eyes began to fill with tears, she turned and

walked toward the square, leaving him feeling like he'd been kicked in the stomach. He watched as every step took her farther away, and he just didn't know what to do.

Maybe I should just leave and be done with it. She deserves someone who gives a damn about her, and apparently I don't, or I would have been the one to notice.

He made it as far as sliding in behind the wheel and putting the key in the ignition before he remembered his conversation with Margo and the reason *why* he'd decided to cancel part of the tour. He remembered why it was so urgent that he find a temporary replacement for Matty and new handlers for the cats. He could have done their jobs himself, as he did before they'd joined the show.

I expected I was going to be with Tahira and planned that she would wait until I had finished business and could be with her all the time. I just assumed she knows that I love her.

"Except for the fact that I never bothered to tell her," he snarled harshly, slamming his palm down on the steering wheel hard enough to make it vibrate. He pulled the box from his pocket, ripped off the wrapping and opened it. The two-carat, canary yellow diamond solitaire ring still looked beautiful against the black velvet. But now he wondered if he should have spent the time to have it designed and made before asking for her hand. Had he lost her, as Ahmad said, by negligence?

He pulled the keys from the ignition and opened the door. Distant drums, flutes, and bells told him that the ceremony must be starting. He needed to find her, talk to her. Setting out at a fast walk, he bumped his shoulder into something. When he looked around there was nothing there.

But then Rabi appeared out of thin air, easily keeping pace with him in flowing white robes that were embroidered with silver and gold thread in geometric patterns. The soon-to-be crowned leader of the Hayalet turned his turbaned head and said casually, "So, you finally figured it out, huh? Took you long enough. We *sahips* can be notoriously thick-headed and slow, so Ahmad and I decided we'd better push along the process. Nice ring, by the way."

Antoine stopped just a few feet shy of the first white plaster home with flowering cacti and plants that filled the air with sweet fragrance. "What are you talking about? Have you been listening this whole time?"

Rabi looked at him in amusement. "Tahira's my little sister, Antoine. Of course I was listening. I could tell that you were nuts about her in the cave and afterward at the house. But you were ripping her guts out by not calling. I figured it probably wasn't intentional, because it's been a roller-coaster ride for me, too, for the past couple of weeks. But Tahira—well, I think part of her expected that life would just stop and you'd be so delirious in love that you'd both ride off into the sunset."

A sad, almost bitter chuckle rose up from deep inside. "And that's exactly what I should have done. It's what I *wanted* to do."

Rabi shrugged and pulled on Antoine's arm to start them moving again. "Yeah, but reality bites sometimes. Anyway, when I saw you and Ahmad at each other's throat, I cooked up a plan and he agreed to help. He really does want Tahira to be happy, and he did ask her to dinner, hoping she'd choose him." He laughed lightly. "But then she spent the whole night asking him about *you*. That quashed that romance damned quick."

Antoine shook his head in confusion. "I must have missed something along the way. What just happened here? Are you telling me that all this—the installation, inviting us, having Ahmad show up—was *planned*? Just to get me to realize I love her? I already knew that. It's why I brought along a ring."

"Not the installation," he said. "But yeah, the rest was. It was actually Ahmad's idea, and obviously we didn't know about the ring. When he saw how smitten Tahira was, he suggested to me that you would respond *really* well to jealousy, especially if it involved *him*." Rabi pushed him lightly toward the seats and then *isimed* so that only his voice remained. "Go. Sit with her until the formal stuff is done. I have to go dazzle everyone with my amazing powers. Just don't leave until after my speech, because you'll want to hear that. Oh, and if I introduce you or ask you to do anything, be a sport. I don't know if I'm going to. It'll depend on the mood of the crowd."

Antoine looked around the semicircle of kneeling people until he spotted Tahira at the front, once again wearing her head scarf and talking to Matty, who restlessly shifted beside her. There was an empty space next to her, right at the end of the row. He skirted around a small stand of pistachio trees until he was even with her row. He could smell her sorrow even over the myriad of emotions bleeding from the crowd.

"Tahira," he said softly as he stepped next to her. She looked up with a combination of joy, hope, and worry. "Is this seat taken?"

She reached up and grabbed his hand, pulling him down beside her. He tucked his legs underneath him and knelt on the sand. "I was afraid you'd left. I didn't mean to upset you. It's just that—"

He pressed a finger to her lips. "Shhh. I've been an idiot, and I'm sorry. I should have spent every moment of the last two weeks telling you how I feel about you. I don't know—maybe I thought you would know it by my scent."

Her voice was soft, somehow fragile. She kissed his finger lightly and stared into his eyes with warmth. "Scent helps, but words are important, too. When I walked away, I nearly ran back because I realized I haven't said it either. I'm just as much to blame." She took a deep breath, as though steeling herself. "So, here goes. Antoine, I—"

A solid, heavy drumbeat was followed by a gong that vibrated in the air, and all of the people fell silent.

"Later," he whispered. "It's your brother's moment right now." She sighed but then nodded, and they turned their attention to a gilded chair sitting inside a heavy iron cage on the raised stone platform. There was no door that he could see, and the squares created by the iron bars would only permit something the size of a squirrel to get inside.

A stooped, elderly man in embroidered robes walked out of a tent at the edge of the crowd. Antoine realized he must be Tahira's grandfather, the present leader of the Hayalet.

He walked with confident authority toward the throne and then clapped his hands twice. At the signal, a dozen well-muscled men armed with heavy curved scimitars approached the small cage and surrounded it on three sides, facing outward. Only the side open to the crowd remained clear.

On a second clap from the *Sahip*, the guards dropped into defensive position and scanned the surrounding terrain with blades extended and arms linked. There was murmuring from the crowd, and even Tahira seemed to be confused about what was happening.

The *sahip* forcefully said a few words in a language that wasn't quite Turkish, and the whispering grew louder and more intense.

Tahira motioned for him, Matty, and Ahmad to move

closer, and she whispered to them. "Grandfather just said that if Rabi is man enough to lead the kabile, then he should be able to defeat our best warriors to claim the throne. But even if he can defeat them, how—*ohhh*!" Then she smiled and smelled of amusement, leaving he and the others confused. "Just watch," she said. "This is going to be good."

Again the *sahip* spoke, the force of his voice a challenge, and Tahira translated for the three of them. "He commanded Rabi to appear and be judged on his worth to lead. Grandfather's going all out for this." When Antoine looked questioningly at her, she just shook her head and smiled.

Silence followed, broken only by the screech of some sort of bird on the top branch of the barren pistachio.

The *sahip* stood to his full height and crossed his arms over his chest. Then he pulled a scimitar to brandish in front of the crowd. Even Antoine could tell that the tone was taunting, sarcastic. The crowd cheered and laughed. A whisper from Tahira followed. "He asked if Rabi wasn't even man enough to defeat an old king, nearly on his death bed. He told the crowd that perhaps such a coward is better off hiding in the brush like a prey animal."

A loud voice suddenly bellowed in English, seeming to come from inside the cage. "I am far greater than a mere man and I hide from no one. I am Rabi Umar Kuric, grandson of the great *Sahip* Mazin, and I claim the throne of the Hayalet Kabile. None may defeat that which they cannot touch."

He appeared on the throne in the center of the cage, his white robes shining almost blindingly in the sun against the black cloth worn by the guards. The *sahip* made a slashing motion across his throat and all the guards turned as one. The squares were just large enough to admit the scimitars, and the cage was narrow enough that Antoine realized the blades would meet in the middle. There would be no room for Rabi to escape being impaled. Rabi *isimed* suddenly, but even that wouldn't save him.

Tahira didn't seem worried, even when her grandfather uttered a rolling tiger's roar of challenge and sliced his blade viciously through the front of the cage again and again as the guards slashed from side to side as well as diagonally. The faces of the warriors matched the stunned, confused ones in the audience and probably Antoine's own. They pulled out their blades and waited for instruction from their leader.

There was a moment of silence and then the *sahip*'s sword was yanked away. In nearly a blur of moment, he flew into the air and was slammed to the ground. His throat was exposed as though it was being held against the stone. The throw hadn't been hard enough to harm the old shifter, but it was impressive.

Rabi's rich baritone split the air again. "And none may defend against the wind." He made himself visible and he was on his knees over the old man, a knife blade held at his grandfather's throat. Antoine couldn't figure out how the trick was done. "Yield your authority or I will take it from you by force. Your time as leader of the kabile is ended, Mazin."

Mazin sneered and spoke in slow, accented English. "You speak the language of the outsiders and live in a foreign land. How will you defend against our enemies and protect the kabile?"

Rabi pushed the blade a little deeper so the people in the front row, including Antoine and the others, could see a small stream of blood that flowed from the cut. "A *sahip* lives with his people. I will do as all other *sahips* have done before me and live here among you, learning your language and your ways. A *sahip* lives for his people and defends them through claw and blade. Your enemies will be my enemies—if I, and *only* I, deem them a threat."

Antoine nearly leapt to his feet as he saw Mazin pull a narrow dagger from his robes. Only Tahira's hand on his arm kept him still when the scent of anger filled the air. "Never forget that a *sahip* dies for his people, too!" But as he swung the dagger, Rabi disappeared and the arm swept through empty air.

"I share the powers of the legendary Khalid, who struck fear into the hearts of all who challenged him. I am *Hayaleti vefa*—true ghost. None may touch me unless I will it." The voice, now a snarling bass that said he had changed to animal form, sounded from above them, and Rabi appeared on top of the cage. He let out a great, triumphant roar that vibrated Antoine's chest and scattered the birds from the trees. Then he disappeared again. Before Antoine could blink a second time, Rabi was inside the cage as a tiger. Once more he *isimed*, and then there was silence for a long moment. When he appeared again, he sat regally in his white robes on the throne. It was hard not to be impressed at the show.

"Do any doubt my skills? Do any object to my rule?"

His grandfather stood up slowly, straightened his robes, and held his head high while he stared at Rabi through the cage. Then he dropped to his knees and bowed low at the edge of the iron bars, touching the stone with his forehead. Rabi nodded with his hands remaining firmly on the arms of the golden chair. It was a sign of respect to the old *sahip*, but it didn't lessen his position.

Then he looked out over the villagers with cold, sure

eyes—and the bearing of a king. One by one the guards bowed low, touching their foreheads to their swords. The villagers prostrated as a single wave until only Antoine, Tahira, Matty, and Ahmad remained upright.

Tahira looked at Rabi, appearing unsure about their role. While everyone was bent down, Rabi carefully mouthed the words, "*You and Matty, but not Antoine and Ahmad.*" Tahira nodded and tapped Matty's arm. She signaled for him to bow with her, and then he and Ahmad were the only two left.

"You may rise." One by one the villagers peeked up and found Rabi standing next to his grandfather on the stone. He stepped down the two steps slowly, looking from face to face sternly. "I've heard that some of you have questioned my judgment in inviting outsiders to my ascension. I know that most of you understand what I'm now saying, and for those who aren't familiar with this language, I will allow others to translate my words while I speak. Basir and . . . Nuha, you will repeat my words to those who require in the tongue of the Hayalet until I am fluent and may speak for myself. But be warned—the esteemed Mazin and my grandmother will inform me if you speak false." He walked slowly as though inspecting troops, but occasionally reached down to touch the head of a child and smile down warmly.

"The men with my sister are visiting *sahips*. The snake that you have smelled and have struggled not to attack is known as Ahmad al-Narmer. He is a great and powerful were-cobra and *sahip* of all the snakes in the world. He fought by my side to defeat one of his own kind, to defeat one of his own line. He is *Sazi*, and I call him friend." Once again, there was murmuring from the crowd as the translators repeated his words. They cut off quickly when Rabi turned around and glared.

"The dark-haired man is Matthew Thompson. He is a healer of tigers, widely renowned in his country for his skill. He treated my wounds when I battled the great snake, and those of my sister. He is human of Sazi blood, and I also call him friend."

Antoine could hear the bird in the pistachio tree again, so silent was the crowd. All eyes turned to him. He knew they smelled him as *cat*, but had they ever encountered a cougar? Could they even grasp what he was?

"The man with hair the color of the moon is Antoine Monier, *sahip* of all the Sazi cats in the world. He, too, fought by my side in battle. He saved my sister from death at the hands of the human police, and saved my life by taking a blow meant for me. But he is much more than a friend to the Hayalet. I name Antoine *brother* and call on you to do the same."

The crowd erupted into angry cries that were punctuated with drawn blades and several men leaping to their feet. This might well grow ugly. He and Ahmad glanced at each other, but Rabi was suddenly beside the man with the knife standing nearest to him. Without a sound, he clutched his fingers around the blade, drove it into the man's stomach and pulled it out in a blur so fast that most of the crowd hadn't seen it happen. Kemil was on his knees on the ground, clutching his bleeding stomach with pain and fear etched on his face.

"You won't die, Kemil," Rabi spit into the man's face. "But I *should* kill you. I know of your treachery in allying with Sargon to capture me and my sister. But you are Kabile, so I will allow you to live. However, you will learn *respect* for your new *sahip*, and I will be watching you very closely." The crowd silenced, and nervous eyes followed his movements carefully.

Rabi held up his hands, holding the blade aloft until red drops marred the smooth white cloth covering him.

"The time for war between the Sazi and Hayalet is *done*. Their leaders have proven themselves honorable. They could be powerful allies to help and protect us from our enemies. They have asked for my voice—and through me, the voice of all of the Hayalet—to help them find a path of truth and honor. The Sazi council, where members of each shifting race meet, not to war but to *discuss* and agree, has offered a governing seat to our tribe. I have accepted on behalf of our people. Without their help, my sister and I would have been the first of many Hayalet to die in a war that would have turned brother against brother and shifter against human. But to further cement the tie between our two great peoples—"

He walked over to Tahira and Antoine, and then winked down at them before his face grew stern again. "I offer the hand of my only sister to the leader of the Sazi cats, with hopes that their union will produce children of shared blood." Antoine looked at Tahira's dropped jaw. For a moment, she was angry, but then she probably realized what he had—that Rabi could announce their relationship no other way without starting a riot he might not be able to quell. "For this, I call him *brother*. Antoine Monier, do you agree to consider my sister for one of your mates and become brothers with me and those I rule? She is not without defects, but she is of my blood."

Rabi drew his knife and cut down his wrist until it dripped blood. The sweet copper scent filled the air and blended with the fur and adrenaline musk that rose from the new Hayalet *sahip*. He held out his dripping hand, and it was spread too wide for a simple handshake. He waited silently for a reply.

Tahira looked at Antoine with startling golden eyes that caught the colors of the sun. Her scent held both hope and fear. He longed to pull off her scarf to reveal the wide orange stripes he found so beautiful, to show her tribe and the world that they weren't a defect. But instead he whispered to her. "Cats don't mate for life, but they *do* fall in love. I don't need to *consider* you for a mate, Tahira, because my heart has already decided that." He pulled the box from his pocket and pressed it into her hand. "I love you. That's what I should have said two weeks ago, and I can think of no better way to show it."

He reached for the knife and sliced through the skin of his wrist. He didn't even notice the pain as he grasped Rabi's forearm in a powerful grip. "I gladly accept your sister as my *one and only* mate, *Sahip*, if she will have me."

He could smell Tahira's happiness and a sharp intake of breath when she opened the box. The deep cinnamon of her hair was blended with a thousand other spices that said exactly how she felt. She clutched his hand tighter, and he noticed it was shaking. It was a struggle not to look at her, but the kabile would expect him to close the promise of marriage with *Rabi*.

Rabi glanced at Tahira and then fought back a grin. "Then it is done. On my word as *sahip*, you are mated and one." He leaned down and kissed Tahira on the forehead while still holding firm to Antoine's arm. His whisper almost made them laugh. "But I will expect an invitation to the wedding. I can't wait to see a cougar in a monkey suit, and you'd damn well better open that hundred-year-old bottle of cognac."

Howling Moon

CATHY CLAMP

and **C. T. ADAMS**

CATHERINE GROWLED AS the clock on the night stand emitted an ear splitting buzz. Every day for the past week, the volume seemed to increase until today it was nearly unbearable. She rolled onto her side, holding the pillow tight against her ear, and slapped at the snooze alarm. The plastic button cracked under her palm, and the resulting silence made her sigh with relief.

Last night setting the alarm at 5:30 had seemed a good idea. This morning: not so much. Grumbling under her breath, she threw off the sheet and climbed out of bed. She needed to get moving before Violet woke. Once her aunt rose for the day Catherine would have no chance at all of managing what she wanted to do. She set the shower cooler than she would've liked, hoping it would help wake her. As she opened the purple floral curtain, the warm mist raised goosebumps on her flawless skin. Skin that absolutely should *not* be flawless. But there was no mistaking that the puncture marks on her arm were healed, the scratches on her stomach gone without a scar. She glanced down at her leg, bandaged from ankle to hip. Part of her didn't want to see what was underneath the wrappings, even though the lack of pain told her what she needed to know. Should she remove the bandage and finally see what couldn't possibly be?

Taking a deep breath she could hear over the hiss of water, she reached for the first strip of tape. She tugged sharply, almost hoping for any hint of pain—anything *normal* enough to convince her to leave it alone. But there was no pain. None at all from a leg that had mauled by a wild animal just three short weeks ago.

The doctors said she might never walk again; and certainly not without a limp. The surgeons hadn't been able to *find* all of the long muscle in her thigh. The stretched what remained as best they could and took some from her calf in a desperate attempt to save the leg. The doctor's face had been serious when he had explained what it would mean—that she would have disfiguring scars and it would take months of therapy after the stitches were removed to retrain the pieced-together muscles.

She unwound the bandage slowly, watching for any sign of fresh blood on the snow white gauze. It was only when she reached the third layer down that she saw the dark, nearly brown stains. She touched the fabric tentatively. The stains were dry and crusted hard, but she could still smell the blood, mingled with her sweat from a week without air to her leg.

Catherine closed her eyes as she removed the last layer, but opened them again when a scattering of . . . *something* falling tickled the top of her foot. Sweeping her gaze along the shiny, pink skin covering half of her thigh, she noticed small bits of black, like little spiders, covering the ground near her toes.

"What the hell?" She shook the black things off her foot and stepped back quickly. Nothing moved or crawled—except for her skin as she finally recognized the black bits for what they were. She reached down and picked one up to examine closer. There was no mistaking that she was holding one of the black thread stitches that just a few days ago was all that was holding her leg together. It was a perfect circle, tied with a tight knot, and there were dozens, maybe hundreds, on the pale purple throw rug.

"I can't let Violet know." The words slipped out of her mouth unconsciously, but she knew it was true. She loved her aunt, and truly appreciated having this refuge from the crush of press that had been hounding her. But Violet would *not* be able to cope with this.

Catherine sat down on the edge of the tub and stared at the perfect little stitches while the shower pounded her back through the plastic. Minutes passed as steam filled the small room, raising beads of sweat on her brow. It felt amazingly good in the warm, moist air.

Finally she took a deep breath, slapped her hands lightly on her knees and told her reflection, "Just give up asking why, and deal with it. You need to get some caffeine and real food so you can think what to do next. And you need to do it before Violet wakes up and *feeds* you."

A shudder that had nothing to do with her leg passed through her. God how she missed milk, and *cheese* and, oh but what she wouldn't give for a strong black coffee. She respected Violet's wishes and didn't bring any of *that stuff* into her home. But that didn't mean that she intended to go vegan alongside her. *Not a chance in hell.* Part of it was Violet's cooking. *The woman could burn water. But I can't tell her that, not without hurting her feelings.*

So, this morning Catherine was going for a walk. A nice, healthy walk on her newly healed leg—first to the ATM at the convenience store on the corner and from there, past the park a couple of miles to a little family burger joint she'd found tucked away off the access road to the subdivision.

She started to pull on her clothes and realized that

shorts were *not* going to work. People would notice the leg, especially since the one hadn't been shaved for three weeks. If she took the time to do that, Violet would have climbed from her bed and gone into the kitchen to fix them both some "nice" oatmeal and decaffeinated herbal tea.

There is nothing nice about oatmeal, and if I ever see another cup of tea . . . She didn't finish the thought. She wasn't sure what she'd do, but it wouldn't be pretty. Still, chances were, as long as she was living in Boulder she would be drinking more tea, eating more tofu, and Boca, and fresh green salads.

Catherine pulled on a pair of navy sweatpants and a gray sports bra. It took a little rummaging around, but eventually she came up with a matching pair of sweat socks to wear under her Nikes. Once her shoes and socks were on she ducked back into the bathroom to brush her teeth and pull her long blonde hair up into a high ponytail. A critical look in the mirror showed her a tall, slender woman in her early twenties—with enough bags under her large blue, no make that *turquoise* eyes, for a two-month tour of Europe.

"Not the eyes too. Please, not the eyes—" As if her words had summoned him, a suave male voice entered her thoughts.

Good morning kitten, Nice to see you up and walking again. I told you it wouldn't be long. Yes, the eyes will be next.

Oh shit, not again! This was why she kept pushing herself until she was utterly exhausted, to keep that damned voice *out of her head*. It entered her thoughts first thing in the morning, or last thing before bed.

I'm losing my mind! Tears filled her eyes and she balled her hands into fists. *It's just been too much.*

She'd been thinking long and hard about finding a

good therapist, but she didn't want to start with somebody here and then have to switch doctors when she moved back to California.

You're not losing your mind, kitten. I'm very real.

Well, of course you'd say that.

He laughed, long and hard. In her head, she could hear office noises and someone talking to him in the distance. It was very much like hearing background noise over the phone, *inside her head. Too weird.*

Not now Muriel. I'm busy. The voice became exasperated. Oh very well. We'll have to chat later, darling. Have a nice run.

Just like that the voice was gone.

Catherine shuddered. *It is definitely time to find myself a good shrink.*

She tiptoed down the hallway, holding her breath as she snuck past her aunt's bedroom door. *This is so ridiculous. I feel like a teenager sneaking out to a party. Not that I had any experience at that, but it's still what it feels like.*

She managed to make it all the way downstairs and to the front closet without rousing her aunt. But as she opened the closet door she heard Violet muttering and rolling around in her sleep. She froze, waiting and listening carefully. When Violet's breathing deepened and steadied, Catherine let out the breath she'd been holding and quietly took out her purse. She slid her ATM card and keys into the pocket of the sweatpants, returned the purse and closed the closet door. Moving with exquisite care she crossed the tiled entryway and undid the various locks and slid out the front door. *Free at last, free at last! Thank God almighty I'm free at last!*

She stretched a few times to limber up her muscles, taking long deep breaths of cold fresh air. In the distance she could hear traffic, and the sound of the few birds who lived in the city year-round chirping. The sun was just beginning to rise, its rays tinting the thin clouds to the east pink and orange. The nearly full moon had nearly set on the opposite horizon when Catherine started walking down the sidewalk toward the convenience store. She hadn't gone a full block before she knew her leg would carry her and she started to jog, reveling in the sheer pleasure of running after so many days of worrying that she never would again.

The store clerk nodded to her, but continued carrying the bags of trash to the Dumpster as Catherine hit the various buttons to access her money. She didn't want to get *too* much, but she was running low on cash, and she didn't dare use any of her credit cards. It was amazing how the paparazzi could be counted on to use that sort of thing to hound her down. *Why the hell can't they just leave me alone?*

She tucked the money from the ATM into her sports bra. She trusted the pants pockets for her keys and the card, but the cash was more bulky and the pockets were too small to be trustworthy. She felt a surge of rage at the press. Damn them anyway. They'd started hounding her for the first time when the truth about her mother's past had surfaced and her engagement to Brad crumbled. But this, this was infinitely worse. Bad enough to lose her parents in a senseless accident. Having the press stalk her with cameras and shove microphones at her shouting "How does it feel to lose your parents? Did you make up with your mother before she died?" from every direction had been utterly intolerable.

She started running again, faster this time, the adrenaline of her anger fueling her footsteps. It wasn't a full-out sprint, the distance was too far for that, but it was a quick pace nonetheless. It took surprisingly little time before she had made it past the park and was turning onto the access road that led to the restaurant.

The smells wafted to her even before the building came into sight: fresh coffee brewing, and the incomparable smell of bacon cooking. Her mouth watered, and she put on a burst of speed. By the time she reached the glass doors her stomach was growling audibly.

It was obvious the restaurant hadn't been open long. A young woman with short cropped dark hair and wide brown eyes was bustling around, getting things started, while a stocky middle-aged man tended the food on the grill. Still, Catherine wasn't the first customer of the day. A group of three young men sat in the east corner. The smell of alcohol on their breath was not *quite* hidden under the strong scent of cinnamon gum. She tried to ignore them, but it wasn't easy. They were staring. One, in particular, couldn't seem to take his eyes off of her.

What? Haven't ever seen a girl before? I mean, give me a break. Then she shrugged. *I suppose I should be flattered.* But she was actually more irritated. They reminded her too much of the frat boys in college who had hung out in packs and harassed her endlessly because she was just a kid the whole time she was there. Still, she had to admit that the big one was handsome. He looked a lot like Brad—big, muscular build, sandy hair cut to always look just a little bit mussed and hang into the wide brown eyes. His clothes were casual, but obviously expensive. It was a very calculated look, and it worked well for him. *Probably gets all the girls. Brad certainly did.*

"Sorry about the wait." The clerk's voice interrupted Catherine's musings. She'd come behind the register while Catherine had been lost in thought. "Can I help you?" She actually seemed to mean it when she smiled. Her spotless white uniform blouse was crisply pressed and tucked into black dress pants with a perfect crease. She was perfectly pulled together and *much* more alert and friendly than Catherine had ever been able to manage at this time of day. It was then that Catherine realized that the girl was the same one from the night before, and the morning before that.

"No problem." Catherine looked up at the menu posted overhead. To her surprise the breakfast offerings weren't limited to a couple of muffins with meat or a breakfast burrito. There was a bacon and eggs special with hashed browns. *Oh and they have steak breakfast!* God was definitely smiling at her this morning! "I'll have the steak and eggs special, rare, with a side of hashed browns and the biggest coffee you've got."

"Having trouble waking up?" The girl teased as she rang up the order. She quoted the price, which Catherine gladly paid.

"Oh yeah." Catherine slid the change back into her bra.

"All right then." The girl's eyes sparkled with mischief. "I think I may have a solution for you." Grinning, she walked away from the counter. She disappeared into the kitchen, only to reappear a minute later with one of the 40 oz. thermal coffee mugs they sold at the Quicki-Mart.

As she began filling the mug with fresh black coffee Catherine said. "If you were male, I'd marry you for this."

The girl laughed and passed the mug across the counter. "You can grab a seat anywhere. I'll bring out your food when it's ready."

"Thanks." Catherine took a deep pull of the scalding liquid, her eyes closing in ecstasy as the scent wafted up to her. "This is *so* wonderful. I can't believe you don't need any yourself. You seem to *always* be here."

The girl laughed. "Hazard of blood, I'm afraid. My dad owns the restaurant, and I'm the resident slave labor. By the way, I'm Holly Sanchez." The girl offered her hand. "I figure if you're going to be a regular, I should know your name."

Catherine set the mug on the white tile of the counter so she could shake the other girl's hand. "Catherine Turner."

"I hadn't seen you around much before the past few days."

"I'm new in town."

"Well it's good to meet you." Holly gestured at the wealth of available tables. "Take your pick."

The restaurant wasn't large, but it was sunny and bright with the décor of an old fashioned diner. Three of the four walls were mostly windows. The parts that weren't were covered in white tile with red and black accents. The booths that lined the outer walls were red, as were the chairs at the center tables. The tabletops and blinds above the windows were glossy black. Every surface had been cleaned until it sparkled.

Catherine chose the booth closest to the front door, sitting at a slight angle that gave her a view of the entire place. She sipped her coffee, watching Holly bustle about her business while subtly keeping an eye on the boys at the back booth. She didn't make eye contact, didn't want to encourage them. But she didn't want to turn her back on them either.

Holly delivered the food to the table on thick white diner plates and plain flatware. The steak was huge, cut thick, and cooked exactly the way she had wanted it.

Catherine finished her breakfast in record time. Never in her life had food tasted so incredibly good. The scent of the meat alone was intoxicating. Considering the portion size, the price had been very reasonable. Catherine decided that this was definitely a restaurant to frequent even more than she had been. She was debating whether or not to have another mug of coffee when she caught a glimpse of the clock behind the counter. *Shit. Gotta run.*

"See you tomorrow, Holly." Catherine called and waved as she dropped a sizeable tip onto the table. The other girl returned the wave before Catherine vanished out the door.

She ran back to the house at a fast, steady jog, but stopped abruptly right before she was about to bound in the door. *Hell! The leg.* The next few moments would have been funny, if they weren't so sad. Trying to remember which leg had been injured after the comfortable run was nearly as difficult as trying faking a limp.

It was probably silly to hope her aunt had slept late, but she couldn't help it. Unfortunately, Violet was wideawake, dressed and waiting with arms crossed and a tapping foot when she slowly came through the front door. "Where have you been?"

Catherine could tell how difficult it was for her aunt not to snap the words, but her eyes told the truth. A small, birdlike woman, Violet had short, permed brown hair and bright black eyes that saw *everything*. And right now, those eyes were seriously annoyed. Violet liked things "just so." Everything in her life was kept perfectly organized and under her absolute control. Except that nothing recently had been controllable.

"I went out." Catherine answered with a smile. It was easy to smile. It was easy to smile. For the first time in two weeks she was actually *full*.

Violet didn't even blink. "Your oatmeal has gone stone cold."

"It's all right. I ate."

"Ah." One word, but it was heavy with disapproval. Maybe she could scent the meat on Catherine's breath. Or maybe she just guessed what her niece had been up to.

Catherine met her aunt's gaze without any hint of apology. She didn't want to hurt Violet's feelings, but there were limits to what she was willing to do. She was, after all, an adult. She had done absolutely nothing wrong.

Violet pursed her lips. Her disapproval hung in the air like an almost visible fog. When she spoke her words were tight with annoyance. "You have a spot of coffee on your bra."

She turned away before Catherine could answer, going into the office and pulling the door *very* firmly closed behind her.

RAPHAEL'S HAND SLAPPED against his clock radio several times before he realized it was the phone ringing.

"Hullo?" The word into the receiver was muffled by warm pillow and he turned his face a bit and cracked open his eyes.

"Raphael, it's Charles."

Raphael threw off the sheets and sat bolt upright in bed, trying desperately to jump start his sleep-fogged brain. "Mr. Chief Justice!" Morning was *so* not his time of day and it was only, he glanced at the red numbers of the digital clock, 5:00 a.m. *Shit. The sun's not even up yet.*

"I need a favor."

The head of all shapeshifters was asking *him* for a favor? Granted, they were shirt-tail relatives of a sort, but it was certainly not a relationship either of them had ever presumed upon. Charles Wingate was not a casual man. If he said he needed a favor, he *needed* it, and Raphael wasn't about to turn him down. He tried to slow the frantic beating of his heart. "Of course, sir. What can I do for you?"

Raphael ran his left hand through his bed-mussed tangle of curls and swung his legs off of the bed and onto the carpeted floor so that he was at least marginally "up."

There was a long, awkward silence. "I'm not sure where to start."

Raphael blinked stupidly. This did not sound like the Chief Justice. Oh, it was his voice all right, but something had shaken the old bear's confidence to the core. There were so many nuances to his voice—anger, sadness, and the one emotion Raphael would never have expected, fear.

"Sir?"

The old man sighed deeply. "I'm not *positive*, because someone has been trying to block my gift . . ."

"Is that possible?" Raphael couldn't keep the shock from his voice. Charles was the Sazi's best foresight seer. *Nobody* should have the power to block his ability to view the future.

"Oh, it's possible. It isn't *easy* but it is definitely possible." There was a heat to the words that made Raphael flinch. He almost felt sorry for whoever had done it. Because sure as hell they were gonna pay. Judging from Charles's anger, they'd pay dearly.

"*Anyway*, I've just learned that Jack Simpson has done it again. He attacked a girl and killed her parents." There was a pregnant pause. "The girl's name is Catherine Turner. She's my goddaughter."

Oh fuck! "The full moon is tonight." Raphael tried to keep his voice neutral. He failed. It was a little higher and breathier than usual. On the plus side, he wasn't sleepy at all anymore.

"Yes, it is. And Catherine will be facing her first change."

"What do you need from me, sir?" Raphael's voice was wary. He was afraid he knew where the conversation was leading, and it was nowhere he wanted to go.

"I just learned that Catherine is staying with her Aunt Violet, in Boulder."

Right on our doorstep. "I'll contact Lucas."

"No!" Charles blurted out the word, then backpedaled a bit. "Please don't."

"Why not, sir?"

There was a long silence on the other end of the line. "Lucas would simply murder the girl." The Chief Justice's voice softened. "I'd rather avoid that if I can. She. . . ." There was a catch in his voice, but he plowed onward. "She means a great deal to me."

"Sir," Raphael spoke very carefully. "There's a good chance she won't survive. If she does, and goes feral—"

"If she is feral, she will need to be put down. I understand that." Charles's voice was tight, as though with unshed tears. "But I don't believe she will be. Catherine has always been an . . . exceptional young woman. Will you at least try?"

"Of course sir. But I can't make any guarantees."

"I know. I know." He sounded tired, defeated. But beneath it all simmered an abiding rage. Raphael was so incredibly glad that he was here and Charles was . . . wherever the hell he was. "Get a pen, Raphael. I'll give you the information."

Raphael pulled a pen and pad from the drawer of the

night stand and started writing. Even as he listened his mind was racing. An attack victim—a jaguar, one of the large cats—in *Boulder*. It was a recipe for disaster. At least the address was on the outskirts of town, near one of the big parks. But a cat that size could cover ground very quickly, and jaguars tended to roam. *Shit, I'll need my weapons. I hope there's plenty of silver ammo in the safe. I haven't needed any in how many years?*

It had been a long time since Raphael was in Wolven, the Sazi police force. Yes, he went to the range often, as much for entertainment as to keep up his skill. At least the weapons hadn't been "rusting" from disuse. But this was the kind of thing Wolven sent teams of two or three agents to handle. Because when it came down to it, there was nothing more dangerous than a feral were-animal.

Charles had finished speaking and was waiting for his reply. Raphael needed to say something, but the problem was, he wasn't sure *what*. A girl Charles loved was facing death tonight. There was a good chance Raphael wouldn't be able to save her, or would have to put her down.

"I'm going to need help, sir."

The reply was a warning rumble. "Raphael, I told you—"

He summoned all his courage, and spoke to the head of the shifters as though he *were* still on the force. He kept any annoyance from his voice, but the reality of what he'd been asked was sinking home. "I need information, Charles. I'm not in the loop anymore. At the very least, I need photos, vehicle descriptions, license plates. Is there *anyone* I can call? If I have to step outside the rules far enough to lose a strip of hide if I fail, then I want to have a marginal chance at succeeding. My son, your *grandson*, maybe?"

There was a long pause and Raphael was afraid he was going to turn down the request. But his son, Raven Ramirez, was second in command of Wolven. He could get the information without anyone asking questions—even if he was presently on mandatory health leave. And, he held confidences like no other man Raphael had ever known. If Charles would trust *anyone*, it would be Raven.

Finally, the old bear sighed. "Call Raven. Find out what you can. I could tell you myself, but I'm afraid that I . . ." He took another deep breath. "Just keep it in the family—no one else. I trust your judgment, Raphael. It's why I called."

In the end, too many other lives were at stake. Raphael knew it and so did Charles. He wouldn't, *couldn't* risk everything for one girl.

"I'll do my best sir. I swear it."

"Thank you." There was undisguised gratitude in his voice. "I appreciate that more than you know. Call me tomorrow on my private line. I'll be waiting for your report." Charles dictated the number where he could be reached. When he finished he hung up without bothering to say goodbye.

Raphael leaned back against the headboard once more and stared into space, desperately trying to think how to convince his son to ignore all protocol, disobey every rule that he lived by, to give him classified information. If Senator Jack Simpson had attacked someone in Lucas's territory, it was a sure bet that Wolven knew all about it. Would he have to find a way to the girl *around* the agents who would be arriving tonight?

The coffee was brewing by the time he decided how to approach the situation. If he called in a Beta Six alert, then *perhaps* Raven would get to a secure phone line to return a call without telling the higher-ups in the agency. But Beta Six was not only seldom used, it might well be an old code that Raven wouldn't even recognize. He'd been retired from service before his son joined.

He stirred sugar into his coffee absently and took a sip, trying to clear the remaining fog from his thoughts. A rooster crowed in the distance, and it was incredibly loud to his ears, reminding him all the more strongly that the full moon was just behind the rising sun, waiting to pull the animal out from inside him—and from inside *her*. He had to hurry if he was going to have any chance at all of finding her before her animal nature took control and forced her far away from humans to change for the first time.

There was no time to lose.

He glanced at his watch as he reached for the portable phone next to his coffee mug. The sultry scent of the dark roast helped him relax and think in "cop" mode again.

"Let's see," he muttered. "It's six in the morning here, so it's . . . what? Lunch, or just after, in France? Is it six hours or seven? Aw, hell. I'll just call his cell and hope for the best."

The phone rang twice before he heard his son's familiar voice, "Ramirez."

"Raven. It's me."

"Oh hi, Dad! It's good—"

"Raven, *stop*. Call me back. Beta Six." He disconnected the call and set the phone down, feeling his heart pounding and adrenaline racing for the first time in a very long while. He tried to imagine what his son would do next. Beta Six was an internal agent code that was the equivalent of *trust no one*. If Raven understood the code, he should know not to contact anyone in charge—

there was a breach of security, and everyone was suspect. Even his own father.

He didn't wait for the phone to ring again. Even understanding the code, it would take awhile for Raven to verify that Raphael had indeed called him on his own cell phone. He would probably also check to see that the triangulation of the signal was Boulder, Colorado, and that he had not left the area by any commercial transportation means before the call was placed.

So, there was plenty of time to get started gathering what was needed to track a rogue feral. He shook his head as he headed down the hallway to his office, feeling very old and out of condition. He was still a very young shifter by Sazi standards. As an alpha male, he would probably live until he was two or three hundred. But that was no substitute for daily training and regular field work.

Once all of his handguns were scattered across the top of his desk, the tops of chairs and the bookshelf edges, he stopped to take stock. A rifle would be better, or even a shotgun, but all of his long guns were in the safe at his pack office. Plus, handgun fire, if it became necessary, was much easier to muffle or "bend" so humans didn't notice it by using his magic than bigger guns.

Checking his ammo cans pretty much determined his choice of weapons. He only had silver ammo loaded for the Ruger Blackhawk and the 9mm Colt. There was more ammo for the Ruger, so that would be his choice. But the Colt would probably come along, too—just in case.

He checked the fit of his Kevlar vest, wondering if it would stop jaguar claws. The vest had been an impulse buy from the internet. He'd never actually expected to *use* it. Still, if there was any chance it would help, he was going to wear it. He was still adjusting it for comfort when the phone rang.

It rang a second time before he made it back to the kitchen. "Ramirez."

"Okay, Dad. What in the hell was so important that you had to use a thirty-year-old code to drag me out of the office and make me buy a brand new phone to call you?"

"What do you know so far?"

Raven sighed. "I know I had to dig through piles of paperwork before I could even *find* what Beta Six meant. Then I checked your position, and the phone's position and did a satellite track. Then I made an excuse to leave the office, bought a phone and called Granddad."

Raphael cursed under his breath. He hadn't expected it, and probably should be insulted, but would probably have done the same damn thing. "So, he told you what the situation is?"

"He didn't tell me a frigging thing. He just said, 'Yes, your father called. Call him back,' and hung up. Big help there."

Nodding even though he knew Raven couldn't see it, he replied with a laugh. "Yeah, that's what I figured. Okay, I need whatever information you have on Jack's latest get. Background, aunt's address, the car she drives, license plate—everything." A long pause made him ask, "Raven? Did you get that?"

His son's voice sounded strange when he responded. "Yeah, I got it. But Jack's last attack was nearly a decade ago. Why would you need it?"

Raphael nearly dropped the phone. Could Wolven possibly *not* know about this? They checked into *every* animal attack in the world, regardless of what the papers reported, and even Raphael had heard the girl's name in the press—just not the details. Is that why Charles had called him? Because he didn't want the rest of the council to know? And if not, *why* not?

"Dad? Talk to me. What's going on over there?"

"*Shit.*" He ran his fingers through his hair again. "Are you *sure* you're on a secure line?"

A pause. "As secure as I can make it in the middle of Paris."

He blew out a slow breath and sat down. Then he proceeded to tell Raven about the call from Charles and what he had been asked to do. "So, do you have any information, or can you *get* any information?"

"Jesus, Dad! Nothing like dropping a nuclear bomb in my lap. This is the absolute *first* I've ever heard this. I know about the Turner girl, but no hint of Jack's involvement ever reached Wolven. There were multiple witnesses to the event. Her parents were killed by a wild animal, all right. But all parties agreed that it was a *cougar* attack. Hell, according to what I heard, someone got a *photo* as the animal ran off! Councilman Monier personally checked with all of the cougar shifters and verified their whereabouts, so it was shunted into the wild animal files. Are you *certain* our spotted friend was involved?"

Raphael shook his head and took another sip of his now-cold coffee. Bright sunshine was bouncing off the copper bottoms of the pans over the stove, and he had to shift his chair to turn his sensitive eyes away. "I'm not certain about a damned thing right now. I can't imagine a reason why Charles would lie about it. He seemed . . . *shaken* when we talked . . . almost afraid. He said that someone had been blocking his ability to see the future, so he hadn't been able to stop the attack."

"Good God! If you're right about this . . . but why wouldn't Charles tell Lucas? Or Fiona, or even one of the council? Why *you*?"

"He asked for a personal favor, which I'm hardly in a position to refuse. After all, it's only because of him that I'm still *alive* right now." Raphael's chuckle had bitter overtones. He was going to have to once again face the very thing that had nearly caused his death. A mistake that had made Jack Simpson his mortal enemy nearly fifty years ago.

"Yeah." Raven paused. "So, what do you need me to do?"